"I wasn't going to come. I tried my best not to," Ross said.

"What made you change your mind?" Lorna asked.

He stepped toward her until they were almost touching. "You're unbelievably desirable in that nightdress."

"Did you have a reason for not coming earlier?"

"I needed to think. I needed to stop fighting myself." He put his hands on her shoulders and drew her against him. "I'm going to kiss you," he said.

"No, I don't think you should—"

She should have known that the instant he touched her the battle to retain her composure would be lost.

He kissed her then, again and again.

TIGER DANCE

JILLIAN HUNTER

AVON BOOKS ◆ NEW YORK

TIGER DANCE is an original publication of Avon Books. This work has never before appeared in book form. This work is a novel. Any similarity to actual persons or events is purely coincidental.

AVON BOOKS
A division of
The Hearst Corporation
1350 Avenue of the Americas
New York, New York 10019

Copyright © 1991 by Maria Gardner
Inside cover author photograph by Garth Pillsbury
Published by arrangement with the author
Library of Congress Catalog Card Number: 91-91795
ISBN: 0-380-76095-9

First Avon Books Printing: September 1991

AVON TRADEMARK REG. U.S. PAT. OFF. AND IN OTHER COUNTRIES, MARCA REGISTRADA, HECHO EN U.S.A.

Printed in the U.S.A.

RA 10 9 8 7 6 5 4 3 2 1

*To Judge Harry J. and Doreen Gardner . . .
for all the love, laughter, and unfailing
support over the years.
Thank you both.
You are the perfect parents.*

Chapter 1

The Indian-Malay Archipelago, 1853

The sudden stillness should have warned them. One moment the two young women could hardly carry on a conversation for the raucous clamor of birds and bullfrogs rising from the green darkness of the nearby jungle; the next their voices sounded abnormally loud in the unexpected silence.

Even the incessant chirping of the cicadas had stopped. The pair of monkeys jabbering in the palm tree that overlooked the *kabung,* the black lava pool where the girls had sought relief from the sweltering heat, had disappeared.

The pool, frequented by the island natives for the restorative powers of its mountain spring waters, stood at the base of the massive cliffs that bordered the lonely beach. Every newcomer to the island was expected to purify himself within its surprisingly cool depths.

Lorna Fairfield rose slowly to her feet. Facing the sea, she felt a rush of moist warm wind lift the hem of the lavender silk gown she had slipped back on and hastily refastened. Although she had emerged from the pool only minutes before, the humidity again enveloped her like a Turkish steam bath. The coiled length of her red-gold hair, only partially secured by a mother-of-pearl comb, was curling into waves upon her neck.

She made a lunge for her straw bonnet as a current of

1

wind hurled it skyward, and managed to catch the tail of a satin ribbon. "Never mind your corset, Ilse," she cried to the sturdily built blond woman struggling to dress behind her. "It's starting to rain. We'll have to take shelter until it stops."

She stared up at the dark gray cauliflower clouds that had amassed to blot out the sun. The wind was rattling the gubbong and fishtail palm fronds into a frenzy, and fat globules of rain began to pelt her upturned face and soak through the fabric of her gown. "Ilse!" she shouted, a strange excitement coursing through her. "Do you think it could be a monsoon?"

There was no response. But then, her own voice could not compete with the rising shriek of the wind. Or was that Ilse's scream? she wondered as she spun around to survey the wall of jagged black rocks that stood behind her.

The storm-weathered carving of a sacred island goddess leered down at her from the summit of rocks that enclosed the kabung; its human face and eagle's body had assumed a lifelike appearance in the sudden false darkness. Lorna could have sworn the stone eyes were staring directly into hers. She shook her head to dispel the illusion.

"Lorna! Help me!"

"Where are you, Ilse?"

"Down here—behind the pool. Oh, damn it, Lorna, I think I've broken my knee."

Jamming on her kidskin shoes with the buttons left unfastened, Lorna scrambled across the barrier of abrasive rock and traced Ilse's cries to a narrow crevasse behind the kabung. The wind fought her every step, pushing at her like an invisible hand as she finally crawled between the rough outcrop of rocks that surrounded the pool to see Ilse's white, frightened face peering up at her from a volcanic fissure that had been concealed by a tangle of wildly swaying ferns.

"Be careful, Lorna. God knows we don't need both of us down here like a pair of boobies."

The water level of the bathing pool was rising dangerously, sloshing over the lava banks, running in a hundred rivulets over the rough-textured rock. Lorna could feel it seeping into her shoes as she flattened herself out on her stomach to reach down into the ten-foot-deep crevasse. Above her head, rain gushed in wild torrents from the beaks of the lesser bird gods that had been immortalized in the lava face of the cliffs overhanging the pool.

"Give me your arm, Ilse. I'll try to lift you." She stretched every muscle, her arm sockets burning as she got and then lost her grip on the other woman. "Try to get a foothold, Ilse!"

"I can't stand up properly, Lorna. No, no. Don't pull at me again. You'll just have to fetch help."

Lorna shoved her loosened hair from her face, her green eyes worried. "Syed!" she shouted toward the palms where she had last spotted the young Malay guide they'd hired to escort them. But there was no answer or sign of him, and she decided that he must have run off, though whether from fear of the winds or from the recognition that they needed help, she wasn't sure. It would take her ages to find her own way back into the village, wending through the hilly jungle vegetation. This was, after all, only her first afternoon on the tropical island of Kali Simpang, a neglected British Protectorate in the Indian-Malay Archipelago, six days distant from Singapore by steamer.

She hardly knew her way around her own father's hillside plantation house yet. Nor had she met the skeletal staff who had remained behind when he had mysteriously disappeared about nine months ago. She only knew she and her uncle had left England to find her father in this wildly alluring land and that they were totally reliant on the expertise of Ilse's older brother, Kurt van Poole, a world-renowned hunter and jungle guide who had sailed from his native Java to assist them. Trust her luck to need his services her first day on the island.

"There was a little palm hut on the hillside as we

passed,'' Ilse said, her voice faint from pain. ''I only noticed it because of the Union Jack flying from the roof.''

''Which way?''

''Back toward the beach—behind the cliffs. Oh, hurry,
Lorna. There are *things* down here.''

Things. Poisonous centipedes, snakes, scorpions, lizards. Lorna drew back with a shudder of empathy.

''Here. Take my shawl. And put your shoes on. They
say there's fever in the mud after a rain. I'll find someone
to help us.''

She was praying she could keep her promise as she made
her way down the steep path that led through the rocks to
the beach. It was all she could manage to keep her footing
while she scanned the hillsides for a sign of the hut Ilse
had mentioned. The sky had darkened to pewter. More
than once she lost the path as wind-blown palm fronds and
the pelting rain obscured its markings. After a few minutes
it became impossible to know if she was even following a
path at all, so uncontrollably did the rain wash down the
slopes, carving its own roadways in the red island soil.
Another quarter mile of relying on blind instinct, and she
finally climbed the leeward side of a hill to regain her
bearings.

The sight that met her eyes took her breath away. The
wind had stirred the sea into a maelstrom of frosted green
foam and wildly tumbling waves. The leaves of the trees
on the outer perimeter of the jungle were flapping about
in a kinetic fury, their pale green undersides exposed like
the bellies of tropical fish in a fisherman's net. In the distant background the sails of the packet boats strained as
though they would tear from their masts, and the Chinese
junks rocked to and fro as if to batter themselves against
the customs wharf where Lorna had disembarked only this
morning.

A dizzying sense of freedom such as she had never before experienced seized her, and she threw back her head,
drawing a deep breath as her concern for Ilse was temporarily stilled by the untamed beauty that embraced her.

London and its filthy congested streets, its poverty and neglected children, seemed like a fading nightmare to her now. To think that she had believed it the most fascinating place in the world. But that was before she had discovered that her fiancé was engaged in a romantic liaison with her best friend. Before her beloved father had mysteriously gone missing somewhere in the vicinity of this island and her Uncle Richard had proposed they launch a search to find him.

A fierce gust of wind howled across the sea. Raising a hand to her face, she was annoyed to find it damp with tears as well as raindrops. Especially since she had forbidden herself to cry any more over Spencer and Emily Pounders, her best friend since they had attended Miss Simmon's Country Boarding School for Young Ladies. But she could not so easily dismiss her father from her mind. Somewhere in the murky tangle of jungle behind her, or on one of the little islands that was a misty blur on the horizon, he had disappeared. She would not believe he was dead. He had always been such a vital man that even now it was as if she could hear his voice.

"I have found my Eden, Lorna. And if you weren't marrying that pompous bugger Lord Kirkham, I would say come to Kali Simpang and select a husband from one of the strapping young natives who inhabit the nearby islands. Laka-Bulu, for example, is a cannibal chieftain's son who has recently become a widower. If you were to marry him, we could invite Spencer to the reception and see how long it takes his blue blood to boil. Afterward, while you went on honeymoon, I should write a splendid story about my daughter, Queen of the Man-Eaters."

A sigh escaped her. She was too accustomed to her father's black sense of humor to take offense, too aware of his artistic self-absorption to believe he had given her future happiness more than a few moments' thought. An eccentric who delighted in shocking people, he was famous in Victorian London for his horror novels, his most celebrated work being his *Twilight Tales*. His readings in

St. Martin's Hall drew throngs from miles around, thrilling everyone from the prime minister to the overworked clerk. He had come to Kali Simpang to begin what he believed would be his finest work yet, and Lorna could only hope that there was a logical explanation for his disappearance, that it was somehow connected with his work, and that they'd have a jolly laugh over it as soon as she'd soundly chastised him for giving her such a fright. Nevertheless, although this wasn't the first time he'd vanished from sight, in her heart of hearts, she sensed he was in trouble this time . . . desperate trouble.

She roused herself, again scanning the beach below for a fisherman, anyone, to help her. But there was no one in sight, and she was thoroughly drenched, her skirts so heavy with water, soil, and sand, she could barely struggle down the hillside without falling against the sharp rocks along the way.

The logical thing to do was to return to the pool and wait until Ilse's brother tracked them down. Undoubtedly Kurt would be suspicious if they did not come back in this rain. Unless he had secreted himself in his room to smoke the opium Lorna suspected he was addicted to. Heaven help them if Uncle Richard attempted to find them. He couldn't walk from one end of the hall to another without getting lost.

But as she began to retrace her steps, she stopped suddenly and tilted her head, her skin prickling at the sounds coming from deeper inland. *Kulkuls,* Kurt called them. The relentless, disturbing drums of the natives attempting to drive the wind by magic back out to sea.

And then another sound caught her ear, sweet and high-pitched, with a subtle magic of its own.

She turned around, straining to hear. It was only the wind again. Yet for a moment she could have sworn she had heard the faint piping notes of a flute—

There! She heard it again. . . .

"Handel's *Water Music?*" she questioned aloud. "But how on earth—"

It was the most maddening task, to trace the elusive melody to its source through the ceaseless onslaught of wind and rain. Her search led her back around the hill, toward the beach, and at last to a partially sheltered bluff that overlooked the sea.

At first she did not see it, distracted as she was by the high bamboo hedge and prehistoric-looking ferns and tropical fruit trees that grew in lush disarray like a private forest. And then it was actually the Union Jack that she noticed, flapping from its pole mount on the shaggy nipah-palm roof. The poignant music was tauntingly clear now, and only as she struggled up the steep incline, then turned around the back of the cliff, did she realize she had found the hut Ilse had seen. Whoever lived here, she thought, did not wish to be found.

A *sulap*—that was the word for the queer little hut on stilts that stood trembling in the wind before her. Smoking smudge pots had been laid out under the foundation to discourage damp and sand flies. A collection of water crocks had been set along the path worn through the swaying saw grass, and rain fell upon them in a lyrical medley of clinks, plops, and splats.

She brushed the hair from her face and looked up. Above her, reclining on a hammock inside the sulap's split-bamboo veranda, was the most splendidly handsome man she had ever seen. Even from her limited vantage point, Lorna was prepared to concede that.

She plunged down the path and clumsily began to climb the slippery notched-log ladder that leaned against the hut, mesmerized by the music, by the man who played it. Judging by his tall frame and longish black hair, she thought it possible he was a native, although he could be a European.

She reached the uppermost rung, pausing to reestablish her balance. She could see his face clearly now, the squarish jaw, the prominent nose, the thick slashes of his eyebrows. His damp hair was slicked back on his scalp, curling around his nape as if to defy his attempts to tame it. His frame appeared several inches too long for the hammock, his suntanned feet dangling over the end, waving to and fro in time with the music. The equatorial sun had baked his skin to a warm teak color, and the moisture in the air seemed to highlight every deep indentation of muscle and sinew on his bare arms and chest.

Even in repose, there was something at once elegant and elemental about him. He seemed to Lorna to fit the savage splendor of his surroundings as perfectly as the fierce teakwood carved gods that had greeted her on the plantation wharf when she'd first arrived. His posture bespoke a relaxed self-indulgence, but his physique indicated a man of action.

"Excuse me." She staggered forward, not certain that he spoke English, although he was definitely of European descent. In fact, he seemed not to have heard her, and she wondered whether he was in some sort of music-induced trance. His eyes appeared closed. At least they were until she remembered poor Ilse at the pool, and she raised her voice to an imperious shout.

"Excuse me!"

His head jerked up. His gray eyes snapped open, widening at her appearance, drinking in every detail in what Lorna could only describe as an expression of the rudest disbelief.

It was one thing that his leisurely gaze made her feel like a filthy mudlark displaced from the Thames, but it was quite another that with the same glance he made her acutely aware of how her dampened gown emphasized her physical attributes . . . or in her case, she thought wryly, her lack of them.

"Ka-bung," she enunciated slowly, as if she were talking to a simpleton. "Water hole. My friend is hurt . . . she's hurt her knee—"

She broke off in agitation, wondering whether he would continue to stare at her while she jabbered on in broken English, and then she followed the direction of his gaze and saw that he was now staring at her feet. Or more precisely at the twisted rattan mat beneath her feet on which she was dripping enormous puddles of sandy water.

"Oh, dear," she said, examining her sodden skirts in dismay. "I'm making a dreadful mess of your mat."

He laid aside his bamboo flute and sat up slowly, his face registering a hint of some fleeting emotion that Lorna did not care to decipher.

"It—it's only a mat," she said, heat rising from her neck into her face.

Ross St. James was, in fact, not in the least concerned with his floor but rather was recovering from the shock of opening his eyes to find this strange young woman standing before him. His first impression had been fanciful, that with his playing he had summoned a Botticelli Venus from the sea. But on closer inspection, he saw that this Venus appeared to have been assaulted by the surf rather than spawned by it.

Her hair hung in dripping rattails down her back. Her finely boned face was smeared with streaks of mud. Raindrops and grains of sand spangled her gold-tipped eyelashes. The determined chin bore a nasty graze. And however attractive he suspected she might be after a lengthy toilette, she was far too tall to fit into a scallop. He sighed. It could mean only one thing: Miss Lorna Fairfield of London had arrived.

"Where are your shoes?" he demanded, his heavy eyebrows drawing into a reproachful scowl.

She leaned against the railing in relief. At any other time she might have been offended by his brusque demeanor. Now she was simply grateful that he spoke English—and in a cultured voice that indicated he was a person of some authority on the island.

"I must have lost them in the mud. My name is Lorna Fairfield. We only arrived this morning, and it was so unbearably hot that we couldn't resist taking a swim, and then the wind . . ."

Her voice trailed off. He wasn't listening anyway, more intent on shoving his feet into a pair of leather moccasins and reaching for the madras shirt that had been folded beneath his head. Lorna knew she should look away while he dressed, but she was spellbound by the fluid grace of his movements. There was an unusual combination of roughness and refinement about him that fascinated her even as it aroused her self-protective instincts. Although he appeared outwardly civilized, he wasn't anything like the London fops or artistic libertines she'd met back home.

"I am Ross St. James, Miss Fairfield. The Resident of Kali Simpang."

Lorna felt another surge of relief at his introduction as the senior British officer on the island, accountable to her father's close friend, the reigning English-born Rajah, Charles Montclair. If her memory served, her father in his letters had approved of this Mr. St. James and had said that the Rajah was in fact Ross's uncle. Still, she didn't think it would please her father now to see the man frowning at her as if he longed to throw her over the railing and return to his flute.

"I am fortunate indeed to have encountered your esteemed personage," she said dryly when it seemed he was waiting for her reaction.

His frown deepened. "As chief administrator of this island, it is my obligation to advise you that in future you must not take such foolhardy risks with your safety. Under no circumstances are you to leave the village without a government-certified guide."

Another wave of warmth crept upward from Lorna's neck into her face. "I had a guide, Mr. St. James, but he vanished at the first sign of the wind."

"Vanished."

"Yes." Her voice was as haughty as his. "He was sitting by the river while we were bathing, but when I tried to call him, it seemed that he had taken it upon himself to run off."

"And you are sure he was not washed away?"

Lorna's face went pale. "No. But surely the water level could not rise that fast."

"It could, and often does. Kana!" he shouted toward the interior of the hut. When there was no immediate answer, he brushed past Lorna and disappeared into the sulap. Seconds later he reemerged with a rope, a towel, and a dark-skinned young man whose bespectacled brown eyes widened in friendly amusement at Lorna's appearance.

She stared back in curiosity. The man Ross referred to as Kana was obviously a native, his lithe body and lean buttocks clad in a *chawat*, a spotted leopard loincloth. There was a wrinkled leather pouch at his waist, to hold the betel nuts that had stained his lips a hideous red, and he carried a *parang*, a large knife for slashing jungle paths, in a deer-antler scabbard. His long black hair was worn in a neat oiled bun.

"Hello," he said to Lorna, his distended earlobes swaying with the weight of the brass earrings that touched his shoulders. "You look very wets."

"I am." Lorna returned his grin. At amusing odds with his primitive looks were not only the wire-rimmed spectacles but also the copy of the *Illustrated London News* he had tucked under his arm. How admirable of Mr. St. James to teach him how to read, she thought.

"Kana is my valet," Ross explained, handing her the towel. "He's going to look for your guide while I help your friend. You were at the bathing pool outside the village?"

She pressed the towel to her face. The rough cotton smelled of sandalwood soap. "Yes. Beneath the lava shrine of the Eagle Goddess Penala."

If he was impressed by her knowledge of the native animistic gods, gleaned from an intensive study of her guidebook, *A Wanderer's Guide to the Indian-Malay Archipelago,* he did not show it. "Please wait inside the sulap until I return, Miss Fairfield. You will find a tunic and trousers in my wardrobe. I would like you out of those wet things before I get back. And clean off that graze on your chin. We don't want it turning septic."

"Trousers, you said."

"Yes. One is forever catching colds and fever on the island—unless, of course, you would prefer one of Kana's loincloths."

"I think not."

He snatched the paper from Kana's arm. "Here. It's old by now, but you can read it while you wait. Kana only uses it to swat the cockroaches the rain brings out. We grow them as big as rats on Kali Simpang."

The interior of the sulap was close and damp. Despite apparent efforts to waterproof the tightly thatched roof and split-bamboo walls, there were beads of moisture on the ceiling and the sparse furnishings were sticky to the touch. But if one was to remain cool in the constant heat, ventilation was necessary, and the price was paid when the rains came.

Cockroaches aside, Lorna was impressed at how clean he kept the surprisingly comfortable hut. After she had rinsed off her feet with the water stored outside, she towel-dried her hair and changed into the overlarge embroidered Chinese tunic and trousers she found in the camphorwood wardrobe in Ross's sleeping quarters—a cubicle really, partitioned off by a bamboo curtain.

Feeling like a little girl in her father's nightclothes, swimming in the folds of the black silk garments, she hung her gown on a peg by the window to dry and turned to inspect the spartan room. There was the requisite mosquito netting draped around the ironwood bedstead, a telescope on the ivory cotton coverlet. At the washstand mirror she grimaced at her appearance and washed her face with the tepid water in the chipped porcelain bowl.

At least now she looked halfway human, she thought. And though she did not mean to pry, she wanted so badly to tidy her hair that she began to search for a brush in the teak chest of drawers by the door. Her own haircomb could never untangle her heavy curls.

Sharp fumes of cedar and camphor shavings, used to protect against insects and mildew, rose to her nostrils as she opened drawer after drawer. Finally she found an exquisite silver-backed brush, comb, and mirror, wrapped carefully in yellowed lace. The silver was tarnished, and there was a faded lace ribbon tied around the scrolled handle.

Sensing she had come upon something that had been hidden away for a personal reason, she quickly rewrapped the set and resumed her search until she found Ross's own comb. Mr. St. James possibly entertained a special lady love, or perhaps he had a wife living inland.

She was standing at the door watching the rain when Ross returned. His dark head downbent, he hurried up the incline with Ilse in his arms. She was a pretty young woman, plump and youthful looking with sky-blue eyes. As they drew nearer, Lorna couldn't help noticing how Ilse was clinging to his chest, her cheek pressed to the hollow of his throat.

"Hold the ladder steady for us please, Miss Fairfield!" he shouted toward the veranda.

Lorna hastened to help, suddenly concerned by Ilse's pallor. But when Ross deposited her on the rattan settee inside the door, she gave Lorna the most impudent grin over his shoulder and then proceeded to hitch up her filthy skirts with an utter lack of propriety. She'd told Lorna on the voyage from Singapore that such relaxed standards were her due as a wife and mother of three children.

"It's not broken, he says," she announced, wriggling her badly swollen kneecap. "Damn, but it does hurt, though." There were several large bruises on her legs, and Lorna thought fleetingly they could not have appeared that soon after her mishap.

"Perhaps I should make you a compress," she said, but before Ilse could agree, Kana came bounding up the ladder and into the hut, raindrops beading on his oiled back.

"I found guide. He hiding in coconut tree. I make him go back to village with message womens is safe."

"The little devil might have warned us there was a monsoon coming," Ilse said indignantly.

"He say he did. He shout 'Musim!' three times and you tell him that good."

Lorna and Ilse exchanged embarrassed looks. "That's true," Lorna said. "But we thought he was saying, 'Me swim,' and wanted our permission to bathe. I understood the monsoon season was over. At least my guidebook says—"

She hesitated as Ross hunkered down beside her to re-examine Ilse's knee. The same masculine scent of soap that had been on his towel emanated from his dampened skin. "My guidebook says—"

"Officially the season is over," Ross said without glancing up. "However, Mrs. Klemp should have told you that it's not unusual for a monsoon to hit us earlier or later than expected. We have another fortnight to go before we're safe. Perhaps your guidebook neglected to mention that. I'm sure van Poole is aware of the fact. I understand he's leading your little expedition."

Ilse leaned back against the settee, shaking her head in mock chagrin. "Living like a hermit at this outpost has made you quite ill-mannered, Ross. I believe you offended Lorna just then, but she's too polite to show it."

"Have I?" He looked at Lorna, his eyes locking with hers before lowering to the masculine clothes she wore and then lifting back to her face. "Have I offended you, Miss Fairfield?"

She hesitated. Ill-mannered was not at all how she would have described him. Preoccupied was more appropriate. "No," she said. "Actually, considering the circumstances, you have been quite hospitable." His face did not change, and she was unaccountably frustrated by her inability to guess what he was thinking. Ilse, on the other hand, was an open book, as her broadening grin attested, and suddenly Lorna realized that the familiarity between Ross and the Dutch woman indicated a prior acquaintance. It was not surprising. Ilse and her sea captain husband, Wouter Klemp, lived on neighboring Java. Quite possibly he had cleared port under Ross's approval.

"What do you think we should do for Mrs. Klemp's knee, Kana?" Ross asked, finally looking away from Lorna.

Kana reflected for a moment. Then he tapped his forefinger to his chin, spun on his bare heels, and left the room. When he returned, he was brandishing a huge jar that contained a half dozen tiger-striped leeches and three silver bells attached to respective leather thongs on the lid.

"We use them primarily to forecast the weather," Ross explained at Lorna's puzzled look. "They're supposed to climb to the top of the jar and ring the bells when rain is in the air. Of course, they are thoroughly unreliable, but they do serve the occasional medicinal purpose—"

"Oh, no." Ilse moaned and covered her face with her hands. "I'll be sick all over myself if I watch. I detest the very sight of them."

Lorna took Ilse's hand and stole another peep at the undulating leeches before she had to look away herself. "They really don't hurt. Try not to think about it."

"Miss Fairfield is right," Ross said. "The leech seems to operate as a natural anesthetic on the skin. There—you don't feel that, do you?"

"Just get it over with," Ilse said between her teeth.

"It's almost done. Kana—"

Curiosity overcoming her repugnance, Lorna watched as Kana deftly removed the blood-engorged worms from Ilse's knee without the aid of a match as she had read described in her guidebook. Rolling, squeezing, plucking. He made it look so simple that she was determined to try this technique herself should the need arise.

"I feel even worse than before," Ilse said as she rearranged her skirts over her legs. "You might at least offer me a glass of arak, Ross. After all, you gave Lorna your trousers and she wasn't even hurt."

"Kurt should be here soon," Lorna said before more attention could be drawn to her peculiar costume. "You'll probably have to be taken back on a litter, or maybe even in a bullock cart. I'll make some nice hot tea and cucumber sandwiches when we return to the house.''

Ross got up from the floor and stretched his arms above his head, touching the cross-beamed ceiling. Still seated on the mat beneath him, Lorna glanced up at his shadowed face and felt again a disconcerting tug of fascination. For a moment, from her admittedly inferior angle, he reminded her of a pirate raider from bygone days, his black hair stirring in the breeze that whistled through the cracks in the wall, his long legs planted apart in a conqueror's stance. The false twilight in the room heightened the illusion. In the gilded darkness of the oil lamp, his profile was hawkish, and his half-closed eyes gleamed like silver coins.

''You will not be able to return to your house tonight, Miss Fairfield,'' he said unexpectedly. ''It's more than a good twenty-five-minute hike around the cove from here, with all pathways flooded, and van Poole won't venture out in this weather.'' He lowered his arms and turned into the golden circle of light that relegated him back to the realm of everyday life. ''I realize it is inconvenient,'' he continued, ''but the wind is worsening, and I cannot take the responsibility of some calamity befalling you on the way back to the village.''

''I see,'' Lorna said, with far less distress in her voice than what was appropriate for a young lady of her upbringing. Yet she could not argue the point. If she had not been so engrossed in her schoolgirl's fantasy, she would have noticed the increasing velocity of the wind. The bamboo walls were shaking with the force, and the long stilts that supported them trembled like a spider's legs.

''I can offer you some tea,'' Ross said politely. ''But supper will undoubtedly not be up to your usual standards.''

''Tea would be lovely, Mr. St. James.''

He nodded, a shock of dark hair falling onto his forehead. ''Kana, put some water on to boil. I'm going to the cove.''

Lorna hesitated several seconds before she got up and followed him to the veranda, her feet tangling in the sweeping trousers. "Will you be back in time for tea?" she asked. "Shall I set a place for you at the table?"

No sooner had she asked the questions than she realized how absurd they must sound. For all she knew he did not even own a tea table, let alone a formal service, and she sounded for all the world like the fretful English wife calling after her husband as he left for his cricket match.

Apparently the humor of the situation was not lost on Ross. For the first time since she had met him, he smiled, his eyes lifting at the corners where numerous squint lines fanned out against his suntanned skin. The smile so transformed his face that he appeared years younger, far less forbidding, even a little vulnerable. She wondered suddenly whether he were actually as arrogant as he seemed, or whether he was merely unaccustomed to social contact.

"Set a place for me at the table, Miss Fairfield. I shall not be long."

Lorna glanced down at the telescope in his hand. "Surely you are not expecting another ship in this weather?"

He hesitated, as if uncertain he should confide in her. "Several islands in our vicinity have been attacked by Illanun pirates and Sea Dyaks of late."

"Sea Dyaks," she repeated slowly, knowing she had read the term in her father's letters.

"Practicing headhunters, if you will. Until we are placed under the protection of the Royal Navy, only the occasional steamer from Singapore patrols our shores."

"But even headhunters would not sail here in this weather."

"The discipline of the watch should not be broken." His tone was light, but she had the impression he was deadly serious about the danger of an attack. "You look alarmed, Miss Fairfield. Perhaps you are wishing you had never left England now that the romantic fantasy of living on a tropical island has assumed a grimmer reality.''

His disapproval of her presence on Kali Simpang was so implicit that Lorna could only stare after him in stunned silence as he slid down the ladder. Obviously he did not realize that she had been encouraged to come to the island by his own uncle, Rajah Charles. Or perhaps he did not understand the strength of her commitment to find her father.

She turned and walked slowly back into the sulap, the floor slick beneath her feet. Perhaps he was not being cruel, after all. Perhaps, like so many others, he believed her father dead and did not wish to see her following a phantom dream. The thought depressed her. She would rather think that Ross was opposed to her presence for personal reasons than that.

"He's such a maddening man," Ilse said as Lorna entered the room. "You mustn't let him upset you."

"It wasn't him."

Ilse gave her a skeptical look. "No?"

"I was thinking about my father."

"Well, if anyone can find him, Lorna, Kurt will. My brother has his faults, I don't deny that, but when he wants something, he always gets it."

Lorna nodded, fighting the disheartened mood that engulfed her whenever she thought of her father. She knew he was in terrible danger. She sensed it. And the image of Kurt van Poole, florid-faced, so overloud as to be obnoxious, did little to lift her spirits. If Uncle Richard had not held the Dutchman in such high esteem, she would have dismissed him on the spot that first morning she had met him in Singapore, swaggering down the wharves with the reek of beer, opium, and a whore's perfume clinging to his wrinkled clothing. But even if Kurt disgusted her, she could not deny he was the most qualified man for her purposes. From hunting lions in Tanganyika, to leading treks across the Transvaal, to penetrating the breathless jungles of Borneo, he was the most experienced guide

Lorna had interviewed. And Uncle Richard, usually passive in these matters, had insisted.

"Gad, Lorna, there's no one more qualified. He was six years a corporal in the Dutch army learning how to track. And the French hired him as a guide in the Congo for their territory-seeking expeditions."

"He's vulgar," Lorna had countered glumly. "And he must be expensive."

"But he's giving us a special rate, my dear. He's rescued missing explorers before, and he's a legend in the archipelago for his skill in hunting man-eating tigers . . ."

"Man-eating tigers," Lorna murmured with a dubious shake of her head as the sound of the wind outside brought her back to the present. "I'm going to change back into my own dress, wet or not, Ilse. And then I'll help Kana in the kitchen with tea."

Moments later, behind another bamboo curtain, she found the humid cooking cubicle that was furnished with a combination sink and sideboard, a rattan cupboard, and an ironwood hearth over which was suspended a blackened cauldron and several pots. Water boiled furiously in the dented kettle, its steam escaping through a flap in the roof. Every so often a few drops of rain would fall onto the burning logs below to release hissing smoke. Kana was sitting crosslegged on the floor with another folded newspaper in his hand, steam fogging his spectacles.

"They always come out when Kana cooks," he said with a grin.

"Well then, you take care of the cockroaches, and I'll make the tea."

Lorna turned to the tall cupboard and began an inventory of the tightly tinned foods, flinching a little each time she heard the paper smack the floor and Kana's ensuing exclamation of glee. When in Rome, she thought philosophically. There was nothing to be gained by going into hysterics every time an insect crossed her path. After all, other white women had been living on the islands of the archipelago for centuries now. She would have to adjust.

She glanced distractedly at the dog-eared copy of *David Copperfield* on the counter. "Is that for squashing bugs, too?"

"Oh, no. That for reading in bed."

"Is there any fresh fruit, Kana?" she asked, smiling to herself.

"In that basket, missee."

There was only one basket that Lorna could see, and that was moldering away in the corner. And the fruit in it was the most unappetizing she had ever—

She gasped, staring in horror at the shriveled object in her hand, which on closer inspection had taken on the gruesome aspects of a smoke-dried human head.

"Not that basket, missee!"

She dropped the skull back into the basket and turned, staring down at the knuckles of Kana's hands for the tell-tale dot tattoos that proudly proclaimed he had taken heads in battle.

"You—you've taken heads, Kana?" she asked in a quiet voice.

"Not since Tuan Resident come to island." He grinned proudly. "In my tribe, a woman not even look at a man unless he take heads to prove him braves."

Lorna lifted the kettle from the hearth, scarcely feeling the heat of its wooden handle, her mind unsuccessfully trying to reconcile headhunting with reading Dickens in bed.

"Tuan Resident like sugars in his tea," Kana said behind her. He got up and followed her to the crude wooden sideboard, watching her pour the steaming water into Ross's cracked Wedgwood teapot. "Tea get cold before Tuan Resident return. Tuan Resident like it very, very hots."

"Then we'll make Tuan Resident a fresh pot when he comes back from the cove. Oh, good, there's milk."

"Tuan Resident not like milk."

"Well, Ilse and I do. And you may tell Tuan Resident that I'll replace his tin later," Lorna said blithely and reached into the darkest corner of the cupboard, past the canister of Donkin's preserved meat, to the tin of F. S. Grimwade's evaporated milk.

She was reveling in her newfound self-sufficiency and growing courage, oblivious to Kana pulling on his lower lip behind her in disapproval. She was going to find her father, and when she found him, she would settle down on the island while he finished his book. She would stay here having little adventures while Emily and Spencer pondered her prolonged absence, and when Spencer finally followed her to Kali Simpang, and begged on his knees for her forgiveness, she would step over him like—

"Missee!" Kana shrieked suddenly. "Missee!"

She was so jolted from her daydream by Kana's outburst that she dropped the tin of milk onto her bare toes. "Ouch," she cried, bending at the same moment to retrieve it as Kana did. Their heads cracked together, and then Kana snatched up his newspaper and waved it at Lorna as she straightened, her hand lifting to her forehead.

"No, no, Missee!" he shouted, hopping up and down for emphasis. Her first thought was that he was acting like an angry child because they had bumped heads.

He raised the paper to her shoulder and before Lorna could protest, she saw from the corner of her eye what had caused his excitement. Entangled in the hair she had brushed over her shoulder sat a shiny black scorpion, its stinger twitching directly beneath her chin.

She screamed. Kana screamed. And they were still screaming when Ilse hobbled into the kitchen, followed by a rain-soaked Ross. Then Lorna fell silent as the scorpion dropped to the floor, and Kana squatted to smash it into oblivion with his newspaper.

"Evil spirit of the cupboard," he said in answer to Ross's questioning look.

"Did it sting you, Miss Fairfield?" Ross stepped into the cubicle, scanning her for signs of injury.

She shook her head, too embarrassed to speak. He sounded out of breath, presumably from hurrying up the ladder when he heard the screaming. He was holding a net that contained several blue mangrove crabs, their pincers wriggling.

There was a long silence. A huge cockroach scuttled over the battered scorpion; Kana was suddenly engrossed in scratching sand fly bites on his buttocks. Then with an utter lack of sensitivity, Ilse said:

"Isn't the tea ready yet?"

"Yes. Yes, it is." Lorna swallowed the lump in her throat and looked at Ross. "We are using your milk. I hope you don't mind."

Chapter 2

Twilight falls suddenly in the tropics.

An hour after dusk the rain stopped, but the wind continued to shriek across the sea. They ate supper on a bamboo mat on the floor, by the light of an oil lamp whose feeble glow had attracted numerous black rhinoceros beetles and emperor moths into the room.

Kana had somehow managed to prepare a palatable meal of steamed rice, crabmeat, and boiled palm hearts—served in banana leaves, for want of enough plates or the facilities to wash them. Lorna and Ilse devoured every mouthful with shameless enjoyment, not having eaten a thing since their arrival that morning. It seemed incredible to Lorna that she had been on Kali Simpang less than a day, and that her first night was to be spent stranded here in this hut. With Ross St. James.

She stole a glance at him. He had spoken little during the meal, then excused himself to the rattan chair in the corner by the lamp, where he sat perusing a thick file of documents. Every so often he would look up from his reading and stare at her intently, his handsome face thoughtful until Lorna would distract him with her nervous fidgeting. Once or twice he even smiled to himself—while still regarding her—which was almost as disconcerting as the faint, seductive grin he gave her when she actually worked up the courage to look him in the eye.

"Ross," Ilse said sweetly, after another half hour had passed, "I hate to take you away from those fascinating papers, but Lorna and I have been awake since before dawn, and I can barely keep my eyes open. Where shall we sleep?"

"There's only one bed, I'm afraid, and you and Miss Fairfield will have to share it."

"Too bad." Ilse sighed. "I snore like a dragon and poor Lorna will never sleep."

Ross stood up to show her the way, gathering his papers from the chair behind him.

"We're putting you out of your bed, aren't we, Mr. St. James?" Lorna said. "Where will you sleep?"

"The hammock on the veranda, I suppose. I can lower the screens to block the wind. Since I'll be back and forth to the cove throughout the night, it's really no inconvenience."

"Of course it is," Ilse said. "But Ross is trying to atone for his earlier lapse in manners. You must have made a good impression, Lorna."

By this time Lorna was becoming inured to Ilse's annoying impertinence, and she merely looked away as Ross and the other woman moved past her to disappear down the other end of the sulap. She rose from the floor, at a loss as to what she should do. Kana was back in the kitchen, chewing betel and smoking foul-smelling cigarettes wrapped in banana leaves, lost in the colorful world of *David Copperfield,* which he read by the light of a stubby candle. After the incident with the tea, she had the impression he didn't want her underfoot again.

She glanced down at the folder Ross had inadvertently left on his chair. The heading glared up at her like a beacon in the night:

CONFIDENTIAL REPORT TO RAJAH CHARLES MONTCLAIR
FROM THE FOREIGN OFFICE ON THE DISAPPEARANCE
OF SIR ARTHUR WARREN FAIRFIELD.

Her heart began to pound with nervous anticipation. Before she could stop herself, she had opened the folder and lifted the single page to the lamplight.

Should his death be ascertained, which is often never made official in the case of missing persons, all of Sir Arthur's properties, including his tobacco plantation on Kali Simpang, fall to his only child and specified heir, Miss Lorna Fairfield of London. At the time of this writing, Miss Fairfield is engaged to marry Lord Spencer Kirkham of Kirkham Hall, Hampshire.

Should his death be ascertained . . .

The words burning into her brain, Lorna dropped the paper onto the chair and turned toward the sleeping cubicle. She could hear Ross and Ilse talking, and though she had no intention of eavesdropping, they were clearly too engrossed in their low-voiced discussion to notice her anyway.

"Why don't you take Lorna and me on the grand tour of the island tomorrow, Ross?" Ilse was teasing him. "Between the two of us, we might be able to thaw you out."

"More likely, I'd spend the entire day reviving her from a series of fainting spells," he replied dryly, glancing up from the chest of drawers he had been rummaging through for a clean shirt. "We've no Hyde Park or Covent Gardens to placate her delicate sensibilities, and I don't have the time to spare squiring around a—"

"I've never seen you react like this to a woman before," Ilse broke in thoughtfully. "If I didn't know better, I'd think you fancied my friend."

"That's ridiculous. I've only just met the girl."

"You didn't take your eyes off her all evening. Even when you were reading, you watched her like a hawk."

Ross jammed his shirts back into the drawer. "One more remark about my behavior, and I'm packing you off on the next boat to your husband. Take your brother along, too. It's criminal that he's taking money from that girl when there isn't a chance in hell that he'll find—"

"Don't say it."

Lorna entered the cubicle, shaking her head in superstitious dread. She was terrified that somehow by saying the words, Ross would make the possibility of her father's death a reality.

"I will find him, Mr. St. James. With or without your assistance."

He straightened, his lean features hovering between concern and impatience. "I don't think you appreciate what an impossible task you have set for yourself. If he had remained on the island, I would have known of it by now. And if he has left the island, as is believed—"

"Are you suggesting I simply forget about him then?"

He raked a hand through his hair and shook his head.

"Let your uncle and Ilse's brother risk their lives if you choose. But if you ask my advice, I must tell you to return home to your fiancé."

Lorna stared up into his austerely carved face, all the emotions of the past month that she had struggled to suppress rising to the surface. It was one thing to have discovered Spencer's infidelity, and the wound of that betrayal would take a long time to heal. But to have traveled this great distance to be told her father was surely dead was more than she could accept.

"Excuse me," she said in a controlled voice. "I think I need a breath of air."

She turned to the screen, her steps wooden. She could no longer hold back the tears burning beneath her eyelids, and she didn't know either Ross or Ilse well enough to feel comfortable exposing her deepest feelings to them.

"There now, Ross, you big tactless fool," she heard Ilse whispering behind her. "You've really upset her this time."

The elemental fury of the wind rivaled the chaos inside Lorna as she stumbled through the hut and out onto the veranda. Even as she stood with her hands gripping the bamboo railing, fragments of the sulap's palm-thatched roof were snatched away by the wind and flung into the darkness before her tear-blurred eyes.

"Come with me, Miss Fairfield."

She turned from the railing. Ross stood before her with his hand outstretched. In the shadows she could not read the expression on his face, but his deep voice stirred an odd sense of trust inside her that temporarily subdued her private turmoil.

"You aren't afraid of the wind, are you?" he asked.

"Not at all."

He nodded in approval and moved toward her, his warm brown hand covering hers for the briefest of moments. It had an uncanny power, that fleeting touch, and the heat of it brought a faint blush to her cheeks.

"Follow me down the ladder," he said. "There is something I would like you to see."

Midway down the ladder she lost her footing on the slippery notches and half-slid to her knees. Ross saved her before she fell, and as he helped her up, she leaned against his chest for support and felt the strong cadence of his heartbeat against her hand. In the sky above them the southwest monsoon clouds floated across the moon, flooding the island in silver radiance one moment, swathing it in mysterious shadows the next.

With surprising gentleness he lifted his hand to her cheek to smudge the traces of tears the wind had not dried. "I never meant to upset you. I was only thinking of your welfare."

"I realize that," she whispered. "I am overtired, perhaps."

He lowered his voice. "If I was rude, it was probably because you took me off guard earlier. In fact, I doubt any man could keep his equilibrium around you for long, Miss Fairfield."

Suddenly Lorna felt as though every sense she possessed was awakening for the first time ever, so attuned to her surroundings as to be almost painful. The warmth of Ross's skin penetrated the wind's chill and sent tingling heat through her fingertips. The high-pitched keening of the wind and the pounding surf against the shore became a medley of wild delight. The air smelled so clean and pure as to hurt her lungs when she inhaled.

And as she looked up into Ross's face, she saw mirrored in his eyes the same sense of pleasurable confusion that had stolen over her.

"What did you want to show me?" she asked, to break the strange spell that had fallen over them.

He led her behind the thrashing clump of bamboo, shielding her from the cool droplets of rain they dislodged in passing, then around a twisting hillside path, their footsteps leaving a trail of crushed saw grass behind them.

"Be careful here," he warned her as they approached the forbidding face of a seaside cliff. Lorna could not see how they could possibly climb to its summit until he grasped her hand and guided her onto a deeply engraved series of steps that brought them to a shallow cave that faced the beach.

The air inside smelled damp and cool. Lorna was puzzled to see a small puddle of moonlight in the back of the cave until she realized that there was a wide natural hole in its ceiling. Beneath the hole sat a heavy boulder.

"Take my telescope and climb up onto the boulder, Miss Fairfield. I will hold you by the waist so you don't slip."

Lorna took the telescope from his hand. She did not know why, but if he had instructed her to stand on her head and recite Hamlet's soliloquy, she would have obeyed.

"Now adjust the lens toward Mount Belakan—that is the village at the rim of the ancient volcano in the middle of the island. Tell me what you see."

The wind hit Lorna full across the face as she emerged from the hole, tearing her hair from its comb. Glancing behind her at the sea, she swallowed down a surge of panic at the realization of how high they had climbed. To plunge down into the hidden coral reefs in the raging sea meant certain death.

And yet she had never felt more protected. Ross had

risen to his knees beneath her, his shoulders pressed into her spine. His face was directly below hers, and she felt an unexpected shock of pleasure at the pervading warmth of his face upon the coolness of her neck.

"What do you see?" he repeated patiently.

She raised the telescope. "Darkness. Just darkness and strange little specks . . . oh, dear, I think they might be dust motes."

"Turn the telescope around, Miss Fairfield."

Lorna glanced down at him, noticing how the moonlight caught the glint of humor in his eyes.

"And now?" he asked, pursing his lips as she lifted the telescope again and gazed across the island in silence.

"Nothing—wait. It looks like there are figures moving up the mountain, but it might be anything in the moonlight. It—it appears to be some sort of procession. But whatever would anyone be doing out at this time of night, and in this weather?"

Ross sighed. "Come down into the cave."

He helped her back down onto the ground, his hands holding her firmly around the waist. "What you have just seen are the adherents of the Agung-Mani. The Cult of the Underworld. There was sickness reported in their village today. There will doubtless be a human sacrifice on Mount Belakan to appease the bloodthirsty gods."

"But I had no idea there was anything of that sort still going on here," Lorna said, her voice low with horror. "I understood that most pagan practices had been suppressed."

"Actually the Rajah is very tolerant of the natives' religious beliefs, headhunting and human sacrifices excluded. The cult's followers are a very small segment of our population and inhabit in far greater numbers several of the surrounding islands."

Lorna was silent. She knew the islanders were composed of many diverse cultures: Hindus, Moslems, Malays, Chinese, the Ranjan hill people, and the Gibungs, who lived along the jungle riverbanks.

"I am shocked, Mr. St. James," she said. "Shocked and horrified, which I suddenly realize is precisely the reaction you intended. Nevertheless, this will not dissuade me from my search. Nor do I understand what it has to do with my father."

"I suspect your father was researching the cult for his latest book."

"Then you think . . ."

She moved to the mouth of the cave, fighting a gripping vertigo as she stared down into the restless sea. She struggled to stem the fresh tears that filled her eyes. Tears of fear and frustration.

"When I suggested you go home, it was for your own good," he said. "I did not mean to be cruel, however it may have sounded."

Shaking her head, she fought to regain her composure. Even in her distress, she was acutely aware of his presence, alternately thrilled and disturbed by it. "No," she murmured, weariness sweeping over her in waves like the surf below. "I supposed you did not."

"You have a fiancé in London, as I understand," he went on. "I cannot comprehend how he could allow someone like you to come here alone—"

"I am not alone. I have my uncle."

"Yes, but any man who loved you should want to be with—"

He broke off. Lorna swung around to look at him, catching a softening of his austere features that she had not glimpsed before. Although she did not dare to interpret what it could mean, she was conscious of a flush of heat within her that suddenly counteracted the cold fear of the previous moment.

"I have nothing left in London," she said, not knowing why she felt compelled to make such a personal admission to him. "No one."

He shifted forward so that she could no longer see his face, but before he moved she thought she noted a spark of something in his gaze that made her feel she had gotten his full interest now. "Indeed?" he said.

Her heartbeat quickened, and she shivered in unconscious anticipation. The special intonation he'd given the single word might have been her imagination, but she did not think so.

"Indeed," she replied softly.

She could not sleep. The wind abated and then returned with renewed force. The sulap shook and insects scurried about seeking refuge in the nooks and crannies of its rattan-lashed roof. Turning onto her side, Lorna opened her eyes to see a centipede crawling across the exterior of the mosquito netting.

She squeezed her eyelids shut, trying to tune out the discordant sounds of the wind, Ilse's snoring, Kana scratching himself in the kitchen. The image of Spencer and Emily as she had last seen them flitted uninvited across her mind, two shadows embracing within the bedchamber of his three-story townhouse on the Thames. They had not even had the discretion to draw the curtains or extinguish the candles that threw their figures into such revealing silhouette. But then, they had not counted on Lorna's returning a week early from Paris, where she had gone to be fitted for her wedding trousseau. She had sat inside her carriage for three hours and cried, ignoring her driver's kindly pleas to take her home, waiting for Emily to emerge. When it became apparent that Emily was going to spend the night in Spencer's house, Lorna had finally left, her heart so numb that it could only reject the pain from that moment onward.

Not even Spencer's tearful entreaties the following afternoon, when she confronted him with his betrayal, had moved her. At first he had tried to deny anything had happened between him and Emily, and that so angered Lorna he finally broke down and confessed the truth.

"We didn't intend for it to happen, Lorna. I swear it. We met inadvertently at Billy Steele's supper party, and believe it or not, we spent most of the time there discussing you. And then her carriage was late, so I offered her a ride.''

"You don't need to tell me the rest," Lorna had managed to say, turning away as he put a hand to his face. "Thank you for admitting the truth.''

"Then—then does that mean you've forgiven me? That we shall proceed with the wedding as planned?''

"No, Spencer," she replied, steeling herself for one of the ugly outbursts that she'd foolishly believed would abate after they were married. Oddly, it was only now, after his betrayal, that she was seeing him in his true light. "I—I've decided to accompany my uncle to the island of Kali Simpang to search for my father. You do recall he'd gone missing, and now it seems even the Rajah is quite concerned.''

"You're joking, Lorna. What good would a young woman like you do in the jungle? I shall have to talk to Richard about this, demand he put—''

"It was my uncle's idea that I go.''

"But he knows we're to be married.''

Lorna's mouth tightened. She wasn't about to inform him that Uncle Richard had suggested she and Spencer move up their wedding date and actually spend their honeymoon on Kali Simpang.

He'd attempted then to take her into his arms and kiss her, but she had recoiled from his touch with such instinctive revulsion that he had instantly released her.

"If you go to this heathen island, Lorna, and leave me in the lurch with all the wedding arrangements pending, I shall not wait for you to return.''

"Perhaps I'll never return," she had countered recklessly, aware how he had manipulated the conversation to make himself appear the injured party. "At any rate, Spencer, I shan't return to *you*. Not after what you did.''

For the first time then, she saw panic in his eyes. "It was a mistake. You can't let it change the years of our courtship, and before that the childhood friendship we developed in Hampshire . . .''

"Good-bye, Spencer."

"I will wait for you, Lorna. But only until you return. You'll have to have forgiven me by then. . . .''

The unhappy memory of that last meeting faded, and for several moments, she did not think but listened to the wildness of the wind.

Next Monday was to have been her wedding day, she remembered with a humorless smile. And the week after she would turn twenty-four.

She opened her eyes and focused hard on the centipede before the forbidden tears of hurt and humiliation had a chance to form. The sulap, she realized suddenly, was rocking on its stilts as Ross returned from his latest moonlight vigil.

Ross. The thought of him unleashed a flood of confusing sensations which she would have liked to attribute to fatigue but could not. The touch of his strong hands around her waist earlier that evening. The smoky intensity of his eyes in the cave when she had caught him watching her. Even the urbane detachment of his manner. These things intrigued her, frightened her. What a puzzling man he was. So unlike Spencer, with his hunts and card games and other tedious social addictions. She could not imagine Spencer living in a leaky hut with an impudent headhunter, nor could she envision him ever having the dedication to stand watch in the wind. But what did a man like Ross St. James do for pleasure?

She peeled back the coverlet. Perhaps he had a woman. Remembering the brush hidden away in his chest of drawers, she felt a sudden sting of inexplicable curiosity. He seemed so brusque, it was difficult to imagine him having a tender side. But then possibly *she* had brought out the worst in him. At any rate, he hadn't seemed particularly overjoyed at her sudden appearance today.

* * *

It was almost daybreak when the wind gave a violent heaving gust and blew the roof off the sulap.

Lorna had finally fallen asleep. But her sleep had not been restful, disturbed by fragmented dream images of first Spencer and Emily together, and then her father, who was running for his life through the jungle, his cries for help so clear they jolted through her consciousness. She wanted desperately to help him, but something held her back so that she couldn't run. And when she turned to free herself, she saw a ferocious tiger, its paws weighing down her skirts. She could feel its foul moist breath on her face, and it was shaking her, playing with her, batting her between its great paws as if she were a mouse.

She woke with a startled cry, looking up to see an inky sky and shifting clouds as the roof was wrenched from the hut and thrown against the hillside. It was raining again, sheets of it soaking the floor, the bedding, the furniture inside the exposed sulap.

"God above!" Ilse cried, lifting her face to the nonexistent ceiling. "Now what's happened?"

"The wind blew the roof off," Ross shouted from outside the screen. "Miss Fairfield, do you think you could help me?"

Lorna and Ilse traded mystified looks. "Of course. Has something happened to Kana?"

Ross didn't answer her until they were outside on the veranda. "In Kana's tribe, it is considered taboo to rebuild a house that falls apart. Supposedly it is a sign from the gods. An unholy spot."

Lorna looked out into the predawn turbulence. She was tempted to tell him that in her native Hampshire there was a similar taboo, but he didn't look as if he were in the mood to appreciate any attempt at humor.

"What shall I do, Mr. St. James?"

"For now all we can do is spread a canvas cover over the sulap. You're going to have to climb the ladder, I'm afraid, and hold the canvas while I temporarily secure it.

Unfortunately, there's no way we can keep the rain off. I hope you don't catch cold easily.''

It was trickier work than Lorna anticipated. The physical demands of balancing on the ladder with her arms extended to flatten the canvas and the rain flaying her back left her aching and exhausted. The wind challenged Ross's every movement, and by the time he'd finished fastening the canvas to the frame with liana vine, his face showed the strain of his efforts.

''Good work, Miss Fairfield,'' he said as they stood alone together afterward, breathing hard and gazing up into the rain to admire their handiwork.

She smiled tiredly. She did not know why, it was quite absurd, but his simple words of praise made her feel as though she had just helped Michelangelo decorate the Sistine Chapel.

Inside the sulap, he gave her a glass of banana sap to relax her so that she could get back to sleep. The deceptively sweet concoction slid down her throat and spread through her system with alarming swiftness.

''Oh, my,'' she said. ''That's gone right to my head.''

''It will be dawn in another hour,'' he said as he took the empty glass from her hand. ''I suggest you try to get some rest. And change out of those wet things again.

Lorna smiled. She felt utterly relaxed and as limp as a rag doll in the large rattan chair . . . until unexpectedly Ross leaned toward her, his sensual mouth lifting at the corners into a smile that sent a frisson of anticipation down her spine. She dug her nails into her palm and stared up at him, transfixed as he reached down and drew her from the chair.

She laughed uncertainly. ''Where are we going now?''

''I'm going back to my hammock. And you've little choice but to retire to my bedroom. There should be dry linen in the iron-bound chest under the window.'' He glanced around the room. ''That is, if Ilse hasn't used it all mopping up the place.''

''But won't the mattress be wet?''

"I'll bring another tarp in to cover it."

"I'm really quite an annoyance, aren't I?"

"You would call me rude again if I admitted you were."
He squeezed her hand, his voice low and mocking. "Go
to bed before the foundation gives way beneath us."

Lorna leaned back from him, holding her breath as his
fingers tightened around hers before he released her hand.
She could have been wrong, but it seemed he was hesitant
to let her go. "I should like you to confess something to
me," she said.

His eyes glittered with amusement. "And what would
an ill-mannered hermit like me have to confess?"

"Tell me what you were thinking when you smiled at
me a few moments ago."

He gave a rueful laugh. "Oh, no, Miss Fairfield. That
particular thought was far too—well, let's just say it was
not fit for a young gentlewoman's ears."

"Now you've really aroused my curiosity."

He placed his hand on her forearm and guided her to
the bedroom partition, his eyebrows lifting in mock alarm
at Ilse's dragonlike snores filtering through the screen.

"I'll leave the tarp out here," he said. "I plan to see
the Rajah tomorrow regarding your father. Rest well, Miss
Fairfield."

"And you, Mr. St. James."

Chapter 3

The early morning sun turned every particle of moisture to steam. Ross peeled off his damp linen shirt, folded it neatly, and placed it with his other belongings in the *prau*, the native hand-hollowed canoe that provided the fastest mode of transportation across the island.

The rains had swollen the river six feet overnight. He would travel swiftly through the jungle to the British fort, provided he didn't lapse into inattentiveness while negotiating the boulder-pitted rapids. One mistake at the cascades could have tragic consequences.

He relaxed as he felt the dugout escape the sluggish jungle stream to catch the current. It would be easy to let his mind wander this morning, as active as it was assimilating his impressions of the previous day. Although he had been expecting Lorna Fairfield's arrival for over a month, he had not anticipated she would enter his life with quite such dramatic flair. He had also been prepared to dislike her. Instead, he had lain awake until dawn, thinking about her sleeping in his bed, picturing her as she had looked at the mouth of the cave with the moonlight outlining her slender form. He shifted forward, pushing the pleasing images from his mind with the practiced ease of one accustomed to disciplining his own thoughts.

"Tuan Resident! Tuan Resident!"

He waved at the group of Gibung children playing along the riverbank. Naked, their thin brown chests ornamented with necklaces of tigers' teeth, they chased and were chased in turn by a pair of mange-eaten mongrels. Farther back behind the trees, he could see the mud hut village of their families. Each dwelling gate was surmounted by a bamboo altar, and on these were trays of fresh fruit, roasted chicken, and flowers as offerings to the gods. Fighting cocks in bell-shaped baskets had been placed outside for the day while the women of the household walked the many miles to market and the men cultivated padi on the hill terraces.

"Tuan Resident! You come inside today?"

Ross glanced up at the enormously pregnant woman on the bamboo bridge above him. To deny such a request in her advanced condition would be to put a curse upon her unborn child.

"Only for a little while," he called back, plying his pole toward the muddy embankment.

The smoke from cooking fires was so acrid and thick inside the hut that Ross's eyes watered and his nostrils twitched in irritation. The family's grandmother, her body as brown and shriveled as a peanut shell, was passing out bananas, mangoes, and jackfruit to the three ebony-haired children seated on the floor.

"And what did you dream last night, Murit?" she asked of her eldest grandson, casually examining a louse she had extracted from his hair.

"I dreamt that the men of the village caught the rhinoceros that killed old Hajim the cloth merchant last month."

"That is a good dream, Murit," she said, giving him a toothless smile. "It means we will have peace for as many days as it took to catch the rhinoceros. And you, Tuan Resident, what did you dream?"

Ross swallowed the slice of mango he had been eating and shook his head in apology. In the Malay culture the sharing of dreams took on the utmost significance, and such important events as weddings, funerals, and the harvesting of padi were often planned around their interpretation.

"I can't remember, Grandmother. I slept very little last night and . . ." He hesitated, suddenly recalling the elusive snatches of the dream he had been having before the explosion of tropical sunrise awoke him. He was surprised to realize he had slept at all, and even more so to think that Lorna had so deeply impressed his mind that she had already begun to invade his dreams.

"I dreamt of a woman."

"A woman, Tuan?" the grandmother echoed, sending an intrigued look toward her pregnant daughter. "A woman of the island?"

"No." He almost laughed at her sudden air of importance. Ever since his uncle the Rajah had been overheard encouraging Ross to take a Malay wife, he had been plagued by a string of prospects, a few of them undeniably appealing. But he did not think another marriage was in the cards for him, despite his uncle's ardent efforts to arrange one. Since the death of Ross's young English wife, Vanessa, and their son during childbirth, a fate for which he assumed full responsibility, he had sealed away the part of himself that loving another woman would demand. Remarriage was not impossible, of course. At times he felt the ache of loneliness for companionship and physical union that his occasional casual encounters did not even begin to assuage. But, until he felt that the future of Kali Simpang was secure from headhunting pirates, he did not have time for romance. Work had become both his absorbing passion and his escape—providing an insidious self-flagellation and at times an almost monastic discipline of solitude. But above all, there was little time left between his duties to brood over what he had lost.

Not that he had been above taking a native mistress, for his was a self-imposed isolation of the heart. He had recently ended a two-year relationship with a young island woman when he realized that she was well into marriageable age, and he wasn't prepared to make her his wife. Their affair had ended amicably enough when he arranged a marriage between her and a handsome rice farmer on the island.

His gray eyes amused, he sliced through the succulent orange flesh of a papaya. "This woman had red-gold hair, Grandmother, like the copper cooking vessels they sell at the Chinese bazaar."

Her gaze widened. "It is so, Tuan?"

He nodded. "And green eyes the color of the sea during the musim. And I"—he wavered as the images flashed across his mind—"I dreamt that she and I were sailing over the sea together." He lifted another sliver of papaya to his mouth and subsided into silence as the old woman and her daughter conversed excitedly in their Malay dialect.

"It is a good dream, Tuan," she announced at last.

"Well, that's a relief." He smiled thoughtfully. "You foresee good things for me and this woman then?"

"Yes." She gave him a shrewd glance. "You lift the loincloth for woman soon?"

"I don't think so," he said, rising from his knees with a wistful laugh. "The Rajah has placed the young lady under my protection. It would not seem proper to lift the loincloth for her."

She shrugged her stooped shoulders, as if she had long since ceased to wonder at the white man's complicated rules of courtship, then she pulled aside the screen that divided the room for their sleeping quarters. A young boy of about ten lay curled on a dirty mat, his eyes bright with fever.

"What happened to him?" Ross asked quickly.

"He hurt foot in trap. He brave boy and not cry once."

Ross knelt, his face hardening as he unpeeled the filthy bandage to reveal the ominous red streaks that indicated gangrene radiating from the boy's ankle. "You were bad not to fetch me right away, Grandmother," he said sternly. "I'll have to stop at the fort for the doctor to be sent here right away. You'll be damned lucky if he only loses his foot."

"I burned offerings to the gods for him, Tuan," the woman said in an injured voice. "I walks all the way up to the Temple of Penala."

Ross arose, his voice grim as he made his way outside. "Whether or not the goddess heard you, Grandmother, I wish you had informed me of this."

He returned to the riverbank in a far darker frame of mind than he had left it.

It was something he had not grown used to in all his years on Kali Simpang, the stoic acceptance of suffering and premature, often unnecessary, death and mutilation. The natives laughed at their own physical misery, no matter how debilitating, and looked upon dying as merely the pathway to a higher spiritual reincarnation. And although there were two British doctors who practiced on the island, their services were as often ignored from sheer laziness as they were sought after.

"If you are to be my successor, Ross, you must learn to accept their way of life for what it is," the Rajah had repeatedly counseled him, for his own policy had been noninterference and the preservation of native custom insofar as possible.

The landscape changed as Ross penetrated deeper into the jungle, the dugout racing beneath a canopy of creepers that tumbled down from the hills on either side. He poled skillfully around a massive water buffalo wallowing in the muddy stream, and watched a sacred long-tailed eagle alight in the parasitic growths that sprouted in bizarre configurations from the trees overhead.

For reasons he did not understand he felt more alone this morning than usual, more aware of his deeper emotions. Perhaps it was knowing that the young boy he had just left would surely die. Or perhaps it had been waking up to see Miss Fairfield's haircomb on his chair, her mud-stained stockings hanging out to dry from the window where she slept. Damn but the woman had a way of slipping into his thoughts.

He tensed as the waters beneath him quickened, his back

muscles flexing in anticipation. Shooting the jungle rapids had become second nature to him, and today he did so with deliberate reckless daring . . . as if a confrontation with danger would subdue the personal demons rearing inside his soul. As he paddled swiftly, the river, fed from its mountain source, spewed a plume of refreshingly cool water onto his sun-bronzed face and chest.

Trees on stilted aerial roots fell behind him in a blur as he descended into the still water below. He glanced up at the weathered temple shrine to Shiva on the hilltop. Many of the natives had converted to Mohammedanism and others had adopted Hinduism while continuing to practice their native aboriginal religion. The American missionary who had recently arrived on the island to convert souls to Christianity had his work cut out for him.

"Good morning, Ross!" the Scottish sentry shouted down from the blockhouse as he paddled past Fort Anne. "Coming in for a game of cards today?"

"Can't. I'm expected at the GH." Ross squinted up at the ruddy-faced soldier. "Send word that Dr. Parker is to go to the Gibung village. There's a young boy there with gangrene. I don't expect he'll live."

"Shame," the sentry said, his face somber beneath his helmet. Then, "There's been another raid off the coast of Maleh. Looks like you were right all along, Ross. The pirates are working their way here."

It was not the news Ross needed to hear to improve his mood. For almost a year now, he had been anticipating an attack on the island from the raiding parties of headhunting Sea Dyaks and Illanun pirates who sailed in their warships from as far away as the southern Philippines under the patronage of the Sultan of Sulu. Ross had taken it as his personal mission to prepare both the natives and the few British residents stationed here for an attack, which no one except him really believed would occur. But he had studied the raiding pattern carefully, and Kali Simpang was a highly vulnerable target, her shallow coast no longer protected by the British navy.

A surprise attack would mean mass slaughter.

He was still mulling over how to use this latest piece of news to convince the Rajah they needed more protection when he reached the shores of the Government House twenty minutes later.

Passing beneath the building's cool arcaded corridors that were strung with purple bougainvillea, he strode directly into the heart of the house to the bathroom. A young Malay attendant greeted him with a cool rice beer, then sponged him down with scented water and pressed the fresh change of clothing he had brought.

The Rajah was in court when Ross entered the marble-tiled hall. The case involved a dispute over a crocodile that was accused of eating a man, and the defense was arguing that the animal should not be put to death as it was only following the laws of nature. Besides, everyone on the island knew the crocodile was a favored being of the gods, respectfully referred to as "grandfather."

When it was over, and the crocodile in question had been acquitted, the young native prosecution lawyer left the hall in a temper, yelling from the doorway to the defense.

"May you reincarnate as a pig tick, and all your children as maggots!"

"Good morning, Ross," the Rajah said as he shuffled a stack of papers across the table to the *mentri besar,* his Moslem prime minister and personal advisor, Abdul Mezid. Erudite and soft-spoken, the middle-aged man gave Ross a faint nod as he prepared to leave. He was Ross's staunchest supporter in trying to convince the Rajah the island needed naval protection.

"You're looking a bit grim today," Charles told Ross. "What dismal news have you brought me?"

Ross gripped the edge of the table. "Miss Fairfield and her party have arrived."

"Wind blew them in, did it?"

"In a manner of speaking, yes."

Charles leaned back against the fan-shaped rattan chair,

his deep blue eyes kindling with interest. His skin was as darkly burnished as his nephew's. But his long-term illness, consumption, had given it a translucent sheen so that it stretched like parchment across his regal cheekbones. His once robust body had begun to waste away too. He had fine white hair, which he wore to his shoulders, and he was stroking the flowing white beard that Ross half seriously maintained he had grown to make him look more like God.

"Sit down, for heaven's sake, Ross. You look for all the world like a parrot perched on the table. Have you spoken at length with Richard Fairfield about his brother's disappearance?"

"I haven't even met him. Miss Fairfield and I did not have the standard introduction."

"I detect a thread of tension in your voice. Bit of a tigress, is she?"

A lock of hair falling across his damp forehead, Ross drew a patient breath and sat down as he was instructed. The Rajah's penchant for labeling people as animals was only one of the elderly man's peculiar traits that Ross had learned to tolerate. No wonder Charles and Lorna's father, the eccentric Sir Arthur, had been fast friends. They were both a pair of certified Bedlamites.

"I had not thought of her in those terms," he said carefully. "But the truth is, she's quite a lovely young woman, if rather stubborn—"

"Lovely, Ross? Yes, that doesn't surprise me. Of course, she was still a child in plaits and pinafores when I met her in London. But lovely? Coming from you that is indeed a compliment. However, you are hardly one to remark on another's stubbornness—"

"She's got it into her head that she's going to be allowed to participate in this search for her father."

The Rajah's eyes rolled suddenly back in their sockets before he lowered his lids and lapsed into silence. Ross sat forward. He wasn't sure whether his uncle was ill or merely feigning mystical contemplation.

"Uncle Charles," he said urgently. "Are you all right?"

The blue eyes finally opened, dark with pain and the discipline required to control it. "Sir Arthur is a very dear friend of mine, Ross, back from the days when we attended Eton together. Furthermore, he has promised to write my biography and a history of this island. If I were well, I would launch a search for him myself. It is not hard for me to understand his own daughter wishing to do so. Did she not hire a reliable guide to help her?"

Ross's face darkened. "That's another thing. She's got that damned butterbox Kurt van Poole from Java. For the life of me, I can't understand why he'd waste his time locating Sir Arthur. Van Poole usually goes after bigger game. Or glory."

"Van Poole is an unpleasant character, I must agree, but indisputably competent." Charles frowned thoughtfully. "Wasn't there talk about him and a fatal accident when he worked the African diamond mines?"

"Murder," Ross said grimly. "And not just one. It's believed he had his own wife killed by one of his hunting dogs because she cuckolded him."

"But this only means that you will have to watch over dear Lorna all the more."

"Watch over her. Now just a minute. It's one thing to take a courteous interest or to offer formal protection, but . . . watch over her?"

"Yes. Protect her as best you can from van Poole's influence."

"The man has been hired by Miss Fairfield of her own volition. Do you propose I chain myself to her side to 'watch over her'?"

"I am only asking you to be nice to Miss Fairfield, Ross."

"Be nice. What exactly does that rather banal order entail?"

The Rajah smiled and folded his hands across his blue silk sarong. "Everything."

"Everything. Oh, God." Ross flexed his fingers to help

tamp down his rising irritation. "Have you heard the news this morning, Your Highness?" he asked in a voice of lethal calm. "Do you know about the attack on Maleh Bay?"

"Indeed, I have. Remind me later we must relay a message of regret and support to the prince."

"They had a standing army of thirty thousand natives and a protected harbor. We have a plodding East India Company steamer that cruises the coast when the weather strikes the captain's fancy."

"When you succeed me, Ross, which God knows will not be long, you can build up your own army and deluge Her Majesty with endless petitions for royal protection."

The Rajah's reference to his illness took the wind out of Ross's sails. Charles was dying; the man who had lifted him out of the mire of self-pity and depression he had sunk into six years ago, after taking a bullet in the spine during the Opium Wars when Ross was a young naval lieutenant.

The injury had ended Ross's career only a year after it began, leaving him not merely physically debilitated but faced with a sense of personal failure. His father had been a British Royal Navy admiral whose dying wish had been that his son attain maritime prominence. But it wasn't surprising that Stephen St. James had expressed more disapproval than concern over his son's injury. Nothing Ross had ever done had pleased his harsh, demanding father.

Still, it was that injury that had brought Ross to Kali Simpang. Laid up in a Singapore hospital, brooding over a prognosis of permanent paralysis that could spread from his spine into his legs, he thought his life was over when Uncle Charles arrived to insist a Chinese physician examine Ross. After a risky operation that might have worsened his condition, Ross had the bullet fragment removed and the afflicted nerves freed. On Dr. Liu's orders, he had begun rebuilding his health by practicing the ancient art of T'ai Chi Ch'uan. To this day he still used the deceptively graceful exercises to discipline his mind. Skill in self-defense had become an additional benefit.

As he recovered, he began to work for his uncle on the island, first as his secretary, then Assistant Resident until the original Resident retired and Ross replaced him. The recuperation, the healing process, had been slow and frustrating for a young man who thrived on activity. Vanessa Eveland, the daughter of a British diplomat in Singapore, had been a bright spot in the darkness of those days and had contributed greatly to his recovery. Theirs was a whirlwind courtship; she had gotten pregnant the first time Ross made love to her, and he had married her out of gratitude and an infatuation that had never fulfilled his expectations. But then—

"Ross."

He looked up, startled, at the sound of his uncle's voice.

"I have another case now," Charles continued as murmuring voices sounded outside the door. "You still haven't learned to relax, have you? Perhaps a visit to that brothel on the wharves would help."

Ross passed a hand over his face.

"Whatever happened to the botanist's daughter who so fancied you a few weeks back?" Charles continued. "I seem to remember your being caught in a compromising position with her in the government carriage."

"She was thrown into my lap when the carriage hit a palm stump." Ross lowered his hand. "Her father packed her back off to England when a marriage proposal was not forthcoming."

"You did not care to marry her?"

"I did not."

"But it's been four years since Vanessa died and you cannot blame yourself forever—" Charles stopped, warned by the sudden tightening of Ross's features that this was a subject he still dare not broach. "Help Miss Fairfield find her father."

"He disappeared from the island, Your Highness. Not on it."

"Be nice to her, Ross. That is an official order. And my final request of you as your uncle."

My final request.

The three words echoed like a counterpoint to the pounding between Ross's temples as he wended his way through the throng of tribesmen, soldiers, and Malay officials waiting outside the door.

My final request.

He stepped outside into the blistering sunlight, nodding his thanks to the serving woman who glided across the manicured lawn to hand him a glass of green pineapple nectar.

"Be nice to her," he muttered, and all he could think about, as the thick sweet juice quenched his thirst, was how warm and feminine Lorna had felt in his arms as he held her in the cave. How the moonlight and rain had bathed the soft curves of her body in a tantalizing glow. How he had ached to kiss her teasing red mouth again and again as she bade him good-night that final time.

"Cockfight in courtyard, Tuan," the serving woman said, interrupting his thoughts as she tugged at his arm. "You place bets?"

"I don't care for the sport, Sanal. Besides, I have to rebuild the lookout so that the Sea Dyaks don't take us by surprise."

A look of fear replaced the playful expression on the woman's face. Hers was a peaceful people, rice farmers and fishermen, easy victims for the bloodthirsty pirates who took slaves and collected children's heads as trophies. Although headhunting was still practiced here in the remote jungle regions, it was far less prevalent than it had been when Ross first came to the island.

"I burned an offering to the spirits for protection, Tuan, when I was a little child," she said, her face brightening. "They send you to island. Bring good lucks to us. You stay and we safe."

Ross wiped his forehead and put on his pith helmet with a wry smile. "I hope so, Sanal. I truly hope so."

Chapter 4

Lorna slid deeper into the copper-lined bathtub and closed her eyes. Even the hint of an offshore breeze that blew in from the opened doors of the veranda did little to relieve the heat. It was far hotter here, on the second-floor bedroom of her father's plantation house, than it had been in Ross's sulap that morning when she'd awakened, her arms and legs covered with sand fly bites, her back stiff and aching.

She was slowly realizing that her father's two-story white wooden house was sturdier than it looked, weathered by constant storms and corrosive salt air. Although its porch was warped from the rains and its facade sadly in need of painting, it possessed a simple charm. Backed by climbing fields of withered tobacco, it stood perched on a sunny hillside and overlooked the island and the surrounding clear green seas of the bay.

"You ready for towel now?" asked Chiang, the Chinese amah, for the fifth time in as many minutes. "Skin rot if you stay in water for too long." She hovered over the tub to smack a mosquito between her palms. "I iron your dress for party tonight."

Lorna rose with a sigh of reluctance. "Thank you, Chiang. You're a treasure. I don't—" She stopped in mid-sentence, clutching the bedpost for support as the stout woman began to vigorously rub her skin dry with a pair of coarse cotton towels. When Chiang had finished, she ran a cloth saturated in rose oil over Lorna's tingling flesh and helped her into a gauze dressing robe.

"I finish unpack while you at party, missee. And then I iron other dresses that still in trunk."

Lorna gazed ruefully at the battered trunk at the foot of the bed. It seemed she had lived out of the monstrosity all her life—at least since she was ten, when her mother had died. Unable to adjust to widowerhood, her father had at first dealt with his grief by either surrounding himself with witty companions into the late hours of his lonely nights, or by sitting in moody silence and then devoting days on end to his writing.

There had been little time for the upbringing of his precocious only child, who suddenly found herself in the heartbreaking position of losing not only a mother but, for all practical purposes, a father as well.

Then when Lorna turned eleven, he unexpectedly dismissed the governess she'd become attached to and pulled Lorna from the security of their rural Hampshire home to spend a year traveling across Europe. At one point he disappeared, leaving her with an elderly French couple, when he decided impulsively to spend a summer with a band of gypsies.

Research, he claimed. Inspiration. And only as she reached adulthood had Lorna realized it was all escape to him, escape from the aching loss he could not accept.

He felt guilty for leaving her alone that summer, and so to make up for his neglect he began to drag her along on his travels—first, for a sojourn in a castle on the Rhine with an impoverished German baron; her father had the habit of making friends with the queerest sorts. There the twelve-year-old Lorna had learned to tickle trout, shoot a bow and arrow, and discern beneath which toadstool the fairies had danced the previous evening. All very useful abilities for when Lorna made her debut into society, Aunt Julia had scathingly remarked. Then there was an interlude in the Spanish Basque country where Lorna was abandoned to a Spanish housekeeper and her bullfighter husband while her father absorbed the "atmosphere of orange blossoms and rural poets." Afterward they went to Greece so that he could soak up the inspiration of the "ancients."

On Lorna's sixteenth birthday, she found herself in Egypt, and it was on her return to London that a horrified Aunt Julia demanded that her niece be placed in boarding school before she became an utter gypsy with "no social or domestic inclinations to ease her passage into womanhood."

"Blister it, woman," Arthur Fairfield had argued back. "The girl can read, write, cook, and even sew better than you. What more would you have her learn?"

"You miss the point," Julia had replied with self-righteous scorn. "It's not what Lorna hasn't learned, but rather what she is learning that frightens me. She's far too . . . independent and free-spirited to fit in with other young people her age."

The enforced separation had not pleased either father or daughter. Sir Arthur was certain he could not survive without Lorna, and she privately feared the same. To make matters worse, she had trouble adjusting to the tedious discipline of boarding school. Fortunately her good humor and high spirits made her popular among the other pupils, if not the schoolmistress.

But in her heart, she always felt different from her peers. Most of the other girls had normal families to visit on holidays, while more often than not when she went home, Papa was locked away in his room or visiting friends because he had forgotten, with his total disregard of time, that it was a holiday. Lorna would eat Christmas dinner with the servants, which so scandalized Aunt Julia that once she actually endured the ride from London to Hampshire in the cold weather that so aggravated her crippling arthritis, just so that her niece would not have to celebrate alone.

Chiang's voice drew her back to the present. "Trunk is locked, missee," she said, rising from the bare wood floor. "You unlock for me?"

"The rest of the unpacking can wait, Chiang. Except for one dress I would like you to carefully store away."

Lorna walked to the black teak wardrobe and opened it to remove the ivory-silk wedding gown she had been fitted for in Paris while Spencer was amusing himself behind her back with her best friend. Aunt Julia's featherbrained young Irish chambermaid had apparently packed it by accident. It was a painful reminder of the humiliation Lorna was determined to forget.

The middle-aged housekeeper gasped in admiration of the needlework, coming forward to examine the Chantilly lace sleeves and pearl-seeded overskirt with its flounced hem.

"Why you not wear to party tonight, missee?"

"It was to have been my wedding gown," Lorna said in a wistful voice. "Unfortunately, now I cannot even bear to look at it, let alone try it on. Still, it's far too costly to go to waste. Wrap it up carefully for me, please, so that the moths and mildew can't destroy it. I'll donate it to charity rather than let it waste."

"But you find husband one day," Chiang said, reverently draping the dress over her arm.

"Perhaps. But right now it is more important that I find my father. You haven't any personal theories on his disappearance, have you? You were here with him every day and night. Did he confide in you?"

Chiang moved toward the door, her eyes lowered to the gown in her arms. When she returned her gaze to Lorna, it was devoid of expression, although her fingers had tightened noticeably around the doorknob as if she were eager to leave.

"He not tell me anything, missee. He secret man. Put on paper what he thinks."

"Yes, but surely—"

She fell silent, perplexed as the housekeeper mumbled something about returning to her work and then left the room. Either Chiang knew more than she cared to reveal about her employer's disappearance or, like Ross St. James, she believed Sir Arthur was dead and did not want to give Lorna false hope.

Blocking that last thought from her mind, Lorna walked onto the veranda and savored the last remnants of the dying breeze. The perfume of frangipani blossoms wafted to her from the garden, where a pair of peacocks, gifts to her father from the Rajah, strutted in their colorful finery about the lawn. From her vantage point, she had a panoramic view of the island that had so enchanted her father.

In comparison with its neighbor, the Dutch island of Java, or even the more distant Singapore, Kali Simpang was of minor political importance to the British Crown, a forgotten island that lay on the volcanic belt connecting Asia with Australia. Its few gold mines had failed to produce impressive yields. Its pearl fishermen more often lost their lives than found wealth. The island's primary exports were pepper, honeycomb, birds' nests, and shark fins— prized by the Chinese and disdained on the European market. The island was too far-flung to be built up as a naval outpost, and had it not been for the passionate devotion and financial backing of its wealthy white ruler for the past forty years, Charles Montclair, Kali Simpang would have been destroyed by the rebel forces he had subdued. Certainly it would never have become a British Protectorate.

Lorna shaded her eyes from the white-hot glare of the sun and gazed inland. Even in the shimmering haze of daylight the dark volcanic prominence of Mount Belakan with its mist-shrouded crater lake took on an ominous appearance. How strange that her father had never mentioned in his letters the gruesome rituals practiced there. Surely, in his research, he had uncovered the sacrificial rites. Or was there a connection between what he had found in that pagan mountain jungle and the fearful tone of his final letters to her?

There is danger for me everywhere. You must not come here now, Lorna.

Masculine voices from beneath the banyan tree below drifted up on the humid air to the veranda. Frowning, Lorna looked down to see her uncle and Kurt van Poole strolling forward with glasses of rice beer in hand. She drew back hastily, conscious of her immodest attire, but she wasn't fast enough. Kurt had already glanced up and noticed her.

She supposed it was an indication of his survival abilities to notice every subtle shift in his environment. But it still made her feel uncomfortable—as she had when she had first met him in a shabby hotel in Singapore.

Despite her uncle's protestations that van Poole was an eminently qualified guide, she had wanted to look him over for herself. Remembering that interview now, she wondered whether she'd done the right thing in hiring him.

"Your experience in the jungle is undeniably impressive, Mr. van Poole," she had noted. "You have no wife to resent your adventures?"

He had leaned forward, speaking in a heavy Dutch accent, his opaque blue eyes drifting from Lorna's face to the scantily clad Chinese serving girl who'd brought his beer. He had a full squarish face that sat upon a bull-like neck, its fleshy folds burned reddish brown from the sun. Although he was muscular and indisputably strong, his double chin and thick midsection showed a tendency, in his late thirties, to run to fat.

"My wife died several years ago. Attacked by dogs in a hunting frenzy."

"How horrible." He did not seem overcome with grief, and she did not know what else to say on the subject. "And you are the same man who rescued Dr. Miles Mattson from the Congo two years ago?"

"I am. Your own government paid my fee."

"Which was no doubt considerably more than I can afford. I'm puzzled, Mr. van Poole, why you have agreed to help me when it appears there might be danger involved and so little compensation?"

"To face danger is to live." His voice deepened with suppressed excitement. "To face *death* and conquer it is the ultimate challenge, isn't it?"

"I suppose so," she said, suddenly uncomfortable without knowing why. "At least it was one of my father's favorite literary themes." She sat forward. "But I don't understand—"

She broke off, leaning back against her chair as the massive black mastiff at Kurt's side leapt up and began to growl at her.

"Nadji," Kurt said with stern affection to the ugly dog. "He's still not sure of you, Miss Fairfield, and you don't have to understand anything except that I will find your father."

"Is that . . . that animal going to help you?"

"Probably not."

"Good," she said heartily.

Kurt grinned. "He's more comfortable around men, but I'll keep him leashed if you'd feel better about it."

"I think I would." She glanced up as Kurt's sister, Ilse, returned to their table.

"I've told him repeatedly to get rid of the beast," Ilse said, squeezing her round frame in the chair next to Lorna's.

"Why were you so long outside?" Kurt asked her, frowning.

"A little boy was getting beaten because he overturned a rickshaw—"

"And you had to come to his rescue," Kurt interjected, shaking his head.

"I think you should go outside and caution the boy's father against such cruel punishment."

"Let's mind our own business, Ilse," he said in irritation.

Ilse folded her arms in front of her on the table, her eyes glittering with angry tears. "I thought you of all people would understand."

He glared at her for a moment, and though Lorna was utterly bewildered by the silent communication between brother and sister, she sensed it went beyond the incident outside that Ilse had spoken of. Lorna fidgeted in her chair as the silence lengthened.

"All right," he said finally, leaving the table with Nadji at his heels. "I'll hang the boy's father up by his toenails, but for all I know the child deserved a whipping."

Ilse called after him defiantly, "It's probably too late now anyway!" Then, smoothing back her straight blond hair, she gave Lorna a crooked smile. "Do you have any idea what you're getting yourself into?"

"You mean—"

"This search for your father."

"I believe so."

Ilse subjected her to a long scrutiny. "You couldn't possibly know, but I suppose Kurt would say that's half the fun of it."

When Kurt returned several minutes later, his white-blond hair ruffled, his face red from what Lorna could only assume had been a confrontation outside, he addressed her from the end of the table but did not sit down again.

"I make an agreement with you, Lorna. I will lead you to your father as long as you do not turn into a flighty female who sobs at every little scare."

"I will hold my end of that bargain." Her voice was cool. "And as to the matter of your drinking and smoking—"

"I touch nothing once we begin the search. Until then, my life is my own."

Kurt had spent that same night locked up in his room, smoking opium with two singsong girls, and Lorna had decided then and there that she would have to overlook his faults if he was to lead her to her father. She didn't completely trust him, but she could not doubt his expertise. His name was well-known in the streets of Singapore, and as he passed, people would point and whisper, *"Shikari,"* a term she vaguely understood referred to his hunting skills. Of course, his tigerskin-lined leather jerkin and the German steel hunting knife strapped at his hip did tend to set him apart.

Besides, Ilse seemed a pleasant enough sort, and Lorna was too tired after the weeks of sea travel, the worry over her father, and the shock of what Spencer had done to her, to calmly assess the situation. If she had, she might have listened to the faint stirring of unease she felt when she had first met Kurt van Poole. As it was, she had let it pass unheeded.

"Come join us, Lorna," Kurt now shouted up to the

veranda, making no attempt, as good breeding dictated, to pretend he hadn't noticed her.

"It's lovely in the shade," her uncle called up, although his ruddy face and perspiring brow made him look anything but refreshed.

"I'll come down in a few moments," she called. She returned to the room and on impulse knelt before her iron-bound chest to remove the letters she had received from her father over the past two years. There had to be some clue in them that she had overlooked. She did not want to spend a day more in Kurt's company than was necessary.

She untied the red ribbon that held the packet of envelopes together, smoothing down the pages, scanning the opening paragraph of the very first letter he had sent her from the island.

I have found my paradise, Lorna, a place of indescribable magic and mystery untouched by time. My good friend, the Rajah Charles Montclair, whom you may remember meeting once long ago in London, has encouraged me to stay with the intention of writing his biography. What a vain old peacock he is. I hesitate to invite you to visit, as deeply as I miss you. Your dear mother, God rest her delicate soul, would have detested it here, but I am happy, Lorna, even though my tobacco withers in the fields, my writing is neglected . . . I am blissfully content.

She sorted through the following months' letters, her eyebrows drawing into a frown. How disturbing was the difference between his first impression of Kali Simpang and that of his final days here.

She raised the mosquito netting and sank down onto the bed. It required her full concentration to decipher the wavering handwriting and to follow the illogical jump in subject matter which indicated his distress.

There is a rare flower that grows deep in the mountain jungle of this island, Lorna, that is known as the Eden Flower.

It is said that if a man touches it, this blossom of incredible color and beauty, it shall wither instantly on the vine. And the man who has not resisted it, though he shall receive the gift of eternal life, shall know fear and misery from that moment onward. Yet oddly the Eden Flower is immune to the insults of its environment and to every jungle creature you can imagine . . . apes, snakes, the frogs and insects that dwell within it. . . .

Lorna looked up at the window. If he had penetrated the jungles of this island, then there was a good chance indeed that he had encountered the Agung-Mani, the dark cult Ross had spoken of the previous evening. Her heart heavy, she continued to read.

On Kali Simpang and its neighbors, there exists another flower of fascination. It is a hideous thing that the natives call the Corpse Flower, a parasitic growth with monstrous warty petals that give off the stench of putre-fying flesh. . . .

She sank down against the pillows, her frown deepening as she read on to the final paragraph of that same page.

Danger. There is a danger for me everywhere. You must not come here now, Lorna. For I have touched the Eden Flower and it cannot be undone. . . .

She closed her eyes, unable to fight the heat-induced lassitude. The letter fluttered to her lap, forgotten. But as she drifted into a light sleep, the warning it imparted echoed in her mind.

Lorna sat up with a start, her head swinging toward the door as the knob twisted tentatively and then stopped.

''Who is it?'' Who would try to enter her room without knocking? ''Who's there?'' she cried.

Hurried footsteps answered her, fading away down the hall. Flinging up the tangle of netting, she bolted from the bed and ran to the door. To her frustration the jamb was warped, and by the time she got the door open and looked outside, the windowless hallway was dark and deserted. It was probably only Chiang anyway.

She glanced at the clock, grimacing as she realized she had slept about two hours. Her head felt thick, her body so sluggish that she returned to the veranda for a breath of air. To live on Kali Simpang was to battle constantly against the draining humidity.

It was only as her head began to clear that she noticed Ross St. James sitting in the garden with Kurt van Poole. Her uncle was ambling across the lawn toward them with a fresh round of rice beer. She leaned against the railing, intrigued as she heard her name mentioned in the course of the conversation. The confusing lethargy of the moments before had vanished, and in its stead she became aware of a rising sense of anticipation that would not abate no matter how hard she willed it to.

She turned back into the room and hastily donned the violet batik gown with a beribboned bodice that she had bought in Singapore. It clashed brazenly with her coppery hair, but she felt a delicious sense of freedom in its unconfining lines. Besides, it was far more practical in the killing heat than a pinching corset and heavy flounced silk.

She remembered Ross had planned to meet with the Rajah that morning to discuss finding her father. As she flew barefoot down the steep staircase and out into the garden, she told herself that was the only reason her heart was pounding with mad excitement and she was tempted to break into a run across the lawn.

Chapter 5

Ross regarded the two men seated opposite him with growing contempt. Richard Fairfield was typical of the English visitors to the island, scornful of the native customs, eager to bag his tiger or rhinoceros to have stuffed and shipped back to his hunting cronies in London. He was a tall man, with little of his brother's winning charm. He wore his wiry brown hair in a fashionable center part to compliment his fashionable sideburns. He had an annoying habit of sucking air into the gap between his two front teeth, and Ross couldn't help thinking that the Rajah would classify the man as a rabbit. The garden variety.

"Don't know why you're worried about our Lorna," Richard said, apparently so unnerved by Ross's silent scrutiny that he felt compelled to defend himself again. "Gel's got a good head on her shoulders, constitution like a Clydesdale. No one could ride like Lorna to the hunt."

Ross covered a yawn behind his palm and glanced toward the house, his face brightening at the flash of violet he glimpsed on the second-story veranda. "Mr. Fairfield, hasn't it occurred to you that there's a world of difference between the tropical rain forest and the well-traveled woods of a squireen's estate?"

"Of course I know there's a difference," Richard said defensively. "Doesn't take a university degree to tell one from the other, does it?"

Ross studied the other man in surprise. So, Fairfield's

lack of formal education made him feel inadequate, he thought, remembering the scant information on Richard's background in the confidential report. Richard had been confined to a factory to work to support the family when he was a lad while his brilliant older brother went on to Eton. Then Richard had managed to rise from office boy to a senior administrator in the navy office, until his recent retirement. No small feat for an uneducated man. Still, he wouldn't be human if he didn't occasionally resent his older brother's success and easy life.

Kurt van Poole squinted into the sun, elbows braced on his massive thighs. "We'll take care of Lorna," he said in thickly accented English. "Don't you worry, St. James. I'll have my eye on her every minute."

I'll bet you will, Ross thought, his own gaze traveling over the Dutchman before returning to the house. If Richard Fairfield annoyed him, Kurt van Poole aroused in him a deeper, more palpable distrust. He was of medium build, about twenty pounds overweight, with straight blond hair, watery blue eyes, and a ruddy complexion from overexposure to the sun. He was also a tracker of world renown, what the natives called a *shikari*—the consummate jungle hunter. But Ross could not forget the confidential reports he had read of Kurt's involvement in unproven thefts, even a murder, when he had been the *voerman*, the overseer of a mine. And Kurt was an outspoken bigot, a flagrant womanizer whose young wife had died brutally several years ago. As a widower himself, Ross decided it might be charitable to assume that Kurt's amoral, danger-seeking lifestyle stemmed from repressed grief. But in his heart, he knew it wasn't true.

Richard swatted ineffectually at the swarm of gnats attracted to his hair pomade. "That's right, Ross. Kurt and I will protect her unless Spence arrives to relieve us. God, I hope he comes."

Ross glanced up at the black-faced monkey swinging from the branches above them. He had a feeling he wasn't going to like the answer, that he already knew what it would be, but some imp of curiosity got the better of him, and he said, "And who exactly might 'Spence' be?"

"Spencer, Lord Kirkham. Lorna's fiancé, of course. Splendid chap, no matter what my niece is currently claiming. Old money and all that."

"Miss Fairfield led me to believe that she had broken off the engagement."

Richard worked the tip of his tongue between his teeth. "That was just a lovers' quarrel. They've had 'em before. Gel will get over it and run straight into his arms when they meet again."

"I still don't understand why you insist she accompany you," Ross said, taking an instant dislike to splendid old Spence.

Richard and van Poole traded glances. "We couldn't stop her if we wanted to," Kurt said.

Ross shrugged. "You could damn well try. Force her to accept your terms."

"There have been rumors," Richard added in a confidential voice, "that my brother has lost his mind and doesn't want to be found. If anyone can bring 'im back to his senses, it's—"

"Mr. St. James," Lorna said, sounding breathless despite the pains she had taken to glide—not gallop—across the lawn. "You weren't there this morning for me to thank you for your hospitality."

The three men rose from their rattan chairs in deference to her. "Good afternoon, m'dear," Richard said, giving her a quick kiss on the cheek. "You're looking much fresher than you did a few hours ago. That's quite the scandalous little frock you're wearing, isn't it?"

Kurt removed his pipe from his pocket. "It's practical in this climate. No sense for even a female to sweat like a pig. The bloody natives never sweat, you'll notice."

Lorna glanced at Ross, choosing to ignore Kurt's indelicate remarks. "What do you think, Mr. St. James? Shall I run inside and put on my crinoline and stiffened muslin? Am I too indecent for your island?"

Ross took a moment to reply, more intent on enjoying the lovely picture Lorna made, her sea-green eyes luminous, her cheeks already pink from the sun. The roughly woven batik enhanced the slender curves of her body, hugging her small, firm breasts and narrow waist. If there was any reason at all to disapprove of her appearance, it was because he found it difficult to keep from staring at her. As did Kurt van Poole. But that, he reminded himself, was none of his business.

"Considering the fact that the majority of the female population of Kali Simpang go about practically *au naturelle*, you are, in a manner of speaking, overdressed. I am forced to agree with Mr. van Poole. The cooler fabric is more practical."

"Nevertheless, I shall change for the reception tonight."

He nodded. "The Ranee—the Rajah's wife—who is Balinese by birth, loves nothing more than to view the latest European fashions. She is as enamored of our ways as her husband is of hers." He reached down for the pith helmet he had placed on the table. "The government carriage will collect your party at five o'clock. I've been instructed to tell you that you should plan to spend the night at the Rajah's home, in the likely event of rain. At any rate, it isn't safe to travel across the island after dark."

Kurt sucked vigorously on his pipe and exhaled a stream of smoke into the air. "They sacrifice young maidens like you to their gods, Lorna," he said with a chuckle. "Right now the natives are afraid of the stomach sickness, and they are desperate to appease their Lord of Hell."

"I wasn't aware you were so well versed in the secret rituals of this island," Ross said quietly.

"Secret?" Kurt shrugged. "The Cult of the Agung-Mani is more widespread than anyone realizes. It has a sizable following here, and an even bigger following on the island of Jalaka." He glanced at Lorna. "That is where we will search for your father."

"You must be mad," Ross said, his disdain for the

Dutchman blatant in his tone. "No white man has ever left that island alive. The natives refuse to go there unless their gods ordain it, and even then it is considered a suicide mission."

"There is always the exception to the rule," Kurt said, unruffled.

Ross's mouth twisted in contempt. "What possible reason would Sir Arthur have had to go there in the first place?" He glanced at Lorna, remembering his own words to her the previous night, the warning that her father had been researching the cult for his writing. But even then, he did not want to accept it. He did not want to encourage this determined young woman to venture out on a mission from which she might never return.

"I am the shikari, St. James," Kurt said with implacable self-confidence. "You leave the hunting to me and take care of your duties here. I have never failed to return yet from any quest."

An awkward silence fell, Ross breathing deeply to control his sudden anger, Kurt leaning back in his chair with an insolent air as if he would welcome an outburst of violence.

"Remember one thing, van Poole," Ross said at last. "While on this island, you are accountable to me, and Miss Fairfield is under my protection—"

"Am I?" she interrupted.

He nodded faintly. "Through no choosing of my own, the Rajah has placed you under my protection, Miss Fairfield. But if you are so pigheaded as to accompany van Poole on this wild-goose chase, thereby risking your life, then I can't stop you. And even if Sir Arthur had gone to Jalaka . . ."

He wavered, hesitant to say anything more to upset Lorna as he had the previous night. "I will see you at the reception tonight," he said abruptly. "If possible, I'll try to ride alongside the carriage."

He nodded to Lorna and then turned, helmet in hand, and strode off across the lawn to the gate. Lorna stared after him for a moment before impulsively brushing past the two other men to follow him.

"Mr. St. James!" She quickened her pace to compensate for his long-legged strides, but he was out the gate and standing in the shadowed arbor that overlooked the hillside before she reached him.

"Mr. St. James!"

He wheeled at the sound of her voice, his face surprised as she swung around the gate. He thought he had offended her, and though he wasn't proud of his bluntness, he felt justified in speaking his mind.

"I want a word alone with you, if you have the time."

"I have the time," he said.

She laid a hand on his forearm and gently urged him beside her on a stone bench. "You spoke with the Rajah on my behalf?"

He glanced down the hillside, suddenly aware of his conflicting feelings. There was so much hope in her voice that he couldn't bring himself to extinguish it. For all he knew, her father might indeed be lost on Jalaka.

"He is convinced your father is still alive."

He paused as she released a sigh of relief, his gaze lifting to her profile, the small straight nose, the stubbornly rounded chin, the graceful line of her throat. "And he asked—ordered—me to do everything in my power to help you."

"And will you?"

"It is my duty."

"That's not what I meant, and you know it. Will you really try to help me?"

"You are the second woman today who has asked me to do what might be considered the impossible," he remarked. "Except that the first only wanted me to single-handedly protect the island against mass slaughter."

"I understand your position, Mr. St. James. Truly I do. But surely it is not so difficult to understand mine. Kurt believes he can find my father."

"How?"

"What does it matter? The point is that it won't be a wild-goose chase, after all."

It was dark in the hot shadows of the arbor, the sunlight absorbed by the heavy masses of tropical vines that formed a natural arch across the sky. A lizard darted out from an invisible crevice and zigzagged over the garden wall.

"I don't trust him," Ross said after a long silence. "I can't understand why a man with an ego as inflated as van Poole's would expend so much effort searching for a novelist."

"He's being well paid for his efforts," Lorna said dryly. "I dislike him immensely myself, but what does it matter if he finds my father?"

She looked up at him without a trace of pretense on her face. Returning her gaze, Ross felt a pang of tenderness stir in his heart that was as painful as it was pleasant. It had been a long time since he had acknowledged anything except physical attraction for a woman.

"I'll do what I can," he said after a long pause, unable to believe he was hearing his own words. "I don't know how much I can help, but I will try."

Lorna lowered her eyes, so overcome with gratitude and relief she was afraid she would embarrass them both by saying something inane or inappropriate. Instead, she shocked herself even more by springing up and impulsively bracing her hands on his shoulders to kiss him on the cheek. At least that was what she intended to do.

But the moment her lips brushed Ross's jaw, his arm slipped around her waist and pulled her down across his lap. She gasped in startlement, too stunned to resist, and by the time she had regained her senses, it was too late. His mouth had captured hers in a sensual, dizzying kiss that was nothing like the friendly gesture she had planned.

"I am not your uncle, Miss Fairfield," he whispered mockingly against her lips. "And you cannot placate me with a mere peck on the cheek, *my dear gel.*"

"But I didn't—"

Lorna left the sentence unfinished, forgetting what she

had begun to say, struggling simply to draw a breath. Slowly she felt her hands lifting to his shirtfront, absorbing the muffled beat of his heart through her palms. More than once last night, as she lay awake in his bed, she had imagined what it would feel like to have Ross kiss her, to touch her, and her mind had spun, her skin had burned, with her naive imaginings. But what she had not anticipated was the power of her own unbridled physical response, the stirring of raw sensuality in her blood as he brushed his mouth across hers with practiced refinement in a slow, slow kiss that simmered with promise.

In the back of her mind she knew that someone might interrupt them—her uncle, Kurt, or Ilse. But she made no effort to break away—she couldn't have saved herself if she tried. And when he gathered her even closer, his tongue flicking against hers like a flame that ignited every fiber of her being, his strong fingers lifting to tangle in her hair, she stopped trying to resist at all.

"Lorna. Lorna," he repeated hoarsely as they broke apart for air. "I don't think you realize what you're getting yourself involved in. . . ." He shook her gently, but she gave no sign she noticed, the heat of his body, of her own arousal, and the sultry afternoon drugging her senses.

His words had only dimly filtered through the haze in her mind. Was he warning her against him or the search for her father? I don't care, she thought with reckless defiance. I don't care.

As if he sensed that he had not reached her, he anchored his fingers in her hair and dragged her head back, not hard enough to hurt but just until she opened her eyes and met his gaze. Suddenly the veneer of the responsible British officer was gone, and the man he had become since leaving England was revealed: a man who had adapted to his environment by becoming part of it. In order to survive over the years he had been forced to absorb into his soul some of the strength and savagery, the pagan enchantment of the island.

"I don't want to hurt you," he said, his thumb caressing the flushed curve of her cheek. "I do not want to see you hurt."

She stared up at him in silence. After what Spencer had done to her, she did not want to be hurt again either, and there was no doubt that Ross was far more experienced and mature than her former fiancé. But did that not make him even more dangerous?

"I can take care of myself," she assured him softly.

"I wonder," he murmured as he bent his head to kiss her again.

In the end it was Ross who drew away. His hands fell to his sides in a gesture of rigid self-control. His gray eyes seemed almost black in the shadows, dark with unsated desire. His face looked impassive except for the bluish vein throbbing in his forehead. His voice low, he said, "It is very fortunate for you, Miss Fairfield, that you did not choose to convey your gratitude in a more private spot."

Lorna slid back onto the bench beside him and inhaled deeply to slow her heartbeat. Her mouth felt achingly tender. Her bones felt like melted wax. "And if I had?" she asked, her eyes meeting his.

He stood up, his tall frame blocking out what little light could penetrate the foliage overhead. "Few women of your class would venture this far from civilization to find a loved one," he said. "Apparently you are a young woman of great loyalty who is also not afraid of tempting fate. However, I must warn you of one thing, if indeed you still want my help after what has just happened between us."

Lorna sat forward. "Yes?"

"I have lived alone for four years now. No doubt I have forgotten whatever niceties of social convention I ever practiced. I cannot always promise to exert as much self-control as it required for me to end our embrace a few moments ago." He glanced away, his tone strained. "I cannot guarantee that I will always be the proper English gentleman."

A shiver passed over her that was part apprehension, part excitement as he swung around to face her. His

unwavering gaze held the explicit warning that there could
be no room for compromise between them. Perhaps he
meant to possess her as the price of involvement in her
search. And if she accepted, she could not honestly look
back upon this moment and claim she did so solely out of
her desperate need to find her father, or to forget Spencer.
There was something more . . . something wild and dangerously alluring about the man who stood before her.

She got up from the bench as he turned again to stare
down the hillside at the withering tobacco fields that belonged to the plantation house. "I think I understand, Mr.
St. James." She tugged nervously at the ribbons threaded
through her bodice. "And I am willing to take you on
your terms."

"My terms," he repeated, his eyes narrowed with what
might have been triumph, or mockery. The truth was that
he didn't know what his terms were. But he knew he
wanted her. He had since the moment the monsoon had
brought her to him. "I wonder whether your fiancé would
approve."

"I have no fiancé," she said, raising her chin for emphasis. "And if Uncle Richard has been gossiping behind
my back like an old woman, then I can assure you he has
no comprehension of what really happened between me
and Spencer. There is no chance of a reconciliation."

Ross reached around her for his helmet, his eyes never
leaving her face. "I will see you tonight, Miss Fairfield.
Try to rest before then if you can. The Ranee Amayli does
love her parties."

"One more thing," she said, trailing him to the winding dirt path. "My father wrote that he had been cursed
by something called the Eden Flower. Can you tell me if
it's a fictitious creation, or does it really exist?"

"As far as I know, it exists only in fertile imaginations
such as your father's."

"And the Corpse Flower?"

"Ah, yes. *Rafflesia arnoldi*. It is quite real."

She stood quietly as he departed down the path, his lean

figure moving with elegant grace. The sweet turmoil of sensation she had experienced in his arms was at last beginning to fade, and in its place she was conscious of a poignant yearning that emerged from the very depths of her being. Dear Lord, she had never felt like this about Spencer, and she had been prepared to spend her life with him!

Perhaps it was as her father had written. There was magic on this island, and she had already fallen under its enchantment.

Chapter 6

The government carriage that took them to the palace in the middle of the island was an uncomfortable conveyance from the previous century, poorly sprung, swaying from side to side as it lumbered along the water-buffalo track like a clumsy beast. Every so often the driver would jump down from his perch, cursing in Malay, to hack at the liana vines impeding their progress.

"Judging from the smell, the Rajah's last honored guests must have been a Hindu dignitary and the proverbial sacred cow," Lorna said, waving her beaded reticule to and fro to circulate the stale air and swarms of tiny gnats.

"All I can smell is Kurt's pipe," Ilse said. "It's unforgivably rude of him to foul what little air there is to breathe."

"All right. All right." He tamped down the leaves in the bowl of the pipe and flung the ashes out the window. "But I'll stop only because Lorna looks so nice and not because you nag me, Ilse."

"I don't feel nice." Lorna smoothed down the skirts of her apple-green watered silk gown with its heart-shaped bodice that revealed the lacy white chemisette she wore underneath. "I feel decidedly overdressed with all these loincloths and naked limbs about the place."

She turned her face to the window. For the greater part of the ride the road had twisted between river and jungle. Now they were passing a *kampong*, a community of mud

71

huts that lined the riverbank. The villagers had just begun to straggle back from the fields to their smoky dwellings to share an evening meal of fish and rice.

"Have you ever bagged a rhino?" Richard asked Kurt, and Lorna closed her eyes, feeling the humidity drain her energy.

The carriage jolted to a halt with such unexpected force that she slid forward into Ilse. There was the sound of excited native voices outside, and then the carriage rocked crazily as the driver jumped to the ground.

"We've broken an axle," Ilse said, crowding against Lorna to look out the window.

Kurt slid across his seat to the door. "I'll see if it can be fixed. Come on, Richard."

"But your clothes—the reception," Lorna said, watching in astonishment as the pair bounded out the door like overeager schoolboys.

"We won't make the reception at all if we're stuck here all night," Kurt called back over his shoulder.

A half hour passed. Clusters of naked children began to gather around the unmoving carriage, giggling and peering inside the door Lorna had opened to admit fresh air. On the gates lining the village, coconut husks had been twisted together into the shape of crosses and lit to drive away the devilish spirits the darkness would bring.

Finally Kurt rapped against the door. "Richard and I are going to walk ahead to the istana for help. Do you want to wait here or join us?"

"Won't the driver go for you?" Lorna asked.

"No. He refuses to leave the horses. They're extremely valuable in the archipelago, bred especially for endurance in the heat. We won't be long," Kurt reassured her. "And no matter what your guidebook says, Lorna, you're in no danger of losing your head to the Gibungs."

Another half hour dragged by, Ilse and Lorna fanning themselves with a couple of palm fronds Lorna had climbed outside to retrieve.

"I'm going for a walk," Lorna announced suddenly. "I can't stand it in here another second. I'm suffocating."

"My knee still aches too much for me to join you," Ilse said. "And you'll ruin those white satin slippers in the mud. Anyway, it's getting dark, the nasty spirits are about, and the natives are as dirty as sin. They have all sorts of horrid rotting skin diseases, and lice as fat as peas."

"I don't intend to dance with them, Ilse. I just want to walk by the river alone."

But as she lifted the flounced skirts of her gown to alight, she noticed the striking figure of Ross St. James riding toward them on the track. He looked enviably cool, even in formal black evening attire, which included a frock coat and polished boots, and he sat astride a muscular gray Arabian mare that made the carriage drays look like nags.

"That must be our Resident coming," Ilse remarked over her shoulder. "You look as if you're about to have heat stroke."

"Oh, really," Lorna said in annoyance. But Ilse's observation was more perceptive than Lorna cared to admit. It had been less than three hours since she'd last seen Ross, and scarcely a minute of that time had elapsed that he hadn't crept unbidden into her thoughts. Her heart thumping against her breastbone, which was aching enough as it was from the constriction of her bodice, she stepped to the ground.

He pushed a strand of hair from his forehead. "Good evening, Miss Fairfield."

"Mr. St. James."

She chose to believe it was the humidity, and not the sight of him, that caused the sudden cascade of tingling waves over her skin. Around her the children scattered, shrieking with laughter and feigned alarm, as she walked among them. Lorna smiled at them and then looked up again at Ross's face, its dark elegance set off by the whiteness of his stark cravat. Moistening her lips, she reminded herself she'd known him only two days.

As he swung down beside her, her stomach gave a queer little lurch that was an entirely inappropriate reaction on her part. So was the warm surge of blood that traveled through her veins and throbbed in her temples. This wouldn't do at all. It was insane even to harbor thoughts of a romance while still recovering from Spencer's betrayal.

"Lorna, you look lovely."

"Do I? I feel like yesterday's wilted lettuce." She smiled nervously. "You cut quite a dashing figure yourself, but honestly, don't you think the pair of us look rather silly standing here in Court dress among the Gibungs?"

"I don't think you look silly at all," he said quietly, then glanced down the road with a frown. "Why is your carriage stopped here?"

"The axle broke. Kurt and Richard walked on to the istana for help."

"I must have just missed them," he said, guiding her around a fallen palm tree. Reassured by his familiar presence, the children were crowding around them again, some tugging at the loose strands of Lorna's hair that had been curled to fall upon her shoulders.

"Go away," Ross said. "Leave the lady alone, or I'll carry you off to Penala's aerie for supper."

"Is this the lady in your dreams, Tuan?" one of the older girls teased, dancing around them. "The one you sailed with across the sea?"

"Whatever is she talking about?" Lorna asked, mystified.

He gave her an evasive smile and turned away briefly to entrust his horse to one of the village boys. "Walk down to the river with me, Lorna. I'll stay with you until the cart comes."

"The cart?"

"We've only one government carriage," he said, amused. "Actually, it's a very short walk if you can find the way."

It was nearly dusk, that magical interlude when the tropical rain forest launched into its twilight symphony of screeching birds and monkeys, frogs croaking in a bass chorus, and unseen night-feeders thumping about for their next meal. As Lorna and Ross reached the riverbank, they were beset by swarms of butterflies of every size and color, from tiny metallic blue ones to an enormous cream-colored species with orange spots. Lorna laughed, trying to dislodge the delicate creatures that clung to her clothing. It was a trial not to damage their frail wings or trembling antennae.

"Hold still," Ross said in a quiet voice.

Lorna obeyed. She assumed he meant to pluck off a butterfly she'd missed. But as his fingers brushed her face, he reached out with his other hand and pulled her by the waist toward him. "Damn it, Lorna, you are a distraction," he said in a fierce whisper. "I haven't been able to put you out of my mind all afternoon."

She lowered her eyes. "Perhaps it's the heat."

"The hell it is. I was supposed to finish off my biannual reports to the Rajah this afternoon, and I couldn't concentrate. I had luncheon on the Sultan of Djuil's yacht, and all I could think of as I watched his viceroy stuffing his fat face with lamb curry was kissing you in the arbor."

"That's not very complimentary." She looked up. "Is it?"

"I don't know what it is." He frowned, his expression hovering between annoyance at himself and stark desire for her. "All I know is that yesterday afternoon a red-haired woman walked into my life and that same evening the roof of my hut was blown into the sea."

"You make it sound as if I possessed some sort of supernatural powers."

"It's the red hair and green eyes. Anyway, Kana's convinced you're an English *leyak*. A sorceress."

"Kana, that bastion of reason himself, of the evil spirits and cockroaches?"

"He happens to be quite intelligent."

He gave her a lazy smile and leaned into her, tightening his arm around her waist. "He also thinks we should get married and have five children to join his staff when I appoint him Inspector of Police."

"How preposterous."

"What? A headhunter as police inspector or our producing offspring?"

"Both."

"Preposterous," he said, and lowered his head to kiss her until a curtain of blackness dropped behind her closed eyelids and she lost the train of conscious thought. She was clinging to the lapels of his black frock coat, and she did not care. He was raking his fingers through her carefully styled hair, and she reveled like a cat in the sensual roughness of his touch. Even when she felt him stiffen and withdraw with an irritated inhalation of breath, she could not seem to shake off the daze of desire that had enveloped her.

He tore himself away with a soft curse, his head thrown back, his breathing uneven. "I must be losing my mind, trying to ravish you under a bloody sacred waringen tree with an audience that includes an entire Gibung village, Ilse Klemp, a pair of gibbons, and heaven knows how many tree frogs."

She couldn't help laughing. "You're exaggerating."

"About what—losing my mind or trying to ravish you?"

"Both," she said, and turned toward the river with her head bowed. He didn't approach her again, and she was relieved. She needed to gather her own confused thoughts. It had never been like this with Spencer. No flirtatious banter. No white-hot bursts of passion. With Ross, she did not know what to expect—from him or from herself.

She stared at the delicate white jambus blossoms that trailed down across the river like shooting stars. The rocks at her feet were smothered in purple terrestrial orchids. She was thousands of miles from home. She wished suddenly, with all her being, that her father were here to confide in, or that her mother were still alive to guide her.

Ross sighed heavily. "I meant it when I said you distract me. You made me forget I rode all the way out here to tell you that the Rajah has just tracked down the man who last saw your father."

She whirled around, her skirts foaming over the orchids at her feet. "Where is he? When can I talk to him? Oh, Ross, does he know where my father is?"

He took so long to answer that the excitement rising inside her began to dissipate. "My father isn't—"

He glanced away. "Not as far as anyone knows. But his chances for survival aren't good. He was last seen on—"

"The island of Jalaka," Kurt said behind them, a glint of triumph in his eyes as they turned to face him. "Isn't that right, St. James?"

Ross's face darkened. "How you learned that before anyone else is frankly disturbing. But yes. He was last seen on Jalaka."

"What does it matter how I found out? The point is, I know he's on Jalaka."

"Jalaka—butas!" several young voices whispered around them. "Jalaka—pati!"

Jalaka—Devil Island. Jalaka—Island of Death.

Lorna gazed past the two men, suddenly aware of the fearful whispering among the native children. She didn't need to understand their dialect to realize the mere mention of Jalaka terrified them. Within moments they had disappeared into their huts, no doubt to implore their parents to make an extra offering to appease the demons invoked by speaking of the accursed island.

She glanced back at Kurt. "What is it about Jalaka that so frightens them?"

"The Jalakans have attacked this island several times in the past," Kurt explained offhandedly. "When their volcano erupted and their crops were ruined. They're a singularly bloodthirsty people with strange practices."

"They came here to take heads?" Lorna asked, sensing he'd left something out of his explanation and that perhaps she was better off not knowing what.

"Oh, no," Ross replied in a deceptively pleasant voice. "There are not only headhunters on Jalaka."

She shook out her skirts distractedly to evict a black butterfly hiding in their folds. "Well? Exactly what are they then? Buddhist monks?"

"Cannibals," Kurt said, his broad face reddening with shameless enjoyment at the instantaneous look of shock that froze her features. "Ja. They are cannibals."

"Cannibals?" she repeated, waiting for the remainder of what surely was a ghastly joke. "My father was last reported stranded on an island of—"

"Cannibals," Ross said, a muscle twitching in his cheek. "Now perhaps you understand my concern, Miss Fairfield."

Chapter 7

The Rajah's istana was a sprawling white Gothic-turreted mansion nestled in the jungle foothills that faced the River Bungas, the River of Flowers. The traditional English garden was strung with Chinese lanterns that gave the appearance of a fairyland palace to those approaching on the arched bridge. A pair of pink marble bulls flanked the stone entrance steps. There was a circular lily pond in the interior courtyard, inhabited by fat whiskered fish and horned frogs.

The Rajah greeted Lorna in his private audience chamber before she was announced in the marble-paved reception hall. His flowing purple sarong and gilded breast-cloth gave him a regal aspect, and she had begun to curtsy before him when he lifted her by the hands and enveloped her in a fatherly embrace.

"You were only six when I first met you in London," he said, emotion crackling in his voice. "How like your enchanting mother you've become, and how sorry I am about your father. Still, between the pair of us, we will find him, I promise you. If it is the last thing I do."

Lorna nodded as he released her, not trusting herself to speak. He had felt as insubstantial as a cobweb in her arms, his ribs prominent beneath the breast-cloth. She feared that finding her father would indeed be his last act on earth.

He and her father had been best friends at school, but

their lives had taken distinctly separate paths when Charles began serving in the British-Indian army. The story of how Charles, with only a large inheritance and a love of adventure, had crushed the rebel forces on Kali Simpang to build it into a self-sufficient, peaceful Raj, was one that her father never tired of recounting.

The Rajah's gaze drifted to Richard and Kurt standing by the window. "You were so late arriving on the island, we had begun to worry. Why didn't your fiancé join you, Lorna?"

"Because I don't need his help." She hesitated, aware that Ross had just entered the room and stood within listening distance, seemingly engrossed in studying a Ming Dynasty vase. Embarrassed that the Rajah's observant gaze had caught her staring at Ross, she forced her own attention back to the older man's face. "Our engagement has been broken off."

"I see," the Rajah murmured.

Lorna bit her lip, wondering exactly what the Rajah saw. Perhaps he was referring to the tension between her and his nephew. At least, as far as Lorna was concerned, it had changed the very vibrations in the air, charging it with a palpable excitement.

The Rajah smiled at Lorna. "How peculiar. This is the first time I've ever seen Ross pretend an interest in the room's priceless Chinese vase collection. How do you find our Resident, Lorna? I notice he's dressed for the occasion—a compliment to you, I suspect. Has the rogue been treating you well?"

She glanced around at Ross, shivering unaccountably as he regarded her from his intense gray eyes over the rim of the vase. "Aside from the fact that he seems to think I should sit home doing petit point while everyone else looks for my father, I suppose I cannot complain."

The Rajah pursed his lips in amusement. "At last, Ross, someone who isn't intimidated by your menacing looks. He scares me sometimes, Lorna, I do admit it. Perhaps because he's so much taller. Now come. We'll discuss our plans for finding Sir Arthur later. Forgive me for rushing you to the table, but our guests have grown ravenous, and in this part of the world, that is a dangerous situation. Amayli—''

He turned and, as if by magic, a small-boned Balinese woman in a gold-silk blouse, a *kabju,* and a silver sarong embroidered with pink orchids glided into the room. Her glossy black hair hung in oiled loops to her hips.

Lorna sank into a curtsy before the Ranee, a golden-skinned beauty who looked decades younger than her fifty-two years. "I am honored, Your Royal Highness."

The woman smiled warmly, clasping Lorna's hands and speaking over the jingling of her own numerous gold bracelets. Fluent in seven languages, she was a high-caste Balinese, a member of the royal Satria Dalem, and provided the steadying guidance to her husband's whimsical bent. "It is I who am honored, Lorna. You will come tomorrow, with your uncle, to take tea with me?"

"Pray make your social arrangements later, ladies," the Rajah said. "At last glance, the Sultan of Djuil looked irate enough at the delay to have us all beheaded."

"Djuil." Ross replaced the vase on its shelf and looked at the Rajah with interest. "I mean to get him alone later to discuss forming an army together for our mutual protection."

"Don't you ever relax, Ross?" the Rajah said with a little laugh as he guided his guests from the room. "This is a night for pleasure, not for talking about pirates."

Lorna hid a smile of sympathetic amusement as she followed Ross into the reception hall. He was frowning again, obviously so deep in thought about headhunting pirates that he'd forgotten her presence. But then he swung around suddenly at the door to the banqueting hall and she had to rear back to avoid colliding against him.

"You must sit next to me at supper, Miss Fairfield," he said with mock solemnity.

"Oh, dear. We aren't dining with visiting cannibals, are we?" she asked.

"One never knows with the Rajah. But just in case—" He took her hand and tucked it into his arm, giving her no opportunity to deny him.

Arm in arm they entered the huge marble-tiled room in the corners of which servants stood before cascading marble fountains. Lorna was aware that her appearance with Ross drew openly speculative stares from the Rajah's Malay staff.

Supper was a formal affair served in endless courses on a solid rosewood table around which servants were strategically positioned with palm fronds to fan away annoying flies. Lorna was seated next to Ross, who sat at the Rajah's right, a place of honor considering how many important personages were present: the Sultan of Djuil, a Moslem-Malay island to the north, and his viceroy; Mr. Barrings-Brown, a representative from the Singapore Chamber of Commerce; a Javanese judge; a native prince, Datu Melam; a French naturalist, Monsieur Henri Corneille and his wife Yvette; and the American missionary who had come to Kali Simpang to convert the heathens, the worst of whom he secretly counted as the Rajah and his British subjects. Finally, there was a very distinguished-looking gentleman from the Foreign Office, Colonel Moody, who said little but seemed to observe everything.

"Unless you have exotic tastes," Ross whispered as he reached for his wine, "I would not eat anything I don't recognize."

Afraid to ignore his advice, Lorna settled for a savory lamb stew served with fried rice and sweet green pineapple. By the time dessert came, she couldn't even taste the universally esteemed durian fruit, but that didn't break her heart since it looked like a thorny-spiked medieval weapon and stank like cow manure and rotten eggs.

Around her conversation flowed in so many different directions that she could hardly squeeze in an opinion of her own. Ilse had just embarrassed the American missionary with an offhanded remark about the increased size of her breasts after multiple pregnancies. The Sultan of Djuil was threatening to leave the table if Kurt didn't stop describing a recent pig hunt. Amayli and Madame Corneille were discussing haute couture.

"It's been missing for several months, but the theft has only recently attracted notoriety," Mr. Barrings-Brown from Singapore was saying. "The authorities were hoping to keep it quiet."

Ilse smothered a yawn behind her palm. "What theft is this?"

"The White Tiger of Palleh," Mr. Barrings-Brown replied. "It has special religious significance for the people of this area, but it is a great treasure for all who appreciate lost civilizations."

"It is rare, this tiger?"

"It's not a real animal, Madame Corneille, but a statue of one. A jewel-encrusted ancient ivory tiger that originated in the perhaps mythical volcanic village of Palleh, which some say was located on one of the islands hereabouts. It had been brought from France on loan to the British government for a showing at a museum in Singapore. It was stolen on its first day of exhibition."

Monsieur Corneille cleared his throat. "I saw it once, with my father in Paris. I have never forgotten those emerald eyes. In fact, I had nightmares for a week afterward. It is believed to have some sort of mystical power—"

"Mystical, my foot," Barrings-Brown grunted. "It'll bring a king's ransom on the black market. The British authorities are most distressed."

"I should say," Madame Corneille agreed in mock indignation. "Your government will owe mine a small fortune."

Kurt laughed. "Your government, madame, has been stealing the major art treasures of the world for years."

"He has a point, my dear," Henri Corneille said. "Considering the fact that the statue was stolen by a Swedish naturalist from the natives in the first place, we can hardly claim it as our own."

"It is not the cost of the statue that is my government's prime concern." Colonel Moody spoke for the first time. "The two men assigned to guard the statue were murdered horribly, the caretaker who had accompanied it from France and had watched over it for half a century died of stab wounds moments after reporting the crime, and, of most concern to my government, three innocent English bystanders were killed, presumably because they witnessed the crime."

Ilse shook her head. "This is not the most pleasant suppertime subject, is it?"

The American missionary at her side nodded vigorously. "For once you and I are in agreement, Mrs. Klemp."

Lorna turned her head and caught Ross studying her. He raised his wineglass in a mock toast. "Our culture must seem strange to you. It is, after all, a long way from London, isn't it, Miss Fairfield?"

"Yes," she replied, catching her breath as she felt his eyes caress her like smoke. "And I am glad."

"Ross." The Rajah spoke in an undertone intended only for his nephew's hearing. "Did you find out if there was cholera among the Ranjans or not?"

"Dr. Parker says no. The Ranjans don't believe, of course, that the two deaths were unrelated, and so they will continue to make sacrifices until their insane gods are sated."

"It must be stopped."

"I'm trying."

"Yes." The Rajah leaned back in his chair, looking worn and worried as he surveyed his guests. "I know you are. I shouldn't have brought it up."

The unspoken reference to the Agung-Mani reminded Lorna of her father, and in a voice as loud as good breeding allowed—perhaps a little louder—she said:

"Excuse me. Has anyone here ever visited the island of Jalaka?"

She might have asked if anyone had visited Hades recently, so sudden and replete with tense expectancy was the silence that fell. Datu Melam, the native prince, looked as if he wanted to hide under the table. The servants in attendance had backed into the corners.

"That's the ticket," Ross said with a wry smile. "You've got their attention now."

"That place is the devil's own playground," the young American missionary said in a low voice. "The religion practiced there is too gruesome to be described."

"They eat people to avenge the deaths of their ancestors," Yvette Corneille said, spooning a lump of durian into her mouth. "Personally, I'd love to visit to add to my botanical collection, but Henri is such an old *couard* these days. A coward."

Lorna put down her glass. "Hasn't anyone been known to leave there alive?"

"Only the guide who accompanied your father," the Rajah said in a gentle tone. "And it took him until now even to admit it."

There was another lull of silence. Lorna wanted to scream in frustration because she knew that every moment her father remained on Jalaka his life was in jeopardy. And his disappearance still made no sense.

"Madame Corneille." She glanced impulsively at the attractive Parisienne brunette. "Have you or your husband ever heard of the Eden Flower?"

"*Qu'est-ce qu'elle a dit?*" Henri Corneille asked, squinting over his spectacles at Lorna. "What is this, mademoiselle?"

"*C'est une fleur tropicale,*" his wife said, lacing her fingers beneath her chin and staring hard at Lorna. "I have never come across it, my dear, but it does sound fascinating." She sighed. "But then, these days Henri is too timid to venture into the more remote areas where one makes the exciting finds. A man-eating tiger was sighted on Mount Belakan and all our servants are in a stir over the significance. Henri is refusing to budge from the garden."

"An exaggeration, chérie. We can leave as soon as we find a reliable guide."

"The tiger only rarely troubles us on this island," the Rajah said. "Yet it has a special significance to the Malays, hence the origin of a statue to represent its power. Long ago it was worshiped as the deity of deities among the volcanic islands of the archipelago. I shouldn't be surprised to learn Henri's servants are eager to avoid it."

"The White Tiger is still both feared and revered in the Far East," Mr. Barrings-Brown said.

Ross glanced up. "You're referring now to the missing statue or to the actual animal?"

"Both, to be accurate. Legend has it that the White Tiger was born from the molten lava of an erupting volcano of some obscure island and that its spirit still resides within the core. It is said to have bred a line of human royalty from which favored Malay princes descended."

The Rajah nodded. "The Malays call him Tok Belang, the Striped Prince. In China he is Ch'ang Kwei, the god of wind and water."

"When I hunt a man-eater," Kurt said, his face animated, "the natives will not say the word *matjan* during daylight for fear the sleeping tiger will hear it in his dream and hunt down the man who dared disturb his sleep."

"That's true," Ross said. "And there are similar beliefs throughout the continent of were-tigers—comparable to the European were-wolves—who wander the earth in search of human mates."

Lorna took a sip of wine and then stopped guiltily, realizing she was enjoying herself when only an hour ago she had learned her father's predicament was even worse than she had feared. She finished her wine quickly, her mood darkening.

Ross stared at her, his gaze falling to the empty glass. "Do not despair," he said. "If it is true that fortune favors the bold, your endeavors shall be rewarded." He leaned toward her. "How lucky your father is to have such an enchanting guardian angel. I envy him."

"You do not strike me as a man who has either need of or tolerance for angels, Mr. St. James."

"Looks can be deceiving."

"My friends." The Rajah rose from the table. "Our entertainment is about to begin."

Lorna's mind was so busy puzzling over Ross's last remark that she didn't think she could possibly sit through the hours of entertainment the Ranee had planned. However, from the moment the first notes of the gamelan filled the room with their sorrowful wail, and the troupe of Balinese dancers filed onto the stage lit by the flickering flames of coconut-oil lamps, she was transfixed.

The first performance was a dance pantomime of the courtship between Barong, the warrior lion god, and the powerful eagle goddess Penala. The dancers played out the battle of the sexes with frank eroticism. Ross had seen this particular dance at least a dozen times before and hadn't found it remotely stimulating.

Until tonight.

Never before had the wild rhythms of the tjeng-tjeng cymbals and buffalo-hide drums stirred such fierce male aggression in his blood. The swaying oiled bodies on stage evoked so many voluptuous images of mating in his mind that it became physically uncomfortable to watch them.

He slid his fingers inside the cravat at his neck, wishing he could dash the damn thing to the floor. Suddenly a flicker of lightning outside threw the room into silver shadows. Lorna glanced up at the windows, caught Ross's eye, and gave him an absentminded smile before returning her full attention to the dance.

It was her fault he was getting so aroused, he thought. They were squeezed together like kernels of corn on a cob on the red brocade settee, pressed shoulder to shoulder, thigh to thigh. He had only to angle his head a certain way and he could smell the faint rose fragrance on her skin. Another half inch to the left and he could see through her chemisette the swell of her soft white breasts, rising and falling with the rhythm of her breathing. But the greatest torment came when a late-arriving guest crowded onto the settee beside Lorna, and she had to reposition herself with her right hand resting primly on the side of Ross's leg. When she started to tap her fingers to the music, he knew he had reached his limits.

"Miss Fairfield," he whispered in her ear, "the integrity of the entire British Empire will be compromised if you don't remove your hand from my leg."

The music had reached an ear-shattering crescendo of palm strings, glass tubes, flutes, and the gamelan. Lorna found herself stirred by the exquisite music. "What did you say?" she asked without even looking at Ross.

He raised his voice, annoyed that she could drive him mad without giving it a conscious thought. "I said, take your fluttering little fingers off my thigh!"

His request resounded across a room plunged into sudden silence as the final notes of the climax faded. Lorna lifted her fan to her face to hide a choking fit of laughter. Ross looked around him in an agony of embarrassment. Tomorrow he'd be the joke of the fort—there wasn't an eye in the room not trained on them. Especially on Lorna, he realized with a stab of jealousy that took him unawares. The Sultan of Djuil was eyeing her as if she were another of the dessert courses being offered.

The Rajah led the audience in a round of applause. Ross stood abruptly and helped himself to one of the drinks being served in coconut shells, a frothy brew of coffee, rum, and scalded coconut milk. He almost yelped as the drink blazed a burning path down his throat.

Lorna came up behind him, her face innocent. "Is something wrong?"

"Oh, no, Miss Fairfield. I only intended to court the Sultan's favor tonight and think instead I shall end up blackening his beady eyes."

"Resident St. James."

Ross pivoted, gulping down another scalding mouthful of the drink as he saw the Rajah and the Sultan of Djuil directly behind him. "Your Highness," he addressed the Sultan, "I had been hoping for a moment—"

"Later," the Sultan said ungraciously. "The evening is for pleasure, and it would bring me the greatest pleasure if you would introduce me to the young lady beside you."

The Rajah slipped away, smiling benignly as if he were unaware of his nephew's displeasure. Ross made the requested introduction with grave forbearance, but he had no intention of leaving Lorna and the Sultan alone.

"You must forgive me, Miss Fairfield, if I was caught staring at you earlier," the Sultan said, with an arched brow of acknowledgment in Ross's direction. "It was your earrings, you see. Emeralds are my youngest daughter's favorite stone. She has just recovered from a long illness, and I am an indulgent father. I wondered if you might give me the name of your European jeweler."

Her earrings. Ross stared at the exquisitely cut green stones that caught the light, and knew himself to be in far deeper trouble than he had realized. He had been so busy staring at her God-given attributes, he hadn't noticed her adornments.

"Unfortunately," Lorna said, "these earrings are a centuries' old heirloom from a former acquaintance. However, I have a soft spot in my heart for children, especially little girls." And while Ross and the Moslem potentate looked on in disbelief, she unfastened the earrings and held them out to the Sultan. "To tell the truth, I've grown rather tired of them, anyway."

"But I cannot," the Sultan said, his eyes glowing with delight as he examined the stones. "They are an heirloom, you say, but—I will accept them only on the condition that you let me reciprocate. What can I give you, Miss Fairfield, as a token of my appreciation? Would you like my favorite slave, Osman? So clever and handsome a boy."

"Heavens, no."

"It is necessary in this culture," Ross said quietly, beginning to enjoy her predicament, "for a gift to be reciprocated."

"All right then," she said, backing away from the two men as she saw Amayli beckoning to her. "Grant Mr. St.

James an extended interview, Your Highness. That will be repayment enough.''

"Are you quite mad?'' Ross asked her later as they were reseated to watch the *wayang kulit,* a Malay puppet show. "Those emeralds were priceless. Why did you give them away?''

Her smile was brittle. "Because they were given to me by someone I don't care to be reminded of ever again. Is that all right with you?''

"Yes,'' he said, as comprehension dawned. "Quite all right.''

"Well then.''

He looked her directly in the eye and felt his chest tighten with longing. "He must have wounded you very deeply.''

She shrugged, glancing away.

He lowered his voice. "Dare I hope his loss shall be my gain?'' When she didn't answer, he added, "Don't you think it would have been a sweeter revenge to sell the earrings?''

"Do you have a pawnshop on Kali Simpang?''

"We do. On the Chinese sector of the island, which I will take the opportunity now of suggesting you avoid.'' He turned his attention to the stage as the puppeteer's assistant, the *dalang,* appeared. "It is not a place for young ladies,'' he added. "Not even those who enjoy tempting fate.''

"Your starch is showing, Mr. St. James,'' she whispered to him.

As the oil lamps were dimmed, Ross reached for her hand and gave it a hard squeeze. "The Sultan is giving me an audience tomorrow. I believe he is favorably inclined to my proposal. *Trima kasih.* Thank you.''

She stared straight ahead, feeling a host of unsettling sensations sweep over her. His casual gesture had reawakened all the pleasurable confusion she had felt when he'd kissed her earlier. She must be careful, so careful, not to let it happen again.

The puppet show began with a cloud of smoke as the evil sorceress Rangda emerged from a fiery cave to ensnare a mortal victim. With her wild hair and bulging eyes, her pig's nose, fangs, and taloned claws, the wooden puppet was indeed a fearful sight.

"It's very clever, isn't it?" she whispered to Ross. But when she glanced at him, she saw that he'd fallen asleep. She leaned back slowly, aching with a newfound yearning she wasn't ready to accept. Her feelings for Ross frightened her. And because she seemed unable to control them, she was convinced they must be stopped. She gripped her fan as her gaze traveled over the chiseled austerity of his face, the wave of dark hair on his temple, the deep grooves alongside his cheeks that gave him such a fierce appearance and that even sleep did not soften. It was easy as she watched him in this defenseless position to resolve she would never allow him another liberty with her again.

His head started to slide back against the settee. Before he could embarrass them both by being caught asleep, she gently prodded him in the rib cage with her fan. Obviously he was exhausted from his all-night vigil at the cove.

"Ross," she whispered urgently. "Do wake up."

He opened his eyes, his gaze focused blankly on the stage, and blinked. Almost at the same time a speculative buzz passed through the audience. A ripple of uncertain laughter followed.

"What the hell?" he said in a gravelly voice.

Lorna had no idea why he looked so upset. But as she glanced back at the puppet show, her lips parted in astonishment. Gone was Rangda, the embodiment of evil. In her place a pair of startlingly familiar figures paraded across the stage. One was a man in black evening dress, his teakwood jaw a mocking caricature of Ross's strongest feature. The other figure was a slender redhead in a green silk gown. And they were locked in an intimate embrace that was too similar to the kiss Lorna and Ross had shared at the riverbank to be a coincidence. Suddenly, in the background, two puppets appeared who were undoubtedly meant to represent Kurt and Richard, down to van Poole's white-blond hair and the Englishman's mutton-chop whiskers.

"Good God." Lorna heard her uncle huffing away in indignation. "Someone has a queer idea of an evening's entertainment. Either that or it's rather an elaborate joke."

"This isn't a joke." Kurt leaned forward with an expression of intense concentration.

"Ross—" Lorna began, but he waved her to silence, his gaze riveted on the puppet show.

Lorna sat unmoving as the next scene unfolded. Against a mountain jungle setting, ominous Mount Belakan, complete with plumes of smoke, dominated the stage. With horror, she saw her own puppet image appear suddenly on the slope, dragged upward toward the steaming volcano crater by two figures wearing thick arm bracelets and grotesque masks. That the puppet was about to become a human sacrifice was clear to everyone in the room.

"Ross," she whispered, her heart palpitating wildly, "what does this mean?"

He didn't answer. He had jumped up from the settee and was running toward the stage, his face taut with fury. He'd thought at first that the soldiers at the fort had put old Tejal, the puppeteer, up to an ill-conceived prank. But the underlying mood of the performance had been sinister from the start. And when all of a sudden an explosion sounded from behind the puppet booth and a billowing cloud of theatrical smoke filled the air, Ross knew he would not find Tejal behind that booth.

The three Malay children who helped work the strings stared up at him in wide-eyed trepidation as he ripped apart the curtain that concealed them.

"Where did the *dalang* go?" he demanded. Before they could answer, he heard footsteps fleeing down the hall, and he shoved his way through the throng of speechless guests and ran outside.

A servant bearing a tray of refreshments appeared before him, slowing his progress. On purpose? Ross had no time to decide.

Some instinct led him to the library. The door to the pleasure garden was still ajar. As he ran across the manicured lawn, a flash of lightning brightened the serrated shadows of the palm grove to his left. He slowed, noticing from the edge of his eye the moving shadow revealed beneath the moonlit palms.

He walked with slow deliberation down the middle of a flagged path, cursing his formal attire and the fact that he carried no weapon. When he came parallel to where he'd spotted the man's shadow, he stopped and without warning lunged to the left. The silver blade of a parang glistened in the moonlight seconds before he ducked and flung himself at the masked figure.

The other man was lithe, young, and prepared to fight to the death. Ross pinned him to the ground to tear off his mask and saw him pull a second parang upward to slash at his chest. He swiveled back. The man leapt to his feet, mask still intact. As he turned to flee, Ross noticed that he bore a tattoo on his shoulder: a tiger rising from a smoking volcano. The mark of the Agung-Mani.

Ross stepped back as the servant finished repairing the broken lock of the istana's library door. "Make sure the other doors are all secure, Papan," he said quietly. "Report to me immediately if you find anything else amiss."

"Warn the other servants to be watchful," the Rajah called after the young servant before turning to his nephew. "I have never been one to look on the dark side, Ross, but this incident tonight is most unsettling."

"Unsettling?" Ross glanced down wryly at the tattered ribbons of his shirtfront. His uncle was a master of understatement.

"The soldiers must not have found anything more, or we'd have heard by now," the Rajah murmured.

Ross stared out into the garden. His uncle might not admit it, but he'd been stunned by Ross's report that the elderly puppeteer, Tejal, had been found beaten and gagged in the orchard. The old man could offer no helpful information about his attackers, only tearful confirmation that Ross's suspicion that the Agung-Mani were involved was correct.

The Rajah motioned Ross to the door. "Let us pray Tejal recovers from his beating and can help identify the villains. I still cannot understand why even the Agung-Mani would go to such lengths to intimidate that lovely young woman."

"Lorna?" Ross pivoted slowly. "No, I don't think this has anything to do with her. It's me they're after. I've made no secret of the fact that I intend to destroy their power on the island, both by education and by force if I must. They're hoping perhaps to get to me through Lorna."

"Indeed. Then someone must have received the impression you harbor a certain . . . weakness for Lorna. That riverbank scene in the puppet show—I assume it was not fiction. Might you have changed your opinion of her since this morning?"

Ross stared straight ahead as they walked together down the hallway, flanked by two Hindu guards who glided behind them like ghosts. "As a matter of fact, Your Highness, after tonight I am more convinced than ever that she should go home."

"And it would not bother you if you never saw her again?"

"It would bother me far more if some misfortune should befall her. I would—" He stopped in mid-sentence as the slender form of a young woman materialized before him from a candlelit wall niche. "Lorna—Miss Fairfield, why have you not retired to your room?"

"I—I wanted to make sure you were all right. We heard about the puppeteer, you see, and—" Her gaze fell to his shirtfront. "You *have* been injured."

He tried to ignore the alarmed concern that darkened her eyes, but it was impossible to pretend he wasn't pleased by the attention. "It's only my shirt. No blood spilled."

She shivered delicately. "You mean someone actually tried to stab you?"

"I believe that was his intention." He barely noticed that his uncle and the guards had drifted to the far end of the hall. In fact, it seemed Lorna always had the disconcerting effect upon him of making everything and everyone else fade into the background. "You should be frightened for yourself, Miss Fairfield," he admonished, using his most solemn voice for emphasis. "Someone is considering throwing you into a volcano."

"You don't believe they would— Who are you talking about anyway?"

"The Agung-Mani."

"You had nothing to do with this, did you, Ross? I mean, I know you wanted me off the island, but—"

"Terrorizing helpless old men and young women is beneath even me," he said angrily. "The puppeteer may not survive the beating he got tonight."

"I'm sorry, Ross," she said, her face distraught. "I had no idea. I'm ashamed for even asking."

"I hadn't wanted to tell you." She turned away from him, her shoulders rigid with strain, her hands nervously clutching the fan. Suddenly he had an overwhelming impulse to put his arms around her to console her, but the presence of his uncle and the guards restrained him. "We'll do our best to make sure no one harms you, Miss Fairfield."

"Me? Dear Mr. St. James, it is not for myself that I worry but for my father. If they are not above thrashing old men—" She lifted her face to his, and with a sense of despair, he saw reflected there her earlier determination. "My father is not a strong man."

"Tonight was just a warning, perhaps." He noticed a guard discreetly trying to catch his eye, and with reluctance he forced himself to back away from Lorna. "Good night, Miss Fairfield. Please do not leave your room again until morning. I realize the overnight stay is inconvenient, but it is safer than risking attack on the dark road home."

He strode down the length of the hall toward the guards, his burnished face impassive in the candlelight. He felt far less in control than he appeared. For one thing, that the Agung-Mani had become bold enough to penetrate the istana only reinforced Ross's determination to eradicate the cult. For another, he realized that his mind had not been as alert as usual or he would have thought it odd that the old puppeteer himself had not, as was his custom, approached Ross before the performance to invite him to sample some of his odious cigarettes. And the reason Ross had not noticed this peculiarity was that he had been focused entirely on Lorna.

The incident with the emerald earrings had not helped clarify his feelings for her. It would have been simple to think that she'd given them away in a dramatically impetuous pique, but unfortunately, he had seen in her eyes how deeply her former fiancé had hurt her. He'd already discovered she was charmingly inept at hiding her emotions, and it wasn't easy to forget that her offhanded kindness might help save his island.

He wished she had not suddenly become so real and appealing to him. Any personal involvement with her on his part would be inappropriate. He preferred to think her flighty and inconsiderate, the usual English miss who fainted dead away upon taking her first step into the jungle. But he was afraid Lorna Fairfield was proving otherwise.

Sometime after midnight Lorna awakened with a start. Every nerve straining, she listened for what had disturbed her, and within seconds the sound returned: a faint scratching at the door.

Slowly she arose from the bed and raised the netting to allow her a better view around the spacious moonlit chamber. There was nothing she could use for a weapon against an intruder except for an ornamental spear mounted on the wall, which she couldn't reach, and a porcelain vase of peacock feathers, which looked as though it might belong in the Rajah's prized collection.

She stared at the door and willed the intruder away, her

heart racing beneath the sheer silk of the turquoise blouse and sarong Amayli had given her to sleep in.

Surely the guards were patrolling the halls. Surely an intruder would be spotted. After all, the Rajah himself slept right across the way.

The door opened an inch and she held her breath as a large hand slipped through the crack to feel along the panels. She reacted unthinkingly, darting forward and flinging herself against the door with all her might, holding the intruder imprisoned by his wrist.

"Ouch! What the devil!"

"Ross!" she whispered in relief and astonishment. Recovering, her heartbeat slowing so that she could breathe freely again, she backed away from the door and said, to cover her fright, "Exactly what do you think you're doing trying to force your way into my room? And at this hour."

He motioned back over his shoulder to the guard stationed outside and then stepped over the threshold, hovering there and rubbing his wrist. "I was checking to make sure your lock was secure. Not that it mattered. You hadn't even bothered to use it."

"I had," she said indignantly. "I locked it the moment Amayli left, and then I—"

"You met me downstairs again, don't you remember? Did you lock it a second time?" he asked with a self-satisfied smirk at his own reckoning that made Lorna alternately embarrassed at her carelessness and aching to kick him in the shin. "I thought not."

"I was upset and overtired," she admitted. "Anyway, you should have knocked. I'm hardly dressed to receive callers."

"I was hoping I wouldn't disturb you. As to your dress—" His gaze drifted from her face to the revealing native costume that draped artfully around her slender curves. Under his steady regard, Lorna felt her skin grow warm and drew a sharp breath, a vague anticipation burgeoning inside her as the silence extended. Then unexpectedly he closed his eyes and stood for several moments with his jaw clenched tight as if he were in pain. She watched him in consternation until a horrifying thought occurred to her.

"Your wrist," she whispered. "I haven't broken it, have I? You look frightfully uncomfortable."

He opened his eyes and stared at her as if he had not heard her correctly. "My wrist?" he repeated in a strangled voice of suppressed humor. "Actually, the source of my discomfort is stemming from another . . . more sensitive . . . part of my anatomy."

Lorna flushed, aware she was the cause of his private amusement and not appreciating it one bit. "I'm sorry I asked."

He shook his head ruefully. "An innocent in a temptress's guise. What would you have done had I managed to force my way inside?"

She turned to the shelf behind her. "Bashed you over the head with the vase. Honestly, Ross, I thought you were a cultist intruder. Don't you ever sleep?"

"I require only a few hours a night."

"Well, I require at least eight." She pushed him toward the hall. "Good night, Ross," she said firmly, replacing the vase on its shelf.

He gave her a long, appreciative look as she swiveled back around to face him, her loose hair spilling around her white shoulders, the curve of a slim calf revealed by the slit in the sarong.

"You do something absolutely breathtaking for a sarong," he said hoarsely.

Lorna caught her breath at the stark desire in his voice and knew she must force him to leave immediately or suffer the consequences. Yet for the wildest moment she actually hoped he would stay . . . and kiss her again in the intimate shadows of moonlight with no one to observe them.

"And you do something absolutely shameful to a woman's sense of propriety," she managed at last, unable to control the catch in her voice.

He grinned at that, his teeth dazzling white against his

sun-bronzed skin. The sudden warm humor he projected was even more disarming than his seductive overtures and as unexpected as it was appealing. But then Lorna was beginning to understand he was a man of contradictions, passionately devoted to his duties, responsible and arrogant, and yet not above working his masculine charm on her when the mood struck.

"Do you know how to use a pistol?" he asked her, his face sobering.

"A pistol?"

"It's a bit more efficient than peacock feathers when it comes to repelling intruders. Besides, that's one of the Rajah's favorite vases. We'd both be exiled if he learned you'd broken it over my head."

"I do have a pistol with me," she said hesitantly. "It's still with my unpacked belongings at the house, but I was praying I wouldn't have to use it."

"You do know how to shoot one then?"

"Yes. Spencer and I spent hours in the woods back home practicing. I was better than he was, actually."

"Umm. Well, it's a shame you didn't use him as a target, if he hurt you as deeply as I suspect he did." His gaze was suddenly intent. "You never did tell me the nature of his crime."

Her mouth tightened, and to her horror, she was tempted to share with him the unspeakable humiliation of that night. "There's been enough unpleasantness this evening," she said with a shake of her head. "Anyway, I shouldn't want to bore you with any more of my woes."

"Bore me, you say?" He smiled to himself and stepped back over the threshold, holding her captive with the warmth of his gaze. "Considering that I haven't known a moment's peace since I met you, I don't think that's at all likely."

Chapter 8

Two days later, the Ranee invited Lorna, her companions, and a select gathering of guests to the istana for an informal supper to make up for the memories of the previous unsuccessful affair. At Amayli's request they played blindman's bluff after sharing a light repast of cold chicken, champagne, and French pastries. Lorna suggested Amayli wanted to end the evening on a note of merriment to atone for the earlier fiasco. Ross said no, that Amayli simply loved English parlor games and concluded all her entertainments in a similar manner.

"You look tired," Lorna said as Ross brought her a second glass of champagne in a fluted crystal glass. She hadn't spoken to him since that night in the Rajah's guest chamber, but she had glimpsed him twice on the grounds of her father's plantation house, giving orders to the guards Charles had commissioned to protect her. "Aren't you going to drink at all?"

He shook his head. "I'm afraid I'd conk out on the spot. I've spent the past two days moving the sulap so that Kana can live there too."

"You're not sleeping at the cove?"

"No. I have a bungalow inland where I will stay for the next few days to catch up on my paperwork."

"Not more confidential reports on me, I trust?"

He shrugged. "Actually, the reading is quite fascinating. I'd no idea you led such a . . . nomadic life." His gaze followed the glass to her lips, lingering there long enough for Lorna to feel heat rising to her face. "Have you reconsidered my advice about leaving the island?" he asked unexpectedly.

She swallowed painfully over the sudden knot in her throat, striving not to show how the casual question affected her. "I am not easily deterred, Mr. St. James," she said with a defiant edge to her voice. "If my presence inconveniences you, then that is unfortunate. But it's something you shall have to endure until my father is found." She gave him a cool, dismissive look. "Have you not wasted enough time on me for an evening? Perhaps you ought to be keeping watch at the cove instead."

"My stubborn young woman—" he began with an infuriating smile.

"Don't," she hissed over the rim of her glass. "Don't you dare call me *your* young woman in that wretchedly sanctimonious tone."

"To answer your question," he continued with unperturbed calm, "Assistant Resident Tunridge has replaced me for the night." He inclined his head so that only she could catch his next words. "Perhaps I should also assign him to protect you in my place. He used to wrestle in town squares for a living."

Her green eyes blazing, she brushed past him as the Ranee began to summon her guests back around the settee where she sat amidst a bevy of palm-fanning servants. As Lorna placed her empty glass on the marble-topped sideboard, she was furious to discover her hand was trembling. There was no logical reason why she should allow Ross to upset her this way, but he had.

They played a game of hunt the slipper, Ross standing outside the circle with several of the other guests who did not care to participate. By this time the doors to the courtyard had been opened, and Amayli suggested they finish up with a game of the bellman played outside. In this version of blindman's bluff, all the players were blindfolded except for the one designated as the bellman. It was his job to ring a small silver bell and elude capture. Whoever caught him, however, took his place, and so the game went until every player had a turn with the bell.

The metallic scent of impending rain hung in the air, blending with the musky fragrance of the kambodja trees in the gardens where guards had been discreetly stationed. Atlas moths and small night birds attracted to the lanterns strung along the wall filled the evening quiet with their agitated flutterings. Not even the threat of headhunters and human sacrifices could taint the tropical beauty of the night.

Ross offered to be the bellman, but Lorna wasn't deceived. He was only taking part because he was uneasy about so many guests milling about with his assailant of the other evening still unapprehended. As angry as he made her, she had to admit it was reassuring to know he could be summoned at a call. Still, she thought he had exaggerated the dangers she would face, and she decided he might be a more pleasant companion if he learned to relax his guard occasionally.

"Look out, Lorna," Ilse said as they collided by the fishpond.

"I'm sorry." Lorna peeked out from under her scarf. "I thought you were Ross."

"Sorry to disappoint you. You never did tell me what you were doing with your hand on his thigh the other night."

"The question is too ridiculous to merit an answer. My relationship with Mr. St. James is based solely on our mutual desire to find my father."

"I wonder. Anyway, I suppose I'd stick close to him myself if someone wanted to sacrifice me to a volcano."

With that cheerful remark, Ilse hobbled off in search of the bellman. Lorna readjusted her blindfold, walked directly into a statue, and swore. There was a shrill cry of excitement behind her as Ilse caught Ross and traded places with him. A few moments later a rough hand turned Lorna around by the waist.

"Ross?"

"No. It's Kurt." She had already deduced as much from the unpleasant odor of smoke and alcohol on his clothes. "You were about to wander off into the garden, Lorna. Take care, please."

"But there are guards everywhere you turn."

"And who is to say we can trust the guards? The Agung-Mani work by fear and intimidation. Take care, Lorna," he repeated, leaving her as the tinkling bell sounded behind her. "I have enough on my mind what with finding your father."

Several minutes passed. Lorna began to feel like a blind sheep following a half-witted shepherd. It was hot, and the scarf around her eyes tickled her nose. She could tell by the quiet that the others were nowhere in the vicinity. At least she assumed she was alone, and she was about to remove the blindfold when she walked into a tall iron-hard figure.

He gripped her so tightly that her knees almost buckled with the weakening thrill of anticipation that surged through her veins. She didn't need to see his face to know who he was. Her senses recognized him instantly. The warm male musk of his skin, the restrained strength in the arms that held her, the trembling of her limbs, the kaleidoscope of dizzying sensations that she had never experienced with any other man were all the proof she needed of his identity.

"You're shaking," he said.

"Ross," she whispered, her mouth suddenly dry, her mind paralyzed with fear and longing, anger and a slowly pervading languor.

Without saying another word, he pulled her against his chest and kissed her. The mocking disapproval she had sensed in him earlier was gone, as were the last remnants of polite restraint, replaced by a darker passion neither of them could deny. His kiss became purposefully urgent and tauntingly sensual, demanding a response from her, draining her resistance, submerging her in sensations so intense she would have run from him had she been able to command her limbs to function. Every thrust of his tongue dragged her deeper into an undertow of dark, unknown waters. She was over her head for the first time in her life.

"No," she sobbed, feeling his fingers twine in her hair, his hips rocking forward. "Oh, no. . . ."

She drew away, but he only gripped her harder and backed her to the wall, pinning her there with his thigh pressed to hers. She could not stop shaking; her skin felt both burning and chilled at once. When he lowered his mouth to her shoulder and nuzzled the swell of exposed skin there, she jerked away with a gasp, her heart beating like a captive bird against her breast.

"And I thought you were the worldly one, Lorna."

"I suppose I ought to slap you."

"By all means." He caught her hand and lifted it to his mouth, trailing his tongue over her palm. "It is a small enough price to pay for the incomparable sweetness you just offered me."

She wrenched off her blindfold. "I offered you nothing. You helped yourself."

He shrugged his broad shoulders, his charcoal-gray jacket falling open slightly to reveal the pistol in his belt. "A matter of interpretation, I believe," he said with that unfailing self-composure that seemed to intensify her own confusion. His voice dropped to a whisper. "Or perhaps I merely want you so much that I imagined you were responding to me. Is that what happened, Lorna?"

She drew her hands to her face, burning with shame as she found herself unable to deny or defend her passionate response. She leaned her head against the wall and felt a raindrop splash upon her feverish cheek. The cool wetness was welcome, helping to restore a measure of reason to her frantic thoughts.

"I did warn you," he said in a half apologetic, half resigned whisper. And then abruptly he tore his gaze from her face and stared out over her shoulder toward the courtyard. "We're about to have company, I fear. Let me help you on with your blindfold."

He had gotten control of himself again. The mask of austere authority had fallen back into place. Only in the silver darkness of his eyes did she detect any hint of the desire that smoldered beneath the surface. What was he really like? she wondered. Which side of his character that he'd shown her revealed his deepest feelings?

He pulled the blindfold back down over her eyes and led her into the center of the courtyard. To resist him now would have drawn unwanted attention to them, and she had difficulty enough recovering from the unleashed turmoil of her own emotions without creating another scene.

"There's Ilse and her bloody bell by the door," he said over his shoulder. "Do us both a favor, Lorna. Reconsider what I said about returning to London."

She stood there in furious silence as his footsteps faded away. The gall of him. Seducing her one minute, trying to pack her off the next. To think that if they'd been alone, she would have actually—

She shoved the thought away and turned at the tinkling of a bell behind her. She was tired of playing parlor games. She was hot and weary, and she wanted to be alone.

The bell eluded her at every turn, leading her in a dizzying circle deeper and deeper down one of the arcaded corridors of the courtyard until she finally stopped and pulled off the scarf.

"This has gone far enough."

Silence engulfed her. A strange, trembling silence underscored by the faintest echo of a breeze stirring the copper bougainvillea above her head. She had no idea she'd wandered this far from the party. . . .

She whirled, heading for the flickering light of the lantern in the distance.

Something glinted silver against the bougainvillea. Slowly a shadow slipped forward and resolved itself into a masked figure who held a knife in his hand.

She backed away, hitching up her skirts and kicking off

her slippers to run. Rain was falling heavily in the gardens, thrumming on leaves and enclosing the arcade in humid isolation. No sooner had she put a yard between her and the man before her than a second figure materialized.

"What do you want?" she whispered.

They wore teakwood masks of some unidentifiable animal with hideous ivory fangs that curled down to their chins.

"Not to make a sound, Inglish womans," the nearest one hissed, motioning her backward with his parang. "Not to scream, or we hurt you very bad."

"What do you want?" she repeated, stalling for time, focusing on the distant lantern.

"You go back to Inglangs. You take shikari away. Death for you on Jalaka. You forget father and leave."

"M-my father." She was so taken aback by the mention of her father, she temporarily forgot the threat to her life and the unexpected reference to Kurt. "You've had contact with my father?"

She recoiled instinctively as he thrust a small, glittering object in her face. For several horrifying seconds she thought he intended to slash her throat, but as her panic abated, she recognized the heavy silver ring dangling from the tip of his tattooed thumb.

Her father's ring. The century-old signet ring that had belonged to her maternal grandfather and which her mother had given Papa on their wedding night. He had not once removed that ring from that evening forward and had in fact requested he be buried with it as a token of his eternal love for the wife he adored.

"H-he's still alive, isn't he?" she whispered breathlessly, catching the ring to her chest as her assailant flung it from him. "At least you can tell me—"

They seized her by the forearms and dragged her out into the thrashing rain. Lorna dug her heels into the mud to resist, slipping the signet ring onto her thumb. The Rajah's guards were nowhere in sight.

"Lorna!"

The voice calling her sounded so indistinct in the rain, she couldn't tell if it belonged to Ross, Kurt, or her uncle. In her disoriented state, it seemed likely she'd imagined it.

"Here!" she yelled, wrenching her entire body backward. "I'm over—"

They shoved her to the ground. She had a glimpse of the rain-blurred figures staring down at her, and reflexively she crossed her arms over her face as one of them leaned over her with his hand upraised. For an instant his mask slipped, and because she feared what she would see if she looked into his eyes, she focused on the slender white scar that bisected his brow. Then she opened her mouth to scream in horror only to find she had no voice. Panic flared inside her as something dark descended before her eyes. But the blow, the stabbing pain she anticipated, did not come.

Instead, something small and hard thudded against her chest. Striving to breathe, too frightened to move, she lay still for several moments with the warm rain cascading over her and the sound of their hurried footsteps squishing in the alang-alang grass.

When she could work up enough nerve, she rolled onto her side, shivering uncontrollably, and looked around. The object on her chest—a doll, by the look of it—fell into the grass beside her. She picked it up and got to her feet, running clumsily back toward the arcade. Only then did she take the time to examine the doll.

"Oh, my God," she cried, holding it away from her in horror.

In the watery moonlight it stared up at her from its worm-eaten eye sockets, a shrunken human skull wearing a wig of bright red-gold hair in a chignon just like her own. A crudely twisted coconut husk formed the torso, and covering it was an ivory silk gown.

An exact replica of the wedding gown she had planned to wear this very week in London. Someone had taken great pains to make this dress. Someone who had access to her room in her father's house.

"Lorna?"

Her uncle's voice down the arcade sounded closer now, but not close enough to prevent her from whirling in panic when she thought she heard running footsteps behind her in the garden.

Her scream stopped Ross in his tracks and drained the blood from his face. It ran up and down the vertebrae of his spine like a jolt of electricity. It propelled him down the arcade in a burst of superhuman speed.

"Lorna." He swerved to a wild halt when he noticed her standing immobile in the shadows.

"I screamed," she said, "to get someone's attention."

"Mother of God, I thought you'd been murdered."

"Ross." Her voice broke as she looked up into his anxious face. "They d-dragged me . . . I th-thought . . ."

"Who—" He glanced down at the doll and then back at Lorna's ashen face. "My God, you're in shock. Have you been hurt?"

She shook her head slowly, her gaze falling to the pistol he had drawn from his waistband. "Don't go after them, Ross. Have the guards do it, please."

He edged away from her, scanning the shadows around them. "Your uncle is coming now. Have him take you back inside."

He removed his boots, then stripped off his jacket and draped it over her shoulders. Clasping the pistol before him, he began to back out into the garden. Kurt was already there—it was his voice she'd heard—instructing the Rajah's guards where to search.

"Ross," she whispered, "don't leave me here."

She shivered, huddling into his jacket, the weight of it solid and warm around her shoulders. The sight of him in formal evening attire and brandishing a gun in her defense did nothing to calm her jangled nerves. Not to mention the way the rain molded his shirt and trousers to his virile musculature. She put a hand to her heart and found it beating as wildly as it had when the Agung-Mani had attacked her. No matter how much power Ross wielded on the island, it would stand him in little stead against madmen who thought nothing of committing murder in the name of their pagan religion. She turned her face into the lapel of his jacket, shuddering at the thought.

Footsteps approached. "Lorna! My dear gel, you scared the wits out of everyone. Were you harmed?"

"No, Uncle Richard." She glanced at the hideous doll she held loosely in her hand. "I did get a fright, though."

"This is all my fault. I should have listened to your aunt and come by myself."

Allowing him to guide her down the arcade, she glanced back at Ross in the garden shouting orders at the guards. The rain obscured their figures so that it was hard to tell them apart, except that his powerful frame predominated.

"Uncle Richard," she said in a subdued voice, "do you recognize this ring? The men who assaulted me had it."

He glanced down at the hand she extended, his face turning white. "It's Arthur's—Ye gods, what is that other thing you're holding?"

"An effigy of me in my wedding dress. Ghastly, isn't it?"

"To say the least. If that's the Rajah's idea of a party favor, I confess I'm glad I didn't get one. But what does it mean that those wildmen have gotten hold of my brother's ring? He often said he'd have to die before—"

"Uncle Richard," she interrupted in an anguished tone.

They turned simultaneously at the clamor of raised voices approaching from the garden. Ross and Kurt were striding forward with the Hindu-Malay Captain of the Guard, who wore a white muslin jacket and loosely woven sarong with a curved spear, a native *kris*, at his side.

Ross reached her first, rain dripping from his dark hair onto his neck. "It would help if you could remember the most outstanding features of the men who assaulted you, Lorna."

"I can't. The only thing I can remember is their hideous masks. Aside from that, they had dark hair, dark skin. . . . "

He lowered his voice. "For God's sake, Lorna, think. There must be something you remember. I can't interrogate every native on the island."

"Any tattoos, perhaps?" Kurt asked, his gaze dropping to the doll still clutched in her hand.

"No—yes. On his thumb, but that's not unusual, is it?" She shook her head in confusion. "They didn't want us to go to Jalaka. They said I'd die if—" She looked up suddenly at Ross. "He had a thin white scar above his left eye, Ross. I was staring at it when I thought he meant to kill me."

The captain glanced at Ross. "It is Ulun, the rice farmer's son, Tuan. He was arrested only a month ago for robbing his own family's hut of its chickens."

"He wasn't jailed?"

"His friends broke him out, Tuan," the captain replied. "Agung-Mani is everywhere."

"Well, not for bloody long," Ross said. Wiping his face with the cravat he'd stuffed into his trousers pocket, he demanded of Lorna, "Why did you wander off by yourself anyway?"

She stiffened at his lashing tone, still not fully recovered from her experience to be insensitive to his criticism. "I was lured by a bell."

Bell or no, he wanted to shake her and couldn't understand why. This was just the sort of incident he feared would happen, and it filled him with impotent fury to be unable to punish the perpetrators who dared intimidate a vulnerable young woman. Well, if one positive thing came out of it, she'd no doubt start repacking for the voyage home tonight.

"Tuan!" Two guards came running up behind Ross and the captain, speaking excitedly in Malay.

"What is it?" Lorna asked Kurt in an undertone.

"One of the guards was just found with a parang in his back."

Lorna stared out into the undisturbed darkness of the garden, a shudder convulsing her shoulders. "They might have killed me too. What prevented them?"

Kurt touched her arm. "Perhaps they simply hoped to discourage you from your search. I don't think they were quite prepared for Resident St. James's personal involvement in searching them out since the night of the puppet show."

His explanation only barely penetrated her dazed mind, the derogatory tone—was it envy?—when he spoke of Ross arousing her anger without her knowing why. "Discourage me from my search?" She turned to face him, seeking in his odd blue eyes answers she sensed he would withhold from her. "Why should it matter to them?"

"I cannot say, but that's part of the adventure, isn't it, Lorna? If we knew what we'd find, it wouldn't be half so enjoyable."

"Enjoyable?" She glanced at the signet ring, overcome with dark fear for her father. "Perhaps we should reconsider the whole thing, Kurt—"

"Bravo," Ross said from behind her, evidently not the least embarrassed to be eavesdropping. "I knew you'd come around eventually."

Kurt's fingers tightened on her wrist and as she lifted her gaze to his face, she glimpsed an almost inhuman determination and challenge in his eyes. "We are committed to finding your father," he said slowly. "We made a pact in Singapore."

It was one of the few qualities she admired in Kurt—an almost hypnotic power to bolster one's failing courage— and she understood suddenly how he'd been able to lead native carriers into areas they were terrified of even approaching alone. "Yes," she said, nodding as if to reassure herself. "You're right, of course."

"Bloody charming of you, van Poole," Ross said, his eyes glittering like ice as they flickered over Kurt's triumphant face. "If you and Richard would report to the

Rajah that Miss Fairfield is safe, I'd like a word with her alone.''

He gripped her shoulders the moment the others were out of earshot, exerting just enough pressure with his hands so that she gave an involuntary gasp of pain. The darkness had accentuated the cold masculinity of his face, eclipsing any hint of refinement. His mouth was twisted into a tight, angry line.

"This won't do at all, Miss Fairfield. It will look very bad for me if I have to send you back to London in a casket.''

The rain had stopped. The steady dripping of moisture from a rose hibiscus resounded in the long silence that followed his words. Lorna felt her shoulders go numb where his fingers had not relaxed their pressure.

"You promised me," she said. "Only days ago, you said you would help me.''

"My primary obligation is to protect you.''

A flock of night herons flew screeching across the garden. The moonlit shadows enveloped Ross and Lorna in muggy warmth.

"If someone you loved were missing, Ross, could you simply put him out of your mind for the rest of your life?''

"I don't believe your father would have wished you to place yourself in jeopardy under any circumstances.''

His hold eased, and his fingers slipped lower from her collarbone toward her breasts. Lorna stilled, every nerve pulsating as he began to caress her through the damp lace of her chemisette with the pads of his thumbs. The friction felt like stinging heat, both arousing and relaxing her against her will.

"For several reasons," he said quietly, "my peace of mind being second only to your safety, I wish you would go home.''

"I can't. No matter what happens, I have to try.''

"Why?" he demanded. "To live up to some preposterous pact between you and that Dutch mercenary?''

"To live with myself," she answered steadily. "And I'm sorry you can't understand that."

His face hardened, his eyes suddenly as impersonal as flint. Lorna wondered whether he was more upset by the challenge to his authority or because his powers of seductive persuasion were failing. She would like to think he cared about her, but she would be deluding herself if she pretended he had ever given her any overt evidence of affection. He knew far more about her than was fair, and unlike him, she could not hide behind a pretense of emotional reserve and responsibilities.

"Ross. Try to understand."

"I don't need to understand." He lifted his hands from her shoulders.

"And your promise—"

"Will be kept," he said curtly, bending to find his boots.

"What about this thing?" She held the doll at arm's length. "What shall I do with it?"

"Consider it a souvenir." He straightened to stare at her with cruel mockery in his eyes. "After all, you do pride yourself on being the sort of woman who always keeps her head about her, don't you?"

Chapter 9

C hiang stood before the unlit fireplace of the parlor, forbidden by Ross to sit, alternately biting her fingernails and smoking clove-scented cigarettes during the interrogation.

"You do not deny this dress was your handiwork, Chiang?" Ross said.

A tear rolled down the woman's face. "I do not do bad thing. I work hard. Wash clothes and iron for lady."

Ross leaned back in his chair. "I doubt there's a seamstress in the archipelago who can rival your talents." He reached for the shrunken-headed doll on the tea table beside him. Holding it by the hair, he spun it around and around, glancing only once at Lorna from the corner of his eye.

"The question is, Chiang, how did you get involved with the Agung-Mani?"

Chiang squatted to stub out her cigarette on the hearth. Lorna could see the woman's hands trembling in fear. In his own way, she realized as she watched the interrogation, Ross was every bit as determined, even as ruthless, as Kurt van Poole, except that Ross worked for the greater good rather than for his own selfish interests.

Ross got up and walked to the fireplace, standing before Chiang with his legs spread. "I don't want to put you in prison, Chiang. I'm afraid the disgrace will hasten your elderly father's death."

114

"I must not say," she whispered, covering her face with her hands.

"He will lose his home without you to support him. He will starve without the money you earn to put food on his table. As repugnant as I find the prospect, I will imprison you, Chiang. I will do *whatever* I must to stop the madness on this island."

Lorna started to rise, shaken not only by his deserved callousness toward the woman but also by this facet of his character he'd unwittingly revealed. All at once his all-consuming dedication to the island was so apparent to her that she realized any interest he might have in her could be only a fleeting diversion from the pressures of his responsibilities. Clearly there was little room in his life for a woman, except for a physical relationship, and Lorna despaired at the prospect of such a degradation befalling her.

"You'll be whipped in prison, Chiang," he continued ruthlessly. "Stripped of all you've worked so hard to possess."

"Please, Ross," Lorna said.

"Leave him alone, Lorna," Kurt said from the corner. "A man was murdered last night, and several other people, including you, came close to meeting the same fate."

"I suppose you're right," she said. "But this whole thing makes me feel wretched."

"Then leave the room," Ross said, his eyes cold and uncompromising.

"I think I will," she said coolly. Kana was at the door as she opened it, giving her an impudent grin as their gazes met.

"Hello," she said.

"Hello," he answered.

"I suppose you've heard about my shrunken head. Would you like to examine it?"

His grin broadened. "Oh, yes, pleases."

"On the table."

"Kana," Ross said, looking annoyed.

Kana didn't answer. He was staring at the doll with his hand pressed to his mouth to smother a hoot of laughter.

"This very good jokes, Tuan," he said, lifting up the skirts to peer at the doll's undersides.

"Kana," Ross said sternly, "did you come here to play with Miss Fairfield's doll, or do you have the information I requested?"

"Yes, Tuan," he answered, sobering. "It take me all mornings, but I found out from Missee Li-Li that Chiang's son Kao not dead like Chiang tell everyone. He Agung-Mani now, Tuan. Very bad mans."

Chiang sank to her knees as if she had just received a death sentence.

"Why did they make you do it, Chiang?" Ross asked.

She did not respond for several seconds. Then slowly she raised her head, her face ugly and defiant. "I never tell you, Tuan. I go to prison before I betray Agung-Mani."

He swallowed and stared at her in silence as if he could not believe what he had heard. "Then prison it is. Kurt, I assume I can trust you to keep her here until the guards remove her to the fort." He collected his helmet and papers from the table. "Kana, I am entrusting you with the formidable task of keeping an eye on Miss Fairfield for the next two days."

"What will you do about the Agung-Mani?" Lorna asked, following him into the hall.

"Whatever I have to." He looked up at the sound of voices outside. "I'll no longer tolerate their practices here."

"Good God!" they heard Richard exclaim at the door. "What in the name of heaven is this all about? Lorna!"

"Well, now, Miss Fairfield," Ross said dryly. "What have you brought upon us now?"

Richard was waiting for them at the door. "There's a present come for you, Lorna."

"Not another shrunken head, I hope."

"Look." He pointed outside to a large black man in a sleeveless gown and white turban who stood holding a baby gibbon ape on the veranda. "From the Sultan."

"Who are they?" she whispered.

Ross rubbed his nose. "I don't know the ape. I believe the African is the next Kislar Aga."

She peeked outside again. "What does that mean?"

" 'Master of the girls.' He's the Sultan's chief eunuch-in-training. I told you that in the Far East a gift must be properly reciprocated."

"Well, I suppose I shall have to keep the ape. But what am I to do with a eunuch-in-training?"

Ross walked outside, grinning. "Actually, I believe his function is to keep *you* under control. What a marvelous idea."

She ran down the stairs after him, giving the eunuch an appraising glance as she darted around his bulky figure. "Don't abandon me to handle this alone."

"I'll tell the Sultan you're delighted with his presents," Ross called from the gate.

She turned slowly. The eunuch smiled and gave her a courtly bow. "I am Ali Aziz, mistress. My little friend here is Mahomet."

"Mr. Aziz. I am very appreciative of your master offering me your services, but I'm afraid I don't have a position for you at the moment."

"I am a man of many talents, mistress."

"I'm sure you are."

"I will massage your pale ivory skin with scented oils," he said. "I will brush your hair until it crackles and shines like threads of sunlight. I will interpret what course the stars have charted for you." His voice dropped. "I will even console you over the betrayal of your beloved—"

"News certainly travels fast to faraway places."

"It is my duty to understand the secrets of your heart."

She sighed. "Very well then. You may as well come

into the parlor and meet the headhunter assigned to guard me.''

''And Mahomet?''

''Bring him along too.''

After the strain of the previous day, Lorna slept late the following morning and in fact did nothing more strenuous than bathe and arrange for a new housekeeper to replace Chiang. Eventually she would have to begin supervising a thorough cleaning of the house, but for now it was enough to concentrate on getting the expedition under way.

Her freshly washed hair fell in her face as she knelt before the iron-bound trunk, sifting through her father's letters. At this time of day, with the equatorial sun high in the sky, the most sensible thing for an islander to do was sleep. But her mind would not rest.

It was quiet in the house. Kurt and her uncle had gone off to some secret rendezvous in the jungle with the guide who had sailed with her father to Jalaka, in the hope he would agree to accompany them on their expedition. His help would be invaluable; in fact, Kurt depended upon it and seemed certain he could persuade the guide to venture to the untamed island again. Ilse was writing detailed letters to her children, whom she had entrusted to the care of her sister-in-law, but Lorna couldn't remember where the woman lived. Or perhaps Ilse had never mentioned it. Kana and Ali Aziz were dozing in the garden, and a young Chinese girl named Mei Sing, who'd been sent by the Ranee herself, had taken over the task of overseeing the small household. Lorna liked her quiet efficiency so much, she hoped to persuade her to stay.

She skimmed the handwritten pages of her father's letters, searching for new meaning in the words she'd read a hundred times before. For the first time, she was looking not for clues to his disappearance but rather to one of the characters whose names had frequently cropped up in his correspondences.

August 14, 1852

I played chess tonight with Resident St. James in his bungalow. Pompous bastard. He beat me again, but I pulled him down a peg or two when I casually mentioned meeting his native mistress in the village earlier that same day. The sly fellow confessed he did not want his involvement with her widely known, not wishing to harm her reputation among her people. He actually looked embarrassed when I confronted him with the evidence of his amour and insisted he was attempting to arrange a respectable marriage for her with one of the village's farmers' sons. Didn't mention whether he intended to carry on their liaison after the nuptials, though. . . .

On a more serious note, I fear he will need to become more flexible if he is to replace the Rajah in the hearts of the people. The man is positively obsessed with maintaining order on the island. Yet the capacity for emotion is within him somewhere. That I sense. As with other outstation officers, his life swings between monotony and high danger. Perhaps he was less reserved before his wife and infant son died several years ago in some tragedy no one speaks of to this day. Anyway, Lorna, he would not suit you at all. . . .

"A mistress," Lorna murmured, frowning. She shouldn't be so surprised. She unfolded another earlier letter and began skimming the lines.

The rains are beginning to depress me, Lorna, or perhaps it is another of my melancholy spells coming on. Against the Rajah's advice, I went to the Chinese sector today. Dined aboard a junk on shrimp and steamed rice with an unpleasant character from Singapore. Suspect he's an opium smuggler, for he certainly had lavish appointments about his craft. Nonetheless, my darling, this dark creature and his dangerous schemes may fuel my imaginings for future writings, but they are not suitable for *your* eyes and ears.

A sharp rap sounded at the door, jarring Lorna's concentration.

"Lorna, may I come in? It's Ilse."

Lorna stuffed the letters back into the trunk and relocked it. "Just a moment. The door is bolted."

"I should hope so," Ilse said as she entered the room. "I'm finished with my letters to the children. I thought I might borrow your eunuch for the afternoon and have him squire me around shopping."

"He's not my eunuch. He's his own man."

"And he's not even really that, is he?" Ilse asked with a wicked grin, sitting down on the bed above Lorna. "Actually, I've come to warn you about Ross."

"He's not a part-time cannibal or anything like that, is he?"

"I don't think he's the sort of man you should get involved with."

Lorna pulled a loose thread from the fringe of the coverlet. "I'll bear that in mind."

"You're as stubborn as my eldest daughter. Look, I realize Ross is an attractive man. I also realize how you must feel over your fiancé's betrayal."

"How on earth could you possibly know about that?"

"From your uncle. Apparently, he asked your coachman why you came home so upset that evening. Richard thinks you've made too much of it, that your fiancé and friend were probably harmlessly engaged."

"Rubbish."

"Yes, that's what I thought."

"Then the entire world from Uncle Richard to my eunuch knows of my humiliation."

"I understand exactly how you feel. That's why I fear you're susceptible to Ross's attention."

"How could you understand what I feel?"

Ilse rolled onto her side. "My husband does not remain

celibate all those months at sea. Nor the weeks when he is home.''

"Have you ever caught him?''

"Caught him?'' Ilse gave a bitter laugh. "He flaunts his harlots in our own home—in front of his crippled mother and the children, claiming they're young girls he's hired to clean the house or help me with the cooking. They stay a month or two until he frightens them off.''

"I should leave him if I were you.''

"He has a violent temper,'' Ilse murmured. "And if that weren't bad enough, he's horribly cruel to the children. I would do anything to spare them suffering, Lorna.'' She hesitated. "This is not to be shared with anyone else, but I have in fact already left him. I have no intention of ever returning to our home. He just doesn't know that yet since he's not due back from Holland for another two months.''

"But what will happen to the children?''

"My sister-in-law is taking care of them until I join them in Africa.'' She bit her lower lip. "If he knew how badly Wouter had treated us, Kurt would murder him. He adores my little ones.''

The idea of Kurt adoring anyone, especially young children, came as a surprise to Lorna, but she was too interested in returning to their original subject of conversation to dwell on it.

"So you see, Lorna,'' Ilse said, "there is a secret bond of pain you and I share. Fortunately, I have my children to reassure me that my marriage was not an utter loss, while you have nothing. Poor Lorna. I believe I would lie, cheat, steal, and yes, even kill to protect my babies, but I would never stoop to betraying my best friend with her man.''

Lorna hesitated, then said, "How well do you know Ross?''

"Not intimately. Not as well as I might have had his wife lived. Vanessa arrived on the archipelago about the same time I did. We were friends in mutual unhappiness those first months.''

"Did she die in childbirth?''

"Yes. And the infant with her. I'd promised to be with her at the time, but it came two months earlier than we expected. Vanessa was a very delicate woman, afraid of everything under the sun. According to her houseboy, she begged Ross at the first labor pain to summon the only British doctor who was practicing here then.''

Lorna sat up slowly, knowing she would find a key to Ross somewhere in Ilse's recount. "And Ross wouldn't?''

"The doctor had been called away to attend an outbreak of cholera on the other side of the island. Ross brought in a competent Malay midwife to assist her. But he lost both Vanessa and his son within an hour of each other. There were complications beyond anyone's control.''

"He blamed himself?''

"So it would seem. Dr. Parker reassured him nothing could have been done to save them. Even Vanessa's father did not condemn him at the funeral. But Ross has never spoken of the incident to anyone that I know of since that day. It was four years ago.''

"He must have felt the loss very deeply, that he still cannot bear to discuss it.''

"Ross was always rather reserved in the first place. Vanessa once mentioned that his father was a cold, stern man who never smiled or showed his children any affection. Of course, compared to my own upbringing such a parent sounds perfect.''

Lorna fell silent. She remembered Ilse mentioning once that her father had been a brutal drunkard who had belittled her constantly and had physically abused Kurt until he grew old enough to fight back.

"I thought—I understood that Ross had a native mistress.''

"I wouldn't know,'' Ilse replied. "I've lost touch with him over the years. But he's a man, isn't he?''

Sounds of activity began to filter upstairs. The gardener

yelling at Mahomet for tearing up the wisteria. Ali Aziz's high-pitched laughter at the monkey's antics.

"Ross never cared for my husband from the start," Ilse said drowsily, closing her eyes. "He likes Kurt even less. . . ."

Lorna got up from the bed and walked to the veranda, her throat tight with emotion. Her father had often counseled her that she must never take people at their face value, that every man who walked the earth wrestled with his own hidden pain and inner demons. Her father had possessed so much compassion and insight when it came to dealing with others . . . the reformed forger he'd once hired as a secretary, the woman convicted of petty theft who became his chambermaid.

It struck Lorna as suddenly very ironic and unfair that her father had never viewed *her* as a human being with needs of her own.

She stepped outside and felt the shimmering heat undulating over her in transparent waves. Down the hillside she could see a lone rider ascending the path between the bordering blaze of flame-of-the-forest trees. Even at this distance, his face indistinct, she could identify the horseman by the blue-black sheen of his hair and the tall erect posture.

She gripped the weather-worn white railing and followed his progress up the path. She had been angry enough at him that last night in the istana to never speak to him again. Now she could not find a trace of that anger to help protect her from her attraction to him.

She moved back toward the bedroom as the rider approached the gate. Ali Aziz looked up at her with kindly concern.

She almost regretted now that Ilse had told her about Ross's past. It made her own broken romance seem juvenile and insignificant. Worse still, it made it harder to pretend he was simply an unfeeling, arrogant man instead of someone who had been hurt so deeply that he had isolated himself from all emotion in self-defense. And she wondered whether the scars of his past had become too much a part of his character for anyone to help him heal.

Lorna was surprised when Ross explained he'd come to escort her to a place on the island where her father had been frequently sighted alone.

"It's an abandoned hut on the hillside, not far from here," he said. "I believe he used to go there to reflect."

"That sounds like Papa," she said as she led him into the parlor. "I might find a few clues to his activities there. This is very thoughtful of you, Mr. St. James. Especially with so many other important things you have to attend to."

"Oh, it's nothing," he lied, thinking of the thousand disputes he had to settle among the villagers, the reconstruction of at least twenty huts swept away in a mudslide, not to mention rebuilding his own sulap and finding a priest to reconsecrate the blasted sand so that Kana could live there.

"I supposed I should have a chaperone," Lorna said, tapping a finger to her chin. "Or at least a companion. Ilse could come."

"That poses a bit of a problem. You see, I'm having a horse brought here for you from the istana—it should arrive at any time. They're scarce on the island, and I understand you're a splendid rider."

"Well, I—"

"I wouldn't dream of compromising your respectability," he interrupted with an ironic smile that hinted he found her hesitation amusing.

She was still considering his offer when she remembered that Mary Ashworth, the famous world traveler, had often embarked on such spontaneous outings unescorted and no one had ever accused her of impropriety. Of course, Mary Ashworth had been fifty at the time, but that shouldn't make a difference, and there was Papa to consider.

"I should change then," she said, eyeing with envy his cool white linen shirt and sand-colored cotton trousers.

He always looked so crisp and meticulously clean that she felt like a scullery maid before a duke in his presence.

"Hurry up," he said. "The weather is undependable."

So was the horse he had borrowed for her from the Rajah's stables. In fact, Lorna suspected that no one had ridden it in years, as it stopped every twenty seconds or so to crop at grass or just stare at the ground.

It took them an hour to wend their way down the hillside.

"I think you'll have to ride with me if we hope to make it up another hill before midnight," Ross said. "That is, of course, unless you are unsettled by the idea."

For an instant, noting the glimmer of challenge in his clear gray eyes, she almost believed this was a conspiracy—that he'd planned the balky horse just to force her to ride pillion on his comfortable Arabian, but that was undoubtedly a romantic fantasy on her part.

"You're very light, aren't you?" he remarked as he gave her a leg up onto his horse. Her own mount was left tethered contentedly to a tree in a cool grove.

"I don't know why—I eat enough to sink a warship," she said, and could have bitten off her tongue for making such an unthinking, unladylike comment when she saw him pretend to cough to smother a laugh.

The sudden closeness to Ross, the pleasant intimacy of leaning against his warm, solid back, only added to her growing concern that she was not at all in control of the situation. She was sure she shouldn't enjoy locking her arms around his waist and allowing the easy rhythm of the horse to meld them together.

She drew her hands back to her lap, only to hear him murmur, "You can't do that. It's quite likely we'll hit a stone hidden beneath some palm fronds. I wouldn't want you to fall because of something so silly as social convention."

It was the first time in her memory that Lorna had been accused of overadherence to any kind of social restriction.

"I think you're making fun of me," she said to his shoulder.

She saw enough of his profile to note the start of a smile on his firm lips. "Not at all. Hang on tight," he said as the Arabian gave a sudden lurch. "This is quite a climb."

The hut was more secluded than Lorna realized, at the end of a steep path that provided little protection from the strong offshore breezes. It was also disappointingly devoid of any clues to her father's disappearance. In fact, except for a few of his books, a pair of dusty boots, and an outdated newspaper, she might not have believed Ross's claim that this had been Papa's private retreat.

"I know he used to come here," Ross insisted at the skeptical look on her face. "He said the peacocks disturbed him at the house, and that he could always think better after he'd climbed the hill—" He knelt suddenly, smudging his fingers across the dirt floor. "That explains it."

"What is it?" Lorna asked, imagining bloodstains spilled in violence.

"Tobacco."

"My father smokes a pipe."

"So does Kurt van Poole, and these are freshly burnt leaves. He's been here recently."

Lorna glanced around at the nondescript mud walls and then up at the snugly thatched roof. "I'm not surprised," she said, although she actually was. "I hired him because he's supposed to be thorough. At least he's been earning his pay. Obviously he found nothing important or he'd have informed me."

Ross shrugged as if he wanted to disagree, but he said nothing. Lorna had found a makeshift bamboo shelf above the window and was examining the seashell collection displayed there.

"Has it ever occurred to you that your father may not want to be found?" he asked her unexpectedly.

She whirled around, her eyes wide. "What on earth are you insinuating?"

"This isn't the first time he's gone missing."

"Did my uncle tell you that?" she asked, her mouth tightening.

"There are records. Confidential, of course."

She sighed. "It happened once before, when I was eleven, and he took it into his head to travel with a band of gypsies into Wales."

"He abandoned an eleven-year-old girl?" he asked in disbelief.

"Only once," she said, unthinkingly on the defensive, "and I realize now he was half out of his mind with grief over losing my mother. In fact, I don't think he ever really recovered from her death." She ran her index finger along the serrated rim of a queen conch. "He didn't completely abandon me. I mean, he made some rather vague provisions for my welfare during his absence. We traveled around together for years after his return."

"That's a rather unconventional girlhood, isn't it?"

"It didn't seem so at the time."

"The Rajah remembers you in plaits and pinafores," he said, staring at her as if seeing her in a different light.

"Yes, but mine was never a regular childhood."

"I think I rather envy you," he said. "My father never took us farther than the garden gate unless it was for school or an endless mass."

"Perhaps that's why you chose a faraway pagan island to settle on."

He inhaled deeply, shrugging. "I don't know. I suppose I've more than made up for my conventional upbringing."

Did he sound uncomfortable talking about his childhood? She would have traded places gladly with him if she'd been able to at the time. For even when she was younger, Lorna saw that to strike out against convention had its price. More than once her father had been arrested for debt and incarcerated, with Uncle Richard resentfully having to bail him out. All too well she remembered the humiliation of pawning spoons and chairs, even her mother's jewelry, which had been her legacy to Lorna. Nearly everything of value was sold, except Arthur's precious books. She and Julia had to beg him not to mortgage Mama's Hampshire house, otherwise they'd surely have no place to live one day. As it was they were forced to lease it out more often than not to afford their London lodgings. Papa would smile ruefully and say that one day he might be forced to accept his old friend the Rajah's offer to take over a neglected tobacco plantation on the far-flung tropical island of Kali Simpang. It did sound tempting, he'd tell Lorna enticingly, describing to her in detail the delicious freedom they could enjoy on Charles's private Eden. But Lorna would only shake her head and insist that her days of wandering the earth like a gypsy were over. . . .

The past receded abruptly as she felt Ross move close behind her, so close she could smell the pleasing combination of his shaving soap and the starched linen of his shirt. Her heart quickened at his nearness.

"Still, it must have been a lonely life for a young girl," he said in a reflective voice.

He reached past her for a seashell on the shelf. Lorna's skin tingled where his hand brushed her shoulder.

"I had three marvelous cats and a fascinating library at my disposal."

"But pets and poetry cannot replace human company, can they?"

She turned slowly to regard him, disconcerted by the joyful leap her heart gave as she looked into his eyes. She should have been happily married to another man right now and instead she was fighting internal flutters over one she hardly knew.

"A penny for your thoughts, Miss Fairfield."

"I was just thinking—well, nothing ever works out the way I plan it."

"Ah. That's what makes life interesting, isn't it? Our meeting, for instance," he continued, his voice suddenly low. "It wasn't planned. Who can tell what lies in store for us?"

It was a dangerous moment, and Lorna was not sure she was ready to pit her weakening willpower against his overwhelming magnetism. His heavy-lidded eyes bespoke a desire beyond her comprehension or experience.

Yet he did not touch her, although his gaze lowered fleetingly to her mouth, and his voice, when he spoke, was as devastating to her senses as any caress. "It was perhaps bad judgment on my part to bring you here alone today."

"It—it is as much my fault as yours," she said weakly, suddenly aware of his thigh positioned against her skirt . . . and that she had no way to escape him.

He drew a deep breath, his nostrils pinched. "Either you become more tempting each time we meet or I grow weaker. I cannot gather my thoughts sufficiently to say. I do know, however, that we must leave this hut immediately before we both regret what might transpire."

Relief and inexplicable disappointment flashed through her. "I suppose that would be prudent."

He hesitated for a fraction of a second, watching her closely, his face shadowed with reluctance. "I warn you again," he said quietly, "share my company at your own peril."

The silken threat in his tone made Lorna tremble, not for fear of what Ross would do but of what she would allow.

He held open the door to usher her out into the humid air that swathed them like an invisible veil. He had not even kissed her in that hut, yet she felt as though they had just emerged from the most intimate encounter . . . perhaps because she had shared some of her most private thoughts about herself with him. Yet it was not until they were halfway down the hillside that she realized she had learned virtually nothing more about him.

Chapter 10

The interlude with Ross in the hillside hut had so engrossed Lorna that she'd forgotten until he brought her home how apprehensive she was over Kurt's return from his jungle rendezvous with the guide who had accompanied her father to Jalaka. The success of the search could hinge on the native's cooperation. And so far he had hidden himself away in the rain forest, refusing to answer the Rajah's summons to explain exactly what had happened to Sir Arthur. He seemed to be afraid . . . but of what or whom?

She could tell by the expression on Kurt's face as she spotted him at the gate that he brought good news. Her uncle, however, had not fared the brief excursion into the jungle well. His face was red from heat and exertion, the material of his trousers blotched with the blood of countless leech bites.

She met them under the gnarled banyan tree in the garden. This was the sacred warigen that Ross had spoken of in the rain forest, a tree that legend said had once been connected by an umbilical cord to a powerful goddess. Lorna prayed that the spirit residing within it would look upon her quest with favor.

"What happened? Did you meet the guide?" she asked.

Kurt took her by the arm out of hearing range of Kana and Ali Aziz, who stood watching her every move. "You mustn't let this discourage you," he began. "Your father is still alive, and Mulak will help us find him. But only under the condition that the gods give their approval."

"The gods." She shook her head. "I don't understand."

"The eagle goddess Penala must sanction our search for your father. Her approval is necessary on this island for everything from planting a crop to undertaking a journey. You have to make a pilgrimage to her temple, Lorna, and ask her blessing. If she bestows it, then Mulak will lead our expedition to Jalaka."

Lorna glanced at her uncle, who had collapsed on the grass with his head in his arms. She wondered suddenly where either of them would find the stamina to penetrate miles of mountain jungle.

"If I make this pilgrimage, how will we know I have won the goddess's favor?"

"One of her messengers must alight upon her shrine before morning. A hawk or a long-tailed kite, perhaps. She speaks to the people through her sacred birds."

"You don't really believe this nonsense, do you?"

He hesitated. "If you had lived on the equator as long as I have, you'd have learned there are many things beyond our comprehension. What matters is that the islanders believe, and without their help we won't be able to even begin our journey. We will need carriers in the jungle, rowers to bear our provisions, a sea captain and native crew."

"What if the goddess denies my request?"

He smiled thinly. "We will give fate a helping hand. Pig is a favorite food of the gods, and I will do a little hunting to accommodate Penala's appetite."

Lorna glanced away, weighing in her mind what he had told her. She regretted suddenly that Ross had not stayed a while longer to discuss the matter, even though, inevitably, he and Kurt would disagree.

"Where is Penala's shrine?" she said. "And when would I have to go there?"

"It's hidden in the jungle foothills—inside the Temple

of Two Hundred Steps. You should go tonight. Mulak's services as a guide are very much in demand, and that French botanist Corneille is planning another expedition.'' He pulled off his helmet and pushed the fringe of damp white-blond hair off his forehead. ''There is one condition to the pilgrimage you will not like—you must go alone.''

''Alone?''

''If no misfortune befalls you on the way to the shrine, it is taken as a sign of favor from the gods. There's no other way, Lorna. But I'll be behind you every step.''

''This temple—it's on the way to Mount Belakan, where the Agung-Mani are, isn't it?''

He nodded. ''There is risk involved, I won't lie to you. But the worshipers of Penala are a peace-loving people, the ancient enemies of the Agung-Mani. As long as you reach the temple before nightfall, you shouldn't be in danger.''

''Why do you think the Agung-Mani want me off the island? And you—they specifically mentioned the shikari when they assaulted me. You must have an idea why they spoke of you.''

''Who is to say?'' he answered. ''Perhaps they simply do not want their secrets uncovered, and I am known for finding whatever I set out after.''

''Do you think they're holding my father on Jalaka?''

''I think we will find him there.'' He edged closer to her, his voice exuding a strange excitement. ''Will you go tonight or not, Lorna? Everything could depend on it.''

She looked into his eyes and was unable to read any emotion in his gaze. He and Ilse were an odd pair. It was hard to picture Kurt as a little boy cowering from an abusive parent. Her own gentle father, for all his faults and eccentricities, seemed infinitely precious in comparison.

''I'll go to the shrine,'' she said. ''I suppose we have to clear this with Resident St. James first.''

''He'll be on the other side of the island by now, at the landing wharf. Apparently a dispute arose there between two merchants, and a coolie was sent to fetch the Resident to arbitrate. We saw him intercepting Ross on our way here. It would take hours to locate him.''

"Well, I'd feel better if—''

"If you could see him again? Or is it just an excuse to spend more time in his company? I never took you as being the type whose head was so easily turned.''

"I don't believe I am,'' she said hotly.

"I say, Lorna.'' Richard had risen to join them, scratching his neck with relentless vigor. "I'm not sure whether this is such a good idea, after all. Not after that nasty incident at the istana.''

Lorna stood, torn between her common sense and Kurt's persuasive arguments. "We do need the guide's help, Uncle Richard.''

He nodded reluctantly. From the large wooden shed behind the house where Kurt's mastiff was kept rose a series of ominous growls as the guard made his hourly check. Kurt didn't like keeping the dog locked up, but on its first night out it had terrified the gardener and almost killed a peacock.

"I'll go then,'' she said slowly. "But from now on, I want to be kept apprised of everything that happens concerning my father. Is that understood?''

Kurt gave her a guileless look. "Of course, Lorna. If that is what you wish.''

It was almost dusk when she reached the waringen grove that marked the beginning of the ascent to Mount Belakan. Everywhere she looked—in the hollows of trees, between mossy boulders—were the remnants of offerings made to the gods. The dark stillness unnerved her. Even though she knew Kurt was following somewhere in the shadows, remaining out of sight from native eyes, she felt vulnerable and alone.

An antelope darted out from a patch of wild bananas. Reflexively she groped for her pistol and then leaned against the aerial roots of a banyan tree to give her galloping heart a rest. She was glad now Spencer had taught her how to shoot, even though she prayed she wouldn't need to tonight.

An aerial root came to life unexpectedly around her shoulders, twisting and writhing near her face with sinuous grace. She stood paralyzed in fear, afraid even to call out for help until she recognized the snake as the nonvenomous Lady-of-the-Forest.

"Kurt." She shuddered as the snake dropped to the ground. "Kurt, there are over two hundred species of snakes in the archipelago. How am I to tell if they're poisonous or not?"

There was silence. Lorna surmised he was annoyed she had broken their agreement not to acknowledge each other except in the case of an emergency. The pilgrimage had to be made alone.

Finally his voice floated out from somewhere behind her. "The only way to tell for sure is to kill the snake and examine its teeth."

"Well," she said, hoisting her knapsack higher onto her shoulders, "that's a big bloody help."

The relief she felt on breaking out of the long-shadowed forest vanished as she encountered the unsmiling inhabitants of the scraggling huts on the hillside path. In contrast to the river Gibungs, the Ranjans were an antisocial people who congregated in hostile silence and watched her as she struggled upward along the narrow path.

To add to her apprehension, she could not escape passing beneath the various collections of shrunken heads suspended in rattan nets from the ruais of their huts. New heads or old? She supposed she should be grateful that none of them resembled the one she'd received with flowing red hair and a silk wedding gown.

She reminded herself that this was not the Agung-Mani village, although she thought Ross had mentioned that from here the cult took many adherents—and sacrifices.

She quickened her steps, feeling a light film of perspiration break out upon her skin. Ross. She wished suddenly that she had defied Kurt to tell him of her pilgrimage. True, Ross was impossible to decipher, and his combination of reserve, unabashed sensuality, and male arrogance disarmed her. But she always felt safe from harm in his presence, as if when they were together he insulated her from the threats of the outside world. Unfortunately, she hadn't yet discovered what she could use to protect herself from his powerful appeal.

She reached the temple as darkness fell. Torchlight flared in the outer courtyards as if lit by invisible hands. A figure flitted by and disappeared, the *pedanda*, a temple priest with a long white robe and crystal-knobbed wand.

The massive sandstone carving of the Prophetess Penala, her cruel eagle's features and pendulous breasts eroded by the monsoons and pervasive salt air, faced the heavens with wings outstretched in regal splendor.

Lorna glanced behind her for a sign of reassurance from Kurt and received none. This was where they'd agreed to part. Remembering her father, picturing him held captive on a cannibal island, she lifted her skirts and began the two-hundred step ascent.

A quarter way to the shrine she stopped to rest. The altitude and unaccustomed exertion left her lightheaded and slow-gaited. There was the sound of rushing wings above her. Glancing up, she saw a formation of bats descending upon the shrine's summit to pick at the sacrificial offerings left by worshipers. Cringing at the sight, she forced herself to continue climbing until she reached the shrine.

There were three inner courtyards enclosed within high walls and pointed bamboo gates that were guarded by sandstone dragons. Lorna passed through the gate to her right and heard it snap behind her like a trap. Almost simultaneously the torches that lit this area of the temple were extinguished.

Only then did she notice that the sconces were actually skulls set into the wall. Smoke from the extinguished flames wafted out of the eye sockets in bluish wisps.

Carved into the stone below the skulls were *togogs*—the ugly pop-eyed goblins whose job it was to chase away evil spirits.

There was a faint noise behind her. She glanced back over her shoulder and whispered, "Kurt?" in the remote event he'd changed his mind about leaving her alone.

If he was there, he did not answer. Using the moonlight to guide her, she walked to the end of the passage and discovered it was the start of a maze. Spirits, she remembered, supposedly could not turn corners.

A faint thud sounded from the opposite wall.

She turned in cautious degrees.

An eerie flicker of blue lightning illuminated the maze, throwing the skulls and togogs into macabre relief. There was not a soul in sight. Yet something told her it wasn't the spirits she had to fear.

It took her an hour to make her way through the misleading maze and reach the shrine, a gigantic sandstone eagle's head that gazed out over the island. From there Lorna had an unobstructed view of the smoking peak of Mount Belakan enshrouded in moonlight and fog.

She entered the shrine through the beak of the carving. The altar inside was a rough stone slab adorned with jacinth, tourmaline, rock crystal, and volcanic stones that glowed in the darkness. Incense pots in wall niches filled the clammy air with smoky-sweet fumes.

She unrolled the mat she'd carried on her back, spread it out on the floor, and settled down for the night. After a few minutes in the dark, she decided to light a candle.

The wavering flame revealed the cadaverous face of the priest watching her from a peephole in the wall. When she worked up the nerve to stare him in the eye, she saw that he had disappeared, and a white albino rat was wriggling through the hole to take his place.

Chapter 11

Ross looked up from his desk in irritation to see his Dutch housekeeper standing in the doorway. That ridiculous dispute on the wharves had wasted a good two hours. And the time spent with Lorna had taken most of his afternoon, although he couldn't blame that on anyone except himself. Just as he couldn't fault Lorna because he'd been thinking of her ever since then, wondering again whether he had mistaken her spirited character for stubbornness.

No wonder she was so fiercely independent. From what he'd gathered of her life, she'd had to learn to depend on herself to survive. Her father seemed to have depended on her too—overmuch, in Ross's opinion. But he supposed she'd be furious with him if he pointed that out. She obviously adhered to the current belief that a daughter owed her parents utter, self-sacrificing devotion.

Although outwardly strong, she had an unconscious vulnerability about her that he couldn't resist. Her high spirits were infectious, but he often sensed a sadness behind her smile. Sadness because of Spencer? he wondered, frowning at the thought. Or was it the weight of her responsibility as a good daughter? She never mentioned that she had any friends back in England, though he assumed she had, but when during all her traveling would she have formed the lasting relationships that carried into adulthood? She was an unusual young woman, and he found himself more and more drawn to her.

"Mr. St. James?" the housekeeper said.

He started, unnerved by the realization that he could not concentrate for even seconds at a time without his mind wandering to Lorna. The disconcerting truth was that she intrigued him. And if her lovely face and figure weren't enough to drive him to distraction, the fascinating layers of her character were even more compelling.

"I do not wish to be disturbed, Mrs. Hofner." He returned to the maps of the Indian-Malay Archipelago on which he had marked the course of the pirate raiders. "Whatever you want to cook for supper is fine."

"Ja then. We have boilt socks and moldy cabbage."

He looked up. "Excuse me."

She quailed a little at his expression. It wasn't the first time she'd shown him impertinence, and Ross suspected it had become a challenge for her to see how far she could push him.

"It's Kana I came to tell you about, Mr. St. James. He's been skulking about in the garden for an hour. Most queer it is."

"Kana."

Ross rearranged his charts into an orderly pile and anchored them to the desk with a magnifying loupe. As he rose from his chair, his gaze fell upon the much-reviewed folder he had marked "Miss Lorna Doreen Fairfield."

"What the hell is Kana doing on this side of the island?" he said in a thunderous voice. "I assigned him to the plantation house."

Mrs. Hofner stood back as he squeezed past her into the hall, her wrinkled pink face glowing in anticipation of some excitement.

"There is a cashmere shawl on my bed that I bought at the bazaar today on the way back from the wharves," Ross called from the front door. "Do you think you could wrap it for me?"

"I'd be delighted, sir." Her smile faded. "It's not for Bale, is not?"

"It is not." He shut the door behind him, puzzled that he had not felt the least urge either to visit or to replace his former native mistress. He stared out into the darkness of the garden, listening to the sawing of the cicadas and the shuffling of a nocturnal anteater under the veranda. Fireflies and an occasional flash of lightning highlighted the palm grove that bordered the garden.

"Kana?"

He glanced up intuitively into the tree where Kana squatted with his arms resting on his knees. "I'm afraid to ask what you're doing up in that tree."

"I'm afraid to tell you, Tuan. You be very angries."

Ross brought his hands to the back of his neck to knead the knots of tension there. "Where is Miss Fairfield, Kana?"

"She very naughty ladies, Tuan. She sneaks away while me and my good fat friend Ali Aziz are sleeping in the sun."

"Damn it! Where did she go?"

"Haji the gardener say she go up the Ranjan path with the shikari. That very dangerous place at nights." Satisfied that Ross wasn't going to kill him, Kana swung down from the tree. He scratched at a bite on his buttocks with a long fingernail, then pushed his glasses back onto the bridge of his thick nose. "Agung-Mani meet on that path tonight, Tuan."

Ross swung around and ran up the steps of the bungalow, eliciting a scream of fright from Mrs. Hofner as she emerged from his bedroom with the shawl.

"I—I wondered, sir," she said when she recovered from her startlement, "should I wrap the shawl in tissue or—"

She clutched the shawl to her chest as he turned from the hall stand, tucking a pistol into his waistband.

"I'd wait to wrap it if I were you, Mrs. Hofner," he snapped. "I just may use it to strangle the young woman for whom it was intended."

* * *

Lorna sat huddled on the floor, every nerve alert with apprehension. The temperature had dropped, and the shrine was engulfed in humid darkness, relieved only by infrequent zigzags of lightning outside.

For hours she had listened to the mesmerizing rhythm of moisture slipping off the stones and the faint peal of prayer bells. She had listened and strained to identify every sound:

The death cry of a small animal as a predator caught it.

The scuttling of a lizard across the floor.

The rustling of foliage in the wind.

Except that there was no foliage outside that she could remember. She sat up, drawing her pistol to her side. Come to think of it, there was no wind either. And the crickets had stopped chirring.

Footfalls, soft and stealthy, sounded outside the shrine. A native come to sacrifice at the altar? She got to her knees and then straightened to her full height.

The pistol in her hand, the blood pounding in her temples, she stepped outside. No one there. She shook her head to clear it of fear and exhaustion. Her imagination was becoming as—

She saw it then, far below her lofty vantage point on the mountainside, the procession of masked villagers carrying burning banana stems up to Mount Belakan. They were chanting as they marched—a death knell that made Lorna's skin crawl even though she understood few of the words. And they carried long bamboo poles adorned with tatters of white cloth.

A young girl was sobbing, wearing a white silk sarong and headdress of jasmine and acacia blossoms.

A human sacrifice was about to take place.

Lorna hurried back into the shrine, trying to escape the funereal chanting and the young girl's weeping. Pacing before the altar, horrified and helpless, she trod on the tail of a moonrat and heard it squeal as it fled to an unseen burrow.

The girl intended as a sacrifice had begun to scream, pleading to the goddess Penala for divine intervention. Lorna listened until she could not stand it, then she ran out of the shrine, back through the maze, and down, down, down the steep plunge of stairs. Three-quarters of the way to the bottom, she stopped so that she still had a clear vantage point and yet there was a fair distance between her and the gathering if she had to run. No wonder Ross was obsessed with crushing the power of the cult.

Praying she could not be seen behind the foliage of trailing jungle willows, she fired her pistol into the circle of village elders who were struggling to subdue the young girl. One of the men clutched his shoulder, falling to his knees, and every one of the remaining masked faces lifted to the temple steps where Lorna stood.

She lowered her arm, her mouth dry, her body shaking in horror at what she had done. Never when she'd first learned to handle a gun had she dreamt she would use it for anything other than sport.

Shouting praises to Penala for her protection, the girl in white broke free of her captors and ran toward the stairs. The villagers surged after her in an angry crowd.

Lorna had just enough time to reload and fire again, this time aiming high into the air. Her shot cracked into the branches of a mangosteen tree, showering those below with fruit. Then suddenly, with a rumble of thunder, it began to rain. Their torches sputtering to smoke in the downpour, the villagers scattered down the mountain path.

Lorna started farther down the steps to help the girl, moving clumsily in her skirts. She thought she glimpsed Kurt at the edge of the forest, and the unwelcome thought crossed her mind that he would be furious at her for leaving the shrine.

The girl clung to Lorna, kissing her hands, weeping over and over, "Trima kasih, Penala."

"Please," Lorna said, dragging the girl up over the rough wet stairs. "If we don't hurry, the priest might lock the gate."

They made it back inside the shrine without incident, although Lorna could not relax for a single moment afterward. She disengaged herself from the girl, who looked as if she was only twelve years old, and motioned her to the mat. "It's all right now," she said soothingly, aware that the girl could understand her tone if not her words. "Sit quietly and I'll light another candle. I need to hear if anyone comes."

Lorna could not sleep that night. Nor did the young girl, who crawled across the mat to sit closer to her.

At dawn Lorna heard a rustling on the temple roof. Stretching her stiff limbs, relieved that the long ordeal was almost over, she stepped over the girl, who called herself Sri, and walked cautiously out into the center courtyard.

A white eagle had descended onto the summit of the shrine, its wings flashing in the rising sun, casting vibrating shadows on Lorna's upturned face. As the temple priest came running from his hidden chambers to witness the spectacle, Lorna realized that this was not a common occurrence.

She glanced up at the sculpted sandstone likeness of the eagle diety just as a shaft of white sunlight struck the regal face. For an instant she could have sworn that the cruel mouth curved into a smile of approval. But surely it was only a shadow, a trick of her fatigued mind.

"Penala," Sri whispered in awe from behind Lorna.

Lorna did not speak. Although she knew Kurt had planted special bait to attract the bird, there was something inexplicably mystical about the experience that brought gooseflesh to her arms. And despite the fact that the logical side of her nature could discount what had happened, a deeper, more intuitive voice whispered that she could never find a rational explanation for it.

Ross emptied the contents of his flask over his face and rubbed his burning eyes, waiting for Kana to return from his foray into the jungle and report what he'd seen. It was just past dawn. At the perimeters of the forest foothills, the usual cacophony of awakening animal sounds served to heighten his headache.

They had been to the crater village on Mount Belakan and back in search of Lorna and Kurt, only to learn that the Agung-Mani had not met that night. The Ranjan villagers, normally reticent about their practices, could not stop themselves from telling him how the goddess Penala had rescued the sacrificial victim to serve as her personal handmaiden.

Penala's spirit had possessed the white woman at her shrine, they whispered excitedly.

"What white woman?" Ross had demanded.

But he knew.

He was going to kill her.

He wanted to kill her as much as he wanted to make love to her, and the degree of passion that motivated the disparate desires was frightening.

"Did you see anything, Kana?"

The young Malay nodded, pulling off his spectacles to rub his eyes with his fists. "They on the rhino path, Tuan, moving down the hillside."

"They?"

"Shikari and *cik,*" he replied, using the Malay form of address for an unmarried woman. "Someone else with them."

Ross scrambled to his feet, his face dark. "Another man—her uncle, perhaps?"

"Looked like child, Tuan."

Without another word, Ross started toward the foot-wide path that connected with the hillside. Not the least of his worries was that Lorna had spent an entire night in Kurt van Poole's company . . . and that the realization made him livid.

"You might have told me it was a rhinoceros salt bath," Lorna said to Kurt's back as he preceded her to clear a passageway through the royal ferns. "How would we have outrun her if she'd decided to chase us instead of the leopard?''

He veered off to the right and vanished into the underbrush, returning a few moments later with a preoccupied frown on his face. "You can't outrun a rhino. You have to take refuge in a tree."

Lorna glanced around, unnerved by the look on his face. "What's the matter?"

"There's someone on our trail. Do you notice how quiet it is all of a sudden?"

"What are we going to do?"

"Not panic. Whoever it is isn't being particularly furtive about his approach. But there's no point in taking a chance." He hefted his rifle onto his shoulder. "Take that girl and hide behind the trees over there."

Sri was still clinging to Lorna, glancing back every so often as the crackling of vegetation sounded nearer. There was a casarina oak nearby whose twisted aerial roots and trellis of orchids provided cover. Taking Sri's hand, Lorna guided her off the sloping footpath toward the stalwart tree.

"Bengas," Sri cried, shaking her head in warning, trying to tug Lorna in the opposite direction.

Bengas. The word struck an alarm somewhere in Lorna's memory, but she had no time to analyze why. Plunging through a bush of sticky-leaved branches, she managed to hide herself among the oak's lower limbs while Sri took refuge in a sturdy tree a few yards behind her.

The footsteps grew nearer. The low murmuring voices became distinguishable in the unnatural quiet.

"Where the hell have you got to, Lorna?" Ross shouted into the trees.

She pushed back a heavy vine and clambered over a bridge of roots, so relieved to see him that she almost laughed.

"Thank heavens it's only you," she said with an embarrassed smile that faded as soon as she reached him.

His face looked as if it had been carved from stone. His

eyes blazed at her with unyielding fury. Suddenly Lorna felt too tired and sick to stand up to him again. She was ashamed to admit to herself she probably deserved what she had coming.

"Go on," she said, her voice sounding distant to her own ears. "Lecture me." She moistened her lips and tried to lift her head to look up at him, but her muscles refused to cooperate. A trembling weakness seized her from head to toe.

"I thought, after yesterday, that you trusted me," he said in a tight voice.

She wanted to say that she did, but the words would not form on her tongue.

He gripped her forearms. It was a rough gesture, but she was actually grateful for it because she feared otherwise she might collapse at his feet.

"I feel . . . peculiar." She twisted her head, focusing on the fuzzy image of Kana helping Sri to the ground.

"Bengas," she heard Sri tell Kana, pointing to the glossy plant below the casarina oak.

"Ross," she said, her knees buckling, "I think I'm going to faint."

He shook her until her head snapped back. "Oh, no, Miss Fairfield. Don't you dare start playacting on me now. Considering the audacity you have shown, such signs of feminine weakness are not only unbelievable but very unbecoming."

She gazed up at his face, and for a moment forgot where she was and why he was holding her. She wanted only to burrow against his chest and sleep, to shake off the lassitude stealing over her. "Are you going to strangle me, Mr. St. James? I think you'd like to."

"No, Miss Fairfield. I am placing you under arrest."

"Arrest? Can you actually do that?" She started to giggle, but it required more strength than she could manage. "Tuan."

Ross released Lorna and turned to watch Kana and the young native girl approach. "What is it?"

"Ranjan girl say your lady friends walk in Bengas bush. Poison very bad, Tuan. Work fast."

Ross spun around, dropping to his knees with a shout of alarm. Lorna had collapsed like a broken doll, her red-gold hair spread in soaking strands across her colorless face. When he lifted her into his arms, he saw the beginnings of the dull purple Bengas rash breaking out on her throat and arms.

"Kana, get back to the fort and tell Dr. Parker to meet me at the bungalow. Make him hurry."

He hoisted Lorna into his arms and started down the path, Sri hurrying behind him. Every so often he would have to put Lorna down, with the native girl hovering over her, while he slashed a path through the foliage that had grown up overnight.

Then he would resume walking, staring straight ahead, fighting the dark feelings inside him. She felt so warm and vital in his arms, he couldn't believe she might die. Or, equally frightening, suffer brain damage or permanent paralysis, depending on her body's reaction to the toxins.

He felt angry, frustrated, helpless. And deep inside, he felt he was responsible, that if he had taken her determination to find her father more seriously, that if he had simply obeyed the Rajah's orders to protect her, if he hadn't been so bloody afraid of the feelings she aroused in him that he stopped resisting them, this wouldn't have happened.

He slipped in a puddle of mud and rocked forward, swearing as he clutched her in his arms. She groaned and raised a hand to her throat, then let it drop.

"I'll help you, St. James. She'll be easier to carry on a bamboo stretcher. I've already got one made."

Ross straightened, his face stiff with fury. "You vainglorious son of a bitch," he said to van Poole, who stood half hidden in the ferns. "If anything happens to her, I'll make sure you answer for it."

Chapter 12

───◯◯◯───

"I *did what you wanted, Papa. I got rid of Spencer. Now will you tell me where you are?"*

"You're a clever girl, Lorna. You'll have to find me. Resident St. James will help you. He's far too honorable to fall from grace as I have. He would never have picked the Eden Flower."

"There's no such thing! Why do you have to confuse me with your twisted riddles? And I'm not clever at all! I only pretend to be to please you."

She quieted, then began to struggle as gentle but firm hands pressed something scalding hot and moist to her skin.

"Be brave, my dear. This must be borne. It's only an herbal plaster to draw out the poison."

She opened her eyes and gasped, shrinking back against the pillows, shaking her head in silent horror.

"You're hurting her," Ross said, his hands gripping the bedpost. "Do you have to do that now?"

"Not unless you'd prefer she died."

"Agung-Mani," she whispered, clawing at the plaster. "I'm on fire—"

Ross came to her side, grasping her hand. "It's only Dr. Parker, Lorna. He's trying to help you."

"I'm going to need help holding her down," the doctor said impatiently. "If you haven't the guts for it, fetch your housekeeper, Ross."

147

Lorna started to tremble. *"Agung-Mani, pati bulan,"* she whimpered. *"Api pati. Matjan Besar. Matjan Putih."*

"Ross?" the doctor said, glancing up with a startled frown. "In the name of God, did she say what I thought she did?"

Ross stared down at Lorna, lying suddenly silent and serene beneath the mosquito netting.

"Agung-Mani, Moon of Death," he quoted, his voice deep with disbelief. "Fire of Death. Great Tiger—White Tiger."

It was early morning when Lorna began to regain consciousness. She kicked away the tangle of bedclothes around her legs and attempted to sit up. The madras shirt she wore—Ross's shirt—gaped open to her thighs. With a horrified frown she stared down at the subsiding blotches on her chest and arms, and gasped.

The three people in the room jumped at her movements. Ross, from the corner secretary where he worked, Sri from the floor mat, and Mrs. Hofner from the rocker Ross had brought in from the parlor.

"What have you done to me?" Lorna demanded. "What is this wretched stuff on my skin?"

Ross touched her forehead. "Sit back. You're delirious."

"I am not bloody delirious." She looked at the housekeeper. "What has he done to me?"

"Nothing untoward while I've been in the room, miss. Doctor's put some medicine on you is all."

Lorna rose to her knees. The room spun around before her like a wagon wheel. "I want my own clothes back, Mr. St. James," she said. "And I want you to stop shaking the bed."

"Hold her by the shoulders," Ross instructed Mrs. Hofner, raising a cup of a murky beverage to Lorna's parched lips. "Dr. Parker said we should expect such outbursts just before the crisis passes."

"Resident St. James," Lorna said solemnly as she sank back down upon the bed, "I'd wager my best pair of drawers that you make your housekeeper put starch in your socks.''

"An invalid wager," he murmured as he drew back from the bed. "I am already in possession of your drawers, Miss Fairfield."

"Mr. St. James," the housekeeper said in a shocked whisper. "A gentleman does not mention such articles."

"She mentioned them first, Mrs. Hofner."

"And she is delirious, sir. You are not."

It was the flute that awoke her. The golden notes penetrated the vivid images tumbling through her mind and brought a welcome peace.

She opened her eyes and saw it was evening, guessed that she was in Ross's own room. Ross himself sat at the window seat, playing softly in rhythm with the pattering of rain outside. He was barefoot, dressed in an unbuttoned white linen shirt and tan stout twilled cotton trousers.

The lamplight caught the silver-blue glints in his hair. It highlighted the sternness of his face, and the concern she had not noticed there before.

He turned his head toward her, setting down the bamboo instrument.

She closed her eyes, curious to see what he would do.

He walked to the foot of the bed where she lay, pushed aside the netting, and stared down at her. Her heart began to pound as he leaned over to feel her forehead. He smelled of sandalwood soap and rain.

"Lorna?"

She pretended to stir, her heart tripping over itself as he sat at the edge of the bed to feel her pulse and rearrange the bedclothes.

She opened her eyes, unable to stand the suspense of waiting for him to make a move. In her weakened condition, she wasn't sure she could summon the strength to manage to defend herself if she needed to.

His mouth twisted into a sardonic smile. "I wondered how long you would continue feigning sleep."

She sat up against the pillows, avoiding his eyes. Someone had slipped one of her own nightdresses on her. The drawstring at the collar had been loosened. She was lying in an immense four-poster bed so high off the floor it required a stepladder to reach it.

"What a charming bed," she said, her voice unusually deep. "It reminds me of something from a fairy tale."

"How gratifying that it pleases you." He reached for the glass of water on the nightstand. "I got it from a Dutch brothel in Java."

She flushed and avidly drank the water he gave her until he put his hand to the glass. "That's enough for now."

She eased back against the pillows, glancing around the room to note they were alone. He was leaning against her on his elbow. Lorna had to clasp her hands around her knees to keep from touching his face.

"Shouldn't you be at the cove acting as lookout for pirates?" she asked.

"I should." He drew himself farther onto the bed. "But Assistant Resident Tunridge is taking my place, and I didn't think I ought to leave you."

She clutched the coverlet between her fingers, thinking it a flimsy barrier to the dangerous heat of his presence. She wanted to believe that the sudden spell of lightheadedness, the fluttering anticipation in her stomach, were residual weaknesses from the fever and not from the effect Ross had upon her. She had never been alone with a man in his bedchamber before.

"Have—have I been a great deal of trouble?"

He pursed his lips and nodded.

She met his gaze and became aware of a pleasant ache awakening inside her. "I should thank you for your care."

"You should thank your lucky stars," he said. "You're fortunate indeed to have emerged from a bout of Bengas poisoning unscathed."

"Bengas. My guidebook says it doesn't grow below an altitude of five thousand feet."

"Your guidebook is tripe." He sat up and laid a hand

on her shoulder, rubbing his thumb across a vanishing splotch of red. "I should have hated to see your skin marred, Miss Fairfield. It is so perfect . . . so very soft and pale."

She could not move, feeling a shock of anticipation shoot down her shoulder into the pit of her stomach as his gaze fell to the outline of her breasts and then returned to her face. "You see, I had several opportunities to examine that flawless skin, inch by inch, Miss Fairfield, while you lay helpless in my bed."

"I don't believe you," she said, putting a pale hand to her throat in an unconsciously self-protective gesture. "You're too honorable for that sort of thing."

"Even my honor has its limits." He leaned closer, his gray eyes glittering. "You have a mole on your left hip."

She colored and laughed unwillingly at his audacity, then tried to slide across the bed to the small ladder that leaned against it. With easy agility Ross sprang forward and rose to his feet to prevent her descent.

Lorna stared up at him, her head spinning, her heart jumping. "Where is my uncle? I want to go back to the plantation house."

"Can't. You're under arrest and have been entrusted to my custody."

"By whom?"

"By me," he said with a grin. "It's one of the privileges of power."

"Really, Ross. How ridiculous. How—"

She made a furtive attempt to slide her feet onto the ladder so that she could rise, only to feel his hands enclose her waist as she straightened. For a perilous moment every drop of blood in her body seemed to rush to her head, and the world tilted. As if aware of her distress, Ross tightened his hold, pulling her against his chest. She placed one hand against his shoulder to steady herself and tipped her head back to look at him.

"You—you need a haircut," she said irrelevantly.

He helped her down the ladder, allowing her to lean

against his forearm. "And you need to do as you're told. The doctor ordered another two days' bedrest."

"Surely he did not specify it was to be here?" She gestured to the bed, drawing away from him to lean against the ladder.

"The doctor's orders were that you were not to be moved."

"And does the Resident enjoy incarcerating helpless women?"

"If it is in their best interest and"—his insolent gaze swept her flushed face—"and if they are as beautiful as you are."

She started to smile in acknowledgment of the compliment, but an unexpected fit of shivering overcame her.

"What is it?" Ross said in alarm.

"C-cold."

"Dr. Parker said that part should be over." He pulled off his shirt and draped it over her shoulders. "For God's sake, get back into bed."

"Oh, no, please, Ross. At least let me get a breath of fresh air at the window."

"Only for a moment then. Let me make sure the floor is not too damp for you to walk on first."

Clutching the edges of his shirt together at her chest, she watched him walk to the window. The sheer male beauty of his body stole her breath and filled her mind with images she could never confess aloud. His frame was powerful and lanky, his buttocks taut in the softly woven trousers. He turned back toward her and she glanced away, warmth suffusing her face.

"Are you all right, Miss Fairfield?" he asked as he came before her. "You've gone rather pink of a sudden."

"That scar on your back—"

"A bullet in Canton."

"But you might have died, sustaining an injury so close to the spine."

"Yes." The ghost of a smile touched his lips. "I often wonder why I did not." He held out his hand to her.

"Come then. I'll only allow you another minute of freedom."

"Have you arrested many other young women this way? I mean, virtually imprisoned them in your bedchamber?"

"It wouldn't be gentlemanly of me to say."

Suddenly afraid, feeling both shy and shameless, she gave him her hand and trembled as his fingers tightened around hers, filling her with a surge of strength and bewildering delight. The moonlight swathed them in cool shadows, contrasting with the bright heat their physical contact generated, invisible flames of a growing attraction between them and a more endurable foundation of trust.

She was not surprised when he drew her gently into his arms. She did not resist when his arms slid up her back and he lowered his head to kiss her with slow deliberation, his tongue just touching hers, teasing her lips until she was whimpering, unaware of everything except the aching sweetness of being held in his arms.

He drew away reluctantly, his eyes burning into hers, his hands dropping to his sides. "I apologize," he said in strained tones. "For a moment I forgot how unwell you are."

"Ross," she whispered, watching him anxiously as he went very still. "I want you to know—I need to tell you that I've never—"

"Yes," he said with a rueful laugh. "I know."

"Is it *that* obvious?"

"Oh, yes, my worldly innocent. The first time I kissed you. Your London lord must be the biggest fool on earth to have let you go."

"You—"

"Hush. The more you discuss such matters with a man, the more . . . aroused he becomes."

"I am not entirely ignorant, Ross. My father had libertines among his friends. They led lives that were not at all conventional."

"Yes, but intellectual knowledge is not the same as experience, is it?"

She did not answer. Suddenly, instead of the chills that

had assailed her, she felt faint and unbearably warm. "I really do need some fresh air, Ross."

He walked her to the window, resting a hand on her shoulder in case she should falter. "Don't go any closer. The rain soaked the floor. Thank God it seems to be tapering off. There are times when I feel that every aspect of my life is dictated by the weather."

He stepped closer to her. Through the thin barrier of her nightdress, Lorna could feel the well-muscled contours of his chest and limbs. He held her as if he would never let her go. She wished it could be so.

"Do you feel better now?"

"Yes."

She closed her eyes and laid her head back on his shoulder. His warm brown skin gave off his virile scent. If she were in a London drawing room, she would never allow herself such an intimate gesture. But the repressive conventions of that life were not suited to this island. A man's lineage here did not seem to matter nearly as much as what he made of himself. The social graces that Lorna had never quite mastered anyway would have seemed contrived in such a culture.

"When you kissed me earlier, Ross—what did it mean to you?"

He was silent for endless seconds. "I don't know. It was something I don't fully understand myself."

Her heart sank at the evasive answer. She had not expected an ardent declaration of affection, but just the same, she had hoped for something more substantial to justify her own increasing attraction to him. It reminded her how foolish it would be to plunge from one disastrous relationship into another, especially with a man like Ross St. James, who did not seem the least inclined to change his solitary life-style.

"Look outside, Lorna."

She opened her eyes with a sigh. She thought that he was trying to divert her from discussing the uncomfortable subject of their relationship. But as she stared out into the dripping mists of the garden, she was so astonished at what she saw that every other thought receded.

Scores of orchids. Night-blooming orchids that had opened while they were talking. All along the garden walls, entwined around the thick-trunked palms, smothering the railing of the veranda.

But the breathtaking phenomenon did not stop there. For miles around the orchids had opened, embroidering the darkly clad mountain slopes like ribbons of lace, outlining the black silhouette of the jungle.

The scent they exuded was subtle and exotic. Their petals were the hue of clotted cream, striated with deep violet.

"It happens only once a year," Ross said. "The entire island explodes with them. It's supposed to have something to do with the atmosphere after a rain. The natives believe it is a sign of favor from the gods."

"It looks like paradise," she said softly.

"It will not last." He kissed the top of her head. "Paradise tonight, but by morning they will have withered on the vine and you will wonder if you imagined it."

"How sad," she murmured.

"No." He turned her around into his arms, his eyes like silver in the moonlight. "It is not sad. It sustains us for another year and reminds us that beauty cannot be taken for granted. It inspires us."

She felt her skin tingle where his thumbs began to caress her shoulders. "You inspire me, Lorna. But now I fear it's time I return you to the bed."

She did not argue, weakened from the violent illness that had attacked her, her thoughts confused and tired as Ross took his leave to allow her rest.

It will not last.

It will not last.

But Lorna had never been one to accept what the vagaries of fate would deal her.

Chapter 13

Dear Aunt Julia,

I am writing this letter to inform you that Uncle Richard and I arrived safely on Kali Simpang just under a fortnight ago. I trust you are feeling better than when I left. Do keep your joints warm and take the nasty rheumatism medicine the doctor prescribed.

Mine has been an eventful week. So far I have acquired an ape, a eunuch, a headhunter and a sacrificial virgin named Sri. My eunuch is a lovely man, well versed in astrology so that I believe you and he could have fascinating chats about the alignment of your planets. Alas, I am giving him back to his former master today. I shall miss his oil massages greatly.

"Oh, dear." Lorna glanced up from the desk and frowned, crossing out "oil massages" and replacing it with "daily horoscopes."
She put her pen back to the paper.

We were scheduled to begin the search for Papa in another week but had to postpone it due to the unpredictability of the weather. Mr. van Poole seems not to mind the delay as he's run into a little trouble hiring an experienced sea captain for our voyage.

Should Spencer inquire as to my whereabouts, kindly

inform him I have entered an Italian convent. Or tell him to go to the blazes.

By the way, I was wondering whether you ever found my father's last letters to me—you remember, the two the postman swears he delivered but which never reached me. I fear there may be information in them crucial to locating Papa.

She put aside her pen and walked to the bed, upon which lay the exquisite white cashmere shawl Ross had sent her for her birthday that same morning. No one else had remembered it was her birthday, not even Uncle Richard, but her father had never remembered either, so it wasn't as if she felt slighted.

She lifted the shawl to her face. It *was* nice that Ross had thought of her, even though he'd probably learned her birth date from his horrid confidential reports from the Foreign Office.

She couldn't share her delight with Aunt Julia, though, just as she had been careful to avoid mentioning the fever in the letter. Aunt Julia would die of mortification if she knew that two days ago Lorna had been staying in Ross's bungalow. She would call him a womanizing heathen who was no better than the natives he governed. Then she would demand to know his intentions toward her niece.

And so would I, Lorna thought, as she carefully redraped the shawl over the back of a chair. So would I.

The Ranee had waited until Lorna recovered fully from her fever before inviting her to the istana. They sipped fine Ceylon tea from delicate porcelain cups and played tennis on the lawn with the Orang Tua, a headhunter chief who lived on the other side of the island. None of them observed the rules of the game.

After tea, the Rajah ventured out from his chambers and invited her to walk with him in the arcaded corridors where the Agung-Mani had attacked her.

''I understand your uncle has started making the arrangements for your expedition, Lorna. You must be excited now that you are so close to beginning the search."

They stopped at a stone bench and sat to rest. Lorna noted with concern that he had lost his breath.

"Excited, yes. And more than a little afraid."

He took her hand, his thin chest rising and dropping rapidly under his white muslin jacket. "To be afraid under the circumstances is understandable. From what Ross tells me, the Agung-Mani might cause trouble for a while, despite the fact he has arrested their high priest and temple attendants."

"It is not the Agung-Mani I most fear," she admitted, toying with the lacy fan in her lap. "It's that I might not find my father at all, or that something unspeakable has happened to him. . . ."

Her voice trailed off. The Rajah did not speak. From the far corners of the garden came the screeching of his pet parakeets and monkeys. Lorna fanned the hot air languidly around her face.

"You will find him," the Rajah assured her. "I feel it inside me."

"Ali Aziz predicted the same thing the morning I sent him back to the Sultan. He also warned me that the search would be fraught with danger and betrayals. Not that I put much stock in astrology."

The Rajah did not comment, and she laid aside her fan, remembering the African's last disturbing words to her:

"Gracious lady whose hair and temperament match the spirits of fire, you will achieve that which you seek. The stars have ordained it. But it will not come until the end of a long and perilous journey during which you will do well to remember that those we can trust are few in this world.

"Prepare for betrayal all around you, Lorna. But do not allow it to destroy your faith in love. . . ."

"I could order Resident St. James to accompany you," the Rajah said, interrupting her musings. "He would balk and fuss at having to leave his outpost, but I wield enough power to persuade him—if you would like his company, that is."

She suppressed a smile. "It would not please *him*, to know we were scheming like this. I fear our plan might fail."

The Rajah stared off into the garden, his blue eyes warm with affection. "I have seen my nephew in every mood imaginable, Lorna, from speechless grief to violent rage. But it is not until recently that I've seen him smile so often. Not since his wife was expecting their child, and Ross was filled with pride. My brother-in-law—Ross's father—was the strictest man I have ever known, passionately dedicated to the Church and the Royal Navy. He raised Ross in what I shall politely say was an overly restrictive atmosphere. Even when Ross married Vanessa, he did not easily show his emotions. When she died, he held all his pain inside. It nearly broke my heart that I couldn't help him."

Lorna swallowed, trying to reconcile her impression of Ross as supremely self-controlled with the man the Rajah had portrayed. "He must have loved her very much."

"I don't know. They married young, after a whirlwind courtship. Amayli foresaw problems between them, but we shall never be able to say now, shall we?"

"It really isn't any of my affair."

The Rajah stood up. "Don't play coy with me, Lorna. Do you want Ross to go with you to Jalaka or not?"

"Yes. But he mustn't know I—"

She fell silent, warned by the look in the Rajah's eye that someone was approaching behind her.

"Speak of the devil," he said. "We missed you at tea, Ross."

"I had to see the Sultan off on his yacht." Ross removed his helmet and turned to Lorna, unable to disguise his pleasure at seeing her. "Good afternoon, Miss Fairfield. I trust you suffer no continuing ill effects from your fever."

"No, Mr. St. James, I am feeling quite well now."

"It's fortunate you have such a strong constitution. I've seen hardy men laid up for weeks with Bengas."

"Have you?" Confronted with his implacable calm, she

was tempted to believe the two days she had spent in his home had been part of a feverish dream.

The Rajah had wandered to the opposite side of the arcade, leaving them to their private conversation.

"You liked the shawl I sent?" Ross asked her, the sudden intimacy in his voice sending a shiver down her spine.

"Oh, yes. It was quite the most beautiful birthday present I've ever received." She brought her folded fan to her lips. "Am I still under arrest?" she asked teasingly.

"Unfortunately, no." He stepped close to her, his voice low. "I have thought of you," he said, "every moment, every bloody waking moment of every day since that night four days ago."

She lowered the fan, struck again by the stark masculinity of his face and form. The white muslin shirt he wore enhanced the golden tan of his skin. His hair, still in need of a trim, had been recently washed and lay flat against his scalp with the ends waving at his neck.

His gray eyes regarded her with an ironic desire, but it was impossible to tell what was in his heart.

"I understand van Poole intends to leave for Jalaka as soon as he finds a ship and captain," he said. "He was stockpiling provisions at the wharves this morning."

She nodded, glancing into the bright glare of the garden to hide her disappointment that he had veered the conversation away from their relationship. "We're also waiting for better weather."

"I need to discuss his plans with you," he continued.

"As you wish."

"I need to discuss those plans with you—tomorrow night."

She looked up, unable to misinterpret the personal emphasis he'd put upon his words. The unwelcome weight around her heart lifted.

"Whatever happened to the discipline of the watch?" she asked.

"You happened."

The Rajah coughed discreetly from the marble fountain.

Ross stirred, leaning closer to Lorna, his voice rich with promise.

"Tomorrow night, Lorna. After supper at the plantation house."

It was an effort for Ross to keep his mind on his conversation with the Rajah several minutes later. He kept looking for Lorna in the garden, dressed in a ruffled lemon silk frock that enhanced her striking coloring. He kept remembering her in his bed, her lustrous hair spread out on the sheets like glints of fire, her body so very soft and pliant as he had lifted her for Mrs. Hofner to change her clothing.

"Are you unwell today, Ross?" his uncle inquired dryly, pausing to stare at him as they walked down the arcade to his chambers. "I realize that the subject of sharks'-fin exportation is no competition for Miss Fairfield's charms, but our economy does depend heavily upon it."

"Sorry." Ross grinned as he caught sight of Lorna wielding a tennis racquet like a weapon on the lawn. "What were you saying?"

The Rajah sighed and paused to pluck a peach-colored hibiscus blossom from a column. "Simple pleasures such as looking at my tropical garden are those I will miss most about this earthly life. The complicated coil of human relationships I will find a blessed relief to leave behind."

Ross did not respond. He hated it when his uncle talked about dying.

"Lorna and her party are scheduled to leave for Jalaka soon, weather permitting. Do you approve, Ross?"

"No. But I have recently quit trying to influence Miss Fairfield's actions in the matter. I could not change her mind anyway."

"This is an enormous relief. I assume you'll have no objection in my assigning Assistant Resident Tunridge to accompany her on the search."

"The hell." Ross stopped dead in his tracks, his eyes narrowing. "You're going to send that bumbling ox, that blustering clod, that drunken wrestler with Lorna to Jalaka?''

"As the island's representative, Ross. Who else could I choose? You mustn't abandon your watch for the Illanuans. And Sir Arthur's disappearance has generated great concern at the Foreign Office. The prime minister himself has sent me a personal letter of inquiry. It seems he is one of Sir Arthur's most devoted readers. My hand was forced.''

"The latest reports from Djuil indicate the Illanuans have changed course. They couldn't possibly make it here in under two months.''

"Really? How reassuring.''

Ross shoved his hands into his pockets and stared hard into the Rajah's eyes. "I had thought to accompany her myself.''

"You, Ross? Why, I'd never have suggested such a thing, knowing how immersed you are in your plans to protect the island. Perhaps it isn't such a good idea, though. Tunridge is an adequate protector for the young woman, even if he is a bit of a moron and does love the drink. I do not think we can afford to lose you, Ross, even for the month or less it will take to find Sir Arthur and bring him back.''

"You old fox,'' Ross said. "You conniving—''

The Rajah held up his hand. "If my decision has reduced you to name-calling, then perhaps I should reconsider. I suppose we can struggle without your leadership if we must. Tunridge will be most disappointed, though. I believe he has heard gossip of how lovely Miss Fairfield is and half imagines he will court her. Of course, with her fiancé no longer an obstacle, I suppose it is a remote possibility. . . .''

Ross did not reply. He had stalked off in utter disgust, leaving the Rajah laughing to himself as he entered his judicial chambers and called for the next case to be presented.

* * *

Lorna came across the Rajah's private chapel by accident the following morning, after she had spent a few hours watching him conduct a case in his chambers. She'd walked through the well-tended formal grounds, a guard following discreetly, until she reached the tropical gardens that had been allowed to grow like a jungle so that there were no proper paths, just dim green shadows and leafy archways that trembled with the acrobatics of chattering monkeys.

It surprised and delighted her, the tiny gray stone chapel in the pagan setting with a red jungle cock strutting across the vegetation-fronted porch.

It was a touch of rural England, and she decided it wouldn't hurt to spend a few minutes inside its cool stuccoed walls to pray for her father.

Ross emerged onto the porch before she'd taken another step. "Lorna." He sounded astonished to see her here, and she couldn't help wondering whether he was embarrassed that she'd caught him at worship.

"I didn't mean to disturb you." She pulled off her sun hat and shook her hair free, wishing she had a brush to untangle it.

He frowned, watching her. "You're liable to get lost wandering about here alone. And there are snakes, you know."

"There's a guard behind me."

"That's not much help if a dharmin strikes. Its bite is deadly. And then there's falling fruit."

"Falling . . . fruit?"

"The durian is encased in a spiked shell like a medieval morningstar. If it falls upon your head, it could kill you, or at the least give you a nasty headache."

"You must think I'm very gullible, Ross."

He grinned. "It's the truth. Ask the Rajah."

"I will." She fidgeted with her hat as he continued to stare at her. He looked incredibly handsome this morning in a dark blue shirt and white cotton trousers. His hair was brushed back off his face, showing his sculptured bone structure and strong jawline.

She glanced past him, flustered by the glint of humor in his eyes. "What a charming little chapel this is."

"Yes. Ironically it was the Rajah's Moslem mentri beshar who supervised its construction. There's an underground tunnel leading from the vaults of the istana into the chapel altar. The river isn't far away. At the time my uncle assumed control of the island, it was feared the rebel forces he'd subdued might stage another revolt."

"It's an escape route, then?"

"Yes. I inspect it at least twice a month to make sure no roots or vines have choked off the tunnel."

"Oh. I thought you might have come to worship."

He smiled—with a trace of sadness, she fancied. "No. I haven't felt much religious sentiment for years now. I suppose I did once—" He looked into her eyes. "I lost my faith a long time ago," he finished quietly. "I find it hard these days to reconcile religion with reality as I know it."

There was something wistful in his voice that hinted of old wounds, but Lorna could not bring herself to pry into his private sorrows. She could only hope he would eventually reveal his deepest thoughts to her.

"Are *you* a religious person?" he asked suddenly, and the gentle cynicism returned to his voice.

"I've never been much for church," she answered, leaning against one of the vine-clad trees that surrounded the chapel. "Papa always used to earn us stern looks by scribbling notes for his books during the sermon. But I believe I do have faith. In fact, I don't think I could live without it."

She thought perhaps he would criticize her for the admission or think her naive, but surprisingly he lowered his voice and glanced away.

"I envy you then," he said. "For I have faith in nothing but what I behold from one moment to the next."

His confession made her ache for that part of him he had closed off to feeling and trusting. "The islanders have faith in you," she said.

"Yes, I know."

Suddenly from within the chapel there came a burst of muffled cries, then silence.

"What was that?" Lorna said, distressed.

He glanced around disinterestedly. "A pair of young monkeys most likely."

"No, Ross, it had a human sound."

"Well, it's stopped now."

"We must investigate."

He looked reluctant. "I suppose we must."

He froze as he entered the chapel, sweat dampening his skin as he remembered exactly when he had last come here to pray. When he'd learned Vanessa was pregnant and the Rajah's old priest had married them. Ross had been too busy afterward to bother with God.

Perhaps if he'd had more faith, things would have turned out differently.

"Oh, Ross, come quickly. *Please*."

The quiet urgency in her voice shook him. He hurried down the nave to the altar he had detachedly inspected only a few minutes before.

"What is it?" He knelt at the sight of her startled white face, then froze as she peeled back a large palm frond from a carrying basket on the floor. Inside lay two naked, nearly identical Malay babies squirming in a bed of straw.

"Babies," she said in disbelief. "Two beautiful babies . . . a boy and a girl. How could anyone be so cruel as to simply leave them here?"

He leaned over her, his face unreadable. "They're twins. The natives believe that fraternal twins are evil—that they've committed incest in the womb. It's called the curse of manak salah."

"What idiocy," she said angrily. "And so they're abandoned to die?"

"Sometimes. The only remedy left to the shamed parents is to sell every possession they own to raise enough money to pay a pedanda to lift the curse. Most families have other children to keep and simply can't afford such a price, especially since the village elders force them to burn down their unholy house and build a new one.''

Lorna lifted the female infant into her arms, holding her awkwardly against her shoulder to stop the convulsive sobbing. "It's breaking my heart, Ross," she said. "What will be done with them?''

"The Rajah will find them a good home among the European residents on the island.'' He shifted forward on one knee, his arms outstretched. "You're holding her the wrong way. I had to take care of a pair of these blighters for an entire fortnight once myself. You have to support the head. Like this—''

He eased the baby into the crook of his arms, his face grave, and expertly brought her to rest against his shoulder. The sobbing stopped as if by magic.

"I'd forgotten you once had a child of your own," Lorna said, and the moment she saw Ross's shoulders stiffen she realized that she should not have mentioned the subject. "I'm so terribly sorry," she whispered. Of course his child had not lived long enough for Ross to have held him. Oh, God, how could she have been so thoughtless?

"It's all right.'' He was surprised that she was sensitive enough to let the subject drop. She must have learned about his wife and child from Ilse. That displeased him. He'd much rather Lorna form her own impressions of him without the jaded Mrs. Klemp's influence.

"Here," he said, his voice suddenly strained, as he handed the child back to her. "I'll carry the other one in the basket.''

They made a strange procession, Ross thought, as they passed over the porch and returned to the istana, he with the gurgling baby in a basket, Lorna with the sleeping child against her shoulder, and the turbaned Hindu-Malay guard who followed behind them with an amused expression on his face.

A strange procession, indeed. And yet—

Yet there was something disturbingly satisfying about watching Lorna with a child in her arms, something that penetrated to the depths of his being and whispered, *Yes, this is a glimpse of what could be. . . .*

"I look for you everywheres, Tuan."

Ross stepped from the bathing compartment in his bungalow, a towel hooked around his waist. He calculated he had enough time to dress and make a quick survey of the cove before he visited Lorna at the plantation house.

He glanced again out the window where seconds before he'd seen Kana's face. A squall had blown in off the coast, bringing rain and gusting winds. Perhaps he wouldn't make the cove, after all.

"There trouble, Tuan." Kana followed him into the bedroom. "Two very small childrens washed away in the river. Mothers ask me to find you. They think you good friends with Penala."

"Penala?" Ross slammed a drawer shut, draping his cravat over his shoulder. He supposed he had Lorna's pilgrimage to the temple to thank for his elevated prestige among the natives. In the villages, a rumor had begun to circulate that Penala had chosen the red-haired woman as her handmaiden, and Ross supposed that by association his personal worth had increased also. "How long have they been looking for the children?"

"One hour, maybes."

"Then there's still hope."

"Hope, yes." Kana hesitated. "One of missing boys is my nephew, Tuan."

Ross's head snapped up. "Aralu?" He was himself fond of the laughing seven-year-old who came to visit frequently to sample Mrs. Hofner's pancakes. The boy was bright and lively and showed all the promise of becoming as much of an asset to the island as his uncle was.

"You all dressed up very pretties," Kana said shrewdly as they hurried outside. "Your lady friend be angries if you not come."

Ross stepped off the veranda. "Lorna isn't like that, Kana. She'll understand."

* * *

Lorna paced before the window, her figure gilded by the pink-gold radiance of the globular lamps placed about the drawing room. It was almost midnight, and the rainstorm had grown into a raging squall that beat at the shutters and ripped away the wisteria that covered the veranda railing.

He was not coming.

She told herself he had been caught in the storm. Perhaps the roof of his new sulap had been whipped into the sea. Perhaps the rain had flooded the road here. Perhaps a tree had fallen and blocked his path. There would be no way to get a message to her.

He was not coming.

She looked at her reflection in the window and did not recognize the watery image. Instead of her usual prim chignon, she'd permitted her hair to fall as it would around her face and shoulders, as wanton and untamed as Ross made her feel inside.

The gown she wore was the most daring she'd ever seen on a woman, sheer moss-green Javanese silk that revealed her every curve and dipped down so low at the neck she was afraid to speak above a whisper for fear she would expose her breasts. It had been a birthday gift from Ilse, and Lorna had accepted it with the sole and shameful intention of appealing to Ross.

But he would never see her wear it. She would take it off and hang it in her wardrobe as a reminder of how easily she could be misled. She had only one purpose on this island, and she mustn't forget what it was.

The door opened behind her.

She spun around, her spirits lifting recklessly and then sinking as Kurt entered the room. He shook himself off like a wet dog, his opaque eyes narrowing as he noticed her at the window. There were times when she regretted letting him stay in her father's house. He seemed to observe her every move.

"Lorna—look at you. Did I miss a party?"

She turned away from him with a dejected sigh, pressing her palms to the window. "No. Everyone else is in bed."

"Share a glass of arak with me then."

"No. In fact, I'd rather you left me alone. I'm not in the best of moods."

He grabbed a decanter of rice brandy and a glass from the sideboard, throwing her an appraising look. "It must be contagious among you English. Tonight both you and St. James are not fit—"

She pivoted. "You saw Ross tonight?"

"Ja." He snorted, rubbing his dripping nose on his shoulder. "Drunk as a fish in the dram shop. He had little of his dignity on display this evening, I can tell you."

"He was upset?"

"I gathered so. He was unable to recover the bodies of two children who were missing earlier." Kurt fumbled in his pocket for his pipe. "I told him it was useless. One of the boys was his valet's nephew."

"Where has he gone?"

"The only place possible—back to his hut at the cove. All roads inland are flooded out."

"But you made it back here."

"Ja," he said dryly, exhaling a cloud of smoke. "And I was sober enough to stand on my own two feet."

After Kurt had gone to bed, Lorna lowered the lamps and stood in the darkness, listening to the dying gasps of wind at the window. The need to be with Ross, to give him comfort, to share his anguish was growing inside her with unaccountable urgency. But she could never find her way to the sulap alone, she thought in frustration. She would have to wait—

She whirled at the faint tapping against the window. Kana stood alone in the darkness, beckoning her into the garden. She answered his summons without hesitation, recklessly determined to go to Ross.

Chapter 14

Kana refused to follow her into the newly erected sulap, not from superstitious fear but because he thought Ross would be angry at him for bringing Lorna here. He had been commissioned only to give her a message of apology.

There were no lamps lit inside the sulap when Lorna arrived. She removed her muddied shoes on the ruai and tiptoed through each room, wondering belatedly what she was doing prowling around a drunken man's home in the dead of night.

"Brazen to the core," she said aloud. "That's always been my problem."

"I believe it is actually one of your most endearing traits," Ross said behind her.

She started, dropping her shoes with a clatter. Ross was sprawled against the king-size rattan chair in the corner, naked to the waist, his long legs stretched out before him.

If he was drunk, she could not tell it from the austere composure of his face. But then Ross was hardly the type to act the falling-down drunkard. He would probably force his pain inward. And, too, it had been hours since Kurt had seen him in the dram shop.

"I heard about the children. What a senseless tragedy."

"Their parents do not consider it so. To them it simply means that two young lives have been abbreviated in order to reincarnate in a higher form."

170

"Perhaps they are right."

He shrugged.

She lowered her gaze, aware of a queer tension growing in the air. She almost wished Ross's anger and hurt would explode. His deceptive calm disturbed her.

He uncrossed his legs and swung forward at the waist, his gaze raking her with insolent approval. "What a fetching dress," he said. "Is it for me, or did van Poole have the pleasure of seeing you in it first?"

She flinched at the raw pain underlying his ugly tone. "You are drunk, else you would not insult me like that."

He inclined his head toward her. "I apologize. And in answer to your question, I am not drunk now. But I wish I were. I wish I were drunk enough to forget forever the sight of an entire village looking to me as its savior, the unholy adulation in the natives' eyes when I arrived to help . . . the childlike disappointment and anger when I returned without the missing boys. I heard them whispering, 'He is not like the old Rajah. Rajah Charles would have found the children.' "

He lapsed into silence, one hand lifting to a deep graze on his elbow he had not previously felt, his gaze so abstracted that for a few minutes he did not even see Lorna. "That look," he said. "It was the same look my wife gave me as she died and begged me to save our son."

"Your arm is bleeding," she said, and cursed herself for a fool, for sounding so cool and impersonal when her heart was breaking for him.

"I failed them all, you know," he continued in a low voice, as if Lorna had not spoken. "The natives today, and Vanessa and Ian. If he had lived, my son, he would have been almost as old as one of the boys who was washed away."

"Perhaps . . . perhaps they will turn up, after all."

He lifted his head, regarding her so intently that Lorna took an involuntary step toward the door.

"Well, it isn't impossible, is it?" she said haltingly. "And if the people are disappointed, they will soon remember all you have done for them in the past. All that you do now. No man could possibly devote more of himself than you do, Ross.''

His lips curled upward at the corners. He wouldn't disillusion her. He wouldn't tell her that through his work he escaped his emotions, that it so exhausted him there was little time left to brood over his personal discontent.

"May I—shall I dress your arm?" she said, breaking the long silence. She moved toward him. "Please let me, Ross—''

He arose slowly, showing no signs of inebriation, and caught her in his arms, pressing his mouth to hers in a kiss that spoke as much of despair as of desire.

"Make me forget, Lorna," he murmured against her trembling mouth. His hands slid up her arms, over her shoulders, and dove into her hair. His fingers pressed into her scalp until her head tilted back, and his mouth bruised hers, seeking peace as well as passion, summoning the light of her soul into the darkness of his. "Help me," he said. "Lorna, help me. Heal me.''

"Yes," she whispered. She strained closer to him, responding against her will to the urgent passion of his embrace. She should have bolted for the door five minutes ago. She should have recoiled from the surge of wild emotions he made her feel. Instead, she was more than willing to immerse herself in the dark waters of her own unexplored sensuality.

He backed her to the wall, kissing her deeply, his mouth absorbing her whimpers that were half abandonment, half protestation. In time her lips opened in avid welcome to the penetration of his tongue. Her head swam in a delirium of desire.

"I am afraid," he said thickly as his fingers flicked open the buttons at the back of her gown, "that I'm going to tear this dress in my impatience to feel you naked against me.''

"I—I should leave you now," she whispered, her spine

pressed to the wall to brace herself against the insinuating thrusts of his body.

"Not now," he said. "You cannot leave me now."

"No, not now," she murmured.

In one deft move he worked the gown down over her hips and loosened the tape ties of her petticoats so that they fell together in a puddle of silk and starched muslin at her feet. Her breasts swelled up over the lace-trimmed border of her corset, flushed and aching for his touch. Her drawers were of the thinnest cotton, highlighting the dark vee between her legs.

"Did you dress like this for me?" he whispered, his mouth lowering to nuzzle her shoulder. His hand slipped between her thighs, the palm pressing against the sensitive core of her. "Did you dress this way to give me the pleasure of disrobing you?"

She could not reply, mortified at what was happening to her, yet wanting it to continue.

The drawers slithered to her ankles, and her legs opened at the subtle movements of his fingers. His touch was exquisitely tender, unbearably intimate, arousing a shuddering pleasure deep inside her. Her knees fell apart, allowing him freer access to the damp apex of her thighs. He eased a finger inside her, stretching her with painstaking sensitivity, his other hand reaching upward to grip hers. Just when she thought she could not bear another second of his deliberate teasing, he removed his hand and drew back to look at her. Her loins ached at the unexpected cessation of stimulation. She bit the inside of her cheek to keep from begging him to continue.

She felt ashamed, afraid, and excited all at once. "I—I came to console you," she said unevenly, expecting him to laugh at her.

He did not laugh, and as she looked at him, she shivered at the sensual intensity on his face. "If you want to leave," he said, his breathing harsh, "then do so now before it is too late."

His eyes burned into hers, reducing to ashes the host of

doubts and moral uncertainties she had been fighting from the moment she let him kiss her tonight.

She did not leave.

"Lorna," he said, closing his eyes, leaning into her with a deep frown of concentration furrowing his brow. "Lorna, please don't go away."

He kissed her again, deep and wet, sliding his lower torso between her legs, rotating his hips in rhythm with his tongue. She gasped as the warm pressure of his mouth claimed hers. The trembling began anew deep, deep inside her.

"Ross," she breathed, suddenly terrified. "I don't think—"

"Don't think then."

In a daze, she did not object when he lifted her into his arms and carried her to the bed where she had slept her first night on the island. Her aunt and uncle would be shocked if they knew what she was about to allow. She was not as sure what her father would think. He had always encouraged her to follow her heart, advising her he was hardly in a position to dictate morals to his daughter. She wondered fleetingly whether he had really believed that or whether he had not wanted to be bothered with her.

"Does anyone know you're here?" Ross asked as he kicked aside the mosquito netting.

She buried her face in the curve of his shoulder. The unexpected urgency of her need for him embarrassed her. "Only Kana."

"You must never do this again. You must never leave the house without leaving word where you've gone."

He was trembling as he lowered her to the bed. It was not just the force of his physical need for her that unnerved him—it was the tumult of emotions he experienced whenever he was near her. He couldn't remember ever feeling this way about Vanessa. He doubted that he had, recalling how arrogant and self-absorbed he'd been in his first years on the island, overeager to prove his worth to his uncle, frustrated by the slow healing of his body, the physical limitations he must overcome. He felt guilty now, recalling how he had so ignored his wife that they had never had a chance to grow close.

Deliberately he had built up barriers around his heart after she died, convinced that he was destined to lead a solitary existence and that he needed nothing more. For years, it seemed to be so.

And then Lorna had come into his life with that last, unexpected monsoon, brought to him by the fickle god of the southwest wind.

She raised a hand to touch his cheek. "You look so solemn, Ross. You frighten me."

He quivered at her caress, and then every muscle in his body tensed as she watched his face while he lowered a hand to the waistband of his trousers to unfasten the row of buttons that he feared would burst open without his help. A vein pulsing in his temple, he quickly kicked off his pants and underclothes and stretched out beside her. He saw her eyes flicker from his face downward to his naked body. Her lips parted, and she looked away with a barely audible gasp, her shoulders tensing.

"It's all right," he whispered, kissing her perspiring forehead.

He kicked the coverlet from their legs and brought his palm up to her calf, over her knee, and the shadowed hollow of her groin. Her shoulders sank onto the pillow. Her breathing quickened. Ross raised his head and kissed her with slow deliberation, his tongue playing with hers, penetrating her mouth until she was whimpering, unaware of everything except the sweet heaviness in her loins, the perilous abandon washing over her.

She thrashed against the coverlet, embarrassed at what he made her feel, what secretly she ached for him to do to her. His mouth scorched the private places of her body, and she nearly fainted with shame at the intimate delights he was teaching her. There was not an inch of her skin he did not brand as his own.

He made love to her with the same passionate absorption he applied to every task he undertook, not questioning his desire to please her. Although well versed in lovemaking, he recognized that with Lorna it would be like the first time for them both. He forced himself to take long moments reassuring her, allowing himself to savor the pleasurable torment of exploring her slender white body. In the moonlight, she looked like a marble sculpture, soft and womanly, and he could feel the intensity of his own need mounting as she responded to him with shy but eager passion. Emotions he dared not even acknowledge surged forth inside him and were translated to her in the tender consideration, the giving and taking of his touch. Still, it unsettled him to realize how deeply he desired her. Tonight would not be enough.

A soft breeze stirred the belladonna lilies that grew on the hillside behind the hut, the sibilant whisperings a counterpoint to Lorna's gasps of delight and Ross's low, seductive voice. He bent his head and kissed her, his hand caressing her breasts, cupping their fullness before gliding lower across her abdomen.

"I want you to be mine," he whispered against her mouth.

She couldn't speak as he eased his hands under her hips, raising her to him. Pressing himself against her, his body pulsing with fierce desire, he held her tightly for a moment. His breathing grew harsh and irregular. Then, with slow, erotic deliberation, he began to rotate his pelvis against hers, his aroused sex slipping between her soft thighs. Lorna shook with both anxiety and excitement.

"Oh, Lorna, if you had any idea what you make me feel. . . ."

He shifted back, bracing his knee between her thighs. Her eyes sought out his in the darkness, hesitant, afraid, yet illuminated with desire and the dawning awareness of the female power she possessed and had never purposefully used.

"Lorna," he said, and touched her face with his palm. "No, don't look away."

Her body resisted as he entered her, easing into the slick warmth that encased him. She went stiff with surprise at the unanticipated pain of penetration, perspiration filming her forehead. But he did not withdraw, soothing her with reassuring whispers which she barely understood and the sensual rocking of his body until the discomfort receded, and she stilled.

"Trust me . . . let me show you the magic," he said, the tendons in his neck and shoulders standing out against his darkly tanned skin.

Slowly, to her bewilderment and delight, the pulsing deep within her burgeoned and spread outward until it throbbed throughout her body, until she shook with the powerful spasms and her heart stopped in an interlude of velvet oblivion. Yet even then he continued to stroke her without mercy, heightening the intense pleasure that rendered her unable to control the violent shuddering that assailed her.

He drove into her then, deeply, his neck arched, his own body convulsing as he burst inside her with a deep sound of male domination. Acting from sheer instinct, she lifted upward, straining to meet him in the fleeting splendor that was her initiation into a more joyous intimacy than she'd ever imagined.

They lay in silence afterward, their breathing slowing, their bodies ticking with sublime relaxation. Ross held Lorna across his damp chest and idly stroked her hair, listening to the breeze outside. He tried to think back over the past few days to understand how tonight had happened. His brain refused to function, and he wasn't ready to face whatever feelings had begun to be born inside him. His instincts warned him he was in danger of overstepping the safe confines he had set for himself years ago.

"Did I hurt you?" he asked hoarsely.

"A little. It's all right, though." She turned her face to the window, tears stinging her eyes. She supposed she was ruined now, in society's eyes, but it was not for that that she wept. She was afraid—of what she felt for Ross, of where it would lead. For it was one thing to consider blithely following her father's advice to abandon common sense and moral convention; it was something else entirely to actually *do* so, and to discover there was no turning back afterward. She blinked away the tears that threatened to fall. A few months ago, her entire future was as intricately plotted as one of her father's novels. Now, she did not know what would happen to her from one day to the next. And she did not know Ross's intentions toward her and what tonight would mean to their relationship. She did not even understand her feelings for him.

He eased her out of his arms and turned onto his side. The longish black hair that fell forward to frame his square jawline gave him the ruthlessly handsome pirate's look that had fascinated her from the first.

"Regrets?" he whispered, wrapping his index finger around a strand of her hair.

"Not as many as I should have," she admitted with a self-conscious smile.

He did not return her smile. "Not even a regret that this might have been your honeymoon and instead you are spending it now, with me?"

"Out of the frying pan into the fire, they say." She wished she felt as casual as she sounded, but she had always relied upon humor as a child to lighten an otherwise difficult situation with her father when his melancholy moods would strike.

"Your fiancé is liable to be waiting for you when you return to England," Ross said after a long hesitation.

She turned away. She did not care to discuss Spencer, and she sensed that this might be Ross's very tactful way of reminding her that, despite tonight, they must eventually lead separate lives.

"I don't want to think about him—especially tonight," she whispered, glancing back at Ross.

He leaned down and kissed her lightly on the lips. "No,

not tonight then. Not after you have restored my peace of mind.''

''I should leave soon, Ross. My uncle will be livid if he discovers where I am.''

''I don't want you to leave.''

Their eyes met for a long interval. So much had happened since the day of the monsoon. So much more than either of them had bargained for.

''I will take you home,'' he said at last, his voice reluctant.

They walked along the beach toward the plantation house. It was late, yet Lorna did not feel the least bit tired. She could have stayed awake all night, just being with Ross.

''Your father should try his hand at coffee instead of tobacco,'' Ross remarked, releasing her hand. ''The combination of humidity and hillside terrain are ideal for it, and he'd make a fortune.''

Lorna laughed. ''My father couldn't even grow a weed in a meadow.''

Ross gave her a shrewd look. ''You could use the money, couldn't you?''

''How rude of you to point that out. But doesn't it take capital to start such a venture?''

''The Rajah is always good for a loan to a worthy cause.'' He stopped to pick up an enormous pink-shadowed nautilus shell. ''If I could convince enough Europeans there was profit in coffee here, I'd have the start of a prosperous economy.''

''I'm a tea drinker myself.'' She turned to face the sea, her heart beginning to race. Was he suggesting she stay or merely making polite conversation? Why was she afraid to take him seriously?

''Ross—''

She glanced back to see him facing away from her, his shoulders rigid, his mouth set in a grim line. ''Van Poole,'' he said, motioning to the stocky figure silhouetted in the moonlight. ''He's coming toward us.''

He tossed the shell back into the sea in disgust, and

with a pang of dismay Lorna watched it sink into a wave. She had hoped to keep it as a memento of the evening—a poignant reminder of how she had foolishly given herself to a man who had no place for her in his life. But unlike Spencer, Ross had not deceived or betrayed her. He had promised her nothing, yet she had still offered herself to him willingly. But while the act of their lovemaking had been beautiful, it made her ache for something deeper, something more to fulfill the longings Ross stirred in her heart, not just in her body.

She bent to bang the caked mud from her shoes and slip them back onto her feet. When she straightened, Kurt had reached Ross at the shoreline. He carried a rifle over his shoulder and a Colt revolver in his belt.

"Well," he said, and gave Lorna a long, assessing look that took in her disheveled hair, her flushed cheeks, and the mud stains on the hem of her gown. "Ilse was right all along."

Lorna's color deepened, and beside her, Ross tensed. "Do you want something, van Poole?" he asked in a deceptively even voice.

"Miss Fairfield pays me to protect her. I merely wanted to make sure she returned to the house unharmed."

"I can see her home."

"But if her uncle awakens and sees you both returning to the house . . ." Kurt smirked, allowing insinuation to conclude the thought. "Besides, we're leaving early in the morning to start interviewing a sea captain and crew. You are coming with me, Lorna?"

"Yes."

"I'm coming, too," Ross said. "And I'll walk Lorna to the gate."

When they reached the hillside path to the house, they were immediately confronted by two guards who had been hidden among the flame-of-the-forest trees.

They lowered their muskets upon noticing Ross, and he praised them for their diligence rather than chastising them for not recognizing him.

"Lorna." He caught her hand, furious that van Poole's presence prevented him from saying good-night to her alone. Perhaps, though, it was just as well. If he took her into his arms with the memory of their lovemaking lingering in his mind, he might not be able to let her go.

"I will see you tomorrow. Perhaps I can come for supper in the evening to make up for what happened earlier."

"All right." She glanced uneasily at Kurt, who did not move out of listening distance to allow them a moment of privacy. "I'm sorry about the children. I know you did everything possible to save them."

"The children," Kurt said dryly, "were found safe less than a half mile from their huts about an hour ago. A messenger was sent to your sulap with the information, St. James, but you evidently did not hear him calling you from the ruai."

Ross shook his head in relief. "You were right," he said to Lorna.

"I'm glad." She smiled into his eyes.

He smiled back, deliberately ignoring Kurt's impatient pacing before the gate. "Go on inside," he said finally. "We will find another time to talk."

He waited outside until she was safely in the house. Even then it angered him to think that Kurt would have the final moments of the night with her, moments that should have belonged to him.

He started down the hill, toward the beach. Away from her, his mind clearing in the damp sea air, he wondered how he had allowed tonight to happen.

He had always considered himself to be a practical man, at peace with his loneliness. Then he'd met Lorna, who with her impractical loyalty and zest for life had penetrated the defenses he only half realized he'd built around himself. He had never been much of a womanizer, not even in his younger days. Whatever he loved demanded his full devotion. And so he felt suddenly afraid of his romantic attraction to this strong-willed young woman who surprised him at every turn. He hadn't expected her to show up at the sulap tonight. God, by tomorrow, if not already, she'd be bitterly regretting her impulsive act of compassion. But he couldn't honestly say that he regretted it. Remembering her lying beneath him, remembering the pleasure of possessing her, he felt wild delight flood through him. If it weren't for her uncle, she'd not have left his side until morning.

He'd never known a woman like her before, and it wasn't merely her physical loveliness that appealed to him. It was her spirit and enthusiasm, her genuine warmth, her ability to adapt to situations that would make any other woman quail. And she wasn't frightened by his beloved island and its people; she had made herself part of them. Of course it was unthinkable that anything permanent could come of their relationship. Hadn't she scoffed at his suggestion that she stay on the island? She had another life back in England, and that useless English lord, who wouldn't give her up if he had a brain in his head. She would return home, after the search, and he would return to the solitude that was the self-punishment he had accepted for his part in Vanessa's death. Besides, he had lived without emotional closeness with a woman for so long now that opening up his heart would be as painful as learning to walk again. He wasn't prepared to make himself vulnerable to the loss of another love. Damn it, he was comfortable with his existence. Why would he want to open up the old wounds again?

As he walked through the lacy surf, he stared out across the sea and smiled to himself. He was so accustomed to giving orders that he'd forgotten there were aspects of life beyond even his control. He had almost forgotten his own humanity and its inherent frailties.

Inside the house, Kurt seemed hesitant to leave Lorna's side. He followed her up the staircase and overtook her on the landing. She turned her face to escape the sour odor of smoke and whiskey on his breath. His eyes were blood-shot, his face pink and bloated, his muslin shirt soaked with perspiration.

"My sister worries about you like one of her own children," he said. "I told her you could take care of yourself. But even I thought you had more sense than—"

"I did not employ you to judge me."

He nodded agreeably. "No. It is not my business how you conduct your personal affairs. And should there come a time when you are tempted to pass judgment on me, I shall ask for the same understanding."

"From the very first day we met, I have overlooked many aspects of your character that are . . . disturbing," she said coldly.

He smiled, as if he had understood that all along. "We are both sinners, Lorna, led astray down different paths. The next time you look at me as if I am a lump of dirt, I shall remember that for all your ladylike airs, you spent the evening alone with a man in a native hut. I shall remember you are as human as I am."

The husky tow-haired man lowered his binoculars as Ross entered the cave lookout a half hour after leaving Lorna. "I thought you'd turned in for the night."

Ross took the binoculars from Assistant Resident Tunridge's hand and focused on the starlit sea. "Anything of interest?"

Tunridge yawned. "Not out there. A native came by with news the children were found, but I gather you weren't receiving callers. I didn't see a woman come to the sulap earlier, did I?"

"Not unless you had your binoculars trained where they don't belong."

Tunridge grinned. "The Rajah's hinted I'm to accompany her to Jalaka. I'm the envy of the fort."

"He's changed his mind." Ross couldn't help laughing at Tunridge's crestfallen expression. "I'm going instead."

"You're not serious. Who the blazes is going to save us from the bleedin' pirates then?"

"You are, my good man. I'll even loan you the use of my sulap."

"Thanks very much," Tunridge said sourly.

Ross shoved the binoculars into Tunridge's relaxed abdomen, eliciting from him a grunt and a filthy look. "The young lady is under my protection."

"More's the pity for her then. I'm surprised you don't have her standing watch and making village rounds."

"Remember I'm your superior, Tunridge."

The other man snorted and began to follow Ross outside to the hillside stream where they regularly refreshed themselves. "Do you know what I think, St. James? I think we're behaving like a pair of idiots over Miss Fairfield. God knows a woman like her won't stay long enough on this godforsaken island that she should threaten our friendship."

Ross lifted his head from the stream, water trickling down the sides of his face onto his collar. He had a sudden urge to smash a fist into Tunridge's grinning face.

"Aye," Tunridge continued. "On second thought, I'm glad it's you, not me, that's going with her. A woman like that puts dangerous ideas into a man's head, about home and family and all that rubbish which shouldn't appeal to us hardened bachelor types. She'd be mad to fall for a sorry pair of outstation bastards like us when she's got some la-de-da lord awaiting her in London."

"You talk too much, Tunridge," Ross said idly.

"Another thing," Tunridge went on, "I don't envy you spending all those days and nights in her company and not being able to spit or smoke without permission, either."

"I feel responsible for her," Ross murmured. "Nothing more."

"Smart chap. Stick with that princess the Rajah's lined up for you. Breed yourselves a few burnt-almond babies and forget about flighty English misses."

"I'm going home to bed," Ross said.

"You need a night in Li-Li Kong's place," Tunridge said cheerfully. "Ask for Yun-Sing, and tell her I sent you."

Chapter 15

It rained late into the afternoon of the next day. Kurt postponed the trip to the wharves and spent several hours cleaning his guns in preparation for the voyage to Jalaka. Lorna played cards with Ilse until she caught her cheating, which put an end to that.

Besides, after what had happened the previous night, Lorna was too restless to concentrate, too nervous in anticipation of Ross's visit that evening to think of anything but how she would face him again. She did not understand why she'd placed herself in such a perilous position as to visit his sulap in the first place, save that the impulse to console him had overwhelmed her judgment. Even now, in the clear light of day, she had to admit she was drawn to him not just for his masculine appeal but for the rough beauty of his soul, which she had glimpsed despite his efforts to bury it under a show of arrogance. She could not forget his distress at believing he had failed to find the two boys missing in the flood, or his desire to find homes for the native twins abandoned in the chapel.

Then too there was the way he had treated her. Clearly she had imposed on his time, but had it been necessary for him to care for her personally during her illness? Was he so wrapped up in his work he could not separate it from his personal feelings . . . or was she simply reading more into his behavior than was there because she wanted to believe she mattered to him? Perhaps she needed to assuage the belated shame she felt for having given herself to him last night. It was frightening to realize she had acted so impulsively and that there was a chance it could happen again.

She was suddenly overwhelmed by her emotions, by what Ross made her feel. There was no one she could talk with about what had happened last night. Her uncle would be infuriated and would send her right home. Ilse would disapprove. If only she could confront Ross with her doubts. But, of course, she couldn't. She couldn't bring herself to expose such painfully private thoughts when he was the cause of her inner turmoil.

She oversaw the supper preparations herself, basting a plump chicken until its skin turned crackling golden-brown and then nestling it in a bed of fragrant saffron rice accompanied with sliced mushrooms and onions. To pass the time, and to impress Ross, she made a salad from produce salvaged from her father's forlorn vegetable plot. She even baked a rich cheesecake and decorated it with slices of fresh tropical fruits dipped in preserves: papaya, mango, and banana. For appetizers she prepared pomelo and herbed goat cheese with freshly baked bread.

As the day wore on, her anxiety increased until she was pacing the parlor like a cat kept inside during a rain. After she had delayed supper for over an hour in deference to Ross, she insisted that the others—Kurt, Ilse, her uncle—begin to eat. A knot of dread had settled in the pit of her stomach. She wondered if Ross regretted last night and could not bear to face her. Perhaps he felt ashamed for having used her.

She gazed out into the garden, toying with the wedge of pomelo on her plate but unable to appreciate the tart pink fruit. The rain had stopped an hour ago. A crescent moon clustered around by myriad stars illumined the clear tropical skies. He couldn't use the weather as an excuse for not coming tonight.

The houseboy slipped into the room and approached the table.

"Tuan send," he said shyly, handing Lorna a folded piece of paper.

"Well, what does it say?" Ilse asked, leaning forward on her plump arms to peer at the note.

Lorna unfolded the paper, her fingers trembling. Her temples were pounding as she began to read. She prayed her face did not show what she felt.

Sorry. Unable to make dinner. Hope you are not inconvenienced.

R

She reread the note several times, striving to find a single hint of anything personal in it. If this was the best he could manage after last night, he obviously did not care for her. She felt physically ill. The smells from the rich foods she'd so carefully prepared turned her stomach.

Her throat felt tight as she looked around the table. "Something's come up, that's all. He hopes we're not put out." It required all her effort to sound normal. She longed to run from the room and vent her unhappiness alone.

"I don't envy him his position," Richard said. "The man never seems to have a free moment."

Lorna caught Ilse's eye and could just imagine what she was thinking: Ross made time enough to seduce you, but don't expect it to go any further. His commitment is to Kali Simpang.

She waited up until nearly eleven, but by then it had started to rain again and she knew he wouldn't come anyway.

"You are going to bed now, Lorna?" Kurt said, pausing at her chair by the window. "We will have to leave early tomorrow if we are to start interviewing a sea captain."

She rose, glancing one last time out the window. "You make it sound as if it's going to be a trying ordeal."

"Well, the Dutch-Malay sea captain who is familiar with the uncharted waters of Jalaka is holding out for more money."

"But I have no more money," she said, trailing him into the hall. Everything seemed to be working against her.

"We'll find someone else if the bastard won't take my offer," he told her as they parted in the upstairs hallway for the night. "Don't worry about the details—and Lorna, for God's sake, do not leave the house for another midnight rendezvous."

"I had no intention of it."

Ilse opened her bedroom door and called down into the landing, "Come into my room and chat a moment, Lorna. I cannot stand to see you looking so miserable."

"I'm not miserable. I'm tired."

"Liar. Be quiet coming up, won't you. Your uncle is asleep."

She went up to the tiny room and sat unwillingly on a wicker chair while Ilse plaited her coarse white-blond hair at her dressing table. "You're in love with him, aren't you, Lorna?"

"I don't know." She twisted her hands in her lap. "I don't think I *want* to know."

"And he promised to see you tonight."

"There was a reason he didn't come."

Ilse swiveled around on her stool. "A very good reason, if you ask me. He's trying to tell you as plainly as he can that he does not want this attraction between you to go any further."

"I need his cooperation to help find my father," Lorna said, rising from the chair.

"Not really. You have Kurt."

"Moreover, I do not think Ross is the type—"

"Your judgment is questionable. You were engaged to a man who betrayed you with your best friend. What makes you think Ross is not going to hurt you too?"

"What makes you so certain he will?" Lorna was stunned by Ilse's cruel frankness.

"I've known him longer than you. I've seen him court

the occasional woman visitor to the island and then forget her entirely after the poor besotted fool reluctantly left.''

"A besotted fool," Lorna repeated in horror. "Thank you very much, Ilse, for the enlightening lecture.''

She left the room without another word, tears blinding her as she wrenched open her door and stepped over the pile of clothing in the middle of the floor, and then the trunk Mei Sing had evidently moved in order to sweep under the carpet. For a moment Lorna was distracted by the mess, then she threw herself on the bed.

Her temples were hammering with a full-fledged headache. Her body felt tender and swollen from the unaccustomed sensuality of the night before. Unable to stop herself, she recalled how Ross had pleasured her with his hands and mouth, the piercing joy of taking him deep inside her. She wanted him so badly, she was ashamed of herself. She was horrified that she could still desire him after he—

She flung a hand over her eyes and curled up into a ball, but the remembered sensations continued to wash over her until she was shaking. Even the Bengas fever had not left her feeling as physically weak as this, and she put a hand to her face, almost hoping she was simply ill again and not desperately in love with Ross.

Her skin felt cool.

She slumped back against the pillow, drawing a measure of sanity from the monotonous patter of rain.

At first she didn't hear the chair bang against the bed. When the sound penetrated her mind, she had time only to lift her head and gasp as a dark, furry body came crashing through the netting and landed on her stomach.

"Mahomet!" She whispered his name in relief. He had gotten his leg caught in the netting and was twisting frantically to free it.

When she got him loose, he stuck his little black face close to hers and wrapped himself around her neck, clinging to her in fright.

"Big silly baby," she said. "How did you get in here anyway?"

Kana had built a rattan cage for the small ape in the garden, and Lorna sneaked him back downstairs and across the saturated lawn, hoping the two guards patrolling the grounds wouldn't see her in her wet nightclothes. The Rajah had insisted that they remain stationed there as a precaution after the incident at his reception.

She'd just gotten Mahomet locked up for the night when she had the strangest sensation that someone was watching her. She whirled around, her gaze probing the rain-blurred darkness until she noticed Ross standing beneath the banyan tree.

The watery light picked out the pristine whiteness of his shirt, but his face was in shadow. He was standing with his arms folded across his chest, his long legs planted apart.

She hesitated. She was puzzled and hurt enough to return to her room without even acknowledging him. But then he stepped into the moonlight, and she saw the expression in his eyes, the silent appeal that made it impossible to turn around without discovering why he had come at last. She took a tentative step forward, her hands clutching at her nightdress to keep it out of the mud. He released a long sigh as if he were relieved she wasn't going to leave. Deep inside Lorna knew she didn't have the will to walk away from him. She was drawn to Ross as helplessly as a wave toward the shore, compelled by forces she could not even begin to understand . . . or fight.

"What are you doing here?" she asked in a whisper.

He straightened but did not answer, staring at her through the light rainfall. Lorna realized how ridiculous she must look in the bulky flannel nightdress that left everything to the imagination, her hair in a braid down her back.

"You're getting wet," he said.

"What do you want?"

"I was hoping you hadn't gone to bed yet. I saw you moving about in your room."

"I got your note," she said tightly.

"I wasn't going to come." He uncrossed his arms and shifted forward onto one foot. "I tried my best not to."

"What—what made you change your mind?"

He stepped toward her until they were almost touching. Lorna did not move, her shoulders rigid, her eyes wary. But there was no way Ross could explain how he'd been waging a battle between his head and his heart all day, and that to his astonishment, his heart had won.

What if she did leave the island in another month or so? He'd manage by himself again. For now it was sheer torture to stay away from her. It was torture to stand here and not touch her. It was impossible to pretend that he didn't care for her. He did, far too much.

He knew he would probably regret becoming involved with her, later, after she left and the solitude engulfed him again. But damn it, he already *was* involved with her, like it or not. He couldn't figure out exactly when or how it had happened, but it didn't help to deny it. The best he could hope for was that he'd be able to forget her after she was gone. When she returned to England, he thought it likely that she wouldn't remember that he and the island even existed.

He reached down for her hands and she leaned away, her bare feet slipping over the tree's slick roots. "You're unbelievably desirable in that nightdress."

"Don't touch me."

"Please, Lorna."

"Ilse thinks you're using me."

His face darkened. "Ilse should pay more attention to her own miserable marriage."

"Did you have a reason for not coming earlier?"

"I needed to think. I needed to stop fighting myself."

She nodded, strangely accepting his simple answer. "I find this all . . . very overwhelming. Especially after . . ."

"Last night," he said, finishing the words she couldn't say. "It changed everything."

He put his hands on her shoulders and drew her against him. Lorna could smell the starch and soap on his shirt that the dampness had brought out. "I'm going to kiss you," he said.

"No." She leaned back. "I don't think you should—"

She flinched as his arms tightened around her shoulders. She should have known that the instant he touched her, the battle to retain her composure would be lost. Yet she yearned for his touch. Only the feel of being held in his arms could ease the poignant longing that she'd become so aware of since last night. He dipped his head toward hers. She tried to draw back, but it was a halfhearted protest.

He kissed her then, again and again. He kissed her mouth, her face and throat and breasts through the wet fabric of her nightdress until she was leaning up against the tree, the papery bark pressing into her bare shoulders. For a while she thought neither of them would be able to stop, that they would make love where they stood in the damp shade of the banyan with only its dripping aerial roots and the rain to shield them from the outside world. Finally Ross pulled away with his head thrown back to catch his breath.

"God. I'm not thinking. You shouldn't be out here this soon after your fever." He reached his hands into the rain to splash fresh water onto his face. He looked wild and intense as he regarded her, his body pulsing with savage urges, his chest heaving.

"I'm leaving," he said, backing away from her. "I'm leaving before I cause us both unneeded trouble. I'll return tomorrow to ride with you to the wharves."

She nodded mutely and pulled her nightdress up over her shoulders as he walked away into the silver-gray darkness of the garden. The guards watched him from their stations, their shoulders lifting in respect at his passage. With a shock that was as painful as a physical blow, Lorna realized that Ross would become Rajah when his uncle died. He would rule this island and it didn't seem likely there would be any place at all for her then in his life. It was a complication she should have considered earlier, but then, none of her feelings for Ross had followed any logical sequence. She wondered whether he had given their future together any thought. Perhaps it was a foolish assumption on her part to hope she meant that much to him. Just because he desired her now did not mean his feelings would deepen.

She turned toward the house. As she passed the shed, Kurt's dog emitted a low warning growl at the disturbance. Lorna shivered, then hurried inside, her face pale in the moonlight.

Chapter 16

Lorna did not sleep well that night, mulling over Ross's behavior, as well as her own, and what it meant. She was still in bed late the following morning when Ilse brought her a pot of tea and a plate of warm, sugary yeast rolls.

"Get up, Lorna. Kurt is downstairs fuming with impatience to leave for the wharf."

"Oh, I'd almost forgotten."

She flipped her braid over her shoulder and drank the contents of the cup Ilse handed her. Revived, she placed the saucer on the nightstand and went to the wardrobe for her wrapper, unbraiding her hair on the way. It was then that the disorder in the room—the overturned trunk, the petticoats and clothes on the floor—caught her full attention.

"That blasted ape."

"Are you referring to my brother?"

"No. Mahomet. He's made a proper mess of this place." She knelt to retrieve her clothes, then froze, her hand arrested in midair.

A gibbon ape couldn't pry open a lock, and Lorna knew she'd secured her trunk the last time she shut it.

"Have you noticed anyone entering my room recently? My trunk is unlocked."

Ilse did not look up from her tea. "Perhaps that Ranjan

girl who's always hiding in corners like a little spider was poking through it.''

"I sent Sri to the istana two days ago."

"Then you probably left it unlocked yourself." Ilse helped herself to a roll, then licked her fingers. "Ever since you became Ross's lover, you haven't been behaving like the practical young woman I initially judged you to be.''

"I locked the trunk. A few of my father's letters are missing.''

"I can't imagine why they'd interest a thief. Perhaps Mahomet ate them."

"But he couldn't have picked the lock on the trunk. And I am not Ross's lover.''

The matter of the missing letters still bothered Lorna as she went downstairs and met Kurt in the drawing room. Yet after one look at his face, she decided not to discuss the matter with him. Impatient and ill-humored at the delay, he hustled her and Ilse into the bullock cart outside and refused to wait for Richard to finish shaving.

"I thought Resident St. James was to accompany us," Lorna said, scanning the hillside as the cart set off with a rumbling jolt.

Kurt shrugged in irritation. "He knew when we intended to leave. It's not my worry if he doesn't come. Besides, his presence is annoying to say the least. I work far better without someone breathing down my neck.''

Lorna arched an eyebrow and braced herself for the ride between two sacks of rice as there were no seats in the cart. If Kurt resented Ross's interference now, he would be beside himself when he learned Ross would probably accompany them on the expedition.

"God, here he comes now," she heard Kurt mutter, and she looked out from under her white lace parasol to see Ross riding toward them.

"Good morning, Miss Fairfield."

She contrived to look composed as he greeted her, but

she felt the caressing warmth of his gaze all the way down to her toes.

"Ilse," he murmured in acknowledgment, then more coolly, "Kurt." But still he did not look away from Lorna until she finally lowered her eyes, unable to endure the rush of intimate memories his gaze provoked.

He gave Lorna a slow smile, then moved forward to address the driver about the direction they would take. The muddied roads necessitated a detour around the island, but Lorna did not mind. The lush green scenery enchanted her. To spend another day with Ross made the discomfort worthwhile.

The cart twisted around hills of emerald-green padis, rice fields where children played with ducks and stooped brown men worked in the blistering sun, some worshiping at the tiny shrines planted in the verdant terraces.

"Those men with poles," Lorna said, rising to her knees, "they're not fishing, are they? What could they possibly catch in a rice field?"

Ross slowed to ride beside her. "A minnow or two, perhaps."

"A minnow? Surely it would be more productive to fish at sea."

"Without doubt. But these natives fear the sea and its creatures—they would starve to death before eating something they consider possessed by an evil spirit."

"But all that bounty that surrounds them. Why should they be so afraid?"

He stared toward the hills. "Perhaps long ago an ancestor was attacked by a shark. The fear of being harmed is buried deep but not forgotten. I suppose there's no more sense in many of the beliefs we follow blindly throughout our lives."

His voice was thoughtful, his gaze reflective as he turned his attention back to the ill-defined path. Lorna twisted her parasol around to shade her face, studying him through the gauzy webbing. Politely attentive but not overly so, he revealed nothing of his feelings for her. She wished they

were alone for a moment so that they might speak about
last night.

The sun glinted off the dark sheen of his hair. Watching
him, Lorna felt tempted to reach out to touch the frown
that creased his suntanned forehead. He looked preoccupied. She would like to believe that he was thinking of
her, that she had the same unsettling effect on him as he
had on her. Unfortunately she couldn't quite convince herself of it. He seemed so composed, so detached, he might
have already forgotten she rode beside him.

The sun rose higher in the sky, white-hot shafts piercing
the ragged fans of palms bordering the path. When at last
they reached the waterfront, Lorna thought that Kurt's
suggestion of a cool beer sounded delicious, though she
disliked the beverage as a rule.

She was pleased when Ross dismounted to help her
down. His pith helmet, back in place, shaded his eyes, but
he held her waist more firmly and for longer than he
needed to. The brief contact flooded her body with alarmingly pleasant sensations, reminding her of the bond they
had forged in the sulap. She ached to be alone in his arms.

They made their way along the old stone pier, past
warehouses and various small businesses to a crowded
dramshop on the bay. Within the dank, stale-smelling taproom, they found the Moslem captain Kurt had arranged
to meet. Seated in the farthest corner of the bar, the
swarthy-skinned man was trimming a bright green parrot's
claws with a penknife when the party arrived.

"Sinan," Kurt said in acknowledgment.

"You are late," the young seaman said, not looking up
from his task. "I thought you said English lady was very
anxious to find ship."

"English lady is," Lorna said tartly, brushing her chair
free of discarded peanut shells as Ross pulled it out from
the table for her.

Sinan glanced up at her, his black eyes reflecting indif-
ference as she settled before him. "Where do you want
me to take you?"

She glanced at Kurt. "I thought you'd discussed this."

"Not in detail." Kurt pulled out a chair, leaving Ilse to manage for herself. "We want to go to Jalaka, Sinan. Have you ever sailed there before?"

Sinan did not reply, seemingly engrossed in feeding another peanut to his parrot. For a moment Lorna thought he hadn't understood. Then, abruptly, he pocketed his knife and arose with the bird perched on his wrist. "I'm not interested."

Kurt sprang up from his chair. "Have you forgotten that only four months ago in this very bar I saved your worthless neck when you were stupid enough to insult a man twice your size?"

Sinan's eyes flashed; his wiry frame tensed. "My life was not spared so that it could be squandered on some woman's whim."

"But you haven't heard how much my brother is willing to pay you," Ilse said as Sinan began to back away.

His face dark, Kurt excused himself from the table. Lorna swiveled in her chair to face Ross. He had not said a single word during the interview and was leaning back in his chair with indolent unconcern. "Can't you exert some influence?" she asked.

"No. He doesn't live on the island."

"And wouldn't you be delighted if no one agreed to take us?" she said in an angry whisper.

"It might be fate."

"Damn it, Ross."

His eyes widened. "Such language, young woman."

Lorna glared at him, then turned her attention to the bar, where Kurt was engaged in a conversation with the barkeep, who gestured to a large man, visible through the window, who was seated on the bench outside. After a few moments Kurt went outside to address the man, whose curly red hair reached his shoulders. Lorna watched the exchange through the grimy windowpane, sparingly sipping the light, nutty beer a boy had just brought to the table.

"They're coming inside," Ilse murmured. She had to crane to see around Ross's tall frame. "What an intriguing looking man. Who is he, Ross?"

The man was dressed in a white silk native sarong and batik breastcloth and dwarfed Kurt by a head and boasted three times his girth. Lorna realized that by now she should be somewhat accustomed to the strange mix of nationalities on the island, but the blazing red hair, freckled skin, ragged beard, and alert blue eyes seemed so keenly at odds with the man's apparel that she couldn't help staring.

"It's William Thomas," Ross said. "He's a Welsh shark fin hunter who lives on his ship most of the time. He has about seven illegitimate children and works like the devil to support them."

"A shark fin hunter." Lorna thought he had possibilities. "Then he isn't likely to be daunted by our requirements."

Thomas approached the table, dragging a chair with him. "Ladies. Ross. I understand you need a ship for an unspecified period of time."

He spoke directly to Lorna. She nodded, trying not to stare at the necklace he wore of what appeared to be coral, lava beads, sharks' teeth—and a mummified frog.

"I'll lose a great deal of business," he continued soberly. "I've customers in China who rely heavily on my exports."

"We will pay you," Kurt said before Lorna could interrupt, "whatever you ask."

"You understand we need to go to Jalaka," Lorna said.

Kurt glanced at her. "I've explained that to him already."

"I'll discuss it with my crew then," Thomas said, his eyes glinting with interest. " 'Tis up to them, you see. They're good lads, brave as they come. I'll not have them left out of any venture."

"We need to know by tomorrow," Kurt said.

"Tomorrow," Thomas repeated, and rose, turning from the table with extraordinary grace for a man his size.

"Well, Ross," Lorna said with a triumphant smile. "What do you have to say for fate now?"

"Thomas is an excellent seaman," he admitted grudgingly, "although his personal beliefs run to the bizarre. One day he's a Moslem, the next a Hindu."

"As long as he's not Agung-Mani, we don't have to worry," Ilse said.

Kurt smiled, and Lorna sensed his relief that their greatest obstacle to starting the search was almost surmounted. "Let's take a look at the supplies I ordered," he said. "The warehouse is on the way back to the cart anyway. In fact, Lorna, we'll even have time for a little shopping if you like."

"I'll go with you as far as the warehouse," Ross said, rising to lead Lorna outside. "If you do go shopping, be careful around the Chinese bazaar."

"We won't go there today," Kurt said quickly. "There's enough to occupy us here."

The provisions Kurt had acquired for the voyage—water, salted pork, rice, dried fruit, ammunition, hammocks, and medical supplies such as salves and bandages—were stored in a narrow partition of a warehouse that faced the water.

Lorna sneezed several times as the harried Malay-Moslem attendant escorted them to the musty compartment Kurt had leased. The pungent odors of pepper, tobacco, and dried fish wafted to them from adjacent compartments where the exports awaited loading.

"I thoughts you should at least inspect the provisions," Kurt explained to Lorna as he fumbled with the flimsy bamboo lock to his compartment. "It is your right, and if there are certain feminine articles I have overlooked, I will have to be forgiven."

"A teapot," Lorna murmured as she followed him into the tiny dark cubicle. "I simply—"

She stopped, flung back into Ross's arms as Kurt shouted a warning and shoved her away from him.

A rat scurried over Lorna's toes, rushed under Ilse's skirts, and then vanished.

Then Kurt raised the lamp the attendant had brought him and as the flickering light dispelled the airless gloom, Lorna realized what had provoked his reaction.

The supplies he had stockpiled had been vandalized beyond salvation, the sacks of rice ripped open and saturated with salt water, the gunpowder ruined, the hammocks slashed into hempen shreds.

Lorna felt the tension in Ross's body as he moved behind her. When she turned to face him, he did not look at all smug or self-righteous as she had half expected.

"God damn it," Kurt said, kicking over a tin of oil. "All that money and time wasted. I was so organized, so goddamned organized. Where is that half-assed attendant who swore this was the safest warehouse on the island? His master will recompense me for my losses or I'll take it out of his useless—"

"This would have happened anywhere," Ross said above Kurt's ranting. "You know as well as I do who was responsible."

Kurt swung around, his face furious. "If you were doing your job, we wouldn't need to worry about a cult of murdering pagans, would we, Resident?"

"If I weren't having to spend half my time chaperoning you around the island, I might have more opportunity to take care of my responsibilities," Ross said, his voice cold but calm. "In the meantime, you might start asking yourself why the Agung-Mani is so determined to stop your expedition." He moved away from Lorna, back to the door. "If you don't already know—"

"Arguing isn't going to help anyone," Ilse interrupted, giving Kurt a sharp glance. "None of us is responsible for what happened here today."

Lorna gazed about the room. "But there must be a reason why they've singled me out. It has to be connected with my father."

"I'll question the attendant," Ross said, "though I'm

certain it won't do any good. And I'll order two men to escort the cart back to the house. Be sure you're home before dark.''

Kurt did not reply, staring sullenly at the floor. In fact, he looked so dispirited that Lorna almost hated to speak her mind.

"All the supplies will have to be replaced, Kurt, and I haven't that much money left."

He turned slowly. For an instant the lamplight distorted his features into an eerie-looking caricature, hollowing out his eye sockets, hardening his features so that he did not appear human. Then he moved. The illusion vanished. But Lorna still could not shake off the unpleasant feeling that for an instant she had looked into his soul . . . and had seen utter darkness.

"I will pay for whatever needs to be replaced," he said. "And I'll make up the difference in Captain Thomas's price, if necessary."

"Oh, well then. Thank you very much."

He nodded, obviously too distracted to pay her further notice.

"I suppose I should help clean up this mess," she heard Ilse saying. "It's just like being home with the children."

Lorna was in the garden playing with Mahomet that evening when she heard hoofbeats on the hillside. She thought it was Ross and felt relieved that she'd have a chance to talk with him alone after what had happened in the warehouse. She also had not yet told him about her father's missing letters.

But her visitor wasn't Ross. "Captain Thomas," she said at the gate, striving to keep the disappointment from her voice. "May I offer you some refreshment? There's lemonade on the table."

He rode a mule—not a horse—and left it tethered in the arbor while he followed her into the garden. He seemed nervous, Lorna thought, not at all the self-assured man she'd met earlier in the day. He wore loose trousers and a billowing white shirt.

It was dusk. Sensing he had something on his mind, Lorna asked him to sit with her under the banyan tree instead of inviting him into the house. She waved at the guards to indicate Captain Thomas was a welcome visitor.

"Is something wrong?" she asked, watching as his gaze shifted from one end of the garden to the other. "Is the money we offered not sufficient?"

He swallowed a mouthful of lemonade and wiped his mouth with his wrist. "Ain't the money, miss. I've other obligations, that's all. I wanted to tell you to your face proper like . . . and"—his voice dropped to an urgent undertone—"and to warn you that you must leave this island immediately."

"It has nothing to do with your obligations," she said, her heartbeat quickening with the fear he had transmitted to her. "Why, Captain Thomas? Why is everyone so afraid to help me?"

Something of the desperation in her voice must have touched him, for he said, "I can't speak for the others, miss, but for myself, it's the children, you see."

Lorna's stomach began to churn. "Your children—your children have been threatened because you were going to help me?"

"The woman I live with—her family are Ranjan villagers. If it were just myself, I wouldn't be intimidated. But the children run wild over the island half the time. I can't be with them every moment. I can't—I can't be worryin' they'll end up as sacrifices, you understand."

"No," she murmured. "I suppose not."

"Well, I wish you luck then, miss. But if you'll take my advice, it might be wisest to return home."

She shook her head in frustration. "And leave my father?"

"Wouldn't help him to lose your own life, would it?"

She did not move as he walked back to the gate. She couldn't. She was suddenly so afraid and dejected that she didn't know where she would find the courage to continue. The sound of Kurt's voice as he approached the table did nothing to help her depression.

"I saw Thomas riding off." He was toweling off his face, blotting splotches of soapy water from his neck. "He wants more money, I assume."

"He's refused the job. The Agung-Mani have threatened to harm his children if he helps me."

Kurt did not respond, slowing continuing to dry his face.

"You must have some idea why they are so determined that I not find my father," Lorna said.

He lowered the towel, his expression bland. "Lorna, my dear, that is something we will not know for sure until we find him."

"How?" she asked bitterly. "We have no ship, no supplies."

"Tomorrow I will return to Java and sail back with a captain who will not refuse us."

"A last resort?"

"A damn good captain—when he's sober."

She nodded tiredly. There was not one aspect of her life that she seemed to have any control over since coming to this island.

Ross sent word the next morning that if he were free, he would meet Lorna for a picnic on the beach at the bottom of the hill where her father's estate began.

She couldn't wait to see him. She loaded a hamper with milk-cheese, bread, bananas, papayas, and a bottle of wine from her father's cellar. She trusted Ross more than anyone else on the island; even though she knew he'd approve of Thomas refusing to help her, she knew Ross had what he perceived were her best interests at heart. What she didn't know, however, was whether he merely felt responsible for her and physically attracted to her, or whether he had actually begun to care for her. With Ross it was hard to tell, and as he didn't seem inclined to express his feelings, she was left to rely on her own intuition, which, to judge by her disastrous engagement to Spencer, was horribly unreliable.

A few minutes before Ross was due to meet her, Assistant Resident Tunridge appeared in his place with Ross's apology that he had been detained at the istana.

"Shall I escort you back up the hill?" he asked solicitously.

"No, it's quite all right. The guards can see me from the gate."

She felt a flicker of doubt as she walked up the hill in the wilting heat. Was Ross really detained or had he more misgivings about continuing to see her on a personal basis?

Lost in her reflections, she was startled when a small boy darted in front of her from behind a stand of banana plants.

If he had not been so young, she would have been frightened by his appearance, but when she noticed the letter in his hand, she thought that Ross had changed his mind and had decided to invite her to meet him at the istana.

"Is that for me?" she asked gently, extending her hand.

The boy nodded, thrust the paper into her palm, then turned and disappeared into the trees. One of the guards was already halfway down the hill to intercept the boy but retreated when she motioned him away. She wanted to read Ross's note alone.

But the note was not from Ross. In a careful, swirling script it read:

> Dearest Miss Fairfield,
>
> In the interest of your father's safety, it is to our mutual benefit that we meet over tea to discuss his disappearance.
>
> I shall be at the Chinese bazaar this afternoon at four o'clock. Please be prompt, and for reasons I shall explain during our meeting, I should appreciate that you come alone. In fact, I insist upon it.

The note was unsigned, and to judge by the position of the sun in the sky, Lorna had about an hour and a half to make the trip to the Chinese sector of the island, if she decided to answer the mysterious summons. Obviously its writer was literate, possibly one of the reclusive types her father associated with. She recalled that Papa had spent time on that part of the island. And she doubted whether any volcano-worshiping Agung-Mani sent their victims such formal invitations to tea.

When she returned to the house, still debating whether to risk the meeting, she found Dr. Parker examining Ilse's injured knee in the drawing room. They did not hear her enter from the hall.

"As far as I can tell, Ilse," Dr. Parker was saying, "it's healed beautifully, which is more than I can say for the bruises on your legs. When I think of the beating he must have given you for them to have taken so long to fade . . ."

He was on his knees, his bearded face lifted to Ilse's. Watching them, Lorna was shocked by two realizations—the first that he obviously cared for Ilse, the second that though in his fifties, he was a handsome man, trim, with sensual brown eyes that bespoke both humor and understanding.

Yet to judge from Ilse's reaction, it might be a one-sided affection, for she briskly pulled her hands from his and rearranged her skirts around her ankles.

"I swear to you, Jason, that Wouter has touched me for the last time ever."

"You're leaving him—"

Dr. Parker stopped, alerted by Lorna's polite warning cough and the look of embarrassment on Ilse's face that she and the doctor had been observed in a personal moment.

"I thought you were having a picnic on the beach with Ross," Ilse said, sounding so annoyed at the disturbance that Lorna suspected she had been enjoying her flirtation with the doctor after all.

"Read this," she said, and handed Ilse the note. There

was no one else to ask advice of—Ross was an hour away at the istana, Kurt had left for Java, and her uncle was indisposed with one of his vague ailments.

"I don't know what to make of it," Ilse said at last. "I think Kurt would want to be included."

But for that very reason, that Kurt would not be involved to either manipulate or interpret the situation, Lorna was tempted to reply to the summons. It might be the only way she would get at the truth, and oddly, because Ilse seemed hesitant about encouraging her, she sensed that something crucial would come of the appointment. If only Ross could accompany her, she'd feel more at ease, but there was no way to reach him and then await his arrival in time to make the meeting. She'd have to be satisfied with sending him word of her whereabouts. If she delayed, the mysterious author might never try to contact her again. Perhaps he too was afraid to reveal his identity.

"May I see the missive?" Dr. Parker asked. When he'd finished reading he said, "It's impossible that you go unescorted, of course. I shall take you there myself. I've a patient at the hotel I should visit anyway. Ilse?"

Lorna looked away as Ilse and the doctor exchanged a meaningful glance. A chance for an afternoon rendezvous under the guise of serving as *her* chaperone, she supposed. Well, what did it matter if it helped her cause?

"I'll need a few moments upstairs," Ilse said. "Lorna, you should take your shawl. With our luck it will rain."

They reached the Chinese bazaar earlier than expected, Ilse carrying an ivory-inlaid pistol in her reticule for protection. They had paid their young Malay driver well to follow them through the maze of market stalls that lay between the dilapidated wharves and shabby huts that housed the island's criminal element. Dr. Parker left them with reluctance, promising repeatedly to meet them at the hotel. He seemed to be having second thoughts about the wisdom of entrusting them to only a single native attendant, but both women were suddenly so intrigued by the prospect of an exotic shopping expedition that he finally felt justified in leaving.

No one out of the ordinary approached Lorna. No one made a single remark to identify himself as the sender of the intriguing letter.

"Perhaps Papa was having a passionate love affair with a Chinese washerwoman," she mused aloud. "I'm probably going to learn I've a couple of half brothers and sisters."

Ilse looked up from the basket she was examining. "It's almost four now. I think we should start back for the hotel. It's a good ride from here."

Lorna could sense Ilse's growing trepidation—was it over the anonymous letter, or her eagerness to see Dr. Parker again?

"Are you having an affair with the doctor?" Lorna asked as casually as she could manage.

"Yes," Ilse said in an even voice. "But unlike you with Ross, I don't dream that anything could possibly come of it. For one thing I am married, albeit to a monster. For another, Jason has no idea what I'm really like. He sees a pretty blonde who leads a lonely life with a husband who mistreats her, and he imagines himself a sort of knight protector to an innocent damsel in distress."

"Is that so very far from the truth?" Lorna asked thoughtfully.

"I am anything but innocent, dear Lorna. I am *tainted* by all the years I suffered my husband's abuse and before that my father's. There is something in me that seems to attract such mistreatment. Your eunuch would have said it was my karma. At any rate, I'm far too jaded for an idealist like Jason Parker."

Ilse's self-evaluation struck Lorna as so cynically sad, she almost wished she had not been privy to it.

"Stop frowning, Lorna," Ilse said with a laugh. "You look all the world like Ross, and I'm only half serious. I want my freedom, not to start another relationship with a man."

Lorna bought a bolt of figured peacock-blue silk from a Bombay cloth merchant wearing a fez and curled-toe velvet slippers. She thought it would make a lovely evening dress. Only after she made the purchase did she wonder where and when she would require such a gown. She had few social connections in London, and for the first time she had to face the reality of returning home. Unless she found her father and he encouraged her to stay here. Or Ross—

"Look at this." Ilse dragged her over to a stall that offered magic charms, amulets, and aphrodisiacs. "The tears of the sea cow are supposed to increase a man's staying power," she said, picking out a tiny vial. "Why don't you buy it for Resident St. James?"

The toothless old woman vendor held aloft a black silk bag. "Powdered rhinoceros horn. Make men very hards. Work very good on Inglishmens."

"Berapa harganya?" Ilse asked. "How much does it cost?"

Lorna walked away laughing. The assortment of merchandise displayed was unlike anything she'd ever seen in London. Daggers, beads, shells, lava dolls, honeycombs, and coconuts. Crickets, hummingbirds, orchids, spices, batik, and brilliant green parakeets in cages. She'd almost forgotten why they'd come to the bazaar in the first place, so fascinating were the little bamboo stalls.

No one molested them as they browsed. The vendors were friendly, the exotic food intriguing, and Lorna couldn't understand why Ross had spoken disparagingly of the sector, although she did have the unpleasant feeling she was being watched. But that wasn't surprising. She and Ilse certainly stood out among the natives. And her unknown contact had yet to identify himself.

"Look to the harbor," Ilse said. "Not long ago pirate chiefs used to land there to abduct young girls for their masters' harems."

Lorna glanced past the old stone pier to the mean huts on the hillside. An aura of secret evil seemed to emanate from the tightly shuttered windows. On the sunlit side of the hill was the Chinese cemetery, and from it the breeze wafted the scent of frangipani, the grave flower.

At four they drank arak from gourds and ate a light meal of breadfruit and rice wrapped with curried lamb in banana leaves. The brandy went straight to their heads, and they inadvertently turned from the central market into the winding streets that stank of dust, dried fish, and dung.

"There's a thriving brothel around here somewhere," Ilse said, tossing her unfinished lamb to a pack of stray dogs. "The joy-girls are world famous. Would you like to visit?"

"Not today, thanks. Are you sure this is the way to meet the driver?"

Lorna was suddenly conscious of the absence of noise and sunlight in the darkened alley into which they had turned. There was a small dramshop on the corner of the street, and Ilse had given their driver money to buy himself a beer before they returned to the house.

Lorna glanced up at the tall windowless warehouses that flanked them. "We ought to start back to the hotel. I think the letter writer is having misgivings about meeting me, after all, and—"

"I knew it was going to rain," Ilse said as a single raindrop plopped down on her arm. "Look, Lorna, there's no help for it. I'm simply going to have to enter that dramshop to retrieve our driver."

"Well, hurry up then."

Lorna frowned and glanced over her shoulder, distracted by a faint sound behind her. A small rat darted down a dark passageway that led to a private warehouse and wharves. A large Chinese junk with a black-dragon prow lay at anchor, the waves lapping at her hull.

A sandy-haired sailor stumbled down the steps of the dramshop and lurched past Lorna. She gave him a wide berth, crowding into the entrance of the passageway to avoid him. She pretended to be fascinated by the junk in the harbor, feeling his breath brush her cheek. He asked her something in Dutch, and she shook her head fiercely until he shrugged and went away. It had not started to rain in earnest yet, but the sky had turned gray, and Lorna drew her shawl tighter around her shoulders. Ilse seemed to be taking an inordinate amount of time in the dramshop. *I'll go inside myself and see why she's been detained. It can't be all that terrible and I might even ask if any of the locals knew my father.*

But as she turned from the harbor, she froze to see three unsmiling men blocking the passageway. Two were Chinese, wearing the black jackets and trousers of servants, with their hair in long queues. The third looked to be Eurasian, of mixed European and Chinese descent, rather tall, sallow-skinned. He wore a red silk patch over his left eye, and his tunic was of black silk with red piping. His straight black hair was cut short in the Parisian style. He gave Lorna a smile that chilled her to the bone.

"Excuse me," she said. "My friend is waiting for me."

"Your instructions were to come alone," he said in softly accented English. "But don't be concerned. Mrs. Klemp has been detained and will not notice your absence for some time."

"You said you had information about my father." She glanced toward the harbor, hoping to attract the attention of a passerby. She was only vaguely aware that he had called Ilse by name. "Please tell me what you know now, or arrange for a proper meeting."

"I did invite you to tea, didn't I? It isn't civil to form a friendship in an alleyway, and I do so want to get to know you, Miss Fairfield."

A shiver crawled down her spine.

He nodded, his single eye lifting to a point behind her. At that same instant, she whirled to flee and realized to her horror that the passageway led only to one abandoned warehouse and its connecting wharf. Although she could still hear the indistinct cries of the market vendors in the background, there was no one in sight to help her.

She wavered. She could feel the skin at her nape creeping, and suddenly everything seemed to be frozen in time. If they forced her onto the anchored junk, she would be at their mercy. No one would hear her cries for help. She would no doubt end up at the bottom of the harbor. Perhaps that was what had happened to her father. Perhaps her search for him would end here.

The two henchmen grabbed her arms and forced a blindfold over her eyes. She ripped it off and punched one of the men in the throat, screaming until the other thrust a gag into her mouth.

She should have listened to Ross. She should have realized he knew what he was talking about. This was his world, his savage island, and she had been a fool to think she could conquer it with no more than her strength of will and a guidebook.

Ross ignored the knock at the door. He'd been interrupted all day long, and he was frustrated in his inability to write a convincing letter of petition to the Governor General in Singapore for increased naval protection of the island. A single British warship could secure the future of Kali Simpang. He was determined to have it even if he had to beg.

He put his pen down and rubbed his face, unable to phrase a coherent sentence. It didn't help his concentration that Lorna hadn't been home when he'd stopped by the plantation on his return from the istana, even though the visit took him an hour out of his way. He'd hoped they could still have their picnic together, but her houseboy said she and Ilse had gone out somewhere with the doctor, and hadn't Tuan Resident received the note missee had sent him at the istana?

She's probably angry at me for breaking our engagement again, he thought. She'll think I did it on purpose, and if the truth be told, I wouldn't be able to deny it. If he couldn't stop his feelings for her, he should at least exert some degree of control over them. It bothered him to realize he'd even begun manipulating his schedule just to spend a few hours with her.

The knock sounded again.

He looked up from the large military desk, his face ominous. "What is it, Mrs. Hofner?" he snapped.

"There's a gentleman here to see you from the Aborigines Protection Society, sir."

Ross folded his arms behind his head and stared at the door. "Tell him to come back in another fortnight."

"But you'll be gone then, sir, away to that awful heathen island."

"I know."

She knocked again three minutes later and this time Ross jumped up, swearing roundly, and wrenched open the door. "What the bloody hell—"

He broke off at encountering the distinguished figure in the doorway, a gentleman near sixty with white hair and a meticulously trimmed mustache. Ross vaguely remembered meeting him at one of the Rajah's private dinner parties. In fact, it was the evening he had spent with Lorna, but nothing of that time stood out in his mind so clearly as how she had given away her ex-fiancé's earrings.

"Colonel Edwin Moody," the man said at Ross's continuing silence.

"Moody?" Ross recalled something about the Bengal army and recognition for heroism in the Burmese War, a later association with the East India Company and then—

"From the Foreign Office," Moody said. "Official business. My visit is to be kept strictly confidential, you understand."

"I was under the impression no one in Britain even remembered we existed." Ross led Moody into his study, closing the door behind him. "Normally, Colonel, the Rajah would be the one—"

"The Rajah directed me to you, actually. And I was under the impression he'd mentioned the purpose of my visit to your island."

Ross shook his head. "Quite possibly he did. How can I help you?"

Moody untied the portfolio he carried under his arm. "Do you recognize this man, Mr. St. James?"

Ross reached across the desk, his jaw tightening in displeasure as he stared down at the rough charcoal sketch of Kurt van Poole.

"I regret, as you're well aware, that I do. Has Kurt van Poole committed a crime I should know of?" he asked, thinking instantly of Lorna.

Moody removed his helmet and sat down across from Ross. "Officially, we have only circumstantial evidence to go on. Unofficially, I would warn you that the man is dangerous and quite possibly involved in a heinous plot of theft and cold-blooded murder."

"Are you at liberty to enlighten me?"

"I assume you've heard of the White Tiger of Palleh? That it was stolen from a museum in Singapore several months ago?"

"I heard some talk of it," Ross said. His mind had already begun to wander. He felt immense relief that though this involved van Poole, it couldn't possibly concern Lorna. He wished the man would not waste any more of his time. He also wished he'd received the note Lorna had sent to the istana. It would be dark before the unfortunate messenger tracked him down.

"It was a particularly violent crime," Moody continued, unaware of Ross's lapse in attention. "Three British civilians were shot to death, the elderly French caretaker stabbed. The museum guards were beheaded with a scythe unique to a certain African tribe. It had the earmarks of a sacrificial rite."

Ross sat forward, his interest piqued. "And that leads you to suspect van Poole?"

"He had experience as a foreman with members of the same tribe when he managed the mines in Africa, yes. And our reports from the Dutch authorities reveal he may have taken part in the tribal ceremonies from time to time.

It's rumored he invented his own savage initiation ceremony, requiring murder, to intimidate the native workers
into subservience.''

"You may arrest him this very afternoon as far as I'm
concerned.''

"If only I could. But all we have is the evidence of a
terrified old curator to rely on. Although several witnesses
have verified that van Poole was seen in Singapore at the
time of the theft, he has a watertight alibi. What we need
is your help, Mr. St. James. Hearsay is not enough, and
unfortunately most of our information has not come from
the most reliable sources. There is a chance he's entirely
innocent.''

"There was talk about his wife's death.''

"Yes. She was killed by one of van Poole's own hunting
dogs on their estate. Did he cause it? I don't know.''

Moody had Ross's complete attention now. "Just what
do you expect to catch van Poole doing that will give you
cause to arrest him?''

"I hope to retrieve the statue, of course. Its worth is
inestimable, and if I may be frank, there is pressure on
me from London to have van Poole brought to trial. The
two civilians killed were well connected at Court. We will
need to put him under surveillance—keep him here on the
island if possible.''

"That poses a problem, Colonel.''

"Yes, I'm fully aware of van Poole's proposed search
for Sir Arthur Fairfield. Look at this.''

He pushed another sketch across the desk, and this time
Ross's reaction was striking in his incredulous silence.

"You recognize this man as Sir Arthur Fairfield, of
course,'' Moody said.

Ross felt a prickle of foreboding. "I'm afraid I don't—''

"I suspect he is in current possession of the Tiger,
though whether by accident or deliberate criminal intent
has yet to be ascertained.''

Ross eased out of his chair and paced before the desk.
This was something that would not have occurred to him

in his wildest imaginings. Lorna. Oh, God. Lorna. It was starting to make a horrible kind of sense.

"But how could a man like Sir Arthur have stolen the Tiger? He's done nothing but spend his time with queer sorts on this island, as far as I remember. I don't even know whether he's met van Poole."

Ross didn't reveal Sir Arthur's interest in the Agung-Mani. Protective of Lorna, he did not want to hand Moody information that might hurt her father.

"My records indicate he did meet van Poole, but not that a friendship was established. It's his association with Pierre Lu Chan of Singapore that interests me."

"He's the opium smuggler who fancies himself an art collector," Ross said with distaste. "I've fined him more than once."

"He's also a member of the Samsings," Moody said, referring to the underground Malay-Chinese criminal society.

"I still don't understand his connection with Sir Arthur."

"A sailor in Singapore tipped us off that Pierre Lu Chan might be the mastermind behind the theft of the Tiger, and that he hired van Poole to carry out the actual crime."

Ross pivoted, his face strained. "And where does Sir Arthur fit in?"

"To be perfectly honest, I don't know much more than that Lu Chan has his men searching for Sir Arthur, and that Sir Arthur is said to have spent time aboard his junk in the harbor. Plus the statue is still missing. Why would Lu Chan be launching a private search for an eccentric old man unless he had a good reason for it?"

"Perhaps they were friends," Ross said, not believing it himself.

"Then why hasn't he come forward to assist Miss Fairfield? More likely, if he believes her father has the statue, he will—"

"Now just a minute," Ross said. "To accuse a man like Sir Arthur on the basis of amateur assumption—"

"Have you not asked yourself why van Poole has offered his services for this search?" Moody said cunningly. "He's very much in demand, you know."

"You think—you suspect he's after the statue?"

There was another knock at the door. Ross strode forward to answer it while Colonel Moody shoved his sketches back into his portfolio.

Richard Fairfield stood before him, white-faced, nervously drawing air through his front teeth.

"It's Lorna," he said without preamble. "My niece has gone missing just like her father. You have to help us find her, St. James. Before she vanishes altogether."

Chapter 17

They dragged her into the cabin of the junk she had noticed earlier. For several moments after her gag and blindfold were removed, her abductor sat smoking a water pipe, regarding her with his single eye, and saying nothing. To intimidate her, she supposed.

He sat before her on a dais of silken cushions with gilded fringes. She guessed that the guards had remained on deck to discourage trespassers. She felt intensely vulnerable and frightened, nauseated from the cloying smoke that wafted around her.

"Jasmine tea, Miss Fairfield?" her captor inquired, indicating the low jade-inlaid tea table that separated them.

"I assume it's poisoned." She refused to show her fear, though she was sure he could see it on her face and in her tightly clenched hands.

He took a sip from a delicate cup embossed with blue lotus flowers and sighed.

"Who are you?" she demanded, ignoring the cup he offered her.

"You may call me . . . Peter." He replaced the cup in the saucer, his eyes narrowing. "But my identity is not important. All that matters is that we find your father—and once we find him, that we impress upon him the importance of renewing old friendships."

"I think you've lit one too many joss sticks," she said.

"The fumes have gone to your head. My father never knew you."

But even as she spoke, she was remembering her father's letters and his reference to an unsavory character he had dined with at the wharves. It came to her clearly that his disappearance had more dangerous ramifications than she'd ever dreamed, and that now she was caught in those deadly crosscurrents.

"If he did know you," she continued in a staunchly loyal voice, drawing strength from her own words, "it was only as an acquaintance, I'm sure. My father's friends were peculiar but never . . . debased."

"Your father had an eye for the rare find, my bold young lady. I am so disappointed he did not mention me to you before."

"He's a writer," she said impatiently. "What would he want with an—an—"

"I am an art collector," he said. "Pray do not pretend you have no idea what our little meeting is all about." He leaned back against the wall, his fingers steepled beneath his chin, his eye closing into a speculative slit.

"Either you are a very accomplished actress," he remarked softly, "or you are truly ignorant of your father's recent activities."

"I'm ignorant," she said.

He arose from the dais and came slowly toward her. Her eyes widened as she noticed the jeweled dagger in his hand. Her heart jumped into her throat, pounding wildly as the two guards outside burst into a flurry of Mandarin Chinese.

Peter stopped, his mouth tight, and stared down at her for an interminable interval. "I have been advised that the gods favor you, Miss Fairfield, and it seems to be so. For now I am forced to cut short our encounter. But when you find your father, you may assure him that I am waiting for him."

"Why?" she whispered, her mouth dry. "What could you possibly want from him?"

"You truly do not know?"

She shook her head, unable to draw her gaze from the dagger he held.

"The White Tiger of Palleh."

She knew she had heard the name before, but in her fear and confusion she honestly could not recall when, or what it referred to.

"I—I don't know what you're talking about."

"Then your father has deceived us both." He bent and grabbed a strand of the hair at her nape, viciously hacking it off with the dagger.

"Now I carry the remembrance of your spirit with me always. Get up."

She obeyed, her fright so intense she hardly felt the pinpricks of blood erupting on her neck. There was the sound of a door creaking on its hinges, and then rough arms reached out from behind her. The blindfold tightened again around her eyes.

They dragged her back to the docks and shoved her down on the warped planking. She got up stiffly, removing the blindfold and fighting down a surge of nausea. She could hear voices in the passageway, and just as she noted with relief that the junk was easing out to sea, a tiny Chinese woman burst onto the docks, shaking her fist.

She was under five feet tall and exquisitely proportioned, sleek as a haughty Siamese cat who regarded the world with regal disdain from her kohl-rimmed eyes. She wore a bright rose silk tunic and willow green pantaloons, with gold bracelets stacked from wrist to elbow on both arms. The heavy layer of rice powder on her face made it difficult to guess her age. Suspecting that this curious creature had somehow chased her captor away, Lorna had an urge to kiss her petite, slippered feet.

The woman suddenly noticed Lorna and subjected her to a long, unwavering stare. "Where he go?" she demanded in a harpy's voice, snapping her fingers for the native servants swarming behind her to search the warehouse. "Where go that one-eyed goat who leave Li-Li Kong house without payee?"

Lorna cleared her throat. "Li-Li—"

"Kong," the woman repeated, stabbing her forefinger to her chest and enunciating her name as if Lorna were a half-wit. "My name Li-Li Kong. My house over there."

"Oh, I—I see." Lorna glanced at the junk bobbing out in the harbor like a tiny toy boat and felt a humorless smile forming on her lips. This woman, her shrieking angel of salvation, was none other than the madam of the infamous brothel Ilse had mentioned.

According to the custom, the stone seats in the Chinese cemetery had been designed for the spirits of the deceased to rest upon when they grew weary. Lorna did not think they'd mind very much if she sat upon one for a little while. Judging from the black look on Ross's face as he climbed up the hillside between the crescent-shaped tombs, she was going to be joining the dearly departed soon anyway.

She turned her face toward the harbor and watched the rising wind stir the surface of the sea into playful cats' paws. It was going to storm at any second. Brooding gray clouds had obscured the sun, reflecting the dark emotions she could see in Ross's eyes. Stinging grains of sand and frangipani blossoms pelted her cheeks. If she didn't move, she could well get blown out to sea.

She didn't care. It seemed a safer alternative than facing Ross, and she had wanted to sit here alone and think, having refused Li-Li Kong's offer to earn a night's lodgings in the ramshackle brothel that faced the cemetery. She'd had a sick fright on the junk, and nothing made sense to her anymore.

"Lorna."

She stared down at the sea in silence, and Ross hauled her roughly to her feet, his voice a whiplash in the wind. "I have enough on my goddamned plate without having to explain to the Rajah how you happened to be found alone in the Chinese cemetery." His tone softened. "Look at me."

She looked up at him and could not stop the tears of delayed fright from slipping down her face.

"The bolt of silk you bought at the bazaar today was fished out of the sea," he said, releasing her to stand with his face to the wind. "Ilse is in hysterics. Dr. Parker is waiting for news of you at the hotel."

"There was a man—he was part Chinese, and he had a silk eye patch. He forced me aboard his junk. He—he was asking me about my father, as if I were hiding something."

"Are you?"

"How can you even ask?" she cried. "After today, and that man—"

He swung around to stare at her, his hands jammed into his pockets. "Pierre Lu Chan," he said. "Lorna, I have to talk to you."

"Do you know something, Ross?" Her voice was trembling. "I have a feeling I'm not going to like what you say."

He sighed heavily. "I don't think you will either."

She shook her head and squeezed her eyes shut, hoping to dissolve the dark intensity mounting between them. Then she gave a small gasp of shock, her explanation forgotten, as rain began falling in blinding rivulets and he took two steps toward her and scooped her into his arms.

"No, Ross," she cried, straining against his chest, drumming her muddy heels against his white cotton trousers. "Put me down before someone sees us!"

His mouth compressed in a grim line, he ignored her cries and began to carry her down the hillside, toward Li-Li Kong's thriving joy-house with its mother-of-pearl windows and mud-pile foundation. When Lorna realized where he intended to take her, she began to struggle in earnest for her freedom, kicking and twisting until she slipped to her knees. She realized vaguely she was taking out her fear and frustration on him, but she still couldn't help herself.

"I'll get back home myself." Rain streaming down her face, she clawed in the mud for the reticule she had managed to keep on her all afternoon. She stumbled backward into the alleyway, staring at his stern, handsome face through the teeming rain. "I'll take responsibility for my own safety from now on, Resident. You're absolved of your duties concerning me, all right?"

"Lorna," he said hoarsely, "I've found out something about your father."

She froze, unable to ignore the sincerity on his face. She could not run away from the truth forever, a small voice whispered in her mind.

Ross used her temporary inattentiveness to take her arm and lead her up the short flight of steps and through the throng of fascinated onlookers who were crowded into the narrow doorway of Li-Li Kong's house, prostitutes, sailors, Chinese gold miners, and merchants caught in the storm.

She balked in the doorway, setting her heels to the floor. The entryway reeked of fried fish and garlic, sour beer, and mildew; the lamplight enhanced rather than alleviated the dark shabbiness of the place. Rough-faced men were playing fan-tan at a table with an ivory rake and clinking Chinese coins.

"I would rather end up at the bottom of the harbor than go in there," she said between gritted teeth. "It's absolutely sordid."

He forced her flush against the wall, his voice cracking with the effort it took to retain a semblance of self-control.

"The nearest hotel—the only hotel—on this island is two miles away, and I've had a hellish enough day because of you without tramping through a sea of mud so that your bloody sensibilities are not offended."

Li-Li Kong was sitting at the bar smoking perfumed cigarettes and squinting through her smoke to watch them. "I knew I get you in here one day, St. James," she said gleefully. "But I not guess you bringee you own girl. I only charge half price this time, yes?"

Scarlet warmth washed upward from Lorna's neck to her temples. A door slammed upstairs, and a man emerged tucking his flannel shirt into his trousers. The monotonous notes of a singsong girl floated in the fishy draft.

"You'll get me up those stairs fighting every step," she hissed at Ross.

He pushed his face close to hers. His hand shot up her arm, over the slope of her shoulder, and cradled the nape with his thumb resting on the erratic pulsebeat in her throat.

He exhaled slowly. "Because I believe this is for your own good," he said quietly, "I feel justified in what I'm about to do next."

Speechless with humiliation, she felt him scoop her up into his arms and start the jolting climb up the steep unlit stairwell with the throng in the taproom cheering him on.

In the hallway doors were opened to allow the occupants to observe them. Li-Li had come up a private staircase and led them to her most expensive room. It boasted flocked red wallpaper and scented oil lamps, a huge gilt-framed mirror, a bamboo bed with red silk curtains, and a real glass window that overlooked the harbor.

Ross dumped Lorna on the bed and left her there to seethe while he pulled off his boots and two coolies carried in a tin tub of hot water, soap, and perfumed towels. From the doorway Li-Li told Lorna:

"Men like nice-smelly girl. You washee first for Resident."

"The hell I will," Lorna snapped, ripping the red silk bed curtains together to shut herself off from the room.

The door closed finally, and she heard Ross undress, then lower himself into the bath with a deep sigh. She peeled off her muddied shoes and stockings, and lay fuming with her eyes fixed sightlessly on the crack in the curtains. She was too upset even to cry. Her thoughts wouldn't settle down long enough for her to control them. And, on top of everything, Ross treating her like this . . .

"Get undressed," he called to her in an authoritative voice. "You may bathe after I finish. When you are calmer, perhaps you'll care to listen to me."

She sat up, her heart pounding so hard she thought it would choke her. Perhaps she deserved his anger for disobeying him by going to the Chinese bazaar. God knew he'd been right about its dangers. But even so, she didn't deserve to be manhandled and publicly humiliated.

"I told you to get undressed."

He yanked the curtains apart with a force that set them trembling on their tarnished brass rings. His bare chest and black hair dripping, a towel around his waist, he caught her by the ankles and dragged her off the bed. She scrambled to her feet. Only the warning flicker of his eyes kept her from slapping his face. She didn't doubt he'd slap her back.

"Bengas can cause recurrent fever," he said. "Unless you wish to spend the next week sweating and hallucinating in a whore's bed, I suggest you do as I say."

She began to undress after a momentary hesitation, but only because the thought of remaining in this place horrified her, although, under other circumstances, she thought she might have enjoyed looking around a bit.

A coolie brought in a tray of liquor, sweetmeats, and spiced plums. When Lorna emerged from the bath, she found he had also taken her clothes to be laundered.

"Wear these," Ross said from the bed where he lay against the red silken pillows. He tossed her a flimsy emerald-green gauze blouse and sarong. "It's too distracting for me to talk when you look so appealing."

She glared at him, holding the towel to her chest, and ducked behind the curtains to put on the sarong. When she emerged, she found him standing before her, his face perplexed, his hands resting on his towel-draped hips.

"I'm sorry," he said quietly. "I hope you won't hate me after today."

He was not referring to bringing her to the brothel, and Lorna knew it. "I could never hate you," she said, realizing, despite herself, that it was true.

"Perhaps you should have a glass of wine."

She felt suddenly drained, resigned to whatever bad news he would share with her. "I think," she said, twisting her hands together, "that I would simply prefer that you hold me instead." Her eyes lifted to his. "Please, Ross, would you mind? I haven't the energy to quarrel anymore."

He pulled her against him and wrapped his arms around her waist, pressing his face into her hair. Resting her head on his damp brown chest, Lorna drew strange comfort from the strong, steady beat of his heart. His grip tightened, and she shivered, suddenly aware of how defenseless she was, not against his physical strength but against the yearning for him in her own soul.

"What—what was it you wanted to tell me?" she said between her teeth to hide the tremor in her voice.

He looked down at her. His eyes were like gray ice with flickers of flame in the pupils. "On second thought, I would rather the Rajah discussed it with you. I don't want to be the one to hurt you."

She turned away, unable to imagine what horrible discovery he had made and could not reveal. She felt lost.

"Lorna," he said softly.

He took her by the forearm and drew her back toward him. His kiss, urgent yet gentle, obliterated all thought from her mind. She hardly noticed him lifting her into his arms and pressing her down onto the bed. There was only his hot mouth claiming hers. Only his hands exploring, arousing, awakening the dark passions in her body, removing the sheer garments that were the only barrier to his avid lovemaking.

His fingers slipped between her legs and she stiffened, her eyes glazed as she tried to focus on his face. He was studying her with a look of intense concentration that made her shudder, and brought home to her how useless it was to deny him.

She turned her face into the pillow, forbidding herself to respond as his fingers quickened and the dull ache deepened into an exquisite torment. She could feel the sensations intensifying, the tension straining every nerve, and when he brought his mouth to her breasts, his moist lips encompassing the engorged peak, she reached for him, shuddering.

"Please . . . oh, please. . . ."

His tongue trailed down her belly. His voice shook as he spoke. "I want you to know that I did not bring you here for this. It's just that I cannot help myself. . . ."

She twined her fingers in the hair at his nape and waited in humiliated anticipation, her muscles shrinking at the burning sweetness of his lips at her sex. His tongue flickered against her, and she moaned. She could not help herself, either. She was past even trying.

It was a pleasure beyond belief, a bonding beyond the scope of understanding. And when he raised himself over her, their eyes met for a moment of searing intimacy. Suddenly, intuitively, Lorna understood that she would never feel this way about another man no matter what became of her relationship with Ross. Accepting that, unashamed and no longer afraid, she spread her legs to receive him.

The crashing fury of the rain and the wind and the sea faded into an angry murmur. There was no restraint in Ross now, only savage, driving need. Lorna surrendered to it with wanton joy, wrapping her legs around his hips, running her hands across the straining muscles of his back as the violent sweetness of climax overcame them. It was far easier to surrender to the passions of her body than to face the dark forces of doubt and suspicion that surrounded her.

"I had thought," he said in the breathless interlude that followed, "that after the first time, there could be no greater pleasure. I was wrong."

She said nothing. Her feelings were too powerful and profound to express.

He turned onto his side, his eyes bright as he searched her face. "You trust me with your body, Lorna. But do you trust me with your other secrets as well?"

She stared into his eyes, wishing that the closeness they had just shared would continue, but already it had started to fade as reality returned. "I trust you, yes," she said softly. "And I'd prefer that it was you who told me whatever you found out today."

"Is there anything you've kept from me about your father?"

"I've told you everything—" She hesitated, thinking of the contents of her father's letters, which had seemed so peculiar and illogical that she'd feared someone else might think him unbalanced. "Some of his letters were stolen from my trunk yesterday morning, but I don't suppose that means anything, does it? Are you going to tell me now what you found out?"

He looked down at his hands. He hadn't for a second believed she knew anything about the statue's theft, but she was so fiercely loyal to her father, she wasn't above protecting him. He admired her character. And he deeply resented Sir Arthur for involving her in something so dangerous.

"It's the White Tiger of Palleh," he said in resignation. "The statue that was stolen in Singapore before you arrived here."

She fought the sense of dread building inside her even before he began, and when he explained that it was believed that Pierre Lu Chan had been the mastermind behind the original theft, that possibly van Poole had worked for him, and that her father may have deceived them both by absconding with the priceless statue, she could only shake her head in angry denial.

"It's preposterous. How would someone like my father get involved in such a plot? And as for Kurt, you've always hated him. I *won't* believe it, Ross. And I won't let you stop the search.''

"I have no intention of stopping the search. No one can prove anything yet. The Rajah will agree with me, I'm certain, that you must be protected.''

She slid off the bed, a sheet wrapped around her, and went to the window, snatching up the discarded sarong and blouse from the floor on the way. That the man she'd revered all her life could involve himself—and her—

There is danger . . . The warning in her father's letter echoed dully inside her head.

She turned from the window, her eyes like glass. "My father has never cared a jot for wealth. His life was his writing.''

"And what did he write about? People who delved into dark, mystical worlds. People who were tempted by the devil and the promise of eternal life.''

"But those were characters he invented. He was complex, yes. He was eccentric. He was not always kind, but never evil. Nor greedy.''

"Why has van Poole taken such an avid interest in finding him?''

"If you confront Kurt with your flimsy theories, we'll never find my father.''

"We need van Poole, I concede that.'' He sat up, reaching for his towel. "But I'm not going to let the bastard out of my sight on Jalaka.''

"Perhaps you should not accompany us, after all,'' she said in a constrained voice. "You'd only arrest my father, anyway, wouldn't you, on the chance that your incredible accusations are true?''

His face darkened. "If I arrest him for *anything,* which I have no intention of doing, it would be for the way he's treated you.''

"I think my relationship with my father is my own affair. A daughter has a certain duty to her parents, which if you lived in a more civilized society, you might understand.''

"And where do you draw the line of duty, Lorna?" he challenged. "When you are allowed to live your own life?"

"My own life," she repeated. "I've made a mess of that, haven't I? Running from the arms of a man who betrayed me with my best friend into those of one who would go to any lengths to be rid of me?"

"To be rid of—"

He broke off as she finished struggling into the sarong and walked to the door. "What are you doing?" he said, his voice sharp with apprehension.

She refused to meet his gaze. "I have to think everything over by myself. To tell the truth, I find that when I'm with you, I cannot think at all. I—I know it's not your fault, Ross, but I can't help being disappointed in you."

"You promised you wouldn't hate me," he said slowly. "Do you think I wanted to hurt you?"

She glanced up at him briefly, her eyes shining with unshed tears. "No, but I can't help thinking you've derived some pleasure from showing me you were right, that I don't belong on your wretched little island."

She wrenched open the warped teakwood door, startling the small party of eavesdroppers gathered outside. Li-Li Kong pushed her way inside the room and stared at Ross's half-naked body with crude appraisal.

"You not leave without payee."

"Pay the woman for the room, Resident St. James," Lorna said quietly. "I think you got your money's worth."

She started down the staircase, and as Ross realized she was upset enough to actually leave, he rushed after her, clutching his towel and shouldering Li-Li Kong aside.

"Lorna, for the love of heaven. Where in God's name do you think you're going?" he called after her. "There's a bloody gale blowing, and you're dressed like a—"

He broke off, conscious of the amused snickers of the Malay-Chinese prostitutes in the hallway behind him.

"You go chase her, Tuan," one of them urged. "You looking very nice indeed in that towel."

He flushed and pounded down the stairs, swearing as Lorna reached the front door and tugged it open. Rain-laced wind gusted into the stuffy taproom, extinguishing the lamps and blowing empty bottles to the floor.

"Lorna!" he shouted, staring at her in disbelief.

She froze, defeated. Turning slowly toward him, she closed the door. "I'll wait down here until the rain stops," she said, sounding much more composed than she felt.

He nodded. He was so relieved that she had calmed down, he did not want to insist she return to the room. "I'll get dressed then. Are you sure you'll be all right?"

"I'll be fine."

She took an empty table in the taproom and ordered a brandy, sipping it for something to occupy her time. She was oblivious of the curious looks given her by the other guests. It couldn't be true. There had to be some other explanation. Her father could not have been involved in a plot to murder innocent people and steal a priceless relic. Van Poole, yes, but not Papa.

"Are you all right, my dear? I heard you had been found, but I had to see for myself."

She looked up into the concerned hazel eyes of Dr. Jason Parker. Raindrops clung to his beard and jacket. With a guilty start, Lorna realized he had hazarded the storm to find her.

"I had a very unpleasant experience, but I'm better now," she said with a tremulous smile.

"May I?" he asked, indicating the chair opposite her. At her nod, he sat, sighing heavily. "Ilse was convinced you had been murdered. I take full responsibility, of course. I should never have left you for even a moment."

"But how could you have known I'd be in any danger?"

"Well, after what happened to your father, I suppose I shouldn't have taken any chances."

Lorna sat in silence as he ordered a brandy for himself. "Did you know my father, Dr. Parker?"

"Please, it's Jason, and yes, I did know him. In fact, I believe I don't delude myself in claiming to have grown rather close to him. I greatly admired his work, and as I am an amateur painter, we discussed my illustrating his next novel. It was a brilliant story. Had you read it?"

She frowned, not really interested in discussing her father's writing. "I don't even know its title," she admitted, and realized suddenly that that was unusual in itself.

"It was *The Eden Flower*," he said proudly, sitting back in his chair. "I helped him choose it."

Lorna felt suddenly cold. "*The Eden Flower*. Do you remember what it was about?"

"I shouldn't want to give away the plot, but basically it concerned a man who'd lost a battle with the devil over the salvation of his soul. He chose wealth and immortality over goodness and God. The end had not been—"

She did not hear the remainder of his sentence. She was preoccupied with sorting out the fragments of information that suddenly bombarded her mind.

"You've gone quite white, Lorna," Jason said in alarm. "Is something wrong?"

"No, I'm just rather tired." She raised her gaze to his, feeling his sensitive eyes on her face. "You say you knew my father," she said carefully. "Did he confide in you at all . . . did he indicate something was bothering him?"

He hesitated slightly. "He did not confide this to me in words, you understand, but I was under the impression he was extremely disturbed about something shortly before he disappeared. He began suffering from a host of nervous complaints and said he had trouble sleeping at night."

"Did you confide any of this to either Ross or the Rajah?"

"Of course not. It had nothing to do with his disappearance and was strictly between Arthur and me."

But it had everything to do with his disappearance, she thought. Just as she knew intuitively that *The Eden Flower* was an allegorical recount of her father's involvement with the missing White Tiger. Her father had stolen the statue. Dear God, it was true.

"Ah, there's our Resident now," Jason said, inclining

his head to the tall dark-haired man making his way to the table.

Lorna glanced up at Ross and felt her heart lurch painfully against her breastbone. Even in her bewildered state, his mere appearance had the power to lift her spirits. Although his revelation about her father had rocked her faith, it was in Ross's arms that she longed to take comfort. But she wasn't ready to face him and admit he was right. Some desperate hope inside her kept insisting her father would yet be proven innocent.

Before Ross reached the table, a native entered the taproom and called to him that he had a message from the fort. Ross turned and exchanged a few words with the messenger before finally making his way to the table.

"I'm needed at the cove," he said, nodding a greeting to Jason but staring down at Lorna, who had lowered her gaze to the table. "A distressed ship has been sighted at sea."

Lorna could not resist looking up at him. "I suppose it's too much to hope that Pierre Lu Chan was drowned in his junk."

"He's too familiar with our numerous inlets not to have taken refuge until the weather clears," Ross said. "If I had the manpower and resources, I'd go after him myself. Jason, do you think you could see Lorna home? I'd rather not risk taking her out in the rain."

"I should say not," the doctor answered stoutly. "Don't worry, Ross. I won't lose sight of her again."

"All right then. Lorna—" Ross laid his hand on her shoulder and she stiffened, afraid that if she did not cling to her fading anger she would lose control in front of everyone.

"Good-bye, Ross," she said remotely. "I'm sorry I was so much trouble today."

She turned to Dr. Parker until Ross left the taproom. Jason watched her steadily, his hazel eyes keen. "Well, if I hadn't seen it myself, I'd not have believed it."

"Believed what?" she said, glancing up just in time to

see Ross pass by the taproom window, rain pelting his head.

"That Ross has begun to act like a human being again. I don't think I've ever seen so much emotion on his face since . . . well, for years, anyway."

Lorna did not reply. It was easy to see why Ilse was fighting an attraction to the kind and sensitive doctor, and why her father had felt able to confide in him. For her own part, she wished she could resolve the conflict between what she had learned today about the Sir Arthur Fairfield who had lived on this island and the thoughtless but brilliant man she knew as her father.

Chapter 18

Her uncle did not believe a word of it when she confronted him with Ross's findings about her father early that same evening. "It's an outrage, Lorna," he said as he paced the parlor floor in indignation. "To think my brother would gad about chopping off heads and pinching ancient relics. Only someone who has himself lived among the heathens would suggest such a thing."

"Ross was simply repeating what Colonel Moody told him," Lorna said, surprised to find herself rushing to Ross's defense.

" 'Ross,' is it?" Richard glared at her across the room. "Is it 'Ross' who has you doubting your father's integrity and going about clad in that—that—"

"Sarong," Ilse said from the chair where she sat embroidering lilies on a linen tablecloth. "And Ross's story really does sound quite incredible, Lorna. From what I've heard of your father, he was a quiet man."

"We cannot go on pretending that his disappearance was not suspicious," Lorna said coolly. "If he's involved in the theft, I need to know."

"*If* he's involved," Richard said with emphasis. "Would you judge your own father guilty on circumstantial evidence and rumors while he is unable to defend himself?"

"No," Lorna said, her mouth compressed. "Of course not."

"Then I suggest you begin shunning the company of

Resident St. James, if this is an example of his influence. You'll have a hard enough time explaining to Spencer why you left him in the lurch without having this unfortunate relationship on your conscience.''

For a moment Lorna could not answer for the anger that threatened to choke her. ''Uncle Richard,'' she said between her teeth, ''it is not *my* conscience that is in question where Spencer is concerned—''

He waved his hand dismissively. ''Oh, you're referring to his little mistake with Emily. Well, men will be men, my dear, and it's better he got his philandering out of his system before he marries you.''

''I am *not* marrying Spencer.''

''Yes, you are. I've already written him explaining you lost your temper and deeply regret the embarrassment your abrupt leavetaking caused him. I reassured him the engagement is still in effect, if he can be so patient as to wait—''

''Then I shall write him to the contrary tomorrow,'' she said furiously.

Richard's face fell. ''For God's sake, Lorna, don't you realize I'm doing this for you? A man of Spencer's lineage doesn't come along every day.''

''Of his wealth, you mean.''

''All right. Is there anything wrong with that? Surely you don't want to pinch pennies all your life the way Julia and I have done? Would you have your children work in a factory as I was forced to as a lad to help support your father's education?''

Lorna turned away. She had always suspected Uncle Richard resented her father's success. Now she was sure of it.

''I'm not discussing starting a family, Uncle Richard.''

''No? Then you would encourage an improper relationship with a man you hardly know in favor of Lord Kirkham?''

''If my father were here, I'd wager he'd support me.''

Richard's shoulders stiffened. ''It would be the only time

in his selfish life that he has. Giving you license to ruin your future is scarcely an act of love, my girl.''

"Spencer is not the only man of means in the world," she said tightly.

Richard gave her a sad smile. "You refer to the Resident again, heir to this pagan paradise and all it entails? Yes, he has wealth, I suppose, but has he offered to share it with you? Has he asked you to marry him? Spencer has, Lorna. Do you long for a dream or a reality?''

Ilse stood up, her plump face anxious. "I think you've both had a bad fright today. We all have, and we're not at our best. You will have a different perspective in the morning, Lorna."

Lorna went to the window and drew aside the curtain. The rain had stopped, but the wind seemed to be rising again. "When is Kurt supposed to return?"

"Not for another day or so. Now, are you going up to bed or not?"

"No," Lorna murmured. "I'll have a cup of tea first."

"I'm coming up," Richard said, giving Lorna a last rueful look. "I've aged ten years today."

Lorna was on her way to the kitchen to brew some tea when a quiet knock sounded at the front door. Her initial thought was to summon the guards. But as they were stationed directly outside, she decided it must be someone known to them.

"Ross?" she said, her face pressed to the heavy iron-wood panel.

"It's Wayne Tunridge, Miss Fairfield."

She unbolted and opened the door, looking up into the coarse but pleasant face of the Assistant Resident. "Is something wrong?"

"No, nothing to be alarmed about." He kept his eyes pinned to her face; he was clearly pretending not to notice the native costume she'd neglected to change. It felt so loose and comfortable, Lorna had forgotten herself that she still wore it.

"Ross wanted me to make sure you were safely at home."

And he didn't want to come himself, Lorna thought. Not that she blamed him, after the fuss she'd caused today.

"Where is he now?"

"At the cove. I'm on my way back there now with our supper." He indicated the tiny canvas sack under his arm.

"What is it?"

"Biscuits and bananas."

"I can do better than that. Wait inside until I return from the kitchen."

She snatched up her bonnet and her uncle's worn mohair jacket from the hallstand on her way and returned as promised three minutes later with a cloth-covered basket.

"I'm ready, Mr. Tunridge."

"Ready?" he said in confusion, jumping up from the bottom of the stairs where he had perched. "Ready for what?"

"To take Ross his supper."

"Oh, no, I don't think—I mean, he wouldn't—"

"Please, Mr. Tunridge. I'm afraid he and I parted on awkward terms earlier. I'd like a chance to mend our differences."

He raked a hand through his sandy windblown hair. "That explains his foul humor. Not that Ross is the cheeriest companion to begin with."

"Then you will take me with you?"

"I shouldn't, miss. It's frightfully windy."

"Of all the dangers on this island, the wind is the one I least fear."

He nodded grimly. "I'd have to agree with you about that. And I think—I believe he'd be glad to see you."

From the crevice in the cave Ross watched her struggling up the hillside in the wind. He should have been furious that she'd come out again in this weather. Instead, he felt only a ridiculous relief that he was going to see her again.

He lowered the telescope. The wind lashed his face until his eyes watered, but he was aware of only an illogical urge to run down to meet her. If she'd been alone, he would have done just that. He'd been haunted all evening by the memory of the lost look on her face when he'd been forced to leave her in the taproom. Not to mention the hurt he'd reluctantly inflicted on her by revealing what he'd learned about Sir Arthur.

He jumped down from the boulder, smoothing his hair back from his face. He had relived every moment of their afternoon together repeatedly in his mind since then. And he had come to only one conclusion.

He was obsessed with her. Besotted. There could be no other explanation for his behavior, for his inability to function normally since her arrival.

He went to the mouth of the cave, leaning against the damp limestone wall. She looked absurdly beautiful in the incongruous combination of oversized mohair jacket and gauze sarong.

Lorna approached him cautiously, glancing back to Wayne with his open grin and then to Ross's face, which looked shadowed and fierce in the dimness that was relieved only by a small fire at the back of the cave.

"I've brought you some supper," she said, taking the basket from Wayne's arm.

"That was kind of you," Ross said stiffly.

For a moment no one said anything. Wayne hovered at the entrance of the cave, as if uncertain whether to leave or stay. Lorna pulled her jacket together at her throat and glanced over her shoulder at the restless sea.

"You should not have come out in this weather," Ross said roughly. "Wayne, I thought you had more sense."

"I insisted," Lorna said, a touch of defiance in her voice.

She pulled off her bonnet. Her hair fell in glinting red-gold waves to her waist. Wayne watched her with open approval. Ross glanced away, his face unreadable.

"It's almost ten o'clock," Wayne said with an enormous, obviously feigned yawn. "I've a long hike back to the fort."

Ross did not move as Wayne began collecting his gear. "You're welcome to stay in the sulap with Kana if you prefer."

The other man nodded. "Perhaps I will."

"Won't you take some meat pie or almond cake, Mr. Tunridge?" Lorna asked Wayne as he passed. "Both freshly baked today."

"No, thanks, miss. I've got my biscuits and bananas. Any more sign of that ship, Ross?"

"She anchored safely in an inlet near the istana."

"Not an Illanuan warship?" Lorna said as Wayne made his way outside.

Ross came forward until he stood directly before her. "No." He stared steadily at her. "Are you still upset?"

"Yes, but not with you. And I still hope to prove my father's innocence. Even though . . ." She looked into his eyes and knew then that there could be no secrets between them. She had to trust him completely. If there was one thing she believed in, it was Ross's integrity.

He listened without comment as she told him about her father's letters, about the danger he had alluded to, the fact that someone thought the missives valuable enough to steal. Afterward, they sat down on the blanket together to share the savory meat pie and bottle of wine she had brought from the house. There was a cake for later.

"I don't want van Poole anywhere near you," he said flatly. "There are other guides we could hire for the expedition."

"But there aren't. Not as good as the shikari. Anyway, if it's the statue he's after—and I'm convinced he has an idea where it is—and if that leads up to Papa, then I must confess, I don't really care. You can do whatever you like to Kurt, *after* we find my father."

"Van Poole must believe he has the statue," Ross thought aloud. "I suppose that's where the link with the Agung-Mani comes in too. Assuming that the statue has deep religious significance for them in particular, then they must be terrified that in searching for your father, you and Kurt will find their Tiger. God only knows what powers they believe it possesses.''

Lorna took a sip of the wine he had uncorked and poured into two glasses. ''My father won't be prosecuted, will he? The authorities won't be able to put him away?''

''I'll speak with the Rajah about it in the morning. But if I know Uncle Charles, he'll go to any lengths to protect your father.''

''You don't know how much that means to me.''

''I wish I could do more to help.''

The way he watched her, his gray eyes half hooded and gleaming in the firelight, made her suddenly aware of how sensitive her body had become to his presence. The memory of his hands on her skin made her nerve endings tingle with anticipation. She ached for him, for surcease from the bewildering longings only he could cause and alleviate. Her blood felt hot, surging through her veins. She bit down hard on her lower lip and looked into the fire. She wished he did not have this power over her.

''I should go back to the house,'' she murmured. ''My uncle and I had a dreadful row.''

''Over your father?''

''Yes. And . . . you.''

''So I come in a sad second to Lord Splendid,'' he said with a dark smile.

She secured her glass in the sand. ''Something like that.''

He reached out and caught her wrist, drawing her steadily closer to him. ''Where do I rank with you?''

She felt the effects of his touch throughout her entire body.

''Ross,'' she whispered, placing her free hand on his shoulder. His muscles tautened at the contact, and then he reached up, removing her hand so that he could begin unbuttoning his royal blue regulation jacket.

"Ross," she whispered again, the single word stark with unconscious appeal.

"You shouldn't touch me like that if you aren't prepared to pay the consequences. It seems to be beyond my capability to resist you."

She sank back onto her heels, watching in a daze of anticipation laced with anxiety as he pulled off his white shirt, revealing the sunbronzed musculature of his chest. She would be lying to herself if she didn't admit she had known this might happen again tonight . . . that she had wanted it to.

"I—I came because I wanted to let you know I do not resent you for suspecting my father."

"I hoped," he said, his voice deep, "that you came because you are as powerless to put me out of your mind as I am you."

He drew her onto the blanket beside him, kissing her mouth, her throat, his hands exploring her body until she began to tremble with excitement. Deftly he removed the large mohair jacket and sarong she wore, covering her body with his as she shivered at the onslaught of damp air against her skin.

"I wish I'd known earlier you were coming," he whispered. "I would have sent Kana and Tunridge inland so we could stay at the sulap."

She gripped his shoulders, pressing her face into his chest. She was glad that their lovemaking had been spontaneous and not premeditated. She could not bear to think Ross was interested only in seducing her, although her uncle surely believed that.

She quivered as he kissed her, his tongue flicking against the corners of her mouth. Caught up in her own desire, she had not realized he was naked until the hard length of his sex brushed her inner thigh. The sensation filled her with the shameless urge to spread her legs to receive him.

"I thought—I thought you had the watch," she said, clinging to the last measure of reason she possessed.

"Umm. I do. . . . But the entire Illanun fleet could

wash up on shore right now and I wouldn't care.'' He hooked his ankle around hers, entwining their bare legs and lowering his head to kiss her again.

''If they—''

She fell silent with a sharp intake of breath as his mouth grazed her neck and slipped down to encompass the sensitive crest of her breast. At the same time his hand eased around her hip to caress her belly, his fingers easing ever lower until they dipped into the honeyed warmth between her legs. She tensed, relaxing gradually as his insistent manipulations overcame her inhibitions.

He teased her until he coaxed from her the response he desired, the total surrender that signified she was his completely. When the sensations became too intense, she cried out his name and twisted as if to escape him. He caught her by the shoulders and gently eased her back down beneath him, at the same time kissing her hard on the mouth and driving himself deep inside her. She met him with unthinking abandon, her back arching to cushion him, absorb him, while her heart yearned to be joined with his as closely as their bodies were. All her uncertainties over the wisdom of their relationship receded as the delight he offered deepened into rapture.

There was a strange peace to be found in their passion. There was an emotional appeal in Ross, a lowering of his guard and a deep vulnerability that he did not let show at any other time. Only in this mindless splendor did he seem to escape the internal conflicts that would bind him.

They rocked together in their own private rhythm until that final, frenzied moment when they fell over the precipice and strained in breathless ecstasy. Ross froze, groaning, collapsing onto his side and drawing Lorna tightly against his damp, pulsing body while she struggled to regain her breath, recovering from the sweet devastation of their mating. She felt drowsy, replete, satisfied, her mind lulled.

The fire had burned down to feeble embers that cast the cave into smoky darkness. A humid draft swirled around their perspiring bodies, still clasped in each other's arms. Lorna shivered, huddling closer to Ross. With a sigh, he stirred and reluctantly released her to put on his trousers and rebuild the fire.

"Come sit with me," he said.

She dressed and went to his side. He put his arm around her, hugging her close, pressing his face into her hair, which smelled fragrantly of roses, smoke, and sea air. "You go against your uncle's wishes in seeing me," he said quietly.

She felt depressed at the reminder of the ugly argument with Uncle Richard. "Yes."

"You were on the verge of marrying another man not so long ago. How can you be sure your love will not be renewed when you see him again?"

She brushed a patch of damp sand from her ankles. "I don't think that what Spencer and I shared was love exactly."

He gave her a curious look. "Was it physical attraction?"

"Oh, no. Affection, perhaps, and I think I was rather a challenge to him because I wasn't particularly impressed by his background. I also think—" She sighed, seemingly preoccupied in rearranging the folds of her sarong. "I think I might have been so eager to be married, I allowed him to talk me into it against my better judgment."

"You surely weren't that anxious to be somebody's wife?"

"It wasn't that way at all," she said quickly, avoiding his eyes. "I rather think I just . . . I just wanted a life of my own."

"To escape your father, you mean?"

"Oh, no." She looked mortified. "It is my duty to care for him, but I . . ." Her voice faded to a whisper. Could Ross be right? She couldn't believe he was drawing such private thoughts out of her, thoughts she was scarcely aware of herself. She shouldn't be surprised, after the intimate act of their lovemaking, but still she was.

He threw dry kindling onto the fire. "Then you will return to London with your father, assuming we find him."

She couldn't bear to think of it. She couldn't imagine surrendering the freedom she had here for conformity and congested streets, to living her father's life and not her own. To dying inside in their cluttered house where she could never steal a moment for herself, what with her aunt and uncle, Papa, and his disruptive friends dropping in. She would make endless cups of tea and grow old running her father's errands. The hidden facets of her own character that she'd begun to discover on this island would slowly sink back down under the weight of convention and obligation.

She frowned and drew her knees up to her chest, her face revealing nothing of her despair. Ross could never know how deeply it hurt her that he even suggested she leave the island. Was he hinting he wanted to be rid of her? The thought left a bitter taste in her mouth. She'd hoped, assumed, that after becoming intimate with him, he would ask her to stay.

"I don't know where I'll go," she said after several more moments had passed. "Not to London, if I have a choice."

"Where then? Hampshire—that's where you were raised, isn't it? Your father still owns the estate."

"It's leased out. Papa does not make all that much money. He might—he might even decide to stay here and finish his book."

"And then it's off again around the world?"

"Not for me. I'd rather try to convince him to remain here permanently and make a go of the plantation."

He looked up in surprise. "What would you do if he decided to stay?"

"I'm not sure."

"If I were a young woman of your background, I would not wish to live here. The risks are too high."

"There are risks everywhere, Ross. I don't think Kali Simpang has a monopoly on tragedy." She rubbed her hands together and held them out to the fire. He seemed to have forgotten it was *his* suggestion that she and her father work to revive the plantation. Obviously she had read more into the remark than he had intended.

"You like the island, don't you, Lorna?" he asked her unexpectedly.

"I adore it." She glanced up at his face. "I don't think there could be a more fascinating place on earth. Discounting the Agung-Mani and headhunting pirates, of course."

"Both of which I do not intend to allow to threaten the island for much longer." He smiled at her, his face reflective. "You've not seen either me or Kali Simpang at our best."

She thought Ross was perfect as he was, but she did not say so.

They talked about Ross's hopes for the island until the fire died down again. For the first time he mentioned that he had a sister who was a nun in Ireland and a brother who was a barrister in London. He spoke not a word of his father, but he did say his mother had died not long ago, and he regretted that he'd learned she was ill too late to be at her side.

Lorna listened in rapt silence, aware that he was sharing a private part of himself with her for the first time. Then as their conversation tapered off, he took her into his arms. "I wish you could stay with me all night," he whispered. "It doesn't seem right to make love to you and then to have to let you go."

She burrowed into his chest, slipping back with him upon the blanket. But instead of making love to her, he fell into a restless sleep, his head cradled on her breast, and Lorna found a deep contentment in simply holding him in her arms.

She closed her eyes. She slept, then awakened with Ross to hear that the wind had subsided, its whisper intermingling with the nearby pealing of a bell and the throbbing beat of the kulkul drums.

"What does it mean?" she whispered, easing out from under Ross.

"It's midnight. Kana rings out the time from the sulap when I'm alone at the cove."

"Midnight," she said, aghast.

"I'll take you back to the house. I'd no idea I'd slept so long."

"You never finished your supper."

"I'll eat when I return. Or if your uncle is waiting for you, perhaps I won't come back at all," he joked grimly.

She did not want to leave him. Soon enough they'd begin the search for her father, and the strain of the journey might destroy their fragile relationship. And when they found Papa, there would be no more excuses for Ross to devote his time to her. . . .

They clambered down the cliff together and hurried along the beach. Ross left her inside the plantation grounds with a lingering kiss. He ran all the way back to the cove, the wind buffeting his body and chasing away the warm remembrance of lying with Lorna. It was the first time he had ever slept through a watch.

He ran faster, his feet splashing through the surf, moonlight illuminating the wet sand. He ran as if to escape the fearful joy that filled him. He ran as if he could leave behind with Lorna all the unsettling emotions she made him feel.

He scaled the summit of the cliff and stared inland across the island that soon would be his to protect. As always the sight of its wild beauty, the dark mountains etched against the moonlight, the silver sea foam that surrounded it, aroused in him a fierce pride. Into this land he had poured his passion and his pain. When he'd lost his family, Kali Simpang had embraced him. But suddenly, inexplicably, it was not enough to still the unresolved sadness inside him . . . the longings he had managed to suppress.

His restlessness increased as the familiar crooning of the wind and sea no longer brought him peace. Returning to the cave, he stared at the imprint Lorna had left upon his blanket—the imprint of their connected bodies. When he was with her he felt more content and alive than at any other time. How was she able to open up that part of himself he kept safely locked away?

He flung himself down on the blanket, deliberately obliterating the outline of their bodies. In his mind he reviewed all the work that awaited him in the morning, the village rounds, the court case he would testify at, the dramshop license to revoke. To his frustration the mental ritual did not help.

Springing to his feet, he walked to the mouth of the cave. With the moonlight illuminating the sand he stood upon, he breathed deeply and focused on the *tan tien*, the inner psychic force located in the solar plexus. As energy from this center flowed into his body, he began to move with the studied precision of a T'ai Chi Ch'uan practitioner. His spine straight, his limbs curved, he performed the Thirteen Forms, moving his arms like a fan before his face, twisting his trunk. These same movements could be used for self-defense, but tonight he wanted only the utter mental absorption the discipline required.

In this he failed. He could not gain control of his mind. His body felt rigid and ungraceful. The inner emptiness required of a Taoist master eluded him.

He lowered his hands and gazed down at the beach. But it was not the restless waves he saw. It was the memory of Lorna in all the various moods that he was learning were part of her. And he realized that through her he was starting to live again.

Lorna crept through the darkened house like a burglar, wincing at every creak of the stairs and still blushing over the knowing smile the young Hindu guard outside had given her. It wasn't *that* obvious, was it, that she had just made passionate love? Perhaps the warm glow she felt whenever she was with Ross radiated to others as well.

She breathed a relieved sigh when she reached her bedroom and quietly closed the door behind her. The first thing she noticed was that her bed had been turned down and a glass of papaya nectar had been left on the bedstand.

Ilse, she thought gratefully. The woman could not control her mothering instincts. Lorna hoped Kurt had not involved her in his crimes.

The second thing that attracted her attention was the breeze stirring the curtains of the veranda door. Hadn't she closed that door during the rain?

Her heart stopped as a shadow moved behind the curtains. She knew with cold dread that it was not Mahomet this time.

She whirled toward the door to the hall, but before she could reach it, a tunic-clad figure sprang out to grasp her, clamping a hand over her mouth.

"This will be painless, Miss Fairfield," he whispered in her ear. "As long as you cooperate."

The voice had a hint of a Chinese accent, but sounded far younger than Pierre Lu Chan. One of his henchmen, perhaps.

"If you scream," he continued, "I shall have to use this." He passed a scrolled dagger before her face with his free hand. "Do you understand?"

Pulse pounding, she nodded. He removed his deceptively delicate-looking fingers from her mouth and nudged her toward the nightstand.

"Drink the contents of the glass," he instructed her quietly. "Death will be swift and painless."

Unthinkingly she turned to hazard a glimpse at his face. He looked young, perhaps only seventeen, with straight medium-length black hair, regular features, and unfeeling black eyes. The resemblance to his mother was striking.

"You are Chiang's son," she whispered. "Kao."

"Yes."

"And you expect me to commit suicide because your mother was put in prison?"

"My mother means nothing." He picked up the glass and held it to her lips. The thick sweet nectar sloshed to the rim of the glass. "If you had not interfered with the will of the gods, we would have let you go."

"The will of the gods?"

A centimeter at a time, she eased a hand behind her back and felt along the nightstand. Nothing . . . a comb, which was useless. Stall, she thought. Ilse or Uncle Richard might hear them. Or the guards. . . .

"What—what exactly is the will of the gods?" She scarcely knew what she was saying. Her fingers closed around the neck of a cut-glass crystal bottle. The cork refused to budge.

"The will of the god of death is that the White Tiger remain where it was created to celebrate his supremacy on earth," Kao replied, his young face grave and chilling. "If the statue is removed from its shrine, the wrath of Tok Belang will be fearful and many lives will be claimed. You do not wish to be the cause of countless deaths, Miss Fairfield?"

She flung the perfume bottle in his face, having at last managed to free the cork. He threw up the hand in which he held the dagger, giving an angry cry. The scent of roses sweetened the air as Lorna came to life, shoving him hard into the mosquito netting.

"Ilse! Uncle Richard!" she shouted at the closed door, her skin turning cold when the warped jamb prevented her escape. A flash of silver caught her eye. She pried the door open just as Kao threw the dagger toward her back. It flew above her shoulder and out over the stairwell, clattering with a hollow echo on the wooden steps below.

"Lorna!" Ilse ran down the hall toward her, her rumpled hair spilling over the lace collar of her nightdress. She had a pistol in her hand and seemed prepared to use it. As she reached Lorna, Richard appeared, looking bewildered by the commotion.

"What is it?" Instinctively he had turned toward Lorna's opened door.

"Agung-Mani," she said, placing her hand on his arm as he started for the door. "No, Uncle Richard—"

He took the pistol Ilse passed him, his face set grimly as he rushed into the room. Only now beginning to regain a semblance of reason, Lorna stared after him and then cried, "No, Uncle Richard, you mustn't shoot him! He might know something that can lead us to Papa." She didn't reveal that Kao had spoken of the White Tiger, conscious of Ilse's presence and that she would carry the information back to Kurt. For as long as possible, Lorna intended to pretend ignorance of the connection between her father and the statue.

"Richard!" Ilse joined Lorna in a race for the room. "Don't do anything until the guards come!"

Even as she spoke, two guards were running up the stairs, muskets gleaming in the darkness. They rushed past the two women into Lorna's room, ordering them to wait downstairs. But when they didn't emerge after a reasonable time, and Lorna heard her uncle talking in a low, continued voice, she realized that the situation must be under control.

"Is—is everything all right, Uncle Richard?"

He emerged from the room moments later. "It's over."

"Over?" She glanced toward the open door. "He got away. . . ."

His face gray, he shook his head. "He killed himself. Drank some kind of poison while the guards were questioning him at gunpoint. They said he was the chief executioner for the Agung-Mani. I'm afraid we didn't have a chance to ask him about Arthur."

Ilse moved behind Lorna, slipping an arm around her waist. "Did he say anything to you, Lorna? Anything out of the ordinary that might tell us why he wanted to hurt you?"

Lorna turned her head. In the moonlight Ilse so resembled Kurt that Lorna unthinkingly pulled away.

"I have no idea what he wanted, Ilse. No idea at all."

Her voice must have sounded more guarded than she intended, for Ilse backed away, glancing once at Richard.

"Of course you don't," she said soothingly. "These madmen don't need an excuse to kill."

"It was Chiang's son," Lorna said.

"Chiang?" Ilse repeated with a frown. Then, "Oh, the Chinese amah. Well, that explains it. Revenge for his mother's imprisonment."

Lorna could not return to her room after that, sleeping instead in the spare bedchamber with a guard posted at the door. Nervous at every sound, she paced before the bed, head bowed. It did not seem possible that only a few hours ago she had lain in Ross's arms, restored by his quiet strength. She wished for his presence now, for the security she knew only when she was with him.

At Lorna's request, the attack upon her life was not discussed at the supper party the Rajah gave the following evening. Furious that Kao had gained entrance to the house, Ross had dismissed the two guards who'd been on duty then and replaced them with a pair he himself handpicked. Aside from the fact that Lorna hadn't been harmed, the only positive aspect of the incident was that the power of the Agung-Mani on the island had been seriously weakened. Adherents were rumored to be returning to either their Hindu or animistic worship, now that the merciless Kao would not appear in the dead of night to select a sacrificial victim from the village.

Kurt had returned earlier in the day. He exuded so much confidence over the upcoming expedition that Lorna's anxiety momentarily abated as her hopes for finding her father were rejuvenated. A captain and ship had been found. The weather was stable. The damaged supplies had been replaced—at Kurt's expense. They would leave in two days.

And all Kurt said when he heard of Lorna's terrifying experience with Kao was, "Well done, Lorna. You're a survivor. I am impressed, I have to admit."

The guests strolled in the Rajah's garden to walk off their overindulgence at supper, enjoying the tropical pink-peach sunset. Ross was surly and withdrawn, snapping at the captain of the guards for the laxity of his men in allowing Kao to gain illicit entry to the plantation house. He barely spoke to Lorna, so that she might have assumed his tender passion of the previous evening had been an illusion. He refused to be drawn into small conversation. His behavior reminded her of the warning he had once given her, that he had forgotten the customs of polite society and had never much abided by them in the first place.

She might have been more worried by his behavior had she not begun to understand that it was in Ross's character to turn inward when he was upset.

"We leave the day after tomorrow," Kurt said. They had stopped to watch the antics of a pair of monkeys in a lantana tree. "You'll be glad to get rid of us, eh, St. James?"

Ross made no response, leaving the group without excusing himself to stand alone across the garden.

"Ross is coming with us," Lorna said.

"What for?" Kurt asked negligently. "I've hired more than enough native carriers for our protection. The diligent Resident can get on with the work we've interrupted."

The Rajah strolled forward to join their discussion. "Ross has been officially assigned to investigate Sir Arthur's disappearance, Mr. van Poole. You'll have to put up with him, I'm afraid."

"Officially?" Kurt said, his lips tightening. "But this is a private expedition."

"I'm not at liberty to discuss the nature of his assignment," the Rajah said with an evasive smile. "But Mulak is a government guide—the natives you have commissioned are under my dominion—and if you wish to employ their services, then Mr. St. James must be part of the package. Now if you'll excuse me, I must continue my walk—just to please my physician."

Lorna stared at Ross across the garden and wondered how much he had overheard of the conversation. If she thought for a moment that she and Ross could locate her father without Kurt's help, she would have dismissed him on the spot. But the mission would be dangerous enough even with van Poole's skills to guide them. She had not found a chance yet to talk with Ross about Kao's reference to the White Tiger.

"The Rajah seems fond of you, Lorna," Richard commented as he approached her to watch Charles's frail figure disappear amidst the trees. "There must be some way to advise him to keep St. James here on the island."

Lorna turned to face her uncle. He looked worried and unwell. She felt a flash of pity to think his concern for her and her father was causing him such obvious emotional distress. He was a bit of a buffoon, she knew, and hopelessly narrow-minded, but he had bailed Papa out of many wretched predicaments, loaning out his modest income when there was no chance at all her father would ever repay him, sending Lorna gifts of clothing when she outgrew her own rather meager wardrobe and Papa had neglected to notice her obvious needs. It was the Uncle Richards of the world, the middle-class plodders, the souls weighted down with their sense of responsibility, who enabled the eccentrics like her father to pursue their artistic visions.

She owed Uncle Richard respect, if nothing else. She felt for him a poignant fondness that made his faults easier to overlook.

"It was my idea that Ross accompany us in the first place," she said. "I don't understand why you should object. You'll be with us the entire time."

He considered her solemnly for a moment. "I received a packet of letters from Julia yesterday, mailed shortly after we left."

"Papa's letters?" she asked, brightening.

"Spencer's letters. There are three for you, and one was addressed to me. His father is in very ill health, Lorna. You're giving up the heir to an earldom for a—a pagan prince."

"Not here, Uncle Richard," she said in a tight voice.

She glanced around again at Ross, but he had left the garden.

Richard's voice dropped to an unpleasant whisper. "It's clear I can't get through to you, but since you and the Rajah have struck up such a friendship, perhaps you'll listen to him."

"About what?"

"Just ask him about the marriage he's arranging for his nephew, Lorna, the match the Ranee is working on between Ross and her own niece, who happens to be a Balinese princess."

Lorna's face betrayed no reaction even though inside it seemed she was a mass of roiling emotions. Ross, engaged? She couldn't imagine him leading such a double life, devoting his attention to her while planning to make a life with an exotic bride. She could not believe it. She wouldn't until Ross himself confirmed the news, and if he did . . . She raised her head, aware of a sharp insupportable pain in her breast.

"Ask Resident St. James yourself," Richard said. "Obviously he hasn't seen fit to enlighten you, though even the istana servants are talking of little else."

"Is that where you heard this—from the gossip of servants?" she asked, feeling an inordinate relief.

"It was from Madame Corneille."

"I'll ask Ross myself."

Richard glanced around. "You'll have to wait until he shows up again then. He's taken it upon himself to disappear without making the requisite excuses. He's not the most social creature, is he?"

"Has it occurred to you that he might have been called away on some urgent matter?"

"What occurs to me is that you defend him at every turn," he said with a sigh. "I'm afraid you're even more deeply involved with him than I realized."

So am I, Lorna thought, turning instinctively to stare at the spot where she had last seen Ross standing in the fading sunlight. And it did not seem she could do anything to help herself.

Ross came to the plantation house after supper, finding Lorna alone in the garden with Mahomet. She watched him walking between the overgrowth of shrubbery and wondered how he could have ever kept such a secret from her as an engagement to another woman. And then he reached her, his gray eyes warm and guileless, and she realized she couldn't judge him on the basis of a rumor.

They walked to the beach, the guards insisting they must follow and Ross nodding his assent.

Lorna stood with her bare feet bathed by the warm tropical water, her head leaning back against Ross's chest. The moonlight glimmered on the glossy waves that rolled ashore. The clear ocean teemed with the phosphorescence of microscopic creatures. It was a beautiful night, the sky encrusted with bright blue stars, the air warm and moist.

"Well," Ross said, turning to regard her. "You've gotten everything you wanted."

She looked at him in confusion. "What do you mean?"

"The expedition. Everything is working out the way you wanted, isn't it?"

"Not exactly." But she might have been happy, she thought, if her uncle had not managed to half convince her the relationship with Ross would end up hurting her. "Ross . . . I heard something very disturbing today."

"About your father?"

"About you." His head lifted a fraction of an inch, a gesture that seemed to Lorna to be defensive. "I heard you were engaged to a Balinese princess."

She waited for what seemed forever for him to speak, and then he merely shrugged, looking relieved, and said, "Is that all?"

"All?" She swallowed to allow herself a moment to regain her full emotional equilibrium. "You're saying there's no truth to it then?"

"The truth is that my uncle has been halfheartedly

making marital overtures to her for almost a year—just to please Amayli.''

"And you agreed to it?"

"I agreed to nothing."

"I see." She forced her gaze out to the water, feeling the wavelets soak the hem of her dress.

"Now I find that I am disturbed," Ross said, studying her profile.

She cast him a sidelong glance. "Over what?"

"Over the fact that you believe I could hide something as important as an engagement from you. Wouldn't that make me rather coldhearted?"

"We've never discussed your personal life in detail."

"There will be time for that when we come back." He held out his hands to her, his voice deep with promise as the waves swept around them. "Won't there, Lorna?"

"Yes." She leaned into him instinctively. "Oh, yes. . . ."

For a moment he lowered his head, and she thought he would kiss her. Then he looked up sharply, his gaze swinging to the two guards who flanked them on the beach. Their presence was a somber reminder of the dangers they had already encountered and would no doubt face when they began the voyage to Jalaka the day after tomorrow.

"I'll walk you back home," he said reluctantly. "Your uncle will wonder where you are."

Richard was, in fact, awaiting them in the garden when they returned. One look at his unsmiling face was enough to alert Lorna there would be a scene.

"I thought you were going to bed early tonight, Uncle Richard." She began to edge away from Ross, but he would not release her hand, or try to hide from her uncle the fact that he was holding it.

"I want a word with Mr. St. James first, please," Richard said, his tone cold.

"Not tonight," Lorna said. "We've too much to do."

"Tonight is fine." Ross released her hand. "Go inside, Lorna."

She left the two men reluctantly, glancing back over her shoulder into the garden and praying that her uncle would do nothing to humiliate her or to destroy the closeness she and Ross had begun to share.

"You really should go to bed, you know," Ross told Richard when they were alone. "The voyage to Jalaka is nothing like crossing the English Channel."

Richard's face reddened. "Incivility is second nature to you, isn't it? You think nothing of destroying a young girl's virtue and encouraging her to defy her family."

Ross's faint inclination to make light of the confrontation faded. He had instinctively disliked Richard from the moment he'd met him, and though the man gave enough superficial offense to make him unlikable, Ross was beginning to feel there was a little more beneath the clownish surface than anyone realized.

"That's your assessment of my relationship with Lorna," Ross said coolly. "Not mine."

"Her fiancé wants her back," Richard said. "He's willing to do anything to mend the breach between them. He can offer her a life of ease and refinement, Mr. St. James. What are you willing to offer my niece?"

The question caught Ross unprepared, temporarily banishing his anger at the other man.

"You cannot answer me," Richard said with a smug smile. "That tells me I was right."

Ross turned on his heel and walked down the path, not in a mood to explain his own behavior when he could scarcely understand it himself. What could he offer Lorna? In terms of physical wealth, there was no doubt he could compete with her former fiancé, but how much of *himself* was he prepared to give?

Chapter 19

Shortly before sunrise two days later a series of small earthquakes rocked the island of Kali Simpang.

The natives whispered it was a bad omen, that the expedition must be postponed.

And then it was discovered that a sacred white-tailed eagle had alighted just after dawn on the temple shrine of Penala. Surely the bird goddess was smiling down upon the young Englishwoman and her mission.

Lorna sat on the veranda drinking tea and anxiously awaiting instructions from Kurt on the wharves where the sloop was moored. She hadn't slept all night, convinced something would happen to stop the expedition. In her mind she had reconstructed her last conversation with Ross, the anger in her uncle's voice when he had confronted them in the garden. She would be embarrassed to look Ross in the face this morning. She prayed Uncle Richard had said nothing to change Ross's mind about accompanying her on the expedition. With his quiet authority and calming influence to temper her own impulsive streak, he had become her lodestar in this dark period of her life.

"I've packed you a luncheon, Lorna," Ilse said as she came out onto the veranda carrying a linen-covered hamper.

Lorna got up from the wicker chair. "Probably my last decent meal for ages. I shall no doubt have to learn to love salt pork and soggy rice."

Ilse set the hamper down on the chair and gave Lorna a hard awkward hug. "I never thought I would like you so much, Lorna. In fact, I was quite prepared to find you silly and priggish."

Lorna had the strongest feeling that Ilse wanted to say something more but was holding back, perhaps out of embarrassment at revealing her affection.

"Your friendship has been a bright spot for me too, Ilse, but you mustn't talk as if we'll never see each other again. I will return from this expedition, you know."

"But I won't be here, I'm afraid. I've already made plans to join the children in Africa. And with Kurt not here to protect me from Wouter, I shall have to make my escape while I can."

It seemed an unfortunate way to live one's life, running away from an abusive husband with three young children, but before Lorna could question Ilse further about her plans, the other woman picked up one of the teacups from the tea tray and lifted it with a jaunty smile.

"To the future," Ilse said. "May we both be wildly happy and free to follow our hearts."

Lorna raised her own cup, sighing to herself. Happiness seemed an indulgent pursuit for a woman in her position. From dutiful daughter to dutiful wife would most probably be her lot, unless she landed up a spinster—and that seemed a strong possibility. Her behavior the past few weeks would be considered scandalous at home, but she had never been happier in her life, despite all the threats and the problems she'd faced. If only it would never end. If only her future could be here.

"To the future," she said, and the image of Ross's handsome face slipped unbidden into her mind.

A few moments later Richard appeared on the veranda, his face solemn beneath his pith helmet. "Is the cart here yet?" he asked in a subdued voice.

Lorna clasped her hands together, hoping he would not bring up the subject of the night before last. "Not yet."

"I think I hear it coming up the hill now," Ilse said.

She put down her cup to peer around the trees. "Don't forget your bonnet, Lorna."

Lorna glanced at the piles of luggage gathered on the steps. Anyone would think she was never going to return. She bit her lip at the thought. It *was* a possibility.

She ran inside to fetch her straw bonnet, jamming it on her head with the white silk ribbons untied. In the heat, her blue muslin frock already felt heavy and uncomfortable.

The cart was waiting outside the gate when she emerged.

"Well, Ilse, wish us luck."

"Take care of yourself," Ilse said from the gate. "I'd promise to remember you every night in my prayers except I don't think God pays much attention to women like me." She glanced skyward. "I'll ask Penala, shall I? Perhaps she'll have more compassion because I am a good mother, if nothing else."

Lorna was on edge during the hot, jolting ride to the wharves, sensing her uncle was preoccupied and suspecting he was pondering her relationship with Ross.

"Uncle Richard—"

"I have been thinking, Lorna," he broke in as if she had not spoken. "Perhaps it is not a good idea for you to accompany me and Kurt after all."

"What?" The cart rolled over a rotted log, and she bounced off the sack of rice that served as a cushion, holding her bonnet to her head. "Because of Ross—you're that determined to spoil my friendship with him?"

Richard frowned. "It's not that. But this whole affair has become more dangerous than I ever imagined. Your aunt pleaded with me to leave you home. It isn't too late. If anything happened to you—"

"I'm not going back *now*. You're the one who invited me to come in the first place."

"Yes, but that was before—"

"Before Ross," she said, her green eyes flashing. "I knew he was at the heart of this."

He looked away and did not say another word until the

cart rolled onto the waterfront and Kurt, red-faced and scowling, came forward to help them unload.

"God save us, Lorna," he snapped as he noticed her bulging trunk. "How do you expect to carry this through the jungle?"

"Good morning to you too, Kurt," she said, climbing down beside him. "We're in a pleasant mood, aren't we?"

"The captain of the sloop was found dead drunk in Li-Li Kong's this morning and is only now beginning to communicate coherently. And look at them—"

He gestured to the eight native seamen who would make the sea voyage in a two-sailed prau, sitting on the wharves smoking, chewing betel, and placing bets on a live lizard race.

"A crew to inspire confidence if ever there was one," said a wry masculine voice from the gangplank.

Lorna glanced up at Ross. He was dressed in blue cotton trousers and a white batik shirt. The sun glistened on his dark hair and caught the tiny golden flecks in his gray eyes. She thought again of how the expedition would throw them together every minute of the next month or so.

He walked toward her, his gaze narrowing faintly as he noticed Richard. "Have you met the captain yet?"

Lorna shook her head. Ross took her arm and turned her to face the bridge of the sturdy Malay sloop shifting against the pier. The man she assumed to be Captain Stokker stood with a damp cloth clamped to his eyes, his sweat-streaked shirt hanging open over his flabby abdomen as he bellowed orders across deck.

Ross smiled wryly. "So that was the best man you could find, van Poole."

Kurt grunted. "He's the only one. No other captain in the archipelago would go anywhere near Jalaka. For any price. Well, the damned fool looks as ready as he'll ever be. After you, Lorna."

Lorna felt a strange mixture of apprehension and excitement as she followed Ross aboard the sloop to the starboard rail, where they stood facing the shoreline. "That isn't Kana I see over there, is it, Ross?"

"It is. He's accompanying me—under protest, you understand. In fact, he hasn't spoken to me all day."

They turned simultaneously as the dark-bearded Dutch sea captain approached them, squinting in the sunlight as if he couldn't bear to open his bloodshot eyes. "Miss Fairfield," he said hoarsely. "Resident St. James."

"I hope to God this tub is seaworthy, Stokker," Ross said. "It looks to me as if she's as out of trim as a teapot. Her bulwarks are wormy, and your crew could've come from the chain gangs of Batavia."

Captain Stokker stared at Ross without offense. "They did."

There was a moment of silence as a Malay crewman cast off the hawser, and it slipped through the hawsehold and into the water with a splash. A fresh breeze bore the sloop seaward under billowing sail.

Ross stared at the receding shoreline, his jaw tense. Lorna knew how difficult it must be for him to leave his responsibilities on the island.

"The Rajah should not have asked you to come," she said quietly. She felt suddenly guilty over her part in persuading Charles to force Ross into joining the expedition. "He did it at my request, Ross. I'm ashamed to admit that."

He glanced down at her and smiled. "The Rajah didn't persuade me to come. We both know why I'm here." He was sliding his hand across the rail to reach for hers when a shocked voice behind them stopped him.

"Oh, my God."

Lorna had managed to forget her uncle until she saw him over her shoulder, his face expressing utter disgust. "Don't tell me our very lives are in the hands of that churl."

Richard was referring to Captain Stokker, who had just leaned over the railing to vomit into the churning white-caps.

"Cheer up, old man," Ross said, studying the sky. "At least he had the courtesy to use the leeward rail."

Favorable winds escorted them for two days. The sloop plowed through the waves, her sails full spread and billowing against the hot tropical sky. On the third day the breeze died, and she drifted with her canvas drooping and the pitch melting in the seams as a merciless sun baked the decks. By evening they were becalmed and enwrapped in an opalescent mist. The moon hung above them like a giant pearl. The native prau floated past them like an invisible ghost ship whose chanting voices and rhythmic drumbeats carried with eerie clarity across the water.

Ross had the midnight watch. Lorna left the quartermaster's cabin she had taken as her own and searched for him on deck, hoping they could spend even an hour alone together.

As it had her first day on Kali Simpang, the music of his flute lured her to where he stood lookout on the bow. The pure notes drifted across the misty darkness with poignant melancholy. Leaning up against the rail, he seemed unaware of her approach.

She stood watching him for a long time, her heart aching with a longing so intense it was painful. He was so enrapt in his music she was hesitant to intrude. What did he think about when he played with such absorption? she wondered jealously.

"Lorna." He glanced over his shoulder, his pleasure at seeing her evident in his voice. "Couldn't you sleep?"

She shook her head and stepped toward him, not noticing the coil of rope at her feet until she caught her heel in it. Ross, who'd gotten his sea legs before anyone else, caught her as she stumbled against the rail. He held her in his arms while she recovered her balance, letting go only when Captain Stokker cursed loudly at the wheel.

"Is he lost?" she asked Ross.

"Amazingly, no. He has quite a way with a sextant and

chronometer. I think the old trout might actually get us there, after all.''

"It's a strange feeling," she said, "to be cast adrift at sea in a mist so thick you don't know which way to turn.''

He slid his arms down her back, pressing his forehead to hers. ''That's exactly how I've felt since meeting you. I've never been so blindly out of control in my life, and I don't want it to end.''

''Nor do I,'' she said softly.

She waited for him to reassure her that their relationship would never end, but he remained silent, disengaging himself as a pair of sailors walked toward them. Staring out toward the sea, she resigned herself to the fact that he wasn't prepared to discuss their future—if they even had one together. For all she knew, she was still only part of his obligation to the Rajah.

That he had grown fond of her she could believe. But that didn't mean she had a permanent place in his heart. And with their lives in jeopardy at every turn, it did not seem the proper time to ask.

They caught the hint of a freshening wind after midnight, and by the next morning a squall had blown in from the southwest. Lorna stood on deck and watched Ross climbing the ropes like a spider while Captain Stokker bellowed orders to lower sail. She felt sick to her stomach from the turbulent rocking.

''Get back into the cabin!'' Ross shouted when he spotted her.

She nodded, turning unsteadily as the sloop plunged through a sheer cleft in the foaming sea, her leeward rail submerging. Reeling, Lorna regained her balance long enough to look up and see a gigantic white-topped wave rising before her. She had never seen anything more terrifying in her life.

It seemed to encompass the entire world, a towering cliff of bottle-green glass. She was mesmerized by its growing magnitude, unable to move, waiting for it to sweep her up and hurl her into oblivion.

"Lorna!" Ross yelled. "For God's sake, move!"

His face flashed before her as he shinned down a length of rope, and then a roaring filled her ears as the wave broke on deck. Salt water stung her face and eyes, blinding her. She staggered backward, and then gasped as something hard snapped around her midsection, fighting to hold her against the inexorable torrent of water that struggled to fling everything in its path into the boiling sea.

A powerful arm squeezed the air from her lungs. She clung to it as the wave dashed her like a leaf against the railing. "Don't fight it," Kurt shouted above the noise. "I've got hold of you."

Spindrift and wind whipped her damp skin, and water lapped around her ankles as the world slowly righted itself. She glanced around at Kurt and nodded a speechless thanks, her chest heaving.

"Get down below," he said. His hair was flattened like wet yellow yarn on his scalp. There was a gash on his forehead where a ratline had swung loose and struck him.

As Ross reached them, he yanked off his shirt and handed it to Kurt to stanch the blood. "We're all going down below," he said grimly.

The captain's cabin was the only place on the sloop that had not been flooded. The skeleton crew remained above, setting the storm canvas and making repairs. Richard was huddled on the bunk, looking as green as the rushing sea that was visible through the closed porthole.

"Dear life, Lorna," he exclaimed as she stepped into the crowded quarters. "What happened to you?"

"I had a wash."

"Nearly her last," Kurt said.

Ross went to the captain's bolted-down desk and removed a flask of rum from a drawer, taking a deep swig before he passed it to the others. He thought he had lost her up on deck. The sick trembling inside him still hadn't subsided. If this was any indication of what he felt for her and had tried to deny, he was in deeper trouble than he realized. He swallowed hard, staring at her over the flask, aching to take her into his arms and reassure himself she was all right. Van Poole might have taken other lives, but he had saved the one that Ross acknowledged mattered most to him.

"I'd like a little of that," Lorna said, nodding to the flask.

She took a deep unladylike swig. Scandalized, Richard sat up so abruptly that he cracked his head on the swaying oil lamp.

"You've taken to drinking rum now, too? And from a communal bottle?"

"I don't think Captain Stokker carries champagne." She glanced at Ross. "Do you?"

He grinned at her and lounged back in the captain's chair with his booted feet on the desk. Lorna passed the flask to Kurt. He took it and leaned against a bulwark, drinking steadily.

"How soon do you think we'll get there, St. James?"

"If the wind doesn't freshen to a gale—if we don't run aground on a reef—and if luck is on our side, it should be tomorrow."

"Tomorrow. You said that yesterday." Kurt began to pace before the porthole, the strain of being confined showing on his face. "Why doesn't Stokker ever refer to a chart? How do we know the fool won't land us in Australia?"

"You won't find Jalaka on any chart," Ross murmured. "And if it were, it wouldn't matter. The currents and channels are never the same two days running."

Lorna stretched out on a bunk and yawned. "You were reading your charts earlier, Uncle Richard. Where do you reckon we are?"

Richard tugged at his mustache. "I'm sure I've muddled them up somewhere"

"Tell us anyway. It will take my mind off my stomach."

"Well, according to my calculations, amateur though they may be," he said, "we are—"

The ship gave a violent lurch as she nosed into a trough. The door flew open and Kana catapulted in, brandishing a bamboo pen of squawking chickens.

"Cookhouse roof is leaking."

"At least it hasn't blown off," Ross said, glancing over at Lorna. "Where did you say we were headed, Richard?"

Richard cleared his throat. "According to my calculations, traveling at a rate of ten knots—say, twenty in a storm—by tomorrow evening we should reach the coast of . . . oh, dear, it appears to be Africa."

"North or South?" Ross asked.

Lorna peered over the top of her blanket. "British or Dutch?"

Richard frowned and passed his map of scribbled latitude and longitude to Ross. "What do you make of it?"

"It looks like we've just sailed off the face of the earth."

The chicken pen flew across the floor and hit the sea chest. A chorus of protesting squawks splintered the air. Lorna propped herself up on her elbow and quoted softly:

> *Three days long sails our noble ship,*
> *And three days lost are we,*
> *Three days long sails our noble ship,*
> *And falls off the edge of the sea.*

They sailed through the night on shortened canvas until the storm subsided and the sloop rode on a restless sea. At dawn a fitful wind carried them through the dangerous straits of Jalaka with its riptides and sunken reefs. By mid-morning she picked her way through the treacherous channels where a current caught her and swept her perilously close to the jagged shore. There was tense silence aboard ship as Captain Stokker took the helm and followed the bowman's direction.

One mistake, Ross thought, and it's all over.

Lorna's first glimpse of Jalaka depressed her. The

smoking cones of three active volcanoes dominated the landscape, and an unearthly orange-red haze from the setting sun made it look as if the island was aflame. She had been hoping in her heart to find her father waiting on shore for rescue. But there wasn't a single hint of human habitation in sight.

Jalaka. Island of Death, she thought, and shivered in the still hot air.

The beach of scorched black sand looked barren and inhospitable, strewn with the skeletal remains of ships which Ross speculated aloud had been snagged by underwater volcanic boulders. Even the water below bespoke desolation with the coral that protruded on dark, lifeless stems.

It took them two hours of skillfully navigating the hidden reefs to enter a passageway between two steep cliffs that enclosed them in shadowed silence. By that time most of the native crew had retreated beneath their makeshift tarpaulin awnings to implore Penala's protection. They had just learned one of the oarsmen in the prau had drowned in the storm.

"We're sailing into a lagoon," Kurt said as he returned from the bridge to join the other passengers clustered at the rail. "Stokker would prefer we lower the dinghies and row to shore. He doesn't want to risk damaging the sloop."

"I should hope not," Richard said, staring in horror across the water. "I can't imagine being stranded in a more unappealing place."

"What do you say, Resident?" Kurt asked in a condescending voice.

"There are clams in this water big and powerful enough to decapitate a diver. Not to mention venomous fish."

Kurt turned to stare at the water. Lorna thought, For all his bravado, he is at least considering Ross's opinion.

"We'll test the water then," he said. "I'll go first."

Kana joined them as the dinghy was lowered with a reluctant Malay oarsman into the murky waters of the lagoon. "Mulak say very bad spirits in water here."

Kurt jumped into the tilting dinghy and squatted, balancing an oar on his knees. Richard leaned over the rail, shaking his head.

"Just remember if anything happens to you, van Poole, we're all lost."

Kurt didn't answer. There wasn't time. No sooner had he and his dark-skinned partner dipped their oars into the water than an angular blue fin appeared from nowhere and sliced toward them. A second followed and then a third.

"*Ikan Butas!*" the lead oarsman shouted from the bowsprit, where the native crew had gathered.

Devil fish.

The first shark capsized the dinghy in a single gliding bump. The native fended off a second attack with his oars, his head bobbing, his eyes bulging with horror. Kurt swam for the safety of the overturned dinghy and clung to it, his gaze following the ever-nearing circle of sharks.

"Are you bastards going to stand there just bloody watching?" he shouted toward the sloop. He gave a mighty heave and righted the boat, diving over the gunwale just as a shark resurfaced and plowed into the hull. Water streaming down his face, he snatched up an oar and began to beat at the water. The native flung his oar aside and swam madly for the sloop and the boarding ladder Ross had thrown over the side, his brown body suspended in the air as several pairs of hands reached down to help him. A dorsal fin sliced directly between his dangling heels. His face impassive, Ross uncoiled the length of rope Kana passed him and raised it to toss toward the dinghy.

"We're going to haul you in, van Poole."

Captain Stokker elbowed Lorna aside, cradling an ancient musket over his arm. "I'll cover you."

Kurt nodded tersely. Then as he lunged for the rope, a shark burst out of the water, jaws gaping, and sank its fangs into the oar Kurt was holding. At precisely the same instant, Stokker shot the shark between the eyes. For an interminable moment it clung to life, and Lorna raised her hands to her mouth, not breathing.

Kurt looked up at her face. The shark's body stiffened in death and then slid into the water, taking the oar with it.

"Haul him in hard," Captain Stokker said. "There's enough blood in the water now to lure every shark around for miles."

When Kurt reached the sloop, he sagged back against the rail, his wet face raised to the sun, his chest heaving.

"That was the most terrifying thing I've ever seen in my life," Lorna said, dropping her hands to her sides. "I thought you were surely dead."

Kurt lowered his face to look at her. To her disbelief, he was actually smiling, his light eyes glowing with an odd exhilaration. "It was quite a welcome, wasn't it?" he said. "Just enough excitement to get the blood stirring."

"Excitement or not," Ross said, "there's no way I'll allow anyone to row across the lagoon."

"I'll second that," Richard said.

Captain Stokker squared his shoulders as if he might put up an argument. "We'll none of us leave this place if I ruin the hull on the rocks."

"Then I will help guide you," Ross said, his voice firm. "There is a way to reach the shore, and we will find it."

It was evening when the ship anchored in the lagoon. A row of coconut palms stood sentinel on the stark shoreline, the occasional twitter of a fruit bat issuing from their unmoving fronds.

The volcanic sand was still hot beneath their feet as Ross helped Lorna down the ladder, through the frothy surf, and onto the shore. The native prau had already moored, having found safe passage through a narrow inlet, and its crewmen were huddled in a whispering circle around a small campfire. Captain Stokker locked himself in his cabin with the solemn promise he would not leave the island until the search party returned. No one believed him.

A full moon shone down on the triad of smoking cone-shaped mountains that rose above the lagoon. Even the moon's milky light could not infiltrate the twisted cover of montane jungle that climbed to the mist-shrouded peaks. Here and there a stream glinted silver where bubbling lava had blazed a furrowed path to the sea. But everywhere else there was only darkness.

Lorna stared up through the palms in dispirited silence. She had no trouble accepting that somewhere within those shadows the animistic cult of the Agung-Mani was practiced in all its pagan horror, the human sacrifices to the Tiger God. But even her stubborn faith wavered at the thought of a gently reared man like her father surviving untold dangers for almost a year. The sense of evil was overpowering. She couldn't take a step without feeling as if unseen eyes noted the movement.

A deep-throated howl rose from the foothills to disturb the silence. She glanced uneasily at Ross. "What on the face of creation was that?"

"Adjags," Kana said. "Wild dogs."

There was a shout from farther up the beach, and torchlight flared suddenly to reveal several figures gathered around a crop of boulders that pitted the shore.

"They've found something," Ross said. "Lorna, perhaps you should stay here."

"I need to know."

They found Kurt, Mulak, and Richard squatted over the remains of the schooner Sir Arthur had sailed to Jalaka. The three men were combing every spar and timber for clues. Lorna turned her head away as they dragged a partially decomposed body out from under a shroud of canvas.

"No," she whispered.

Ross glanced at her stricken face. "Mulak says it was one of the sailors who drowned during the shipwreck."

"There's nothing else here," Richard said, his voice flat with disappointment. "Not a wretched thing."

Lorna stared down at the shroud gleaming in contrast against the black sand and abruptly walked away. She was so wrapped up in thoughts of her father, she didn't notice Ross until he spoke.

"I have something I think you should hear." He guided her into the palm grove and lit a match to read from the scraps of paper in his hand. "Mulak found these in a haversack near the shroud and wanted me to see them before Kurt did. Even he doesn't trust van Poole completely."

Lorna leaned against a palm, her stomach clenching as she recognized her father's handwriting and Ross began to read.

" 'He felt it from the moment he set foot upon the island, the indelible shadow of the sleeping evil that would soon claim him for its own as it had every creature that inhabited this accursed place.' " Ross glanced down at her briefly before continuing. " 'No accident had brought him to these shores. From the first ill-fated day when he'd encountered the abominable treasure he carried under his arm, he had been ordained to return it to the eternal hell from whence it was spawned. . . . Even now he was enslaved by its dark magic. . . . ' "

The match died. Ross lowered the paper and shook his head. "It sounds like a page from your father's journal. It proves he had the Tiger."

"He kept no journal," Lorna said. "He didn't believe in them. And this was written in the third person. It's more likely from his last manuscript, Ross."

"Until now I'd assumed he was blown off course and landed on Jalaka by accident. But it sounds as if—"

"As if he were compelled to bring the statue back here." She released a terse sigh. "Is it possible that the lost village of Palleh is on this island? You said Papa was researching the cult. That would explain what Kao meant when he spoke of the statue remaining at its birthplace."

Ross stared up at the mountains. "I don't know as much about the native religions as I should, but it's not impossible. What should I do with these?" He indicated the scraps of paper.

"Destroy them. There's nothing in them that would help Kurt find my father."

Ross nodded. He wasn't about to tell her that he thought their chances of locating Sir Arthur were almost nil. Having heard in her father's own words that he had the statue, she did not need any further discouragement.

They slept between the palms that first night, too weary to discern a single path or even to organize their supplies on the beach. Ross slept poorly, awakening every half hour out of habit, but tonight it was to check on Lorna, lying several yards away in the small vine hammock beneath a protective cover of netting.

He stared at the moon through the fronds, trying to imagine what his life would be like if she returned to England. He should welcome the return to the odd normality he'd known before her. Lord knew he had enough to worry about with the pirate Illanuans. And there were the incessant demands of the island, which would double when he took up his uncle's position as Rajah. Work had filled the bleak, welling sadness within him before when he'd lost Vanessa and Ian. But he knew that it would not be enough to replace Lorna. She had carved a special place for herself in his heart, amidst the guilt, the loneliness and self-deception, the deep scars. She had come to care about him despite his flaws.

He closed his eyes, his breath falling into the rhythm of the surf that rushed toward the palms and withdrew with a frothy whisper. Images of Lorna as he had come to know her in her diverse moods drifted across his mind. He would never again stand watch at the cove without remembering that first night in the monsoon, and weeks later, when thy made love in the cave. And he wouldn't be able to walk past Li-Li Kong's again without a smile—and a tug of loneliness at his heart.

It was the scream that woke him just as he had drifted off, a long bloodcurdling shriek of terror that had him reaching for his rifle and jumping off the hammock before he even realized where he was. His feet splashed through the warm incoming tide as he waded over to Lorna's hammock and found her awake and pushing off the netting in instinctive panic.

"Where did it come from?" she asked. She looked about thirteen years old with her hair hanging in a braid down her back.

"It came from the native camp." Kurt had waded up through the surf behind them.

They turned in unison to watch Kana running through the palms in their direction, holding three flaming frond torches. "What happened?" Ross called to him.

"Two mens hurt. Broken arms and legs."

"How?"

He passed Ross a torch. "Crabs, Tuan."

"What?"

"Nocturnal coconut crabs," Lorna said. "Their pincers are strong enough to break a grown man's bones. They crack open the coconuts to feed upon them."

"How the devil would you know that?" Ross said.

"My guidebook," she said smugly.

"The waters bring them this way fast," Kana said, his eyes bright behind his spectacles. "Mens are running away into the forest. They say this very bad place."

"We'll move inland where we left the supplies," Kurt said. "Lorna, you go with Ross. I'll partner your uncle."

Richard came splashing through the tide toward them. He was the only member of the party who had bothered to change into his nightclothes. "There's a passel of them crabs crawling over the longboat. I hope to God we can outrun 'em."

A wavelet broke around Lorna's feet. Ross glanced down as she hopped back. "You're not wearing your boots."

"I usually don't when I sleep."

"I'll have to carry you then."

"If you insist, Ross."

"There's a mangrove thicket on the other side of the lagoon where the sloop is anchored," Kurt said as he hoisted on his own haversack. "Watch out for the crocodiles. They're particularly nasty at night."

Lorna sat down close to Ross on the cliffside ledge as a bat glided across the lagoon and landed with its webbed feet splayed. Her eyelids burning with fatigue, she watched it wiggle into an invisible crevice. There was a gun and two ball cartridges in her lap, but she didn't feel safe. They had skirted the mangrove thicket and climbed the rocky overhang above the water, intending to move farther inland in the morning. They were both too exhausted to seek another shelter.

Ross lowered his binoculars. "Kurt and the others are making camp in the foothills."

"Did you see the look my uncle gave us when we left?" Lorna asked.

"I was trying to ignore it."

"He doesn't think your intentions toward me are honorable."

"Yes. He told me so in no uncertain terms."

"Uncle Richard can be such an overprotective old silly at times."

"He makes a great pretense of caring for you."

Lorna looked up at him. "A pretense?"

"Well, he's a lot of bluster, isn't he?"

"Yes, but I've never doubted that he loves me. His feelings for Papa are perhaps more ambivalent."

Ross scooted across the ledge and pulled her across his lap, raising his knees and wrapping his arms around her waist to prevent her from falling. The gun dropped from her skirt between Ross's legs, and one of the ball cartridges rolled off the ledge.

"There has to be somewhere safer than this," he said roughly, standing up. He leaned down to help her to her feet. "A cave inside the cliff, perhaps."

She hung back. "I saw a bat," she said faintly. "There must be others."

They found a narrow crack in the cliffside and squeezed

into it after Ross made sure it harbored no unfriendly inhabitants. No sooner had he spread his blanket on the sand than there were footsteps on the ledge outside, and he leapt up with his rifle.

"It's only me," Kurt called inside. "I just wanted to make sure you and Lorna were all right."

Lorna clambered to her feet. "Do you think the islanders know we're here yet?"

Kurt shrugged. "We'll find out soon enough. Get some rest."

"I'll sleep outside on the ledge," Ross told Lorna as Kurt disappeared down an unmarked path. "Just in case."

"In case of what?"

He kissed her chin. "Nothing. You heard Kurt. Go to sleep." She did as he suggested.

A noise disturbed her a few minutes after dawn, and she rose stiffly from the blanket and made her way outside.

Ross was already awake, drinking strong coffee from a tin cup and staring farther down the ledge.

"What is it?" she said when she saw his strained expression.

"I think your question has been answered."

She followed the direction of his gaze and felt the blood drain from her face. A human skeleton was propped up on the ledge with a pipe in its jaw and a plaid forage cap pulled down over its skull.

"They know we're here, all right," Ross said. "Would you care for coffee?"

She didn't answer him. She had taken two steps forward and then frozen with her hands pressed to her mouth. "That cap," she whispered. "I gave it to my father the last Christmas we were together."

Chapter 20

"It's not your father."

Lorna crept farther along the ledge, her courage returning with relief. "How can you tell?"

"The teeth in the skull have been filed into points as is common among the cannibals. And I'm reasonably sure it was a younger man." He passed Lorna the pipe and hat.

"Then what are these supposed to mean?"

"Agung-Mani calling cards, I suppose."

They met Kurt as they headed inland, toward the gradual ascent into the montane jungle via dense wooded hillside and sparse shrub. It was here that Mulak had last seen Sir Arthur before hiding out on the beach for a month and fashioning the crude boat that had carried him out to sea, where he was rescued by a Chinese merchant ship.

They stopped at a stream when the blazing midday sun made progress miserably slow. The nearer they came to the jungle outskirts, the denser grew the foliage. For hours on end the rhythmic slashing of parangs disrupted the heavy silence and sent parrots screeching for cover.

Lorna sat at the edge of a stream and yanked off her leather half-boots to soothe her blistered feet. On the dark embankment opposite a family of wau-waus, gibbon apes, abandoned their play and disappeared into the underbrush with wails of alarm.

"I'd run too if I saw us," Kurt said.

She cupped her hands in the water to drink. Another hand, strong and long-fingered, seized her wrist.

"No," Ross said. "Not like that."

"My guidebook says if the monkeys drink it, it should be safe for us."

"You and that damned book. Look, the water is safe, but what lives in it isn't." He scraped the tip of his parang across a rock and held it up in the sunlight. What appeared to be several flesh-colored threads dangled from the blade tip.

"Thread leeches," he said. "An unpleasant business if they lodge in your nose and throat and start to swell." He handed her a fine sieve attached to a tin cup. "Use this from now on."

Shuddering, she wiped her hands on her skirt. "Are we going to make camp here tonight?"

"That's up to Kurt."

Kurt glanced over at them. "Ja, Lorna. We rest now. But tomorrow at dawn and the next day and the next, we slash until sunset. That will be the most demanding part of the expedition. Once we are in the jungle, we are relatively safe."

"Safe." She stared at the black thicket that embraced the mysterious jungle interior. "My guidebook says a man can easily get killed trying to penetrate that protective layer."

Ross scraped his blade across the rock, squashing the undulating leeches at the same time. "Clever fellow, the author of that guidebook."

"He suggests you travel by river whenever possible."

"He never traveled to Jalaka," Kurt said patiently, drawing a peppermint lozenge from his pocket. "Anyway, I'm not a water man, and I don't fancy making ourselves sitting ducks for some little bastard's blowgun. If your father had his wits about him, he'd have hidden in the jungle where the natives rarely venture. We can return by river if we have to."

Lorna cast a sidelong glance at Ross, at the grim set of

his jaw. He did not even try to hide his dislike of Kurt, and she worried that sooner or later the two men would be drawn into a violent confrontation. For her own part she refused to dwell on the suspicion that Kurt was a cold-blooded killer. It was as if by not accepting the possibility, it might prove unfounded.

At sunset Lorna returned to the stream to collect drinking water, dragging the sieve as Ross had instructed her. Overhead a fairy bluebird hopped from branch to branch of a balsam tree, and a pair of pink-crested doves pecked at an offering of ripening figs.

As she straightened, a shadow fell across her path. A second merged with it and then another until she was encircled by a half dozen Jalakans of an unknown tribe. Small-statured and golden-skinned, with frizzy mops of oily black hair, they wore loincloths of bark cloth fibers and triton-shell armlets above their underdeveloped biceps. The two women present had on brass toe-rings and bone anklets. As they grinned silently at Lorna, she noticed that their teeth had been filed into fanglike points that reminded her fleetingly of vampire bats.

Lorna's heart began to race in alarm. She wanted to shout for the others but feared any sudden action on her part would trigger the women to attack her.

One of the women spoke to her in a dialect she did not recognize. Then she proffered a carrying basket laden with bananas, jackfruit, and mangosteens. From the corner of her eye Lorna noticed Ross, Kurt, and Mulak moving behind a fig tree to watch over her.

"Take the basket, Lorna," Kurt said in an undertone.

She glanced down. "How do you know it's not full of shrunken heads?"

"Because they're cannibals," he said quietly.

"What a relief."

A second woman edged closer and removed the torque of polished teeth she wore around her neck, looking inquiringly at Lorna for permission to bestow it. Lorna did not move. The woman slipped the torque off and placed it around Lorna's throat, her pointed teeth digging into her fleshy red lips in concentration.

"It's rather tight," Lorna murmured. "Not that I'm ungrateful, or anything."

"Just stay calm," Ross told her.

Mulak approached to address the group in his native tongue. The leader of the four men made some reply and gestured over his shoulder with his spear.

"They river people who live in longhouses at the bottom of volcano. Not Agung-Mani."

At the mention of the cult's name, the women shook their heads fearfully and backed away to the stream.

The leader of the band spoke again to Mulak, indicating the basket of fruit at Lorna's feet and pointing toward the trees.

"His peoples have big full-moon feasts tonight," Mulak translated. "They say we come. The gods send us to them, and they receive us as honored guests."

Kurt sauntered down to the stream, his shirt hanging open. "Ask them if they've seen Sir Arthur."

Lorna nervously fingered the torque of sharp teeth that pressed into her throat, straining to make sense of the brief exchange.

"He say the manang see every person who come to island. The gods already told him in a dream to expect us."

Ross leaned forward, the shadowed light falling on the rifle under his arm. "Tell them we would be honored to meet the manang."

There was a long silence as the natives glanced back toward the tall trees that lined the water's edge. Lorna saw the flickering of reverent fear in their eyes as a cadaverously thin figure walked slowly toward her.

The shaman, or manang, had black frizzy hair that reached his protruding hipbones. He wore a crocodile-skin loincloth. Around his neck hung a polished pelican stone, that most prized of amulets. He squatted down on his haunches before Lorna and smiled, revealing sharp foxlike fangs.

"Ask him about my father," she said to Mulak without turning her head.

Mulak crouched before the shaman, talking haltingly and gesturing with his hands. The manang grunted and with his fingernail drew a crude sketch in the damp soil of a man at the summit of a moonlit volcano.

Lorna glanced up as Ross and Kurt edged closer to examine the drawing.

Mulak began to speak again, but the shaman shook his head and rose, disappearing into the trees without another word.

"Your father is alive," Kurt said. He gestured to the vulgar drawing. "Or at least he was about two weeks ago."

"How do you know?"

Ross pointed to the crescent above the volcano. "The new moon. Someone's seen him recently."

"But at the summit of a mountain. . . ."

The women began to chatter in agitation. Lorna stepped back close to Ross, feeling his free hand against her shoulder. "What are they saying now?" she whispered.

Mulak jumped to his feet. "They say the band around your neck is to protect you on your mission."

"T-to find my father?"

He shook his head. "To destroy the God of the Agung-Mani, their enemy. They say that is why their gods sent you."

Lorna was silent as one by one the Jalakans retreated into the shadows of the riverbank. She should have been encouraged to learn that her father was alive, but even so she realized that the search had not even truly begun, and she had far less confidence in her ability to overcome the Agung-Mani than the cannibals of Jalaka seemed to have.

Fireflies illuminated the edges of the small hollow encampment where they stopped shortly after nightfall. In the distance the primitive pulsations of native drums resounded and then faded away. The silence so unsettled Lorna that she envied the Malay natives who slept peacefully in their palm-leaf beds.

Her uncle stared at her across the low fire, balefully setting aside his plate of rice and salt pork. The others, including Ross, were moving about the edges of the encampment as a safety precaution. A makeshift tarpaulin protected the precious food supplies from marauding animals and moisture.

"Lorna, please, won't you reconsider and at least read Spencer's letter?" Richard said. "It breaks my heart to see you giving yourself to—"

"Don't start this again," she said wearily.

"It's my obligation to look out for you," he said in a fierce whisper. "I *insist* you read Spence's letter before you cross him out of your life entirely."

She glanced up, meeting Ross's gaze across the clearing. The faint orange light accentuated the sculpted austerity of his features; his eyes had narrowed into silver pinpoints. She knew he was within listening distance.

"All right, Uncle Richard," she whispered, tossing her head. "Give me the wretched letter, and that's the last I'll hear of the subject, do you understand? And I'll need a lantern to read it by, which is a ridiculous waste of oil."

As angry as she was, she was unprepared for the bittersweet stirrings she felt when finally she settled by the small nearby stream and began to read Spencer's letter.

My Dearest Lorna,

I write this letter exposing my deepest emotions and knowing your uncle will probably first read it and think me the greatest fool in Christendom. But I never dreamed when you left me that life could become so unbearable. A thousand times I have relived our last meeting, wishing I had insisted on accompanying you as I could not persuade you to stay.

I met Emily the other day—quite by accident, I assure

you. She was too embarrassed even to speak to me, and we both bitterly regret our foolishness that night. I think you would find me greatly changed, Lorna. I have forsworn drinking and gambling, and I'm having Kirkham Hall restored to its original style as you suggested. You always wanted to live in the country. If you would come back to me, we'd never have to visit London again. I am lost without you. . . .

Her eyes were sad and resigned as she forced herself to stop reading, unwillingly recalling the memories she had shared with Spencer . . . memories she had vowed to forget. There had been good times between them. She had been fond of him once. And the disappointment and humiliation he had caused her went far deeper than she realized.

She supposed legions of women had forgiven similar infidelities and gone on happily with their lives. But even if she could forgive him, it didn't change anything. There was Ross now. She could never go back to her former life after loving him, for if Spencer's letter had failed to soften her heart toward him, it had made her realize that what she felt for Ross was too deep, too powerful, too wonderful to be anything but love.

There was a sound behind her. She scrambled to her feet, past remembrances replaced by an awareness of the countless dangers of the present. Ross was sitting crosslegged on a flat black boulder behind her.

"So," he said, flicking a twig into the water, "has Lord Byron managed to win back your heart?"

"You were eavesdropping."

"Sorry," he said without a hint of apology in his voice. "Are you going to answer my question?"

"The answer is, no. It's over for me and Spencer. I've told you that."

He considered that for a moment, then said, "What do you think it means that I'm more concerned over your reading another man's love letter than I am about being eaten by aborigines?''

''I don't know.'' She tilted her head back, her green eyes luminous in the moonlight.

The cynical uncertainty returned to his voice. ''You still have feelings for him. I watched your face change while you were reading. I wonder if you're beginning to regret breaking off with him.''

She turned away, struggling to explain the emotions she was only just beginning to understand herself. ''I did care for him—I tried to convince myself it was love. But until I met you—'' She hesitated, aware of the sudden tension in his body. ''Until I met you,'' she continued unevenly, ''I did not understand what it means to love someone.''

''Are you saying that you . . . you—''

She glanced up at him, horrified by the look of incredulity on his face. ''Yes. I love you.'' Her voice sounded uneven; her breath seemed trapped in her chest. And when he did not speak again, her cheeks grew hot and her heart began to hammer in agitation.

Ross just stared at her as if he could see straight into her soul and would find there either a reaffirmation or a denial of those three devastating words.

I love you.

Then just when she thought she could stand the strain no longer, she heard her uncle calling to her from the camp. Without another glance at Ross, she picked up her skirt and ran back through the ferns to wrestle with the vine hammock that kept her safe from the ground-burrowing animals of the night, but not from the turmoil of her own confused feelings. She lay swaying under a mound of mosquito netting, her throat swollen with unshed tears. She wanted to cry for the girl she had once been and for Spencer, for the innocence between them that was gone forever. She wanted to cry for her father and whatever insanity had brought him here. But most of all she wanted to cry for Ross and for herself, for the aching humiliation she had felt at confessing her deepest feelings to him and for his inability to respond or to receive her love.

Their relationship would never be the same. She could never look him in the face again without remembering this night. Obviously he had not guessed she was in love with him. *He had not wanted to know.* She had ruined everything. She did not want Spencer, and Ross did not want her. The realization seeped painfully into her heart. It had been better not knowing, to go on hoping, waiting. She did not think she could endure the remainder of the expedition, knowing that she had offered her heart to Ross and he had refused it.

It took them three days to infiltrate the outer jungle wall. Three days of slashing and hacking, of crawling on their hands and knees through tunnels of choking vegetation and venomous spiderwebs that adhered to the flesh like glue; of suffering the white-hot stabs of insects and the razor slashes of plants that grew protective spines and squirted acidic fluids.

Lorna worked along with the others, exerting every muscle until her body felt numb and she couldn't lift her arms without wincing. Her face was red and scratched, and she didn't care. She was too intent on slashing her way into the bottle-green world she glimpsed occasionally beyond the fortress of snarled foliage. And she was too intent on reliving that wretched moment the night before last when she'd told Ross she loved him, and he'd only stared back at her as if that were the last thing in the world he had expected her to say.

To make matters worse, she could swear he'd been avoiding her. True, he was always there to help when a suddenly liberated rattan swung its thorn-spiked vine down toward her face. And it was his gun, not Kurt's, that dispatched the nest of deadly pit vipers she'd unwittingly disturbed.

But every time he came to her assistance, he pulled away immediately afterward.

It seemed that suddenly he couldn't bear to be near her.

She gritted her teeth as a liana swooped out of the air to smack her face. She turned, her hand to her cheek, and caught Ross staring at her, though he glanced away the moment their eyes met.

Damn the arrogant, aloof bastard anyway. If she'd listened to her uncle, she might have emerged from this relationship with a trifle more dignity and a lot less anguish.

On the third day they made camp just before twilight near a pond that was stained the color of dark amber tea. Of the three natives who had been assigned to patrol the vicinity, only one returned. Whether the lost two had been captured by hostile natives or were hiding in the forest for fear of their lives, the remaining native refused to reveal, keeping stubbornly silent.

Kurt and Mulak left the camp to scout ahead in different directions. Richard made his bed and settled into it with a roaring groan and a torrent of complaints.

"Oh, dear heaven, I ache in every corpuscle. What the blazes is that stench? It can't be them flowers, can it, Lorna? Look 'em up in that guidebook you're so fond of quoting. If I weren't feeling such a cripple, I'd move my bed. This place is as quiet as a mausoleum. And I've yet to even see a single bird."

"*Rafflesia arnoldi*," Ross said from between the massive buttresses of the tree trunks he had taken as his territory. "The stinking corpse lily." He glanced at Lorna. "You were curious about that same plant when you first arrived on the island."

She dropped her haversack onto the shallow jungle soil. If she didn't reclaim it before morning the ants and termites would devour it. Her voice was resigned when she spoke, and she did not look at Ross. "I was curious about a lot of things then that I should have let remain a mystery."

He turned away deliberately as she began struggling to secure her hammock. He was certain they would end up cradled together in it if he so much as touched her.

For three days he had thought of nothing else.

Back on Kali Simpang resisting her had been hard enough, but at least there he'd had the distractions of his responsibilities to balance out his obsession with her. Here it was a ludicrous torture, sleeping only several feet away and pretending they hadn't been intimately familiar with each other.

He might have managed a semblance of self-control if she hadn't told him that she loved him.

He hadn't known a peaceful moment since then. Of course she had been in shock at the time. Finding oneself face-to-face with a tribe of cannibals tended to give the brain a good jolt. The sensible thing was to pretend she had never brought up the subject.

She certainly wasn't the first woman to share his bed and afterward declare that she loved him. But this was the first time he had spent more than an amused moment wondering whether it were true. Hoping it was.

It was the first time he had cared.

Oh, God, he thought, as the realization sank in.

He leaned against the white-barked tree whose branches did not sprout until a hundred feet above and watched Lorna making a tangled muddle of her bed. Without a word he strode to her side and took the sagging hammock from her hands.

"I can manage myself," she said.

"Obviously you cannot."

"Then I'll sleep on the ground. I certainly don't need your help for that."

He turned, having easily slung the hammock between two sturdy saplings. She was angry at him, he realized, probably because she felt embarrassed at having admitted something so absurd as that she loved him. Damn her. Damn her for making him want to believe it whether it was true or not. Damn her for dragging him away from the known dangers of the Illanuan pirates to the far more treacherous dangers of the heart. Damn her for getting him to risk his life over this harebrained scheme to find her father when he was only going to lose her as soon as they returned to Kali Simpang.

If they returned.

They ate supper in silence.

Lorna took her time rinsing the dishes in the sherry-stained water, refusing Ross's offer to help, refusing even to look at him. She was too upset to forget what had happened between them the other night and too confused by his avoidance of her the past three days to pretend their relationship could continue as it was.

She had just gotten the dishes stacked in her arms when Ross came to help her. She stood abruptly, limping painfully a few steps toward the camp. "What's the matter?" he said.

"Blisters," Richard called from his hammock. "Her feet are a mass of 'em."

"Tomorrow," Ross said to Lorna, "you'll go barefoot."

"You told me there was fever in the mud."

"Not in the jungle soil. It has healing properties no one understands. In fact, the natives believe there's a cure for every ailment known to man somewhere in the jungle."

With twilight the uncanny quiet exploded into a thousand discordant voices, the throbbing of tree frogs and cicadas. Gnats descended in clouds so thick you couldn't help inhaling them until Kana lit a scattering of dried grass fires to drive them away.

They went to bed before Kurt and Mulak returned from their scouting forays.

The twelve feet that separated their sleeping areas might have been a chasm. Neither Ross nor Lorna slept. Ross had the late watch again anyway, and Lorna soon discovered she was encamped directly underneath a tree whose night-blooming flowers gave off an offensive stink that attracted fruit bats to pollinate them.

She listened to them rustling above her until she could not stand it and had to leave the hammock.

"That tree's called the 'midnight horror,' " Ross said, as she sat across the fire from him.

She stared into the shadows. Everything she saw wore an otherworldly halo of irradiant green—the mushrooms crowded into the buttresses, the centipede crawling up a liana, the hopping rat under her uncle's hammock.

"Why is everything glowing?"

"It's some kind of fungus."

She bit her lip, acutely aware that he was staring at her and making no effort to hide it. She had slipped off her chemise in the hammock to cool off and left her blouse unbuttoned.

"Come over here to me," Ross said suddenly. "We can't go on like this."

It took all her resolve to resist, and when Ross finally realized he would have to go to her, they were both stopped cold by the sight of a leopard crossing the aerial network of vines and branches overhead.

Lorna held her breath until the cat disappeared. There was a soft purring growl from the darkness. Ross slowly lowered his rifle and stared down at her. "Believe it or not, this is probably the safest place on the island."

She rose to her feet and attempted to move past him. He caught her arm and spun her around into his chest. "I think this is a good time to talk."

"I think I've said enough already. Too much—"

He kissed her before she could move again, the rifle wedged between their bodies. Lorna stiffened and told herself she wouldn't weaken this time. Instead, she raised her hands to his head and sank her fingers into his hair, straining closer to him, pressing her breasts to his chest. His hips jutted hard against hers. His voice, when he drew back to breathe, was harsh and fraught with the same combination of arousal and confusion she felt.

"If we were alone—"

She stepped away from him and then turned to retreat to her hammock. "Cover yourself up well tonight," he

called after her, and she did not know whether he meant
to protect herself from insects or from him.

The combination of a hundred screeching birdcalls and
the soft patter of rain awoke Lorna at dawn. At least she
assumed it was raining until she disentangled herself from
her netting. Amazed, she realized that the steady fall of
moisture was a collection of morning dew dripping from
leaves that nature had inverted to prevent them from rotting as they grew.

The canopy above teemed with life—gibbons swinging
in howling families, orange-blue parrots, golden canaries,
and emerald-green parakeets that appeared in brilliant
flashes and sailed through the gigantic loops of liana that
dangled to the ground.

As Lorna dressed, she discovered that mushrooms had
sprouted in her boots overnight from the humidity. She
banged them against a palm, swatting at the angry white
ants that dropped onto her arms and neck.

"I told you not to bother with your boots until your feet
heal."

At the sound of Ross's voice she snatched up her blouse.
She was wearing only her chemise and drawers and hadn't
finished putting up her hair.

"Do you mind?"

He continued to stare at her through the screen of ferns.
"Not at all. And if there weren't other men present, I'd
advise you to stay in only your underwear until we're out
of the jungle. It's far more comfortable."

She stepped into her skirt and yanked on her blouse.
"Go away—"

She was distracted by an angry shout from Kurt. "Another native disappeared during the night," Ross said
grimly, glancing around at the source of the commotion.
"Excluding Kana and Mulak, that reduces the original
number from eight to four."

"We'll manage," she said.

Ross watched her struggling with her hammock. "Oh,

yes. And it's a good thing you have the 'constitution of a Clydesdale.' We'll all be carrying another extra load today.''

That morning they began to ascénd in earnest into the heart of the montane jungle. They walked in single file, Mulak scouting ahead. Kurt took the lead with Lorna in second position, where she'd be least vulnerable to attack from any snakes he stirred up in passing.

There were no roads, no native paths to guide them. They followed the hillside ridges, struggling up and down trenches, amidst rows of teak and camphor that formed the only barrier between them and a two-hundred-foot drop.

Exhausted, her mind numb, Lorna stared at Kurt's back and followed wherever he led her, through crackling clumps of bamboo, between passageways of rattan, into hillside streams that swam with leeches. As they reached a steep ravine, the light became obscure and danced with elfish shadows. The dark chasm below amplified their every footstep. In tacit agreement no one spoke.

They were cautiously working their way along the narrow shelf when Lorna glanced back at her uncle and noticed he was shivering. The heat was so intense, she could only think he was frightened of falling into the ravine below. She couldn't bear to look down herself.

Kurt's voice interrupted her train of thought. ''Give me your haversack, Lorna. There's a barricade of rocks ahead that you'll have to climb.''

She removed the haversack and crept toward him with her arm outstretched. Suddenly a butterfly hawk soared by, distracting her. She dropped the haversack and watched in dismay as it plunged into the ravine.

''The shelf!'' Ross cried. ''For God's sake, Lorna, don't take another step.''

She glanced down. The porous rocks beneath her feet had begun to crumble. Staggering back, she caught hold of a vine, only to feel it snap forward as if in resistance, propelling her to the very edge of the shelf.

Ross shoved his way past Richard and threw himself against Lorna, flattening them both to the wall of the cliff. Their eyes met for an instant in a look more eloquent than a hundred words.

"My clothes," she said. "Everything is gone."

Ross grunted and inched away from her. "What the devil else did you have in that haversack? It thudded like lead into the ravine."

"Nothing much. Soap, tinned milk for tea, my curling tongs." She sighed. "My teapot—that's the hardest loss."

"Your guidebook?" Kurt asked hopefully.

Lorna shook her head. "I carry it in my pocket, thank heavens. I don't suppose there's any chance of retrieving the haversack, is there?"

"Not bloody likely," Ross said with a mirthless laugh, looking past her to Kurt. "That's it, van Poole. The expedition's over unless you find a safer way to continue the climb."

As soon as they were off the ledge, Kurt turned to block Ross's path as if to provoke a physical confrontation. But before either man could speak again, Mulak returned from his foray, his excited chatter diffusing the situation.

"He thinks he's found a path the Jalakans use when they make their volcano pilgrimages," Kurt explained. "He says if we can cross the ravine, we'll save ourselves a week's effort."

"Where is the path?" Ross asked.

"We have to return to the last stream we forded and follow it to the falls."

"Not more water," Richard said with an audible shudder. "My skin will never dry out. And the leech bites—" He sank to his knees, leaning his head against a camphor tree.

Lorna knelt at his side. "Are you unwell, Uncle Richard?"

"No, my dear. Just very hot and giddy. I'll feel better by evening."

"He can rest later," Kurt said. "We'll never find that

path before nightfall at this rate. God, now it's starting to rain.''

The leeches emerged in droves after the rain, raising up on their behinds, their pink bodies undulating across the jungle floor at the scent of fresh blood. No matter how well Lorna covered herself, they invariably found an opening in her clothes—through a loosened buttonhole, a rent in her skirt.

The search party followed the stream to the waterfall and found that behind the cascading water and overgrowth of vines was actually a hollow tunnel into the hillside. They were soaked by the time they'd waded through the damp foliage and squeezed into the concealed aperture. There was no light. The walls pressed down upon them until they had to proceed on their hands and knees, cobwebs brushing their sweating faces, unseen insects and albino mice darting between their legs. Every so often Kurt shouted that he'd found a bead or a betel nut, evidence of human traffic.

''I can't go on,'' Richard cried suddenly. ''There's no air to breathe in here.'' He was struggling to crawl over the four native carriers behind him, knocking his rifle and equipment aside. ''It's like a crypt in this tunnel, and we're going to be trapped, I know it. I have to get outside.''

''It can't be too much farther,'' Lorna said, her own skin creeping with the secret fear of being buried alive. She took her uncle's hand, trying to instill in him a courage she didn't really feel.

''It's probably just as far back to the entrance now as to the exit,'' Ross said, then paused. ''God, what is that stench?''

''It smells like death,'' Richard said with a hysterical sob. He clutched Lorna's hand. ''This is my punishment, Lorna, for deceiving you. But it isn't right that you should suffer too. It—''

''Shut up, you blithering fool,'' Kurt said from the front of the tunnel. ''You're using up what little air we have with your nonsensical babblings, and you're scaring the hell out of the natives.''

Richard was trembling, taking deep convulsive gulps of the fetid air. "I've always feared suffocation," he whispered pathetically. "Please, please, Lorna, get me out of here.''

She put her hand to his cheek. "He's burning with fever. We'll have to get him outside.''

"Damn it, no," Kurt said impatiently. "I saw a light around this corner, and there's even room to stand. Tell him we've almost made it through to the end. In fact, I think it's safe to light a candle.''

The feeble golden flame caught and cast its glow on the nine strained faces following behind Kurt as he crawled out of sight into a large crevice in the tunnel wall.

"I see the opening," he cried. "I see—Jesus, all of you, don't come any closer!''

Chapter 21

Kurt shouted the warning just as the last of the natives followed him into the hole. He raised his rifle and Ross reached for his in reaction, shoving Lorna against her uncle and squinting to see in the stagnant gloom.

They had entered a large cave. Bamboo cages hung from rattan hooks along the wall. As Lorna's eyes adjusted to the dim light, she began to perceive the outline of human skeletons protruding through the bars, arms outstretched as if in supplication. The only evidence of life was the bats clinging to the latticed ceilings, suspended in twittering clusters of fur.

She edged toward Ross. The natives staggered back against the wall. "What—what is this place?" she asked.

"I'd say it was the Jalakan version of Newgate Prison."

Forcing back her fear of what she might find, she glanced into every cage on the grim chance that one of the prisoners had been her father. With Ross and Kurt at her side, she gazed up at the white husks of human beings and tried not to imagine the tortures they had endured.

The skeletal remains were all too compact to match Sir Arthur's lanky frame. Until they reached the last cage. Lorna stared at the tattered tweed jacket draping the broad shoulder bones, the shattered spectacles that had slipped into the victim's collarbones.

"Oh," she gasped, putting her hand to her mouth. "Oh, Ross, help me."

Kurt lit another candle and placed it at the bottom of the cage. "Did your father ever break his right leg, Lorna?"

"N-no, but it could have happened h-here," she said, her face buried in the creases of Ross's shirt. His arm was supporting her sagging weight.

"What do you think, St. James? This man is taller than her father, no?"

Ross stroked Lorna's hair. "For once, van Poole, I think you're right. Come on, Lorna, let's get out of here."

It was only a short way farther on before they broke out of the cave onto the edge of a jungle swamp whose stagnant miasmas befouled the air. A pervasive silence heightened the grimness of the tableau left behind in the tunnel. Lorna helped her uncle along the slick embankment to a boulder where he could rest. No sooner had she gotten him settled than she saw a deadly draith uncoiling at her feet.

"Don't move, Lorna," Richard said, his voice trembling. "I'll get my gun."

She stayed his hand, swallowing a cry as the snake drew back as if to strike. At the same instant she spotted Kana crouched behind the boulder and watched him send his parang flying through the air. The knife bisected the draith into two writhing pieces that he threw into the swamp. Richard released his pent-up breath in relief.

"You be careful near this waters," Kana said as he retrieved his knife. "Evil spirits dwell here. And many more snakes."

Lorna looked at the swamp and wondered how anything at all could live in its murky depths. "Where is Tuan Resident?"

"With the shikari." He lowered his voice. "Tuan not want to go any farther."

She found Ross and Kurt arguing inside the hillside tomb. Kurt had proposed constructing two rafts from the bamboo cages and poling them across the swamp. Ross maintained the waters were untested and therefore unsafe. The natives were terrified.

Kurt stood with his legs braced apart, his face empurpled. "I'm not going to lose a goddamned week because you and a bunch of half-assed natives are afraid of ghosts."

"And I'm not going to risk all our lives to suit your warped schemes."

"Why don't we let Lorna make the decision?" Kurt said as she appeared behind them. "After all, she's paying for this expedition."

Ross looked at her, his eyes full of dark irony. "Well, Lorna?"

"Please, Ross. . . . I simply could never live with myself knowing I hadn't done everything possible to find my father."

He made a sound of disgust and pushed past her, sweat trickling down his temples as he emerged from the cave. He blamed himself for this, for his own lack of self-control, as much as he blamed van Poole. If he hadn't been so obsessed with Lorna, he would have stuck to his original assertion that the expedition was a suicidal folly. He should never have let her convince him otherwise.

"Ross." She came up behind him and touched his shoulder. "I thought you understood."

He turned, his face troubled. "What I understand is that I'm a fool, and that even if we do find your father, we'll never leave this island alive."

"You can leave now."

"No, I can't," he said with heavy realization in his voice. "I can't leave *you* here. That is something I could never live with."

He moved away from her to the edge of the swamp to watch the natives assembling the rafts. After swiftly dismantling the bamboo cages, they lashed the long lightweight poles together with liana vines to fashion surprisingly sturdy craft.

Kurt, Richard, Mulak, and two of the natives poled their

raft across the swamp first, landing on the opposite side without incident. But as Lorna settled down between Kana and the other two Malays, uneasiness washed over her.

It was silent except for the water dripping off the long bamboo poles plied by the pair of terse-faced natives. Enormous water lilies snagged them as they passed. One of the carriers had snared a pheasant on shore to later sacrifice to Penala; it was tied to the kris resting against his shoulder. The bird was only half stunned, beginning to stir as the raft drifted past the midway point.

"Do they have to kill it?" Lorna asked Kana. "It's only a baby by the look of it."

As Kana turned to examine the bird, Lorna was suddenly conscious of a surge of pressure underneath the raft. She glanced at Ross to comment on it, but he had swiveled around, his face shadowed by the sinuous black vines that trailed into the water from the trees above.

"Ross, what—"

She broke off with a gasp as a crocodile blasted straight out of the water and snapped the pheasant into its jaws. From the shore Kurt fired once, hitting the crocodile in the throat. Even then it thrashed in death throes as it hit the water, the bird's tail feathers squashed between its fangs. Kana threw out an arm to steady Lorna as the raft rocked violently.

"Watch out for the vines above your head!" Ross shouted to her. He lunged to grab the poleman by the forearm as he tottered on the edge of the raft. The raft swayed and then slowly steadied itself. Lorna was too terrified to even turn her head.

By the time they reached the opposite bank, the surface of the swamp had subsided back to its deceptive calm with the raft drifting lazily on the current and a handful of feathers marking the spot where they had nearly capsized.

Once on solid ground, Lorna sank to her knees against Kurt's haversack.

Ross stared down at her in grim contemplation. "I think Lorna should return to the sloop with her uncle."

She put her hands over her face.

"We can't turn back," Kurt said, wiping moisture from his rifle with a dry cloth. "The Agung-Mani have been trailing us since we reached the ridge."

"How do you know?" Lorna asked, glancing at him over the tips of her fingers.

"They send messages through the trunks of the trees. You have to read the vibrations. So no one can go back now—except perhaps Richard."

Lorna lowered her hands and looked at her uncle lying prostrate in the glade. "What's wrong with him?"

"Pig-tick fever," Kurt said. "It will take weeks, perhaps months, for him to recover. He'll only slow us down."

Ross walked across the clearing and knelt at Richard's side, feeling his pulse, examining the calves of his legs for tick marks. "We're taking him back to the ship," he said, rising. "And then we're returning to Kali Simpang."

"No," Richard said weakly. "I'll stay here until I'm better. We've come too far."

"You can't stay here alone," Kurt said brusquely. "We'll see how you are in the morning, and if there's no improvement, Kana and Mulak will carry you back to the sloop." He glanced at Ross, then at the others with undisguised contempt. "What a pathetic little group you are. A girl with more guts than common sense. A British Resident whose self-righteousness will smother us all. A clodding oaf of a sickly Englishman. And a band of ignorant savages afraid of their own shadows. God, what a group."

He spun about to stalk off into the forest, motioning the natives to follow. Furious, Lorna jumped to her feet and shouted after him, "How dare you leave us after all I've paid you!"

"I'm not leaving you," he said imperturbably, not glancing back. "I'm scouting ahead to make sure my bunch of boobies doesn't walk into a trap."

Lorna went to her uncle, hiking up her sodden skirts to kneel at his side.

"Lorna," he said, tears in his eyes. "I'm such a fool."

"No, you're not. Kurt is just impatient and in a vile temper."

"I should never have made you come along. This illness is my punishment. I deserve to die."

"That's nonsense. I insisted on coming, remember?" She glanced up at Ross. Despite her anxiety, despite the ever-present dangers and discomforts, she drew strength from his presence.

She rose tiredly, staring into his eyes. "He needs help."

"Kana knows of a root that can prevent the more serious side effects of the fever if it's taken in time," he said quietly. "Mulak and I will go with him to find it, if you can manage alone for awhile. I'll leave my rifle."

"I can manage."

"We won't wander far," he said. "According to Mulak, there's another waterfall about a quarter mile from here. We'll leave you and Richard there."

Some time later, when they had arrived at the waterfall Mulak had described, Lorna settled Richard in a hollow enclosed by volcanic rocks whose crevices sprouted waist-high ferns. The water ran clear and fresh here, with blue herons alighting to drink and white egrets engaged in picking leeches from the backs of water buffaloes. Twilight shadows bathed the fig tree grove beyond.

Lorna sponged down her uncle, but he seemed to grow worse, shivering convulsively and vomiting the small sips of liquid she gave him. Finally, he slept and she crept off to wash in the river. He was asleep when she returned. She unbuttoned his drenched shirt and began searching through his haversack for a clean one to replace it. A packet wrapped in a protective layer of canvas fell into her lap. She untied it with unthinking curiosity.

She found not only the two letters from her father that she'd never received but also the ones that were missing—*stolen*—from her trunk at the plantation house.

Disbelieving, she started to read.

"Dearest Lorna," the letter began in her father's sprawling script.

I pray you will not be shocked by what I am about to reveal, my darling, but I must tell someone the horrible mistake I've made, and there is no one on this earth I trust more than you. Even as I write this letter, the malevolent eyes of the White Tiger are watching me. I do not possess the statue . . . it has possessed me. . . .

She stared into the shadows of the fig grove, her chest tight with anguish, the letters of damning evidence against her father, and her uncle, in her lap. She wished with all her heart that she could awaken and find that the last nine months of her life had been only a nightmare. Except that then she would never have known Ross. . . .

She reread her father's letters in the waning light. She read his explanation of how he had innocently spent time in research on Kali Simpang. How he had met Pierre Lu Chan and been fascinated by the man's boasting of his art collection, and then, inadvertently, how he'd stumbled upon the White Tiger while Pierre was showing him his most priceless treasures.

Her father had restolen the statue on impulse, fascinated by its legend, by the promise of immortality its possession endowed, and yes, he admitted, even by the lure of wealth that could be his if he sold it.

I thought of you and me, Lorna, of all the luxuries we had gone without for so many years, the humiliation of always borrowing from Richard, and you marrying that odious Kirkham, whom I did not openly oppose only because I knew he could comfortably provide for you. For weeks I gloated over my crime, overcome with greed and vain imaginings of immortality. Then soon I began to realize that I could not keep the Tiger. It emanates an evil greater than any I could create in my fiction. I have resolved, therefore, to remedy my wrong by returning it not to the authorities in Singapore but to the land of its origin.

I do not have much time. Pierre Lu Chan suspects me of the theft by now, I am sure. And I should be ashamed to admit to Rajah Charles that I have kept the statue hidden in my hillside retreat all this time, brooding on its fate, knowing its violent history. It is for me alone to atone for my sin. Countless innocent souls have died since the statue was stolen by a Swedish explorer from its pagan birthplace. Unspeakable sacrifices are made even here on Kali Simpang to appease the bloodthirsty Tiger god who lives in the heart of a volcano. I will return it to the island where it belongs. . . . I will end the curse that follows it, even if I forfeit my own life in so doing.

"Are you still there, Lorna?" Richard murmured, his hands moving restlessly. "Be an angel and fetch me something to drink."

Betrayal all around you, Ali Aziz had prophesied.

"Lorna? Is something wrong? Dear God, you're not ill, too? You look ghastly."

She didn't answer. She just lowered her head and stared down at him as if he were an utter stranger to her. Which indeed he was. It was devastating to be betrayed by the uncle she had always felt such protective fondness for. All the blundering flaws she had overlooked in the blindness of her affection for him. And in a way, it was a deeper disappointment than her father's conduct, for Papa had not deliberately involved her in any danger. At least he had recognized his wrongdoing. But Richard had deceived and misled her. He had used her to find the statue, for surely he cared nothing about her welfare if he was willing to risk her life to help him find it.

"Does Aunt Julia know why we left England?" she asked tonelessly. "Is she also part of your scheme?"

He looked bewildered. "Scheme?"

"The White Tiger, Uncle Richard. Is that not what this so-called mission of mercy is really all about?"

His head fell back. A shudder rippled through his frame.

"Why, Uncle Richard?" she whispered in an anguished voice. "Why?"

"Van Poole talked me into it. He f-found out that Arthur had gotten hold of the statue, and he wanted to combine our resources to organize a search without arousing suspicion."

"Then you did not really care whether you found my father at all?"

"Of course I did. But he was the one who created this whole wretched mess. I couldn't see letting him return that priceless statue to a bloody volcano when the money it would bring could provide for us all for the rest of our lives."

She stared up at the trees, feeling numb and cold inside as her last hope that he would defend himself died. At least now she would know the truth.

"What was Kurt's stake in this?"

"We were to split the money he got for the Tiger on the black market. It—it's said to be worth millions to the right person."

"Millions," she said bitterly. "Is it worth our lives, your integrity?"

"Integrity?" he repeated, resentfully. "Where was your father's integrity when he bled me dry with his endless financial needs? Who put you through boarding school, my girl? It wasn't Arthur who saw to it you were properly attired and presented so that you'd attract a future earl's attentions."

"You hate Papa!" she cried. "I always knew you envied him, but it goes deeper, doesn't it?"

"When I was seven years old, Lorna, only *seven* years old, I had to work in an ill-lit, rat-infested factory to help pay for Arthur's precious education. I sacrificed my youth—my spirit, my future, *my dreams*—so that your father could sit about composing poetry and charming his dons at Eton." His face grew dark with exertion and the pain of remembering. "What will Aunt Julia have left when I'm gone? A pathetic clerk's pension, that's all."

"If you tell me," Lorna said, fighting to control her emotions, "that Aunt Julia actually sanctioned this insanity—"

"Of course she didn't," he said quickly. "But it was because of her—and you, Lorna—that I agreed to van Poole's plans. I intended to use the money wisely, you see. The doctors all say she would do better in a warmer climate with her rheumatism. I thought if I could move her to Italy, she might find at least some relief from her pain. And I wanted to take proper care of you, as my brother never has. I wanted to give you and Spencer a fairy-tale wedding to remember always instead of the deprivation you were accustomed to."

"A fairy tale—against a backdrop of murder, theft, and God knows how many other crimes? How noble of you, Uncle Richard. I don't suppose you intended to spend even tuppence on yourself."

"Well, of course. But it's your father you should be most angry at, don't you see? He's the one who got us into this."

As they stared at each other, a faint suspicion began to take shape in her mind. "You and Spencer have always been close. Did you tell him about the Tiger, Uncle Richard? Is he expecting us to come home laden with riches?"

"Spencer knows nothing of this, I promise you, Lorna."

Without a word, she rose and walked into the forest, too numb to cry, or to fear the rustling shadows.

Ross found her huddled against a lemon-scented laurel, her face buried in the crook of her arm. She had neglected to smear insect-repellant oil on her skin, and tiny red bumps were rising on every exposed inch.

"Lorna, I've talked with your uncle. We found the root to reduce his fever . . . if you still care."

She lifted her face and looked at him, unable to hold back the sudden rush of emotions unleashed by the compassion in his voice.

"Go away," she said, her voice breaking. "I'll be ready to leave as soon as I compose myself. Until then, I really would prefer to be left alone."

He settled back on his haunches but made no move to leave. After a while, her quiet sobs abated.

"Well, Ross, you've gotten your wish. I'm willing to pack up and go home. I assume Richard's told you everything. There's no point in going on."

"I'm sorry about Richard," he said. "I can't say I'm surprised to learn he is involved."

"Can't you? Bloody nice of you to share your insight."

"You wouldn't have believed me," he said. "And I wasn't going to make things worse between us when I had no proof." He passed her a handkerchief. "I didn't want us to fight again."

She blew her reddened nose. "I've no will left to fight."

"I don't believe that."

"You were right, Ross."

"About what?" he asked gently.

"About my father. That my relationship with him has destroyed my life."

"That's a bit harsh," he said. "I never said exactly that. I'm sure he must care about you. How could he not?"

She tossed her head. "Well, he can find his own way out of this mess. He never gave me a second thought, gallivanting from one end of the globe after my mother died, foisting me off on strangers so that he'd have peace to write his horrid books. He never considered my feelings. It's always been the other way around. I'm tired, Ross. I'm tired of being betrayed and used by the people I love." She blew her nose again. "I thought you'd be leaping with joy at the chance to leave."

He shrugged. "I've changed my mind. We've come this far. We've nothing much to lose now."

"Except possibly our lives and probably our sanity. I don't want to go on. I just want peace."

He leaned forward, cupping her face in his hands and looking deeply into her eyes. "Lorna, understand this. I can't go back to the island and tell my uncle we gave up. And once you were back to yourself, you'd hate me for letting you quit."

She frowned, her mouth trembling. "Lorna," he continued softly, "not everyone in your life has betrayed you. I never would."

"You haven't had time."

"Give me time to prove myself to you. If we ever get off this island, I'll show you that your faith in me is well placed."

She sighed like a lost child and buried her face in his shoulder as he drew her against him. "I think, Ross, that you could talk me into anything. No wonder the Rajah has such faith in you. No wonder we all do."

He inclined his head to kiss her tear-stained cheek, holding her until the last remnant of sunlight faded and darkness engulfed them.

When Kurt returned with the natives a few hours later, it was to a chilled reception he could not misinterpret. He threw down the bananas and clusters of figs he had gathered, along with the canteens of water he had refilled at the river, where Kana and Mulak were keeping watch.

"Use this water for drinking, Lorna."

She looked up at him from the campfire and then quickly turned away.

"How are you, Richard?" he asked, halting at the hammock where the man lay.

Richard opened his overbright eyes, his face and throat glistening with sweat. "She—she found Arthur's letters."

Kurt said nothing. He merely glanced at Lorna, his eyes narrowed. "And?" he asked at last.

"She *knows*," Richard replied weakly.

"You told her—"

"Everything."

Kurt's mouth twisted into a cynical smile. "You couldn't keep your mouth shut, could you, you bumbling fool? It was all too much of an adventure for your feeble system to handle. I told you to destroy the letters."

"Leave him alone," Ross said from the fire. "At least he has a conscience."

Kurt paced to the edge of the clearing and returned to help Lorna prepare the fish the natives had caught. "It's up to you what happens now," he said as he handed her the first canteen.

"What do you mean?"

"I'm still willing to find your father. All I want is the Tiger and a chance to get away. I'll even give your uncle the split he asked for after the statue is sold. And you—there'll be enough left over for you to do with as you please."

"Do you really think I could live on that money, knowing men were murdered to gain it?"

"The slaughter in Singapore was unfortunate, I agree. But fear and intimidation are effective tools when dealing with susceptible minds. I needed to make sure I would not be followed or betrayed. Besides, if I don't recover the statue, someone else will."

"There's no way to justify what you're doing."

"I suppose it's different for your father?"

"At least he's trying to return it to its rightful home."

"To placate an island of savages?"

"The gods will not be pleased," she said without thinking.

"The gods? Does that mean you too have come to believe?"

Despite his scornful tone, she thought she noticed a shadow of unease cross his face at her mention of the gods, but it was soon gone.

"I told you earlier, Lorna, that there is no turning back now. Not for me, because I will recover the Tiger if I die in the attempt. Not for you, because you are motivated by love, and love does not give up.''

"How would you know? Who have you ever loved?''

"My sister, my nieces and nephews. Even you, in a peculiar way.''

"You disgust me,'' she said.

He shook his head, smiling. "I'm going to miss you. I truly am.''

"Then you are leaving us—''

"Yes. We'll make it a contest, shall we, to see who can reach the mountain first?''

She jumped up, his soft laughter following her as she returned to the campfire.

"He's going to abandon us,'' she told Ross.

"I gathered as much.'' Ross took a deep drink of water from his cup. "Do you feel better?''

"I feel . . . empty.'' She glanced around as Richard began to moan and thrash in the hammock. "How long does it take for the root to work?''

"It should have already started to take effect.'' He rose, his hand gripping hers. "Stay away from van Poole. There's no reason he should want to help us now.''

Ross's warning was still echoing in her mind as she repeated her earlier task of rehydrating and comforting her uncle. From the corner of her eye, she observed Kurt and the four natives sitting a distinct distance from the campfire, their faces shuttered.

A shiver danced over her skin.

"No,'' Richard said, clutching her hand.

"Are you ill again?'' she asked wearily.

He shook his head, gesturing behind her to the campfire. She turned, straightening in alarm as she saw Ross approach the circle and say something that made van Poole leap to his feet, his face flushed with anger.

She hurried toward Ross, her nerves strained beyond endurance. She was terrified there would be a fight. Both men had been spoiling for it ever since she'd arrived on Kali Simpang.

Neither of them noticed her, but she could feel the primitive tension building between them as she reached Ross's side.

"You call me a coward, St. James," Kurt said in a low, deadly voice. "Who do you think has brought us this far?"

"The natives," Ross said, his breathing harsh. "And courage goes far deeper than courting physical danger to prove one's manhood. Courage has nothing to do with deceiving a young woman and then abandoning her to die in an alien environment. Of course, I would expect anything from a man like you . . . a man who murdered his own wife."

Lorna did not move, expecting Kurt to react to the accusation. Instead, he smiled with chilling unconcern, not bothering to deny Ross's words.

"You murdered your own wife too, St. James, as I recall. Indirectly, perhaps, but in the end is there a difference? And your own son, your heir—"

"It was an accident," Lorna said. She knew Kurt's taunting was intended to hurt Ross, and that it would succeed.

Kurt glanced at her. "Naive child," he said, reaching for his rifle. "There are no accidents."

Ross moved so swiftly Lorna scarcely realized what he intended as he shoved her to one side and swiveled on his heel, his right leg snapping out at the knee to kick the rifle from Kurt's hand.

For an instant Kurt wavered, glancing down at the natives as if he expected them to leap to his defense. Lorna saw the uncertainty on their faces. She knew they feared Kurt; she knew they would go against their own instincts to obey him. But she also knew—she hoped—that they remembered Ross would soon rule them, that it was to him they owed their allegiance.

Kurt lunged at Ross, a parang in his hand. She flinched as she saw Ross's left hand shoot upward to protect his face, the other balled into a fist to ram into the other man's throat. Kurt's face darkened, but he threw his entire weight forward, slamming his elbow into Ross's face to send him stumbling back a few steps until he suddenly regained his balance. His lean face intense, Ross grasped Kurt's wrist and twisted it back until the parang dropped onto the ground.

Lorna quickly knelt to retrieve the rifle, but Kurt moved faster, grabbing the weapon with his right hand and pulling her against him with the other.

Holding her tightly to his chest, he got to his feet and faced Ross. "Mudah," he said, addressing the native sitting directly behind him, "gather up our supplies and see to it that the Resident is left without food or ammunition. Nako, take care of Kana and Mulak at the river."

"You bastard," Ross said softly, his eyes flickering to Lorna's face.

She did not move. She wasn't convinced Kurt would kill her, but she knew he'd relish the excuse to murder Ross. And Ross looked no less menacing, his eyes blazing with unbridled fury, a thin line of blood trickling from the corner of his mouth.

When the natives had finished gathering up the supplies, Kurt shoved Lorna toward where Ross stood.

"Farewell, Lorna," he said with a rueful smile. "You kept to our pact, after all . . . but we'll soon find out how far that admirable spirit will carry you without my help."

Chapter 22

◝◜◞◟◝◜◞

Lorna opened her eyes and saw the vultures circling around the trees overhead. For several seconds she did not stir, reviewing the events of the previous evening, then becoming aware of an exquisite throbbing in her temples and a maddening itch all over her face and hands.

She tore off the huge leaves that had served as her blanket, then sat up with a horrified cry to see that her skin was swarming with scores of orchid spiders.

"Don't panic. I'll get them off you," Ross said.

"They're in my ears! And down my neck!"

She closed her eyes, shuddering with revulsion as Ross crawled toward her and swiftly brushed the spiders to the ground.

"I thought we were dead. The vultures are—"

"One of the natives apparently changed his mind about accompanying van Poole. He was shot in the back." He studied her face, noting the purple shadows like smudges beneath her eyes. "God, Lorna," he said with a deep sigh.

"Is Richard all right?"

"The root reduced his fever, but he'll still have to return to the sloop." He helped her up, swatting a fat spider off her shoulder.

"What are we going to do?"

"Find water first. Lack of it is one of the primary causes of death in the jungle."

"The river isn't very far."

He shook his head. "They killed a water buffalo and left its carcass to rot where the stream feeds down over the rocks. We'll have to climb up higher to where it runs pure."

"My guidebook says you can drink from the lianas."

"From some. Others will knock you dead after a few sips. If we get really desperate, we can collect water from the tanks of the prickly bromeliad plants that act as natural reservoirs in the trees."

"Kurt's trying to kill us," she said as if she could not believe it herself.

He pulled her to her feet, drawing her against him and holding her until they were disturbed by Kana returning to the camp. "Do you want to stay with your uncle or come with me?"

"I'll come with you," she said without any hesitation. "But the vultures . . . Can't you fire a shot to scare them away?"

"There was only one pistol the natives neglected to take, and I'm not going to waste any cartridges on the scavengers. Anyway, it's nature's way of keeping down disease."

"I misjudged you, St. James," Richard said later that afternoon when Lorna and Ross returned with drinking water. "If not for you, my niece and I would surely perish. I mistook your strength for arrogance."

Ross expelled a breath, slinging down the gourds he had hollowed out in place of flasks. "If I had been truly strong, I would never have agreed to this expedition in the first place. But"—he shrugged, pushing his hair off his forehead with his wrist—"we're too involved now to give up."

"I don't understand." Richard struggled to sling his legs over the hammock, clutching at the vine netting for support. "The pair of you can't still be determined to go on. I—I forbid it, Lorna, do you hear?"

Ross and Lorna stared at each other in contemplative silence. Somehow, since Kurt had left them, they had overcome the fears that might have forced them to reconsider. As the shikari had said, there was no turning back now for any of them.

Total exhaustion. It seeped into the bones before it spread to the spirit, claiming Lorna from the instant she awoke in the morning to the blessed moment they made camp at night.

There was always another stream to ford, another rain to wait out, another dozen leeches to pluck off her deadened skin. She could hardly believe it had been only two days since Kurt had left them. In that time she had learned that Ross's keen sense of direction, his physical stamina and knowledge of the jungle, were more than equal to any shikari's skill. If only she knew where they were headed, and what they'd find at journey's end.

They climbed a muddy slope, slipped and started all over again. Crawled through tunnels of vegetation which, if they were lucky, a passing family of rhinos had already trampled down, and then tumbled down and down, over hidden rocks and decaying trees, praying they would not land in a patch of thorny rattan. Which more often than not, they did.

Lorna visualized herself as a human pincushion. If there was an inch of skin on her left to prick, she couldn't find it.

"We'll stop soon to rest," Ross told her repeatedly, like a farmer dangling a carrot before a donkey, and she always nodded, too weary to speak.

They traveled alone. Richard's condition had not improved, and Ross had ordered Kana and Mulak to carry him back to the sloop and return to the jungle as soon as possible.

They relied on their ingenuity, like children playing house. Lorna wove hammocks of dried grasses. They used large leaves for blankets. Ross carved eating utensils out of bamboo and served her boiled lizard eggs for breakfast.

They were like Adam and Eve after the fall from Grace, alone in a savage Eden, all the while climbing higher and higher toward the home of the devil god Butas, the Tok Belang.

Ross was certain that the Agung-Mani knew of their

approach. More than once he was awakened by a subtle whistle carrying through the forest that no other bird or animal answered.

He was afraid, not just for their lives, but because daily he found it harder to believe that Sir Arthur could have made this journey alone. And if the Agung-Mani had captured him, then his chances for survival were even more uncertain.

"Lend me your knife, Ross."

He reached out automatically to help Lorna over a grassy hillock, staring at her flushed face, the tangle of red-gold hair she'd knotted at her nape. He was probably going to get them both killed.

"Your knife," she repeated with an impatient sigh, and he watched as she slashed at the hem of her skirt until it came to her knees beneath a row of ragged lace. "Don't say a word," she warned him. "Not one word while I've still got this knife in my hand."

But if there was adversity, there was beauty, too, to be recognized in the warm moonlit evenings when the anteater and civet cat, whose musk scented perfumes in London, prowled amidst the damp grasses and a thousand night-blooming flowers sweetened the air. There was beauty in the weird twisting of lianas filled with epiphytic orchids and the iridescent blue bees that pollinated them.

At five thousand feet they feasted on raspberries and wild bananas, and Ross caught a mountain antelope in a little ravine. For the first time they encountered the sulphur hot springs that poured down from the cavity of a burned-out crater on the mountain.

"It smells like hell, all fire and brimstone," Lorna said as she waded in the soothing warm water that ran blood-red with volcanic earth.

"It means we're close to the volcano now. To the village where your father was presumably taken."

"Oh, God, Ross, what if he isn't there? What if all this has been for nothing?"

"Bit late to worry about that now."

They regarded each other across the puddle of bubbling

springs, a veil of steam separating them. Slowly, without speaking, Ross came to her. He gripped her hard and she melted against him, inhaling the strong musk of his skin, the hot water lapping around their legs.

"I love you," she said, on the verge of tears. "I can't help it, Ross. I love you."

Something deep inside him broke. He held her to him, his heart pounding, his eyes squeezed shut.

"Don't cry," he whispered. "Everything will be all right. . . ." He didn't know whether he could keep that promise, but for her he would die to make it so.

She drew back, her voice unsteady. "Don't you love me at all, Ross? Even a little?"

"Lorna, Lorna, how could I not?"

He led her to the clearing they had carved out earlier and laid her beneath him on a fragrant grass mat. For the first time he made love to her with his heart as well as his body, allowing himself to experience tender emotions that for so many years he had suppressed. He was shaking as they undressed each other, trembling not only with sexual arousal but also with the belated acknowledgment of his own vulnerability. With the willingness to love again came the chance he would be once more wounded. If only he could know everything was well for Vanessa and Ian, in whatever heaven they inhabited. If only he could release them and move out of the past.

Lorna stroked the damp skin of his shoulders as he entered her, her body straining with his, seeking the pleasure that was so intense it almost stopped her heart as it overcame her. The sunlight faded from the sky and the stars emerged from a smoky heaven. The steam from the hot springs rose into the darkness and warmed their entwined bodies where they lay in drowsy contentment.

Ross fell asleep, planning in his mind the route they would follow the next day. Kurt had been a talented guide, indeed, he thought, to have left no trace of the trail he'd taken. But sooner or later Ross would find some hint as to which way he'd passed . . . assuming that nothing had befallen him on his way to the village.

He drew Lorna closer, her face pressed to his shoulder as weariness washed over him. As he slipped into a pre-lucid awareness, he saw himself walking through the jungle, Lorna trailing behind him. It was mid-morning in the dream, and the shadowed greenness took on an other-worldly glow. A pair of purple butterflies flitted before him, dancing in and out of a drapery of vines. He turned back to reassure himself Lorna was all right, but she was so far in the background he could no longer see her face. She waved to him, signaling everything was well, and as he turned away from her, raising his arm to slash at the vines, he was puzzled to discover they had disappeared and in their place stood a small dark-haired boy dressed in a white shirt and tan trousers.

Ross felt a trembling start deep inside him as he stared at the boy, a wellspring of joyous recognition, intuitive, unquestioning, bubbling up inside him. His hand dropped to his side, releasing the parang. It made no sound as it fell. He could not move. He did not even breathe as the child raised his face to him.

"Daddy." The boy's eyes were gold-flecked gray, his features so like Ross's own that he could not fail to rec-ognize them. The boy looked as if he were four years old, tall for his age, as Ross had been.

"Ian," Ross whispered, falling to his knees with his arms outstretched as the boy ran into his embrace. "Ian," he repeated, his voice thick with emotion.

He did not question how his lost son had appeared be-fore him. It was enough to hold him for this moment, to communicate with that close embrace all the regrets, the sorrow, and the love that he had held inside him.

"You're all right?" he said, leaning back to marvel again at the strong little jaw, the solemn gray eyes.

"Of course, Daddy."

"You know that I never meant to hurt you—"

"He knows," a woman's soft voice said above them. "We both know, Ross."

He looked up, his gaze focusing on Vanessa's delicate features. This was a dream, Ross realized in the back of his mind, but there was a reality to it he accepted on an intuitive level even if it defied rational explanation.

"I don't understand why it happened," he said. "Why you were both taken."

"All you need to know is that we are happy, Ross. Only your sadness clouds our peace. Can you not accept our forgiveness and live the life you were given?"

There was more he yearned to say, but the words would not come. Suddenly they did not seem to matter. Then something compelled him to turn his head, an awareness of love, of a strong yet gentle presence behind him.

Lorna. The clearer her image grew, the less aware he became of Vanessa and Ian. He felt Lorna's hand touching his, warm, strong. He heard her voice, though the words were distant. Her fingers tightened against his; with effort he turned back to the spot where Ian had stood, but now there was only a shaft of brilliant sunlight brightening the jungle floor. Yet Ross did not feel sad.

"Lorna," he whispered, opening his eyes.

She was leaning over him, her red-gold hair loose about her face, her eyes concerned. "I think you must have been dreaming," she said. "I've been trying to rouse you for ages."

He sat up slowly, trying desperately to recall the images that had filled his dream. "Did I say anything while I was asleep?"

"Not that I could understand." She began plaiting her hair over one shoulder, her fingers twisting deftly. As Ross watched her, he was overcome by an inexplicable wave of tender affection. "My guidebook says that the natives consider the hot springs holy ground, that they often spend nights alone here in the hope of receiving dreams of revelation. I don't suppose your dream gave us any clues as to how to continue?"

"Do you know how beautiful you are?" he asked her unexpectedly.

She lowered her hands to her lap. "That's the first time you've ever said anything like that to me and I've believed you."

"Well, I have thought it countless times." He raised his face to the sky, tinted orange upon cobalt blue where the sun was rising. Strangely it was one of the most peaceful moments of his life, to sit here beside Lorna at sunrise. Not even the prospect of what lay ahead could spoil his serenity. For the first time in years, he allowed his true feelings to flow unimpeded.

He thought it ironic that his greatest peace had come when he had begun to accept the possibility of his death. The burden of guilt and emotional self-exile he had suffered for so long was finally lifting, and he did not know whether he could stand the freedom that beckoned. The freedom to love Lorna. To forgive himself and start another family without fearing that a vengeful God would strike them down to punish him for what he had believed were his sins, the pride and willfulness that had contributed to Vanessa and Ian's deaths.

But unless they got off this mountain alive, it was all fantasy anyway.

The rotten-egg stink of sulphur grew stronger now, often overpowering the more delicate perfumes of orchids, white honeysuckle, and laurel. At seven thousand feet the leeches disappeared, and the dense forest began to give way to steep groves of Balih Sumpa draped in grayish lichen and stands of rattling bamboo. The air thinned.

By day they could hear the siamangs howl and the pheasants cry. At night the coughing roar of a mating tiger would drift from the moonlit riverbanks. Soon they would be forced to leave the womblike cocoon of the green jungle for the lava-scarred face of the mountain.

On their last morning in the rain forest Lorna awakened in her hammock to feel Ross beside her, his arm snugly encircling her waist. She stretched, unwilling to surrender the last vestiges of sleep for the grueling day ahead, but he refused to release her, his grip tightening until the pain around her rib cage roused her fully and she opened her eyes to protest.

"Don't make a sound," he whispered in her ear.

She lay unmoving, her nerves jumping at the sound of footsteps not ten feet from where they lay concealed in a natural bower of overgrown ferns. She could feel Ross's heartbeat against her shoulder. Her own agitated pulse actually made her feel lightheaded, as did the tension of waiting, not knowing whether they would be discovered.

"Agung-Mani," he said, long minutes after the footfalls faded away, and the chattering of birds resumed above.

"Do you think they were looking for us?" She sat up stiffly, blood rushing into her cramped limbs.

"I'd assume so. Thank God we took precautions last night to hide ourselves. We can credit Kurt for teaching us a few tricks."

"I'd like to thank him by wringing his neck," Lorna said wryly.

"Not before me, love."

She eased out of the hammock, staring at the area the Agung-Mani had searched just minutes before. "It's only a matter of time before they find us."

"It will be easier when Kana and Mulak return from the sloop."

Lorna nodded, not daring to voice her fears that the two natives might never have made it back to the ship with her uncle. Still, there was nothing to do now but continue onward.

The jungle ended unexpectedly, giving way to bamboo, rhododendron, and mountain passes of alang-alang grass. Lorna missed the raucous morning music of the red jungle cock and tetabu birds. More than anything, though, she missed the protection from the outside world that the rain forest, despite its hazards, had afforded.

The mountain rose steeply now. In the mornings heavy mists engulfed them in a rainbow-edged haze. The black soil stank of sulphur. Now and then the unnerving silence was broken by a siamang calling or a hill wren chattering from the myrtles.

It rained their first night on the exterior, and without the cover of jungle, they were forced to shelter in a *rumah*, the cave of one of the prehistoric-looking dragon lizards Lorna had spotted earlier sunning in a gorge.

"We'll start climbing the cliffs of the main peak tomorrow," Ross told her over the miserable fire of brush and twigs he was feeding. "After that, we wait until Kana and Mulak find us."

"But we've been so careful to cover our trail."

"Not so careful that Mulak won't be able to follow. Anyway, they'll make their own way to the village. There can't be many paths to reach it."

He took a swig of mountain spring water from his gourd. "Strange that we haven't encountered even a single villager." He finished the water after a time, still reflecting aloud. "And there aren't the usual signs of offerings about."

The fire died with a choking puff of smoke. Coughing, Ross grabbed a palm frond to fan the ashen embers. "We might as well get some rest."

But she was already asleep, had been oblivious of him for the past fifteen minutes, curled up on a mat, her head pillowed on her hands. He covered her with a sheet of bark and leaned over to kiss her cheek as a surge of love, fear, and desire rushed through him. He saw no point in telling her he'd heard a tiger in the distance. There was nothing they could do about it anyway.

There was no doubt they were being observed as they picked their way slowly along the precarious mountain path, the sheer drop to their left deceptively hidden by an overgrowth of vines. The dawn mist had not yet burned off, and steaming geysers of mud spewed out of the numerous fissures they depended upon for footholds. Even if they survived a fall from the sheer mountainside, they'd never be able to climb back onto the path.

Lorna glanced up at the ledges that provided the perfect

ambush point, and gasped when a face appeared suddenly from between two rocks. Agung-Mani—she recognized the animal mask and tattooed shoulder—and even before she could cry a warning to Ross, the native lifted a slender blowgun to his lips.

She pushed Ross toward the face of the cliff. The poison dart flew into the air where seconds ago they had stood. His arms lifting to shield her, Ross pulled her down behind a pile of fallen rock, his pistol poised, ready to shoot the assailant. But even after a tense half hour of waiting he never reappeared.

"I'm going to give you my gun," Ross said after a long interval. "I can use the bow and arrows I made in the jungle if I have to."

"We're going to die," she said, standing with her back to the cliff.

"The thought had occurred to me."

The mist had evaporated, and a watery sun appeared as they reached a stream that rushed through a lava bed. Lorna knelt to scrub at her face and neck, but Ross shook his head in warning.

"Just refill the gourd. I don't like remaining out in the open any longer than necessary."

"It can't be too much farther, can it?" Her breath steamed the thin mountain air.

"I don't know. I wish I did."

Less than two minutes later they found the body of one of the Malay carriers who had accompanied Kurt, sprawled across the path that had become so narrow they could no longer walk abreast of each other.

"Turn your head away," Ross said.

"How did he die?" she asked quietly. "Was it a blow-gun dart?"

He hesitated. "No. A man-eater. Let's just hope that its appetite for humans has been appeased. I suppose I should cover him with a few rocks."

"The Tiger god," Lorna said in a subdued voice. "Do you think he could have been left as a sacrifice?"

"It's an unpleasant possibility."

"It's—" She stilled in sudden apprehension, sensing a presence behind her. She glanced upward at the rocky ledge that ran parallel to the path. She saw nothing.

"Sit down, Lorna, with your head between your knees," Ross instructed her. "You look—"

Those were the last words he said. He was standing with a rock in his hand to put on the corpse and then suddenly he was sagging to his knees and falling backward. Over the edge of the path, out of sight.

For a horrifying moment she couldn't react. From behind the rocks overhead at least six Agung-Mani appeared, lean and golden-skinned, their faces masked, their torsos striped with slashes of black dye. Each wielded a long tubular blowgun whose darts could kill a man of average weight within two hours. And when she saw Ross falling and realized he had been hit, her first impulse was to stand and wait in defiant terror for a dart to strike her too.

"Ross!" she cried in desperation. "Ross!"

She wrenched the pistol from her waistband and fired at the nearest native. The shot hit the cliff but succeeded in sending the hunting party scrambling for cover in the mountain crannies where they had previously hidden. As one of them, clearly braver than the rest, lifted his blowgun to his mouth, a white eagle soared downward before Lorna with its wings outstretched, circling above the cliff three times until even the last native retreated in fear.

Lorna gave the eagle not more than a glance of distracted gratitude. She stared down into the dark chasm in dread. When finally she spotted Ross's body sprawled beside the mountain stream, she could only pray that somehow he was still alive.

It was against all odds. She knew that even as she dropped to her knees and began the dangerous descent, digging her feet into the uncertain crevices on the cliff face, grasping the protruding clumps of fern when her bleeding fingers threatened to lose their grip. She refused to look down, knowing the fear of falling would paralyze her.

What took her only a half hour seemed like a lifetime, and she was frantically aware that with every second that passed, Ross's chances of survival lessened. Moreover, she had become an easy target for an Agung-Mani dart. Yet they did not appear again. Perhaps the eagle had given them pause.

When she finally reached Ross, he was lying on his side, the single dart clutched in his hand, blood drying on his forehead.

She turned him over with infinite care, biting her lip as he stirred and attempted to push her away. "Damn it," she said. "Damn it."

"Mustn't swear," he whispered. "Are you all right?"

"Yes," she said brokenly. "But I—I don't know what to do."

"Find us shelter if you can." He flung the dart away from him and reached up to grasp her hand. "Leave me behind if you can't."

Fear shivered along her nerve endings. "There has to be something I can do to help you. Do you know of any antidote?"

He stared at her, his gaze unfocused. "Antidote . . . for a cracked head?"

"But the dart—"

"Hit the rock I was holding on the ledge and somehow became embedded in my shirt. I plucked it out as I fell so it wouldn't stick me accidentally."

She sank back onto her heels, shaking with relief.

His mouth curved into a pained smile. "Featherbrain," he murmured fondly, closing his eyes.

She managed to heft him to his feet, supporting his weight on her shoulder and hip. "That looks like some sort of path leading down through those trees, but I don't know where it ends."

"No." He sagged against her, glancing back to the spot where he had fallen. "There's a cave partway up the cliff you just came down. We'll have to climb up onto those rocks to crawl inside.''

He was semiconscious by the time she half hoisted, half dragged him into the cave that overlooked the chasm. As she stepped into the dim interior, the stench of animal droppings, so pungent that her eyes began to water, nearly sent her reeling back outside. Even the dragon lizard rumahs hadn't smelled so nauseating.

She laid Ross down as comfortably as she could and then coaxed a small fire with a precious match and a heap of dried ferns that had blown into the cave. The miserable flames leaped and then dwindled to smoke, but not before she caught a glimpse of the dark creatures covering the cave walls. Bats. Thousands upon thousands of them, twittering uneasily at the unaccustomed light.

Panicking, she jumped up and ran to the mouth of the cave, taking huge gulps of fresh air, working up the courage to return to Ross. Voices filtered down to her through the ferns, and she looked up, drawing back inside belatedly as a hempen rope swung down in front of her. Before she could fully retreat into the cave, a lithe figure dropped down into the overgrowth that partially concealed the entrance.

''Kana! Oh, thank God, thank God.''

''You hurt, missee?''

''No, it's Tuan.''

Mulak appeared next, armed with a spear and boarskin shield. As they all retreated into the cave, he stopped and sniffed the air, then knelt to examine the ground.

''Bats,'' Lorna said, clenching her fists.

Mulak shook his head. *''Matjan.''*

''Matjan?'' she said distractedly. ''I've heard that word before. What does it mean?''

There was a groan behind them.

''It means,'' Ross said, lumbering to his feet, ''that we've taken refuge in the lair of a man-eating tiger.''

Chapter 23

The tiger wasn't home. But as they ventured deeper into the musty interior of the cave, they stumbled across the fresh carcass of a mountain antelope and realized a return was to be expected.

"There's probably no other way out of cave," Kana said. "Original path, farther up cliff face, crosses into Agung-Mani kampong."

"The path," Lorna repeated, thinking of the nondescript stretch of dirt concealed beneath a tunnel of trees on which she and Ross had been ambushed. "Did we miss the village? Is it farther up the mountain?"

Mulak hunkered down on his haunches to face the others. "Down. Not many peoples left since volcano erupt, perhaps two years ago."

Lorna glanced over at Ross to reassure herself he was finally awake. He'd suffered a mild concussion from his fall, and she wasn't certain whether to believe him when he kept insisting he was fine.

"They must live in constant terror that the volcano will erupt again," Ross said, thinking aloud. "No wonder they are desperate to please their Tiger god."

"*Matjan* return before dawn," Mulak announced, his face impassive.

Lorna glanced around the cave. "Isn't there another way out of here?"

"I doubt it." Ross fingered the gash on his head. "But

326

we'll have to try. We may find somewhere else to hide in case the tiger makes an early return. We have until nightfall to look.''

"What do we do after that?'' Lorna asked him uneasily. The diffuse light penetrating the cave had already begun to wane.

"We'll have to take the path we were on and hope we don't run into another ambush.'' He lowered his hand. "We'll head back down the mountain to the village . . . and hopefully to your father.''

She laid her head against his shoulder. She no longer believed they would find her father alive. It had all been for nothing.

As they pressed farther into the cave, they passed under ceilings dripping with stalactites and iridescent lichen. Kana and Mulak scouted ahead a few yards to search for an exit to safety. Lorna thought she would lose her mind as they plunged down one twisted corridor after another, following a trickle of water that Ross hoped would lead to a stream.

Unexpectedly a mild earthquake shook the entire mountain, disturbing the bats, and Lorna didn't know which alarmed her more, the earth shifting beneath her feet or the masses of unseen creatures rustling and occasionally swooping down out of the stagnant darkness with their webbed feet and wings brushing her face.

"There's a light ahead,'' Ross said suddenly. "I think I can feel fresh air.''

He reached backward and caught her hand, guiding her toward the arc of light. But no sooner had they stumbled a few more steps than he stopped in disgust.

"Bloody wonderful. We've been wandering around in here all day only to come full circle back to where we started.''

"Then we *have* to leave by the path. At least if I'm going to die, it won't be with bats draining the blood from my body.''

Kana brushed past them to look outside, followed a few

moments later by Mulak. Lorna could hear the hushed murmur of their voices as she and Ross finally joined them at the opening of the cave.

The cold air outside felt so invigorating that she couldn't seem to draw enough of it into her lungs. She didn't even care that its purity was tainted by the crater above them, wheezing mephitic fumes and sonorous blasts of sulphur into the night sky. Gazing upward into the vaporous darkness, she could see where cracks and fissures steamed with gases that swirled into the evening mists. Against the moonless black sky the mountain had taken on an ominous aspect that she hadn't noticed earlier in the day.

"It looks like hell." Unconsciously she leaned against Ross.

"Or as close to it as I care to get," he murmured. "I'd guess it is several hours before midnight."

"There's no moon."

"All the better for us to start back toward the jungle unnoticed."

"The jungle?"

"I'm having Kana take you back there while Mulak and I scout around the village."

"No, Ross. I've come this far with you, haven't I?"

"Tuan is right, missee," Kana said softly. "Mulak say this nights very bad nights to go near Agung-Mani kampong. Itam Bulan," he added in an undertone.

Mulak stirred, gazing across the chasm at the shadowed path they must ascend to. Lorna, distracted by the fierce look of concentration on the native guide's ugly face, glanced from Ross to Kana.

"What does it mean, 'Itam Bulan'?"

"The ceremony of the black moon," Ross told her hesitantly. "It—"

He broke off, diverted when Mulak began cocking his head back and forth, then staring intently at the dense scrub cover below them.

"It means that tonight there will be another human sacrifice," Ross finished.

"But not to the volcano," Kana added. "To the Tiger god who lives inside. He very angries tonight. Make mountain shake."

There was an indistinct, peculiar noise from above them. Mulak rose slowly, nodding his head.

The sound that drifted down toward them was not one that Lorna had heard often, but the deep coughing roar could not be mistaken. The man-eater was returning to its lair.

They waited for an interminable half hour, while the lone cat prowled about on an unseen shelf above them, pacing, sniffing, circling in the dirt and stones. Then suddenly, unexpectedly, the tiger leapt down perhaps twenty feet onto a pile of rocks just below them, a graceful streak of compact agility. Lorna stared fiercely into the shadows but could discern only the most nebulous shape. Yet the agitated swishing of the tiger's tail against the ferns, its leisurely pace as it approached the cave, made her rigid with terror.

It knows we're here, she thought.

Then just as suddenly as it had appeared, the tiger leaped upward into a tree opposite them and vanished into an overhang of branches above the stream.

"Now. Go," Ross said, pushing Lorna before him so that she was protected by Mulak and Kana.

"It was an old cat, Tuan," Kana said quietly.

Ross gave a terse nod and motioned forward with his right hand, fingers tightly gripping the pistol. Lorna knew he had only one shot left.

The climb back up the chasm went far more easily than the descent, Kana and Mulak helping her up the hempen rope, pulling her to the relative safety of the mountain path from which Ross had fallen.

Yet she did not breathe until he scrambled to his feet beside her, his face damp with exertion.

"Come on."

She stared back over her shoulder into the chasm. "Won't the tiger follow us?"

"It might."

"What—what did Kana mean when he said it was an old tiger?"

"An old tiger is more liable to have developed a preference for human flesh. And people are far easier to kill than animals."

She did not speak again after that, concentrating instead on tackling the thin, treacherous path. The four of them were connected to one another by the length of rope, looped and knotted around their waists to encourage sure-footedness. Although the total darkness increased the peril of falling, the path back down seemed more smooth than it had been when Ross and Lorna had ascended it alone.

The village was well concealed in a bamboo grove almost halfway down the mountain, on the jungle outskirts where the seaward-bound river rushed through a massive configuration of black lava boulders, some almost fifty feet high. It was behind them that they took refuge, crouching in the shadows of the riverbank to survey the Agung-Mani kampong.

Fog drifted over the water in ghostly shreds, adding to the eerie isolation of the village. There were several native dugouts crowded along the shoreline, and Kana and Mulak moved stealthily in the darkness, devoting their attention to disabling the boats.

The village itself, illuminated by a great central campfire, was nothing more than a cluster of mud-and-grass huts, enclosed by a peculiar bamboo fence on whose pole-tops sat hideous hand-carved relics and human skulls.

"Those would tend to discourage the occasional visitor from dropping in," Ross said with grim humor.

Lorna glanced at him, his face and form half shrouded in fog, half silhouetted against the distant fireglow.

"Has the ceremony begun yet?"

"It doesn't appear so." He leaned forward onto his knees. "I'm not going to ask you to leave with Kana again."

"I wouldn't go anyway."

His eyes gleamed like steel in the darkness. "No, I didn't think you would. But if anything happens to you, Lorna, I would *never* stop blaming myself."

She glanced away, a knot of fear rising to her throat.

"Tuan," Kana whispered, crawling toward them. "Ceremony begin."

With Lorna at his side, the two Malays behind them, Ross watched from behind the boulders as an Agung-Mani witch doctor emerged from a bamboo temple so far removed from the other dwellings that Ross hadn't noticed it until a procession of torchbearers converged on its perimeters.

The Itam Bulan, ceremony of the Black Moon. A young male headed the procession, bearing on a gemstone-studded altar the statue of the White Tiger. Draped in black silken robes, his face obscured behind a mask with reptilian jaws, the witch doctor followed at a slow pace, sprinkling holy water on the crowd gathered to worship the ivory tiger, itself covered in precious jewels that caught the firelight.

Trance dancers undulated in the shadows, bare feet slapping the damp grass, eyes rolling in their sockets. A chosen medium writhed and then froze in a contorted pose, as if the spirit had seized possession of his soul.

Ross picked out enough words to understand that a human sacrifice had been demanded to placate the Tiger deity who controlled the volcano.

He glanced back at Kana. "I trust your judgment. If at any time Lorna is in danger, use whatever means you can to get her back to the sloop."

With Mulak at his back, Ross edged forward, zigzagging in and out of dancing shadows, until he came against the bamboo enclosure. His muscles burned with tension as he strained to hear every noise, detect every movement.

It was one thing to know people were actually murdered in pagan worship, another to witness the atrocity. And he hadn't seen a sign of Sir Arthur, who in all likelihood had already been a victim of the Agung-Mani.

"Shikari, Tuan," Mulak whispered, creeping beside him, his parang held between his chipped teeth.

Ross looked up in disbelief. Not ten yards away a pair of masked Agung-Mani were bearing Kurt in a bamboo cage toward the mountain path, presumably into the tiger's den. He had been obviously beaten and lay slumped against the cage with his arms and legs tied to the hollow bars. There was no sign now of the rebellious arrogance he had displayed during the expedition. In fact, the horrified pity he stirred in Ross surpassed his anger.

The witch doctor began to address the bejeweled statue, raising his arms dramatically to the mountain. Ross couldn't understand a word of the mantra he chanted, but he gathered from the gestures and raised voices that the medium did not agree with the witch doctor on whether—or how—to sacrifice van Poole.

Apparently, the medium won out. A mood of restless anticipation settled over the crowd. The pulsating drums competed with the crashing of the nearby river over the rocks. The medium raised his fist into the air. At that signal the natives bearing the cage resumed their climb up the path and disappeared into the dark mists of the mountain. Somewhere behind Ross a dog began to bark.

There was nothing he could do to save van Poole. He wasn't sure he'd chance his life even if he thought it would help.

"Tuan?" Mulak inclined his head to indicate that if they were going to search the kampong for Sir Arthur, it would have to be now, at the height of the ritual.

"Right," Ross said grimly, and then straightened, only to freeze halfway to his feet as Lorna crept up beside him. "Why in God's name didn't you stay put?" he demanded.

"There was a pair of dogs on our scent," she whispered, staring back at the boulders she had left. "They started to bark, and I feared it was only a matter of time before they set the entire village on us."

"What happened to Kana?"

"He wanted to make sure I reached you, so he decided to divert the dogs back to the mountain. He said he'll meet us at the river as planned."

Mulak shook his head, as if doubtful Kana would return at all.

"The damn fool," Ross said, but there was more fear than anger in the words. "If he had—"

"*Ang, ringa, pen, menpang brong sih,*" the witch doctor began intoning before the altar. "Black fire from my breast, appease the demons of darkness. God in heaven, forgive these heathens and save my miserable soul. . . . "

Ross stared in disbelief as the frail but unmistakably British voice drifted across the clearing. Lorna rose shakily to her knees, her face ashen in the firelight.

"My father," she whispered in a voice dull with shock.

Incredulous, Ross watched as the witch doctor—could that hideous figure really be Sir Arthur?—lifted the statue from the altar and abruptly vanished with it into the skeletal kepuh trees that surrounded the *dulam saki,* the sacred temple.

He looked back at Lorna. "This is our chance. Do you think you can run if we have to?"

"Yes." She got to her feet, her gaze still on the temple.

For a moment Ross did not move, gauging the distance they would have to cover, grateful for the misty shadows that enclosed the village. Mulak waited patiently, his wiry body brimming with nervous energy.

They moved stealthily around the enclosure, Lorna in the middle, Mulak at the rear, and Ross ahead, signaling when it was safe to proceed. His anxiety lessened somewhat when they reached the perimeter of the light given off by the campfire, where a semicircle of darkened huts provided cover for them to proceed to the isolated temple. Breathing hard, crouching together in the stinking mud of a pigsty, they waited in silent trepidation as an elderly man shuffled out of his hut to watch the ceremony from the earthen path in front of his home.

At last a child's voice called to him from inside the house. With maddening slowness the old man turned and began to move, one inch at a time, back up the path. Mulak did not remove his gaze from the man's shuffling bare feet. Ross remained motionless, aware of the tingling numbness in his ankles and lower legs. Only a flimsy palm frond cover concealed them, but at least the snoring pig beside them drowned out any inadvertent noises they might make.

Ross was acutely aware of Lorna. They had both lost weight during the expedition, but while Ross felt haggard and dirty, he thought that she only looked more delicately beautiful, the thinness of her face accentuating her unusual sea-green eyes and strong bone structure.

She refused to raise her face, but with the force of his will, he succeeded in connecting their gazes. His heart tightened at the bewilderment in her eyes. The relief she should feel at finding her father must be tainted by the confusing evidence of what he had become.

They reached the bamboo temple unnoticed, slipping past the two guards who stood laughing and talking several feet away. After passing through a series of connecting cubicles, they finally found Sir Arthur in the largest compartment at the rear of the domelike structure. He was on his knees before an unshuttered window, his face in his hands. Without the grotesque mask, he appeared smaller than he had during the ceremony, and Lorna choked back an involuntary cry when he lifted his head to stare at them.

"Papa—"

He leaped to his feet, his graying, shoulder-length hair swirling around his face. His hazel eyes wide with fright, he backed up against the thin wall and then, without warning, he opened his mouth and began to shout for help.

Ross lunged forward, pressing his hand to Sir Arthur's mouth. "It's all right now, Sir Arthur. We've come to take you home."

The older man ceased struggling as Lorna moved fully into his view. "Papa," she whispered brokenly, holding out her arms to him.

Ross drew his hand to his side, but still Sir Arthur did not move toward his daughter. Shaking his head, he edged away from Ross, toward the altar where the White Tiger sat surrounded by a circlet of night-blooming orchids. His gaze defiant, he snatched up the statue and hugged it in his arms.

"Go away," he whispered hoarsely. "Get away from here!"

"We only want to take you home, Papa. You can do whatever you like with the statue."

"Lorna?" he whispered, stepping toward her as if only now he could believe his eyes. "I never thought—but how—"

"You remember me, sir," Ross broke in, "the Resident from Kali Simpang? Ross St. James. Rajah Charles sent me to find you."

"St. James?" Sir Arthur whispered uncertainly, then recoiled, hugging the White Tiger to him as Ross reached to wrest it from his grasp.

"Sir Arthur, please, you may have the statue later. But come with me now, or all our lives will be in peril, including Lorna's." Sir Arthur looked at Lorna, his face collapsing as Ross carefully hoisted the statue into his arms. It was ivory with onyx stripes, yellow-green emerald eyes, and a ruby mouth above a collar of diamonds. Ross wanted to smash it to smithereens for all the grief it had caused.

From the corner of his eye he noticed Lorna and her father embracing, but suddenly Sir Arthur broke away, his voice alarmingly loud in the still temple.

"I did it all to survive, Lorna," he said unsteadily. "I had no choice, you see—"

"It's all right," she consoled him. "I'm glad you had the wits to fool them."

"But I want you to understand—"

"Guards moving toward temple, Tuan," Mulak said from the curtain at the door where he stood watch.

"Do you know a way to the river without passing by the village?" Ross asked Sir Arthur, anxiety sharpening his voice.

"The river?"

"Please, Papa," Lorna said. "Please think."

"There is no way out of here," he said heavily. "Has this not been my own private hell for months?"

All of a sudden from outside rose the frenzied barking of several dogs. Ross moved to the narrow slit that served as a window. Kana's lithe figure edged past his line of vision and was gone, streaking in the opposite direction of the trees. The two temple guards outside abandoned their post to investigate the disturbance. His chest heavy with admiration, Ross realized that Kana had been aware of their whereabouts and was using himself as a decoy so that they could escape.

Ross swiveled around, bending to replace the statue on the altar. "Let's go."

Only Sir Arthur hesitated, backing away from Lorna to reclaim the statue. With an exasperated curse, Ross turned to usher the older man outside with the others.

The reverberations of the ceremonial drums assailed them as they broke out into the foggy evening. Lorna could feel the loud vibrations penetrating the very earth she trod, moving through her body to rival the wild pounding of her heart.

"Agung-Mani celebrating sacrifice to their god." Mulak's face was impassive as he gestured toward the village.

"Which way?" Ross demanded tersely of Sir Arthur.

"Down that incline. There is a little bamboo bridge across—"

He fell silent, moving closer to his daughter as the drumbeats died to an abrupt silence, then resumed in a frantic tempo.

"Why did they do that?" Lorna said, her blood turning cold.

"Alarm drums," Sir Arthur answered. "We've no time to waste."

She ran so fast she felt as though she were being stabbed in the sides with a pair of red-hot swords. Ross and Mulak snatched her and her father to their feet when they stumbled over a twisted root. Night birds stirred in unseen branches at their passing, and a herd of deer scattered before them, frightened at the crashing footfalls.

They broke out of the grove and startled a pair of Agung-Mani archers walking along the riverbank. They were in the open now, a wide gap between them and the boulders where the canoes for their escape were tied. Only the fog provided them with any sort of cover, and it was dangerously unreliable.

"Cross back behind the last stand of trees," Ross instructed Lorna. "Mulak and I will divert them while you and your father run."

"Be careful, Ross."

"And you." He regarded her, his gray eyes unnaturally bright. There was so much he longed to say, and now it might be too late. She had given him back the ability, the desire to live his life again. It did not seem a sacrifice that he might lose that life to protect her. "Go!"

She headed back the way they'd come, glancing around to make certain her father still followed. Rage swept over her as she realized he still carried the statue against his chest, that he was risking their lives by clinging to his sick belief in its powers.

An arrow whined over her head and bit into a tree. She couldn't see for the heavy mist, but there were footsteps behind them now, and disembodied voices.

"Lorna!"

"Oh, Ross, where are you? I can't see anything."

"At the river. Stay where you are. I'm coming to get you."

It seemed an eternity before he reached her, wending his way through the shadows. "The canoe is ready. We'll have to take our chances on sailing past the search party that's after us."

They stole across the stillness of the grove, aware of shouting voices that grew nearer. Lorna slipped to her knees in the dank mud of the riverbank. As Ross lifted her to her feet, another strong arm shot up to help her climb into the canoe.

"Kana." For a moment she was overcome by a rush of relief and affection. "Are you all right?"

"No, missee. My whole body hurt very bads. And I lost my glasses too."

Ross snatched up a paddle. "Get under the thwart, Lorna. Lie low with your father until I tell you it's safe to come up."

He released her and she swayed unsteadily in the rocking boat, bending at the waist to position herself as he requested. Suddenly, from out of the mists of the grove, came the slap of bare running feet, and a lone masked face, disembodied in the fog, loomed above them.

The solitary warrior slid down the embankment, a long pointed lance held in his hand.

The lance hurtled downward at Lorna. Before she could duck or fling up her arms, Ross knocked her hard against Mulak and lunged for the masked assailant, grabbing him by the knees and throwing him to the embankment. The native twisted frantically. Lorna discerned a flash of silver as Ross lowered his parang. The warrior groaned and fell still.

Suddenly dozens of torches burned against the fog, drawing nearer to the riverbank. Lorna caught a glimpse of Ross's face, dirty, lean, and smeared with blood, before he leaped into the canoe.

A swarm of Agung-Mani neared the riverbank. The canoe resisted the current, caught on a mudbank. Then, suddenly, with Ross, Kana, and Mulak plying their paddles, the boat shot forward, whisked away like a feather in the wind. Yet even then they could not relax, as a steady stream of arrows poured at them from either side.

Lorna, crouched down with her arms around her father, stared up at Ross's face as if she could will him to be protected from harm. "Will they follow us?"

"Not in the boats left along the riverbank. At least not for long."

Even as he spoke, the Agung-Mani were overturning, untethering, and jumping into their canoes to pursue the prau. As Ross manipulated the lightweight boat around a bend, shouts resounded from the bank as the natives discovered the holes bored into the canoe hulls.

"There are other boats," Sir Arthur murmured to Lorna. "They'll follow us, you know."

"Ross—"

"I heard," he said without glancing down. "There's nothing to be done for that now."

Sir Arthur slowly raised his head to stare at Lorna. Her heart contracted as she looked into his gaunt, bearded face, at his snarled hair and shrunken shoulders. He had always been youthful in appearance, but now there were few traces of auburn left in his hair, and his hazel eyes were dull and shadowed with fear.

"They'll torture us if they catch us." He said this with certainty. "They'll feed us piece by piece to the man-eater on the mountain."

"You—you saw this sort of thing, Papa?"

"I witnessed every atrocity imaginable. I—" His voice dropped so low she almost could not hear it over the rushing of the prau against the river. "I participated in more evil than even my own morbid mind dreamed could exist on this earth." He faltered, his voice breaking. "I presided over—"

"Don't talk of it now, Papa. It's over, that's all you must remember."

Still, even as she attempted to console him, she feared the damage done to his psyche went deeper than anyone could see. He had always been too sensitive for his own good, although it had helped him as a writer. And even though she realized he had done what he'd had to do to survive, he could not help but be emotionally, perhaps permanently, affected in his mind by what he'd endured.

He pressed his cheek against the cold white neck of the statue, rocking it in his arms like a child. "They have not yet rung the bell," he murmured.

"The bell?" Lorna said.

"The sacrificial bell on the mountain. It is rung when the tiger has begun to devour its victim."

Kurt, Lorna thought, shuddering at the agonizing end

he was about to meet. It was hard to believe she'd once regarded him as invincible, as a man who could conquer any earthly force. But in the end he was a man who was conquered by his own spiritual darkness. In challenging death, he had dared too much. She should feel little sympathy for him. After all, he had abandoned her and Ross to die in the jungle. Yet she couldn't help wondering what sort of man he might have become had his younger days not been warped by the cruel abuse Ilse had spoken of.

The boat spun about in a wild circle. Startled, Lorna looked up to see Ross paddling furiously around a half-submerged tree looming in the dark waters. The craft pitched into a churning trough, slamming its occupants against one another. Lorna fell back against Ross's knees. He pitched forward, caught by the arm Mulak had thrown up to prevent his fall.

Her whole body shivered in relief. Then as the pounding of blood in her ears receded, she detected several excited cries from the stygian stretch of river behind them.

"They're coming after us," she said, her voice rising in fear. "Dear God, Ross, I think—I think I can see them—"

For miles the Agung-Mani pursued them along the tortuous bends and dips of the river. Once they came so close to the single prau that Lorna could actually feel the cold foam their oarsmen had churned up. Now and then a dart or arrow would whiz past them to scrape the water. But the utter darkness that made negotiating the river so treacherous also provided a measure of protection.

At one point Kana collapsed from exhaustion. The prau lost appreciable speed. Remembering that the young Malay had spent his energy evading pursuit on the mountain, Lorna urged him to take her place next to her father. Her face determined, she snatched up his paddle and straightened on her knees opposite Mulak. It was bliss to stretch her tortured body.

"What the hell do you think you're doing?" Ross snapped, fatigue and fear eroding all self-restraint.

She leaned into the paddle, slowly picking up the rhythm

the two men set. "We can't afford to lose any more speed."

Ross glanced down at Sir Arthur, his mouth thinning in unconscious resentment. "Are you going to allow your daughter to risk her life?"

The elderly man lifted his head. "They'll torture us if they catch us. Lorna's always been a strong girl. She'll manage."

His eyes blazing, Ross bent into the oar and plied it with the renewed vigor his rising anger supplied. God knew it wasn't the time or place to start a quarrel. And yes, Lorna's help might indeed save their lives. But it was Sir Arthur's attitude toward her that infuriated him, his selfish assumption that she existed to serve his needs. To think Ross had worried that she would return to Spencer . . . it was her father he should have been concerned about all along.

The river changed in subtle degrees. By the time Kana regained enough strength to resume his position at the bow, Lorna could no longer fight the crosscurrents and small whirlpools that occurred more frequently as the river was fed by numerous mountain streams.

The Agung-Mani had dropped farther behind. That in itself should have been reassuring. But sunrise could not be far away, and the natives surely knew the turns of the river better than they did. Moreover, the increased difficulty the three men were having maneuvering the craft forewarned them that the easiest stage of their flight was about to end.

Ross had known for almost an hour what they would eventually face. He'd noted the quickening in the central current that carried them. He had felt the insidious drop in the riverbed, the increased size and frequency of the boulders that pitted the gravelly bottom. And even now, in the distance, he could detect the muted thunder of the rapids they were approaching.

He'd run the rapids on Kali Simpang, but never in a

craft this size. Never with the safety of four other passengers to consider.

He flung himself into the paddle, avoiding a rock that appeared as if from nowhere. Backstroking with all his strength, he narrowed his eyes to gauge what lay ahead. The sky had lightened almost imperceptibly to pewter. Shadows of vine-clad trees carved stark silhouettes against the steep-banked shore.

"Tuan!" Kana cried in warning, but Ross had already anticipated the narrow scrape through a sharp-rocked passageway, plying the blade with frantic speed.

Yet before Ross could even congratulate himself on the skillful maneuver, he glanced up at the escarpment that overlooked the river. With quiet panic, he realized that it was the twelve painted archers positioned up ahead along the slope that Kana had been warning him to avoid.

Mulak gazed up at the escarpment. "Agung-Mani sent message ahead to scouting parties. Attack us as we pass."

Ross stared straight ahead, his shoulder muscles quivering. He could feel Lorna looking up at him, but he dared not glance at her. It took all his concentration to negotiate the treacherous torrents that propelled them forward . . . toward certain death.

Suddenly the banks of the river closed in around them. Unseen vines, thorny and wet, lashed at them from above. Massive black boulders, outlined in white foam, whirled at them out of the grayness. Cold spume and perspiration stinging his eyes, Ross twisted his lower body and thrust his paddle against a shelving ledge. The canoe shot sideways, lurching wildly.

With grim irony, he remembered Kurt's warning in the jungle:

I don't fancy making ourselves sitting ducks for some little bastard's blowgun.

As if propelled by invisible forces, the canoe rushed over the dark, frothy waters, drawn toward the as-yet-unseen rapids. Suddenly, without warning, the river twisted. Around a sharp bend the waters dashed, bearing the lightweight craft in its current. Ross cringed as he heard the canoe's bottom scraping against rock. When the spume flying about them finally settled, he saw another bend. There the river split into two directions, white water frothing over the boulders that obscured visibility beyond the farthest curve of the river.

The first route, the straightest and safest to navigate, led them directly beneath the archers waiting on the escarpment. A death trap.

Taking the second route meant shooting the rapids in untested waters.

He glanced at Kana, then at Mulak, nodding tersely.

The three men paddled in a frenzy of coordinated effort, steering the craft between a jagged archway of rocks. For an instant the canoe hovered in flat water. Then before Ross could decide whether he had made a mistake, the craft burst out into space and dropped into the placid basin below.

The second series of rapids, steeper than any he'd ever shot before, came before he was prepared for it. By the third he felt he was losing control . . . but it was too late. The canoe shot forward, plummeting down. . . .

"Lorna!" he shouted as he felt a tremendous pressure force him backward. But his voice was lost in the splintering crash of the canoe bow against a shallow outcrop of rocks and the thunderous roar of water racing over him and the capsized boat. He grabbed her sleeve, catching a glimpse of her startled face before she vanished from view . . . and the current wrenched them apart.

Lorna felt a heavy weight dragging her downward and realized it was not the current but her father clinging to her arm. She flailed out to grasp him as he was torn from her side, but the river heaved her shoreward, swirling her around and around. Her hands scraped rock, and she could not breathe, trapped beneath the overturned body of the canoe. She fought with all her being to reach the surface but only succeeded in draining her strength. At last she could not battle the current any longer. At the horrifying realization that she would probably drown, she drew upon a final reserve of fortitude. Straining, kicking, she broke to the surface of the water to find herself entangled in a strand of reeds along the shore.

It took several minutes for her to work herself loose. Then, in a daze, gasping and choking, she searched frantically across the tumultuous water for a sign of Ross. It seemed her heart did not resume beating until she spotted him flung out across a flat-topped rock, preparing to launch out again into the river—

"Lorna!" he shouted, his face alight with relief. "Stay right there!"

"My father—"

He gestured behind her. She turned to see her father lying prone on the shore, Mulak kneeling over him. The head of the White Tiger, its emerald eyes shining in the purple-gray shadows, lay nestled in the crook of Sir Arthur's arm. He moaned, lifting his hand to his face.

"Are you all right?" Ross asked her. Having made it safely to shore, he'd waded into the reedy still water where she was waiting.

She nodded, leaning against him as he dragged her against his chest. She could not speak for several moments, welcoming the warmth of his face against her neck, the firm support of his arms around her waist. A cool undercurrent nudged their bodies closer together. Her knees gave out, and with a deep frown of concern, he lifted her up in his arms and slogged through the water to lift her onto the bank.

"Where is Kana?" she asked.

"I sent him downriver to search for you in case—"

"In case—"

"Never mind. I don't even want to think about it. You're safe, thank God."

She glanced behind her but saw only the endless rise of snarled foliage. "The Agung-Mani?"

Ross shrugged tiredly and deposited her beside her father. "We've put enough distance between us and them to increase our odds of reaching the sloop."

"Through the jungle again?"

"Yes. It's safer than delaying to build another boat."

"Lorna?" her father called out weakly, raising up on his elbows to regard her. He looked like a wildman, she thought in despair, trying to ignore his haggard face and tangled hair. He cleared his throat to speak again, his voice faltering with emotion. "I was afraid for a moment I had lost you—but then I remembered the Tiger. Its power is stronger than anything we could ever dream up together, Lorna. It kept me alive all those months, and if . . ."

She glanced up at Ross and then hastily away, unwilling to face what she might find in his eyes. Her father's voice faded as the tumult of her own thoughts chased uncensored through her mind. She couldn't blame Ross for resenting her father. She resented him too, but she also loved him, and it was almost more than she could bear to see his brilliant mind convoluted with his weird beliefs.

She closed her eyes. Her body felt numb. Her mind drifted away. . . .

"Lorna."

She jerked upright at the sound of Ross's voice. "What happened?" she asked, fatigue slurring the words.

"You fell asleep," he said. "I'm sorry, but we can't afford to wait."

She got to her feet, fighting down a wave of nausea. In the background she could hear Kana and Mulak already slashing at the wet green wall of the jungle. It was all she could do to put one foot in front of the other.

A chorus of bullfrogs and wild birds resounded from the depths of the rainforest.

Ross knelt to help her father onto his feet, his face gaunt with fatigue.

It was sunrise, and they had survived.

Chapter 24

The return through the jungle went far easier than Lorna had expected, perhaps because they'd already covered so much ground by water. Or perhaps because they knew the pitfalls to avoid. When they finally made camp that same night beneath the forest canopy, she was so exhausted she couldn't have taken another step even if the Agung-Mani had suddenly appeared. The queasiness in her stomach had subsided but not completely—the result of fear and hunger, she suspected.

She lay back upon her bed of palm fronds, staring up into the trees that stretched some three hundred feet above her. She knew Ross was awake, lying a stone's throw beside her. She shifted onto her side to look at him.

"You should try to sleep," he said quietly.

"I think I'm overtired. My muscles keep jumping every time I close my eyes."

Seconds later the uneasy humid stillness was broken by the patter of rain. In tacit harmony they sprang up to erect a makeshift tent of palm fronds on bamboo poles to protect their pathetic camp. Mulak, standing guard by the stream, lifted his face to the sky but did not move.

"Remind you of something?" Ross asked as they settled back under the dripping canopy.

She shook her head. "What?"

"You don't remember . . . the first night in the sulap? I have never felt both so excited and wretched in my entire life as when I was stretched out on that bloody roof with you leaning against me.''

"Lower your voice," she said, smiling at the memory of that night. "Kana and my father will hear.''

"I don't care. Do you want some coconut milk?''

"Only if it's accompanied by a liberal portion of strong hot tea. When we get back, I shall drink gallons of it all at one sitting—so much I'll probably float off your island. My stomach has felt ever so peculiar these past few days.''

"The island," he said with a heavy sigh. "While you're drowning in tea, I'll be buried in paperwork and hearings.''

"I'll never take anything in my life for granted again," she mused. "If we return. . . .''

He lowered his gaze, toying with the fibrous ends of a palm frond. He could not touch her for fear of disturbing Kana and her father sleeping restlessly only a few feet away. Yet he felt closer to her than to any other person in his life. She had seen him as himself and claimed to love him despite his emotional frailties. She belonged in his world, and when he returned to Kali Simpang, he would ask her to be his wife.

There was a startled cry behind them. Sir Arthur began to shout, and as Ross glanced over his shoulder, it was to see Kana on his knees, shaking his head in alarm.

"He think I try to steal Tiger, Tuan. But I only try to move it out of rain.''

Lorna went to her father's side, crouching to console him. Watching the emotional exchange between the pair, Ross felt a sharp fear that only deepened as he caught Sir Arthur's words.

"Take me home, Lorna.''

"Yes, Papa. I will. I promise. The Rajah is waiting for us.''

"What? No, no, no. I mean *home*, Lorna. Home to Hampshire. That's where we belong, you and I. Not in this nightmare.''

Ross swung around and stared out into the watery gray-green forest, his expression bitter. He did not feel the aching discomfort in his lower back. He did not bother to swat away the unseen insects that flitted about his face.

He was still awake an hour later when a golden flicker of light beyond the trees appeared and disappeared before he could be certain he had actually seen it.

He blinked. Mulak remained relaxed and unmoving . . . unless he'd fallen asleep, or something had happened to him.

Ross eased to his feet, sensing Lorna awakening behind him. "Don't move. We've company."

Even before she could respond, Mulak had grabbed his spear, and the footsteps of the approaching party crashed into the encampment. Dancing orange flames of torchlight, blurred in the abating rain, sent night creatures scurrying.

Lorna came to stand behind Ross as the faces of the intruders became visible—Richard, Captain Stokker, and a native crewman from the sloop.

"Lorna . . . Arthur, my God. I never thought to see you alive." Richard rushed toward his niece with his arms outstretched.

She did not move, and Ross could sense her reluctance to go to her uncle. Instinctively Ross put his arm around her shoulder as if to restrain her.

He didn't want to let her go. Because when he did, it would mean she no longer needed him. She had her family now, and they would try to lure her away from him. The bonds of blood, societal pressures, and guilt-ridden love were powerful rivals. Yet he could not lose her. Not after what they'd shared.

He would *not* lose her. She was his. He told himself that even as she drew a deep breath and reluctantly broke free of his hold to go to her uncle.

The Rajah's yacht met the sloop her first day out to sea from Jalaka. Transferred onto the luxurious royal vessel, Ross and Lorna were summarily separated to be examined by Dr. Parker and pampered by Charles's well-trained staff.

The Rajah could not hide his distress at his first glance of Sir Arthur. To Lorna's amazement, no mention was made of the priceless statue her father had secreted in his cabin. Clearly someone—she suspected Ross—had taken Charles aside to explain Sir Arthur's dangerous obsession with the stolen Tiger. She began to worry how her father would be affected when, inevitably, the authorities reclaimed the statue.

She worried even more about Ross and the change in his manner toward her. Since leaving Jalaka, he had begun to withdraw into himself again. There had been a closeness between them on that mountain, and now it seemed to be eluding her for reasons she couldn't comprehend.

Her father's demands on her time left her with scant energy for further contemplation. Sir Arthur could not bear for her to leave his side except for a few minutes at a time. Yet moments later, without explanation, he would order her to go away. His melancholy disturbed her even more than did his petulant outbursts. He had nightmares, too, awakening the entire ship with his haunted screams.

On the evening before they pulled into port, Lorna stole away from the cabin to search out Ross on deck. He stood alone at the rail, gazing out to sea.

"Am I disturbing you?"

He half turned, his eyes lighting up as they met hers. "Only in the most pleasant way."

"You look very serious."

"I was trying to clear my mind." He hesitated. "My uncle's condition has worsened . . . he's begun discussing the funeral already."

She did not know what to say. Preoccupied with her father, she had unwillingly ignored the change in Charles's appearance.

"Is something else troubling you?" She slid her hand up his shoulder to the tense muscles of his neck. Gently, firmly, she began to move her fingers over his bronzed skin.

He closed his eyes, murmuring, "I should warn you, it's very dangerous to touch me like that."

She pressed herself against his back. "You tried to warn me away from you once before, don't you remember?"

He turned swiftly and caught her to his chest, startling her with his intensity. When he looked at her like that, as if she were the only woman on earth, she could not fight the wild longing that took possession of her senses.

"Do you regret not taking my advice, Lorna?"

"No," she answered softly, closing her eyes with an involuntary sigh as his head lowered to hers. Warm, possessive, his mouth found hers in a kiss that smoldered with restrained passion. She arched into him, shivering in delight.

"Damn it, Lorna," he said against her lips. "Am I ever going to have you to myself?"

He spoke not of that specific moment, but in general, though Lorna was too flustered to understand that immediately. His hands dropped to the small of her back, pressing her flush against his body.

"Reassure me," he said, forcing her away from him. "Tell me that I'm not losing you."

"Losing me? How could you think . . . ." She drew back so abruptly that Ross knew someone must be approaching.

He swung around and found himself the subject of Sir Arthur's intensely curious regard as he approached the rail. Arthur's mind might have been affected by his captivity, Ross thought, but his powers of observation were all too keen.

"It's late," Arthur said brusquely. His gaze lingered on the hand Ross had drawn back to his side. "I awakened to discover you were not in bed, Lorna. I began to fear something had happened to you."

She checked the impatient retort that sprang to her lips. Dr. Parker had warned her that her father could not control his fears, most of which were now unfounded.

"It's early yet, Papa. We've not even had supper."

Arthur put a hand to his temple, looking suddenly embarrassed and confused. "Then you must both think me mad . . . which perhaps I am, after all."

"No one thinks any such thing," Lorna said hastily. "You've lived through hell. We all understand that—don't we, Ross?"

Ross leaned back against the rail. "Yes."

"You are the Resident of Kali Simpang," Arthur said to Ross. "Charles's nephew."

"I am, sir. We have dined and played chess together."

"And it would seem you have become well acquainted with my daughter."

"Yes."

"Then I suppose it is safe enough to leave her in your company while I return to the cabin."

Arthur turned, a perplexed look on his face, and began wandering toward the bridge. "Papa, wait. That's the wrong way," Lorna said. "Ross, I have to help him—"

"It's all right," he said. "You can't have him ending up in the ocean."

Her father was subdued as she walked him back to the cabin and got him settled down for the night. The Rajah's personal valet had bathed and shaved him earlier, so except for looking thinner and older, he was quite presentable.

"Why do you keep staring at me like that, Papa?"

"It's your hair, I should think. You've taken to wearing it loose like your mother. It suits you."

She gave him a sharp look. "I never knew you noticed how I wore my hair."

"I noticed many things about you," he said in an aggrieved voice.

"It—it never seemed so." She pulled the coverlet up to his chin—the way he liked it—swallowing the knot that had risen to her throat. This wasn't the time to chastise him for the hurts he'd inadvertently inflicted on her during their life together.

"The laudanum should help you sleep."

"It gives me nightmares." He eased up onto his elbows. "You were to be married by now, weren't you?"

She got up from the bed, disconcerted by his probing gaze. "I broke the engagement. Papa, how long do we have to keep this wretched thing?" She motioned to the elegant statue of the Tiger standing on the chest at the foot of the bed.

His face turned white as bone. "You mustn't let them take it away from me. The curse is that I shall die if I do not guard it."

"It has to be returned to its rightful place."

"To the English authorities, you mean."

"English or French, I don't know. But it doesn't belong to *you*, Papa."

His head fell back upon the pillow. His gaze focused upward on the low-beamed ceiling. "But I belong to it. Such is the price I must pay."

She tore her gaze away from the statue's hypnotic golden-green eyes. "Perhaps if you began to write again—"

"I cannot write," he said tonelessly. "I have no desire."

"But your unfinished manuscript—"

"I believe that arrogant young Resident is fond of you."

"We are fond of each other," she said quietly.

"He is Charles's heir," he mused. "Not a bit like his uncle."

"I think you should rest now, Papa."

"I cannot rest," he said angrily. "Every time I close my eyes, I see pitiful human beings pleading for their lives while undergoing the most gruesome tortures. I will never rest again, Lorna. I was part of their evil, don't you understand? My soul has been corrupted."

There was a discreet knock at the door. Unsettled by her father's outburst, Lorna welcomed the interruption.

It was Ross. "I wanted to make sure everything was all right," he said from the doorway. "We'll arrive very early tomorrow morning."

"Thank you," she said, her tone intentionally terse.

He glanced past her to Arthur. "Good night, then."

"Good night, Ross."

She leaned against the door after she had closed it, staring vacantly across the room.

"When we return to England, Lorna," her father said, "do you think you and Spencer might reconcile?"

"Never."

"I see." His gaze followed her around the room as she extinguished the two lanterns. "Then you would not mind if we did not return to London for a while?"

She sat down on the edge of her bunk. "I wouldn't mind at all."

"Good. I had been thinking I might move us back to Hampshire. What do you think?"

"I think we should discuss this after we return to the island."

"I do love you, Lorna. I know I may not have told you often enough—"

"I don't believe you've *ever* come out and told me, Papa."

"But you know I do?"

She averted her face, her voice low. "Yes. I know."

She waited until the regular rhythm of his breathing reassured her he'd fallen asleep. Then she crept outside, hoping to find Ross again on deck, disappointed when instead it was her uncle she encountered.

"I have wanted to see you alone," he said, his face anxious. "There's so much I need to say—"

"I'd rather forget what happened, Uncle Richard."

"And forgive me?" He grasped her hand. "I realize how terribly shocked you were to find me involved with van Poole."

She turned her face away from him. "I have forgiven you—but let us agree never to let my father or Aunt Julia know what you had planned."

He squeezed her hand. "The Rajah has had a letter from Julia. She's threatening to come here to bring us all home. Can you imagine my wife among the headhunters?

She'd have them all scrubbing out their huts with vinegar and ashes, and practicing bows before the queen.''

He was chattering away in relief, Lorna realized. "Have you seen Ross anywhere?" she asked him.

"Not for an hour or so." He gave her his arm, guiding her across the deck. "Now that we are friends again, I shall have to insist that you reconsider this unfortunate—"

"Not that again, Uncle Richard."

"Hear me out. I've come to realize St. James is a decent enough sort, Lorna. I can't deny he risked his life to save us. But that doesn't change the fact that he's about to inherit the Raj."

"I understand that."

"There are obligations that come with his inheritance. And you have your own."

She stopped, turning to stare at him. "Obligations?"

"Why, to the family, of course. You can't leave your father now, and he's repeatedly expressed a desire to return to England. It's the only way to get our lives back to normal. We don't belong here."

Lorna glanced across the deck and saw Ross at the rail, watching her.

"You consider what I've said," her uncle told her. "I know you'll do the right thing. You're a damn good daughter—better than my brother deserves, but you'll take care of him. I count on that, Lorna."

Ross had disappeared by the time her uncle took his leave. Alone, the breeze stirring her hair, Lorna stood and watched the waves churning in the moonlight. No matter what she did, someone would end up hurt. And until Ross made firm the commitment he had so far only hinted at, there really was no decision to be made.

She could only stay if he made a permanent place for her in his life.

Chapter 25

Ross reached across his desk to examine the stack of letters he had managed to ignore for the past six days since his return from Jalaka.

Nothing crucial by the look of it. No letter from the Governor General of Singapore or the Royal Navy's rear admiral stationed there, offering him the warship he'd requested to protect the island. That was a bitter disappointment.

There was a message from Colonel Moody stating he'd like to meet briefly with Ross to tie up a few loose ends. For all practical purposes the case of the White Tiger was closed. Sir Arthur had at last relinquished the statue. It was being held under guard in the subterranean vaults of the istana until Moody could transport it to the proper authorities. Nothing could be proved against Pierre Lu Chan, though Ross was certain he would be arrested one day for his unscrupulous dealings.

"A glass of cold beer and a sandwich, sir?" Mrs. Hofner asked from the crack in the doorway, hesitant to enter.

"Just the beer, please."

She edged in carefully with her tray. "Have you heard any news on Sir Arthur's progress, sir?"

He hesitated but did not look up. "The last time Dr. Parker examined him he was the same—malnourished and suffering from acute nervous anxiety."

"Well, it's not long since he's been back among his

own, is it? I imagine when his daughter takes him to England, he'll become himself again."

Ross reached for the glass, his voice rough. "Has Miss Fairfield made arrangements to leave the island that you know of?"

"I assume so, sir. At least that was what her uncle appeared to be doing at the wharves yesterday when I went marketing."

"Lorna wasn't with him?"

"He was accompanied by only a native guide that I recall." She clutched the empty tray to her chest. "Surely you've seen her yourself, sir, since your return?"

"Only once, and briefly," he admitted. "There's been so much work to catch up on, you know, and she has her hands full with her father. . . ."

That was not the real reason, and he knew it. He had decided he would give her a reasonable period of time to work out her responsibilities to her father without his influence, gambling on the hope that she would choose to stay. But suddenly the stakes were higher than he cared to wager.

He couldn't believe Lorna would make arrangements to leave the island without informing him first. He should not let his feelings for her, his fear that he would lose her, override his logic. But he also knew that all her life she had been emotionally subservient to her father, and he had to be certain that she could make the break from her family with an unencumbered conscience. God forbid that he should overestimate her attachment to *him*.

He of all people knew how hard it could be to throw off one's self-imposed shackles, the subtle but persuasive inner forces of guilt and self-sacrifice that could ruin a life.

Had he himself not dedicated his younger years to the impossible task of pleasing his father, attempting even to emulate him by plunging into a naval career, with near-disastrous results? Hadn't he dedicated himself to the island, believing his motives noble, when the truth was that he was only trying to forget the unhappiness of his past?

Mrs. Hofner exited the room, but entangled in his own thoughts, Ross hardly noticed her departure.

He arose and strode across the room, opening the door to find Assistant Resident Tunridge approaching from the hallway.

"Whatever it is will have to wait," he said. "I have another appointment."

"This can't wait," Wayne said. "It's your uncle. He's very ill. The Ranee thought I should fetch you."

"How bad is he?"

"All I know is that he's been unable to leave his bed since yesterday morning."

Although Ross had known for long months that this day would inevitably come, he still felt stricken and unprepared to handle it. If it hadn't been for the dream he'd had of Ian, he might have scoffed at Charles's native belief in an afterlife. Now he clung to that belief for reassurance.

Rajah Charles had been the most powerful influence in his life, ever so patiently teaching him the tolerance and compassion he needed to balance out his own harsher inclinations.

He would miss his uncle more than he could ever tell him. And he would live by his example for the rest of his days.

The Rajah's condition had deteriorated rapidly in the past week, and Ross suspected his uncle had clung to life only long enough to see the search for Sir Arthur successfully completed.

"He tires easily," Amayli told him as he entered the bedchamber. "And his mind wanders sometimes into the past."

"I won't stay long," Ross said.

He knelt at the side of the bamboo bed—another of Charles's concessions to the Malay life-style—and took the frail hand in his own, absently tracing his finger over the prominent blue veins.

Charles opened his eyes and smiled. "A display of maudlin tenderness, Ross. I must be very near the end."

"No tenderness," Ross said gruffly. "I thought you'd already gone and was looking for your pulse."

There was silence. Charles struggled to sit upright against the pillows. "The Sultan of Djuil's viceroy is waiting to see you in the anteroom. You must go to him right away. The Illanuns attacked a fleet of trading vessels off the coast of Celebes, and the survivors claim there were at least twenty thousand of them."

"Celebes," Ross said remotely. "Yes, that doesn't surprise me."

"I must say I expected a rather more passionate reaction from you."

Ross said nothing. He felt frozen inside, weighted down by sadness.

Sighing, Charles reached across the nightstand for an envelope. "Perhaps this will impress you then—it's from Admiral Harkwater. The Royal Navy is sending us a warship. Datu Makota won't get to carry your head home in a basket to his harem, after all."

Ross stared at the envelope, then rose and walked to the window with his head bowed.

"What is it?" Charles asked in concern.

"I'm losing everything again," Ross said in a stricken voice, horrified by the rush of emotion he couldn't control. "Uncle Charles, you gave me my life back, and to see you . . . if I could trade places with you . . .'"

"I would refuse," Charles said irritably, and then, his voice softening, "Does this have something to do with Lorna? Has she decided to leave the island?"

"I don't know. Her father has taken over her life again. She scarcely had time to talk with me when last I saw her."

"What will you do if she does leave, Ross?"

"I cannot imagine," he said, shaking his head, finding it easier to talk to Charles than ever before, finding it almost impossible to stop. "I have come to depend on her company more than I realized. There were times when the thought of her only halfway across the island drove me to distraction. To think she would be thousands of miles beyond my reach. . . .''

"I never told you, Ross, but her uncle has tried to persuade me to exert pressure on you to leave her alone. I explained to him that my policy is always to remain impartial in the personal affairs of my citizens. He insisted he wants only what is best for her—"

"What's best for Lorna is that she stay here," Ross said, his voice impassioned.

"Then I'm glad we made only overtures, and not promises, to Princess Kalimri."

Ross nodded. "I'll discuss that later with Amayli. Her niece honors me with her willingness to be my wife. I do realize a marriage to a native princess would be good for the Raj—"

"Never once have I expected you to sacrifice your own happiness for the island. It was not I who insisted you live alone in your miserable little hut when the istana was always at your disposal."

"I never blamed you."

"No. Not me. You always turned your pain inward. And even though it broke my heart to see you punishing yourself for Vanessa's death, I could not help you. I could not change the course you'd chosen any more than you can now change mine."

"I should leave you to rest," Ross said, suddenly realizing his uncle was struggling to carry on the conversation.

"Talk to Arthur about Lorna. He's more reasonable than he appears."

"When I last saw him, he was hardly in a frame of mind to be persuaded to part with his daughter. Considering she's spent almost her entire life taking care of him, I doubt he'll ever agree to let her go."

"Ultimately, it will be Lorna's decision."

"I'd rather she stay with me without feeling guilty for leaving her father. But if I have to fight her father, I will."

"Arthur will be fine without her. I've convinced Colonel Moody not to press charges against him."

"We'll talk later," Ross said softly, moving away from the bed as Charles's eyes began to close.

"If I had a son," Charles said faintly, as Ross reached the door, "I should not love him half as much as I love you."

Lorna leaned down to rearrange her father's pillows, praying the wind would not disturb him. He stirred, whimpering in his sleep, and shrank away from her. In the past day or so, he had actually seemed to improve, although he was still troubled by nightmares. Caring for him exhausted her. She herself had felt vaguely unwell since the search on Jalaka, plagued by an inexplicable malaise she could not shake off.

"I heard him scream again," Richard whispered in the hallway. "I wish there were something I could do to help."

"It won't help me if you fall ill again," she said tiredly. "For heaven's sake, go to bed."

"It's rather early yet. I think I'd like a cup of tea."

"I left a fresh pot in the parlor, just a minute ago," she said, her hand on the banister. "It's probably still hot."

"Let me fetch my papers. I've written down the schedule for the steamers."

"To England?"

Richard nodded. "The sooner we get Arthur home, the better for us all."

"I've not agreed to go yet," she said. "I haven't even had time to consider it."

She walked slowly down the stairs, suddenly missing Ilse's presence and wondering what she would think when she learned of Kurt's death. She and Ilse might have viewed life differently, but at least she'd been another woman to talk to.

She was almost to the parlor when a knock sounded at the front door. At this hour it could only be Ross. She hurried forward to answer it in the hope he'd come to see her.

Yet when she opened the door and looked up into his

unsmiling face, she felt her heart stop in sudden anxiety. "What is it?"

"Nothing."

He followed her into the parlor, glancing repeatedly up the darkened staircase they passed. "Is your father still up?"

"No."

He frowned. "I wanted to talk to him. Do you think he could be awakened?"

She sat down on the settee, watching him as he took the chair in front of her, sliding to the edge with his hands on his knees. "It's not about the Tiger, is it? If so, I don't think it's a good—"

"No. It's not the Tiger."

"Do you want a cup of tea? It's going cold."

"Would it be all right to wake him?" he said, ignoring her offer.

Before she could answer, Richard walked into the room, glancing at Ross with a frown before turning his attention to Lorna. "Arthur's awake and says he can't sleep. He's coming down for a cup of tea."

"I'll make another pot then," she said, rising. "Uncle Richard—would you mind helping me with the tray?" It seemed wise, considering Ross's edginess, to keep him and her uncle apart.

Her father entered the room as she and Richard were leaving. "Papa, Ross says he'd like to talk to you. Are you up to it?"

"My mind is not so enfeebled that I can't carry on a conversation," he said dryly. "However, I can't promise I'll stay awake after all that laudanum you fed me."

"Be polite," she said under her breath.

Ross gave her a searching look as she closed the door, and she wondered suddenly whether he meant to discuss *her* with her father. She wasn't sure if Papa was truly capable of making a reasonable decision at this point, but she did know she couldn't afford to wait, what with her uncle planning to return them all to England as soon as possible.

She knew her suspicion—her hope—was correct when she returned to find her father sitting in pensive silence, and Ross at the window, drinking a brandy he'd already poured himself. She would never know exactly what they'd said about her during the five minutes she had been gone, but it would change her life forever.

"I've brought some biscuits and cheese," she said, clearing a space on the tea table for her uncle, who carried the heavy tray with the silver teapot and porcelain service.

"You'll have a biscuit, Papa?"

He nodded, giving her an accusing look as she handed him the plate. "You didn't tell me that you and Ross intend to marry."

Unable to speak, she glanced over at Ross, but his face was obscured by the shadows of the rose-globed lamp in the corner. Until this moment she hadn't realized how desperately she had wanted him to want her enough to fight to keep her here. Not in the least did she resent him taking control of the matter without her consent. Clearly she was not as independent, as free-willed, as she'd believed herself to be. Without Ross's intervention she might never have found the courage to realize that her own desires were important. Until now she hadn't been at all convinced he cared for her as deeply as she did for him.

Only now did she believe Ross had torn down the last barrier that had kept them apart.

"I tried to explain to your father, Lorna," he said, moving into the light, "that I need you, too . . . that we need each other."

Arthur sat with the plate untouched on his knees. "You should have told me," he said to Lorna.

"I didn't think you—you weren't . . ."

"This is all very sudden," he continued, "especially considering the fact it took you five years to agree to marry Spencer."

"Precisely," Richard said from his chair. "It's too sudden, I say."

"You asked Mama to marry you the first day you met,"

Lorna said, trying not to let her pity for her father overtake her emotions again. "You even used to boast about it."

"I thought the island was in danger from attack by head-hunting pirates," Richard said to Ross as he took a sip of tea. "You can hardly claim to care about Lorna and yet risk her life."

Ross lifted his head, and as Lorna watched him, considering his next words, controlling the anger she guessed he felt, she thought again how effective a ruler he would make, that his doubts about his ability to replace Rajah Charles were utterly groundless. Even now Ross's presence dominated the room.

"A Royal Navy warship is on its way to protect our coast," Ross said. "And you're right, Richard, I would rather send Lorna away than see her harmed. I tried to discourage you both from going to Jalaka, when you first arrived."

Arthur placed his plate on the tray. "I'm going back upstairs."

"Are you all right, Papa?" she asked, rising to follow him.

He paused at the door. "I'm fine, though I might have been better if I hadn't been made aware that I've become such an incredible burden to you." Then, straightening his shoulders, he left.

She turned to Ross, her voice low with disbelief. "You didn't tell him that, did you?"

"Of course not. If he came to that conclusion, it's from his own conscience, not from anything I might have said."

Richard got up from his chair. "I think you'd better go up after him, Lorna."

"Yes," she murmured.

"Walk me outside first," Ross said, blocking her path.

They reached the veranda steps, and he pulled her into his arms, the possessive hunger of his kiss dimming every other thought in her mind but of how much she loved him.

"I'm not going to lose you," he said fiercely. "I could have managed alone the rest of my life if I hadn't met you, but I can't now."

"What did you tell him?" she whispered, glancing up toward her father's brightly lit window. "He seemed terribly upset."

"I only told him how I felt about you, and that I wanted you to stay—as my wife. He assumed everything else—or perhaps he's suddenly realized how badly he's treated you. To say the least, he was quite taken aback."

"It might have been better if I'd talked to him first."

"Why? So he could convince you to leave with him and sacrifice your own happiness?" He shook his head. "I wasn't about to give him that advantage."

He drew her forward again into his arms. With a slow, teasing smile, she tilted her head back to look up at him.

"You never even asked me, you know. You just assumed I would."

"Would what?"

"Marry you. Honestly, Ross, you need a little more self-confidence."

He gave her a disarming smile. "Well, will you?"

"May I have a month to think about it?"

"No, you may not." His smile fading, he caught hold of her arm as she started to pull away from him. "I'd like to let my uncle know. He may not live to see the wedding, but he'll be immensely pleased for us."

She stood very still, her eyes sad, the warm evening wind stirring her hair. "Then you will inherit the Raj. Your life . . . will change."

"No doubt."

"The Balinese princess," she said hesitantly. "The servants were whispering that she's very beautiful. 'Exquisite' was how they described her."

"I don't give a damn, Lorna. I don't want anyone but you."

She touched his cheek as if to soften the stern expression on his face. "We'll tell your uncle together in the morning. I'd like to spend a little time with him too."

Ross nodded, his eyes closing briefly as he stepped toward her to kiss her again before he left. As he moved down to disappear into the black-purple shadows of the garden, a sudden gust of wind rippled through the encircling palms.

Lorna shivered, hugging herself, although she was not cold, and glanced up as a configuration of storm clouds scudded across the sky. Deliberately she forced the shadow of unease from her mind. Nothing was going to spoil her happiness tonight. Nothing could dim the glow of knowing that Ross wanted to spend his life with her.

Bumping noises against the wall awoke Lorna just as she was falling asleep. She snatched up her white silk wrapper from the foot of the bed and hurried to the room next to hers. A bright sliver of light showed under her father's door, but no sound came from within.

"Papa?"

The radiance of at least thirty candles temporarily blinded her as she opened the door. Blinking, she stared at the bedclothes thrown about the room, the drawers overturned, the books and papers strewn everywhere.

"What on earth did you do to this room?" she said angrily. "And where are you, Papa?"

"I'm working," he said calmly. "And I'd never have been forced to ransack my own room if *someone* hadn't moved my belongings where I couldn't find them."

She stepped around the door, afraid of what she might discover. She almost didn't recognize him. He had dressed in his favorite trousers and flannel shirt; his forehead was creased in a familiar preoccupied frown. There was a pen in his hand, and on his desk before him sat a thick sheaf of papers.

She had been on the verge of accusing him of childishly ransacking the room out of his anger at her and Ross. But all she could manage, in her astonishment, was, "You *are* working."

"I'm trying." He sounded broken and full of doubt for a moment, staring around the room at the candles as if only a madman could have lit them. His gaze fell on the papers before him. "I'm having difficulty concentrating. And your interrupting me didn't help."

She was so relieved to see him behaving like himself that she could only smile. "That will come . . . the concentration, I mean."

"Do you think so?"

"I'm positive. Is it a new book?"

His face lit up. "Oh, no. The same one. But I know now how it's going to end."

He turned back to his desk as if he had already forgotten her. Content to watch him, she curled up on the foot of his bed as she had done as a child. "Tell me."

"If you're going to chatter, Lorna, I shall have to ask you to leave."

"Must you burn so many candles? I'm afraid of a fire. Perhaps I could bring up a pair of lamps instead."

"What? Oh, as you like. But you mustn't talk while I'm working."

She eased off the bed and crept to the door, sighing to herself. This was a tremendous step toward improvement in his attitude, but she was concerned that he hadn't even mentioned her engagement to Ross.

"Lorna?"

She pivoted at the door. "Yes, Papa."

His voice was uncharacteristically soft. "Will you ever be able to forgive me?"

She clasped her hands together, moving back toward him. "For what?"

"For all the horrendous wrongs I've committed."

"Oh." She was disappointed. "You mean because you snatched the Tiger."

"Yes, that," he said shortly, "but what I really mean . . . I had no idea, Lorna. I never realized that you had grown up. It—it went so fast, and I—I needed you so much I never dreamed . . . I never meant to ruin your life."

She looked down at the floor, holding back the tears that threatened to spill. "It's all right," she said. "I needed you too."

"But you don't anymore," he said wistfully. "You don't need an eccentric old fool of a father hanging around your neck when you have that young man belowstairs willing to lay his world at your feet."

She looked up, her eyes bright. "I do love you, Papa."

"Yes," he said, his expression sad. "Too much, I fear. But you also love Ross, don't you?"

"Oh, yes."

"I have been thinking, Lorna. I was wondering whether you and Ross would object to my staying on the island indefinitely. There's no real reason for me to return to England. In fact, I'd probably be declared insane at this point and confined to a lunatic asylum."

"We couldn't have that."

"Then you wouldn't mind—"

"Mind? It's the second most wonderful thing I've heard all evening. I can't wait to tell Ross."

"He'll probably have me exiled from the island after the dressing-down I gave him tonight."

"He never told me."

"I disapproved of his allowing you to search for me on Jalaka. He should have stopped you."

"He tried, Papa. But everything turned out well, didn't it? And now you're writing again."

His expression darkened as he turned to gaze out the window, distracted by the wind. "It's not finished yet," he said as if to himself. "Who can say how it will end?"

It was almost a half hour later, as she was crawling into her own bed, that Lorna stopped to reflect on his last remark . . . and realized that although she assumed he was referring to his uncompleted book, he might not have meant that at all. Yet she could not imagine what any of them, not her father, herself, or Ross, had to worry about, except the sadly expected death of Rajah Charles. According to Ross, the Agung-Mani had dispersed and there had been no recent activity on Mount Belakan. And the statue that had caused so much turmoil in untold lives would soon be gone from Kali Simpang.

Chapter 26

Rajah Charles received the news of Ross's engagement to Lorna with warm approval, bestowing his blessing on their union and then asking for a moment alone with Sir Arthur, who had accompanied his daughter to the istana.

Leaving Charles and Sir Arthur together, Amayli invited Lorna into her private receiving chamber, showing her on the way the various rooms of the istana and their functions. The older woman seemed preoccupied as they sipped from tall, refreshing glasses of *khoshab,* a drink of sweetened rosewater, peach juice, and a drop of musk stirred with a sandalwood spoon. It was almost impossible for Lorna to imagine that she would one day sit in Amayli's place, welcoming visiting dignitaries to the island. Etiquette in this part of the world went far beyond pouring tea in a cozy parlor. There was so much to learn—the language, the customs. . . .

"You are scowling," Amayli said. "You do not like the khoshab?"

"No. It's wonderful, but I'm afraid . . . you won't leave Kali Simpang, will you, to return to your family in Bali? I know Ross would be lost without you, and I—I will probably start a war in the archipelago by serving pig to a sultan or something."

Amayli laughed delightedly. "You worry for nothing,

and yes, I would be happy to stay, for as long as I am needed.''

"You were born into royalty," Lorna said in a sudden, overwhelming rush of anxiety over what being married to Ross would entail. "And you are familiar with the island ways. What if the people reject me?''

"Did they not accept Charles and then Ross?''

"Yes.''

"The wedding feast will be a public celebration, an important occasion. Of course, first you will have a traditional English ceremony . . . if you approve.''

"How could I not?''

"The dress I wore when I married Charles is made of watered white silk and gilded toile. And the headdress is stitched with pearls, diamonds, and rubies. It reaches the ground.''

"It sounds divine . . . but it must have been difficult to turn your head—to say your vows, I mean.''

"I used to dance with a heavier headdress before I met Charles. I could take you down into the vaults to see it, if you like. And if it pleases you, you shall wear it for your own wedding.''

"You are very kind to me, Amayli," Lorna said softly. "I don't think I could hold up nearly so well as you under the circumstances.''

"If you believed as Charles and I do that there is no death, only a doorway to another life, then you could not be sad,'' Amayli said, her brown eyes luminous.

"But you will miss him.''

"He will not leave me," Amayli said with calm conviction. "And in the flash of a butterfly's wings, we will be together again.'' She touched her heart with a small-boned hand. "This I know inside me, Lorna. Now let me take you down to the vaults before I return to sit with my husband.''

"I don't want to take you away from him any longer than I already have. Perhaps one of the guards can show me around.''

Amayli frowned. "Ordinarily, that would be allowed. But the White Tiger is still under guard there too, and Charles has ordered special precautions, just in case."

In case. Lorna didn't care to contemplate what that might cover, and the thought of even being in the vicinity of that statue again made her almost refuse Amayli's offer. But that would seem ungracious, and she wanted to start off on the right foot with the Ranee, knowing she would have much to learn from her about the island.

A Hindu-Moslem guard brought the headdress out of the vaults for Lorna's inspection, along with a tray of jewelry that Amayli suggested she might borrow. The stunning array shone in the torchlit darkness of the musty room where Lorna sat, dazzled by the selection, feeling like a small mouse who had happened into Ali Baba's cave.

When she had finished and was being escorted back up the stone steps to the istana, the wrought-iron gates clanging behind her, a messenger approached her. In his hand was a note from Ross informing her that her father had become upset during his meeting with the Rajah and had asked to be taken back to the plantation house. Ross promised he would stay long enough to calm him down and asked if she would mind making her own arrangements to leave the istana.

In truth, Lorna welcomed the respite from having to be with anyone, even Ross, craving the time alone to deal with the diverse emotions aroused in her by the events of the past week. It seemed ages since she'd had a chance to spend an uninterrupted hour by herself.

She set out immediately for the Rajah's private garden. Wandering aimlessly, simply enjoying the feel of the sun on her face, she walked between the plots of overgrown ferns and hibiscus. At the edge of the estate, she passed a pair of guards who gave her friendly smiles and warned her to watch out for snakes.

It was then she remembered the secluded chapel by the river. She recalled the urgent prayers she had said for her father's safe return. She could at least spend a few moments expressing her thankfulness for having him back. She wanted also to say a prayer for Rajah Charles and Amayli, and one of gratitude to God for bringing Ross into her life.

The interior of the small chapel enshrouded her in its cool pink-gray shadows. The only light filtered down through the stained-glass window depicting the Ascension. As Lorna settled down on a pew, she thought that if Ross agreed, she might like to use the place regularly for herself. The private stillness it offered brought her comfort.

But the peace did not last long. Outside in the gathering dusk, monkeys and birds chattered in discordant orchestration, spoiling the illusion of a quiet English church. And then a faint echo, muted and oddly faraway, drew her attention to the space behind the altar.

She arose slowly, recalling the day she and Ross had discovered the abandoned twins in this very chapel. Proceeding cautiously to the altar, she stepped around heaps of leaves the constant winds had blown in. Possibly a family of rats or a tapir had set up residence in the undisturbed coolness. Certainly Ross had had too much on his mind recently to bother maintaining the forgotten retreat.

She saw a dingy white bundle in a basket and knelt, one hand pressed to her mouth. It appeared to be about the size of an infant, but there was no movement from beneath the cloth, no sign of life. Bracing herself for a grim discovery, she lifted the edge of the cloth and swiftly threw it to the floor.

There was no child, thank God, only what appeared to be a small supply of food wrapped in a sack, ammunition, and a hunting knife. But the cloth—the *tablecloth*—was stained with blood and embroidered with a flawless stitchery of daylilies.

Ilse.

Ilse had embroidered that cloth—Lorna had watched her countless evenings. But Ilse had gone to Africa to be with her children, and even if she had remained for some reason, why would she hide out in this chapel?

Unless she had returned to avenge her brother's death. After all, Ilse had been dependent on Kurt since leaving her husband. And she and her brother, perhaps because of the hardships they had shared as children, had managed to overlook each other's flaws to cling together in what they perceived to be a hostile world.

There was a sound of stone scraping against stone behind Lorna from the shadows along the wall. Her heart in her throat, she jumped up and whirled around to see Kurt's enormous mastiff emerge from the darkness and lunge at her with its teeth bared. She pressed backward against the heavy wooden altar, but before the dog could reach her it was jerked up short by the leather leash its owner held.

"If it had been anyone but you, Lorna."

She watched incredulously as Kurt van Poole stepped forward from a narrow recess in the wall. Vaguely she remembered Ross mentioning a subterranean tunnel that ran from the vaults of the istana to the chapel: the escape tunnel the Rajah had built early in his reign when he was unsure whether the rebel forces he had subdued would rise again.

Her heart hammered frantically as Kurt moved into the waning light, his face swathed in filthy bandages, his opaque blue eyes shining with a wild inner light.

"You," she whispered in bewilderment. "But we saw you on the mountain—in the cage. . . ."

"And assumed the man-eater devoured me. Did you forget that I am the shikari, Lorna . . . that the natives say I can gaze into a tiger's eyes and subdue its soul? Did you really think I would blithely walk into an Agung-Mani village without having carefully laid plans for my escape? I had ammunition hidden in the cave. I tainted the tiger's kill with poison before it could return."

"Your face—"

"—will no doubt terrify certain women and fascinate others when it heals. To which category will you belong?"

She stiffened, her lips parting.

"Forgive me," he murmured. "I had forgotten . . . your engagement to the Resident. What a waste."

"Ilse," she said, hope cutting through her frightened confusion. "Is Ilse here with you?"

He lowered the rifle under his arm, his voice grave. "Ilse is almost to Africa by now."

Lorna was running out of ways to prolong the conversation, her mind still frozen in shock.

"Did she—was she aware of your plans all along?"

"Ilse chose not to know the details. But she did try to warn you, Lorna, and she will be genuinely upset when she learns what I was forced to do to you."

"Why?" she cried. "Why would you want to hurt me? Why have you come back to the island?"

He did not answer.

Her mouth went dry. As covertly as possible, she looked around her for a possible way to escape both Kurt and the vicious hunting dog, whose muscular body had still not relaxed its predatory stance. Her gaze drifted to the dark passageway from which Kurt had emerged, and then, distractedly, she glanced back to him and noticed the burlap sack slung over his shoulder.

The White Tiger.

It made terrifying sense to her now. This man who had spent the majority of his life tracking tigers would not be thwarted in his pursuit of a tiger statue . . . especially one that possessed such treacherous fascination.

"You understand now," he said softly. "It will seem as if the guards were overcome by greed and absconded with the statue. By the time their bodies are discovered, I shall be on my way to my sister. Only you, Lorna, threaten my plans."

"You have no reason to hurt me," she said, losing the battle against her rising panic. "I couldn't stop you from escaping now if I wanted to."

"But you could raise an alarm. And I have timed my escape precisely—the guards will patrol the perimeters of the istana grounds in another half hour."

"Money," she said contemptuously. "You've taken countless lives for—"

"—immortality. Even the Rajah of Kali Simpang cannot buy that. And I have earned it."

"Immortality?" She was stunned. "You mean you actually believe the legend? My father's obsession I could understand, but you—you were the one who mocked the gods by using boar bait to lure an eagle to Penala's shrine."

Kurt's fingers tightened around the rifle barrel. "I used no bait. The eagle came of its own accord. I too made a petition to Penala, and she answered me—she rewarded my courage by helping me find the Tiger on the condition I take the statue far from her islands."

Lorna shook her head as if to deny his insane confession.

"I have worshiped the pagan gods nearly all my life, Lorna," he continued. "Since I was old enough to realize the God of my own people had turned His back on me."

"God isn't like that," she said, her body beginning to shake.

"God allowed my father to whip me into unconsciousness for the least transgression until I was almost ten years old."

The patter of raindrops against the chapel roof drew her gaze toward the stained-glass window. Who would think to look for her here? Who, until it was too late, would even find it odd that she had not returned to the istana?

Ross and Arthur had been playing for some time on the teakwood chessboard that Arthur had picked up at the Chinese bazaar. When it started to rain, both men glanced to the window yet made no move to close it as a gust of damp air swirled between the curtains.

"Lorna might have to stay the night at the istana," Ross said, frowning at the thought of being forced to wait an entire day to see her again. "The river will be too dangerous to travel, and the roads are hopeless."

"There's the jungle path, if you're all that anxious.

shouldn't be offended if she's not worrying about you, though. Amayli was taking her down to the vaults to examine some jewelry.''

"The vaults? Yes, I'd forgotten there's a fortune hidden away down there."

"The White Tiger," Arthur said, his lips tightening. "You would not listen to me and have it destroyed."

"It wasn't up to me, or I'd never have brought the damn thing back."

They fell silent, staring down at the chessboard in fierce concentration. But Ross's mind refused to remain on the game. He kept thinking of Lorna, wishing she was sitting beside him. Just the sound of her low, teasing voice, the touch of her hand, would be enough to calm the irrational unease creeping into his awareness. Perhaps it was the incessant rain. Or watching helplessly as Charles slipped away from life. But he wanted suddenly to see Lorna—

Arthur's face brightened with a smug expression. Without glancing up, he took Ross's bishop and announced, "Check."

Ross's face betrayed none of the irritation he felt. In silence he contemplated his next move, forcing all other thoughts from his mind.

"All right," he said, leaning forward, as his queen captured Arthur's knight, taking his own king out of check.

Arthur immediately moved his other knight to Ross's bishop's pawn and said crisply, "Checkmate."

Ross stared down and then leaned back in his chair, feeling drained and frustrated and suddenly unable to bear the stuffy confines of the parlor. Glancing at the bell jar clock on the mantel, at the dim shadows around the room, he rubbed his face briskly and rose agilely from the chair.

"I'm going to the sulap. Tell Lorna if she returns I might drop by later this evening."

"How about another game?"

"No, thanks."

"Then I'll walk you outside. Good Lord, it's coming down, isn't it? Just like home."

They walked onto the veranda and stood listening to the rain and the faintest pealing of a bell in the distance. Arthur shook his head in distress.

"I dislike that sound. Detest it, in fact."

"What's that?" Ross asked idly, wondering whether he should risk going straight to the istana to see Lorna. It was doubtful Amayli would have let her set out in this weather.

"The bell," Arthur said. "I cringe inside whenever I hear one."

"It's coming from the harbor. Nothing to be alarmed about."

"Not here. But on Jalaka. . . . It rang out every time a human sacrifice was made to the man-eater. I shall forever associate that sound with death. I used to pray that it would not peal . . . that the poor victim would miraculously escape that cage."

Ross said nothing. As far as he knew there had been no such activity on Mount Belakan in recent weeks.

"The bell did not ring the night we escaped," Sir Arthur said. "It always rang before when the tiger claimed its victim."

"Perhaps in the excitement we did not hear it."

Arthur considered that for a moment. "It's more likely the man-eater took his time returning to the mountain."

"No." Ross's memory of that night was clear, if disjointed. "It was there when we fled the cave."

"You should go before the rain worsens."

Ross nodded, bracing himself to plunge down the steps.

He had reached the garden gate when he saw a white-uniformed figure hurrying up the hillside path. It was Colonel Moody, shoulders hunched against the rain. He gave Ross a wave of recognition.

"Damn horse ran off and left me stranded on the road on my way here," Moody explained, breathing heavily as he ducked with Ross into the orchid-trellised arbor.

"You must have important news to venture out in this weather."

"Nothing that couldn't have waited. I just thought you might like to know that Pierre Lu Chan was arrested in Singapore last week for the murder of a prostitute. Speaking of which, there was a disturbance down at your wharves this morning—at Li-Li Kong's."

"That doesn't surprise me. What was it over—nonpayment for services rendered?"

"I'm not sure. Seems a Dutch sailor—a drunk, I assume—stole one of Li-Li's fishing boats before dawn this morning."

"I'll see about it later."

"Don't know if I'd even bother," Moody said. "Fellow was in bad shape, the witnesses said. Head in bandages."

"The wharves always attract unsavory sorts." Ross wasn't about to waste his time investigating a stolen boat. "Listen, Moody, I have to go, but if you're a chess player, I'm sure Sir Arthur will keep you amused for the evening."

"Don't I know it," Moody said wryly. "Oh well, I suppose it's better than standing out in the damp. At least we won't have to sit listening to that dog's unholy howling from the shed where it was confined."

"Dog?" Ross said slowly. "I wasn't aware Lorna or her father kept any animals—except the peacocks and an ape."

"Van Poole's hunting dog," Moody elaborated, removing his helmet to shake off the rain collected in its rim. "He left it here when you all set off for Jalaka. Wretched beast broke out of the shed two nights ago and hasn't been seen since. Saves me the trouble of destroying it, you know. I daresay that it was the same dog—or its offspring—that killed van Poole's young wife." With a curt nod, Moody pulled up his collar, placed his helmet on his head, and set off toward the garden gate.

Ross gazed down the hillside at the agitated gray-green sea as a plethora of seemingly disconnected voices clamored in his mind.

I am the shikari, St. James. . . . I have never failed yet to return from any quest.

A Dutch sailor . . . stole one of Li-Li Kong's fishing boats. . . .

Amayli was taking her down to the vaults. . . .

The wretched beast broke out of the shed two nights ago and hasn't been seen since.

The bell did not ring the night we escaped. It always rang before. . . .

Amayli was taking her down to the vaults. . . .

The vaults . . .

The vaults . . .

Chapter 27

Ross ran out of the arbor, rain drumming against him as if to rival the frantic thoughts hammering at his mind. He realized that the missing dog and the drunken sailor could well be a coincidence, but in his gut, he knew it wasn't so. In any event, he was going to investigate for himself to make certain Lorna was in no danger.

Traveling by foot wouldn't be too bad along the rain-sheltered jungle paths, but it would take forever. To canoe upriver in rising water was too uncertain.

He heard footsteps behind him and spun about to see Moody swinging open the garden gate.

"My horse," the colonel said, gesturing to the trees bordering the hillside path. "Blighter certainly took his time."

Ross glanced briefly at the sturdy roan walking toward them. The horse could carry him so far and after that he'd have to run.

"What on earth do you think you're doing?" Moody shouted as Ross vaulted onto the gelding's back and reined him sharply onto the path.

Ross hesitated for the briefest moment. "I think van Poole is still alive and somewhere on the island. Send Sir Arthur's houseboy to my sulap with a message for Kana that he should sound the alarm drums across the island. Tell him to warn the istana of an enemy attack by the River of Flowers."

Moody stared at Ross in amazement and then opened his mouth to speak. But Ross didn't wait. He set his heels sharply into the horse's undersides and urged him onto the sandy path.

Kurt had tied Lorna's hands behind her back with a leather thong, explaining he would not have been forced to take such measures if he were certain she wouldn't try to escape.

As if she'd be so stupid with the fierce hunting dog's black eyes riveted on her face.

She was unfamiliar with this section of the istana grounds that bordered the river. The ornamental ponds and jungle willows looked as though they'd been neglected for years, and nature had finally reclaimed this piece of land where gigantic water lilies and swamp grasses flourished in the soil saturated by the ceaseless rains.

In the distance a small bamboo bridge spanned the wildly rushing river. Kurt motioned toward it, keeping Nadji at his side, the sack containing the statue still slung over his back. Farther downriver, half hidden in a screen of reeds, Lorna could see the painted prow of a small but sturdy-looking fishing boat.

"You can't mean for us to sail the sea in that," she blurted out, stopping several yards from the bridge.

He glanced back at her, his throat working as if his next words were difficult to speak. "*We* aren't going to sail."

She understood then that he intended to kill her, and the stark terror she felt at the realization must have shown on her face.

"It will be quick," he promised her. "God, Lorna, if there were only another way."

"Might you not . . . take me with you?" she asked, an idea forming in her mind. She did not want to die. Every moment alive extended her chances of somehow escaping him.

"I can't," he said, his voice uneven. "Ross would have the Royal Navy out searching every cove and inlet if we were spotted together. As it is now, at least no one will know I was responsible for your . . ."

Death, she finished silently, her heart beating so hard it made her feel ill.

"They'll realize it's you sooner or later," she said wildly. "As soon as the statue is discovered missing, someone will put everything together—"

"And realize the Agung-Mani reclaimed their treasure and murdered you for interfering with their plans."

"Ilse will hate you," she whispered.

He glanced away. "Probably so."

"Ross was right. You *are* a coward."

"Lie down on the ground, Lorna."

"No, oh, no—" She was shaking as he forced her to her knees; but then a sudden flash of movement in the tall acacia trees behind them diverted her attention. Was it the rain or had there been a figure?

Kurt's eyes narrowed as he too glanced toward the trees. "On your stomach," he said, prodding her shoulder. "And for God's sake, whatever you do, don't move."

She thought then that he had decided to shoot her. But to her bewilderment, as he laid her head against a patch of damp red soil, she heard him unbuckling the dog's collar, felt the animal's hot breath on her face, and caught Kurt's softly uttered command:

"Kill, Nadji."

She rolled over, her hands shielding her face, to discover Kurt gone, halfway across the bridge, and the mastiff bounding off in the direction of the acacia trees. There was a shot—she heard it clearly.

Seconds later Ross emerged from the trees at a run, his hair slicked back, a pistol clutched in his hand. He drew up short before Lorna. Falling to his knees, his eyes almost black with fear, he took one look at the red dirt stains on her face and pulled her roughly into his arms.

She felt utterly numb, her breathing shallow and irregular. "I thought—I feared you wouldn't come in time."

"He didn't hurt you?" He forced her head back, his fingers brushing her cheek.

She shook her head. Ross glanced around as three of the Rajah's guards ran past them toward the bridge.

"Stay here," he said, springing to his feet.

"The dog—"

"I killed it before it damn near killed me." He glanced down at her face and felt consumed by a savage need for revenge against van Poole. "Don't move from here."

She nodded. She doubted she was capable of moving anyway. The rain had not lightened, but she hadn't noticed it, sheltered beneath the layered canopy of branches overhead.

She noticed it now, blurring the figures moving along the opposite riverbank, like a grim watercolor come to life. Kurt had reached the canoe and was straining to slide it down the slick embankment and into the river.

She saw the guards thundering across the bridge, Ross behind them. Words she could not discern at this distance were exchanged between him and a guard, who remained while the other two rushed along the bank.

The remaining guard shouldered his musket. Kurt had gotten the canoe into the river and was struggling to throw off the anchor. The sack over his shoulder hampered his efforts, and finally he removed it. Placing it carefully under the thwarts, he snatched up the paddle to steer into the turbulent current. By his own admission, he was an inexpert boatsman.

Lorna felt cold inside with premonition as he raised to his knees to navigate. She stared at Ross's figure, tall and unmoving. Then she turned away.

Three shots thundered in succession from the bridge and the embankment. With each shot fired, she flinched. There was silence then, except for the faint dripping of the rain. Slowly she turned her head, glancing hard at Ross to reassure herself he was unhurt. He stood rigid on the bridge, in charge of the situation as he ordered the guards to the river to retrieve the body.

Unwillingly she looked toward the river. Kurt floated facedown, snagged amidst the flowering reeds. The river had sucked the canoe out of sight, toward the sea, and with it the Tiger.

She rose by reluctant degrees, haunted by the image of Kurt lying dead. He had been raised in violence. He had lived and died by it. Even now she didn't know whether he would have actually killed her or not. Yet the fact remained that he had not. She would never know why.

She glanced up and saw Ross standing before her. He took a hard look at her face and frowned. "There was no choice, Lorna. I could not risk the guards being killed if we'd tried to take him prisoner. I'm only sorry you had to witness the shooting. I don't regret his death."

She swallowed. Ross took her into his arms, hoping only his relief and not his cold rage showed on his face. When he'd seen her lying in the grass, he had been clutched by a fear so profound that he did not think he would ever forget it.

"It will be all right now," he said into her hair, unaware of the faint catch in his voice.

She nodded, her skin warming at his touch, the ugliness that had gripped her receding. She wanted to put the memory of this day as far from her mind as she could, concentrating instead on the life that she and Ross would soon begin together.

Chapter 28

Rajah Charles Montclair died five days after Kurt's death at the river. Dignitaries from the surrounding islands began arriving as early as the following night to attend the royal funeral.

Ross had come to Lorna immediately with the news. She'd taken one look at his face, assessing the unnatural pallor, and knew what had happened.

He was so distressed she didn't want to share her own news with him—that she was pregnant. Her reasons for withholding the discovery were purely selfish. With so many visiting potentates claiming his time, she doubted he would give her the undivided attention she would demand. There were plans now to be made. Her father's needs and even Ross's had quite unexpectedly been usurped by the life growing inside her. For this child to have the security and stability she herself had lacked was suddenly her priority.

"I wanted my uncle to live to see us married," Ross explained as they walked in the garden.

"He'll know," she said. "He will bless us."

He looked at her, her face unusually serene in the moonlight. "I could not bear this without you."

"When is the funeral?"

"Tomorrow afternoon. Lorna, what is it?"

She laughed at his concern, embarrassed that she'd

clutched his arm as they were climbing the steps to the veranda. "I felt a bit giddy for a moment. I'm fine now."

"I'll ask Dr. Parker to check you over. You might have caught a fever in the rain that day."

"Oh, no," she said with a mysterious smile. "I doubt it was anything I caught."

"I'll send Kana to fetch the doctor, nonetheless."

"Kana dropped by this morning, you know. He's insisting I call him by his new title—"

"Tuan Inspector Kana, Chief of Polices." Ross grinned. "He's already out patrolling the island."

He glanced up as Sir Arthur and Richard stepped onto the veranda. Inclining his head toward Lorna, he said in a low voice, "I'm counting the days until you're mine, only mine, and I don't have to play chess with your father just to see you."

"Will the wedding be postponed because of the funeral?" she asked.

"Not even if Mount Belakan erupts and sweeps us into the sea," he said, his gray eyes glittering. "I personally—*physically*—could not stand it if our marriage were delayed. I have to admit your eagerness is flattering, though."

"Coming in for a game, St. James?" Arthur called from the railing.

"No, sir. Not tonight."

"Lorna will make us some lovely lemonade and sandwiches."

"No, she won't," Lorna said, smothering a yawn. "I'm going to bed. The sea air has made me sleepy."

Ross stared after her as she slipped around the door and into the house. He thought she was behaving rather oddly, and he was concerned. He decided to talk to Dr. Parker about her himself.

Lorna was alone in the house for most of the following day, too lazy to stir beyond the parlor after she finally dragged herself downstairs. Dr. Parker had awakened her earlier and, after a brief exam, had confirmed her suspicion that she was pregnant. As if her wretched morning sickness wasn't proof enough. He'd also sternly advised her to avoid any further excitement for the next two months, suggesting she begin by not attending the Rajah's funeral that afternoon.

"The celebrations tend to get a bit boisterous, my dear," he told her at the door. "And after all that activity on Jalaka—"

"Celebrations?"

"Oh, yes. This is a joyous occasion on the island, the freeing of an earth-bound soul."

"I believe Ross will be disappointed if I don't show up. And the people might interpret it as a sign of disrespect."

"Ross will understand—in fact, he'd be furious to think you went against my advice just to please him."

She nodded, aware they were both thinking of what had happened to Ross's infant son.

"In two more months, you can be as active as you please, within moderation." Dr. Parker turned to leave, then hesitated, his eyes suddenly dark with appeal. "I don't suppose you've heard from Ilse?"

"Not a word, I'm afraid. I have no address for her in Africa, and I daren't send word to her husband in Java."

"He was a brute," Jason said quietly. "I think I'd kill him if I ever came face-to-face with him. I loved her, you know. I would have made a place in my life for her children too, if she'd given me the chance."

"Perhaps it's not too late."

"Perhaps," he repeated, doubtfully.

She closed the door and walked into the sun-drenched parlor, sinking into a wicker chair to contemplate how she would break the news of her pregnancy, not only to Ross but also to her family.

She must have fallen asleep. When next she opened her eyes, it was to feel herself being gently shaken awake.

"Ross," she murmured. In the darkness of the parlor,

he stood over her, clad in a white satin uniform embroidered with gold silk thread, a lightweight white cashmere cloak thrown over his shoulders.

"Where is everyone?" she said, sitting forward, her heart not recovering from the lurch it had given when she'd recognized him.

She was amazed at the physical impact he always had on her, how his presence eclipsed everything that surrounded him. In the jungle he had exuded an animal magnetism that fit his environment. But here, amidst the overembellished clutter of her father's parlor, he seemed larger than life, dark and magnificent, intimidating, a storybook figure out of a childhood fantasy. The planes of his face bronzed and taut with worry, he inspired such a feeling of awe in her that she was tempted to curtsy before him.

"Lorna," he said cautiously, "why are you looking at me like that?"

"I—I was just remembering what else Kana said this morning. About your title. Your Royal Highness. I—I feel as if I should dip into a curtsy."

"I'd like that," he said. "Go on."

"I won't. I'd feel ridiculous."

"I saw Jason at the funeral. He said you were in perfect health."

"Yes," she murmured. "Everything is fine."

He backed away from her, pulling off his cloak and then reaching down for her hand. "We're entirely alone," he said, his eyes like quicksilver in the shadows.

"But Mei Sing, and the other servants—"

"—will be feasting on the beach until the early hours. And your father and uncle are on their way to the reception at the istana. I packed them off myself."

She allowed him to lift her off the chair, her head falling back slightly as he kissed her throat. "But you—you should be at the istana, too, shouldn't you?" she said.

"Amayli has arranged for a troupe of dancers and actors to entertain. I won't be missed for an hour or so."

He took her upstairs to her room, lighting the small lamp on the nightstand while she drew the drapes, leaving only a gap for the air to circulate. From the corner of her eye, she watched him remove his boots, throw back the mosquito netting, then sit back on the bed.

"Undress for me, Lorna."

"But the light," she whispered, coloring as she faced him.

"You are to be my wife," he said calmly. "No other man has seen or touched you as I have and will. Do you believe that the pleasure we give each other is wrong?"

She shook her head, then lifted her gaze to his. Ripples of excitement blazed throughout her body at the dark passion in his eyes. She began to undress, her fingers unsteady on the buttons of her bodice. Ross lay back with his arms folded behind his head, watching her intently until she stood naked before him, her red-gold hair streaming down her white shoulders to her slender hips, her petticoats foaming around her ankles.

He sat up slowly, his jaw clenching, his gaze hooded.

"All those days and nights on Jalaka," he said, staring at her hungrily, "I thought I would go mad, wanting you and unable to have you."

"I would have thought you were too tired to even contemplate—"

He threw back his head and laughed richly. "Too tired for you, Lorna? Never."

Her eyes shone at him in the soft lamplight, sea-green, luminous, reflecting the mysteries within her he had yet to plumb. "Come to me," he said, his laughter fading.

He held out his arms to her as she reached him, but instead of joining him on the bed, she placed her hands on his chest and began to undo the small mother-of-pearl buttons of his shirt. His breathing quickened. His fingers tightened around the coverlet as he leaned back on his elbows. He could feel her impatience in her trembling hands, and it excited him. And when at last she worked his trousers off and sank onto the bed with a sigh, he took her swiftly in his arms and laid her beneath him. He could not press close enough to her warm, fragrant skin. It did not sate his hunger, just to *hold* her.

Curbing his own almost painful desire, he began to massage her hands and feet, kissing her closed eyelids and face, her throat, the tender buds of her breasts, and then lower to the softly sculpted plane of her belly.

She caught her breath, feeling the tension melt from her body as his unhurried lovemaking continued and her mind stilled.

"I love you, Lorna," he whispered, his breath a wisp of flame against her flesh. "You will be safe with me."

Safe. Oh, yes. He would always be her haven, her port in a storm, as he had from the first day in the sulap. Quivering with anticipation, replete with joy at the knowledge he loved her and had given her his child, she lost herself in the pleasure of his hands and mouth, reveling in the sensuality he had awakened within her. Deliberately he prolonged the loveplay until, with a low moan, she reached for him, her thighs slipping open in invitation. He slid his powerful hands beneath her hips and lifted her to him, penetrating her with swift male possession.

The worries of the world could not touch them now . . . not for this all-too-brief moment of magic when there was only their love and the incredible outpouring of passion that was its physical expression.

Afterward they lay lazily entwined on the coverlet, allowing the delicate evening breeze to cool their bodies while a chorus of cicadas serenaded them.

"I hate leaving you," he murmured, sighing as he turned to the side of the bed. "The reception will last late into the night."

"For the sake of the Raj, and not just your uncle's memory, you have to be present," she said. "I wish I could be there with you, but Dr. Parker didn't think it was a good idea."

"But he said you were all right." There was a trace of anxiety in his tone. "You are feeling well, aren't you?"

She smiled. "Of course. In fact, while you're at the reception, I shall be attending to the future of the Raj myself."

"What do you mean? And why are you smiling like that?"

She slid a hand to her abdomen. "Your heir, Ross. I wasn't sure, but Jason said it's true."

For a moment he could not speak, overcome with gratitude and happiness at the joy she'd brought into his life. Then he leaned down and kissed her tenderly, placing his hand over hers.

"Thank you, Lorna," he whispered, his voice thick with emotion. "There is nothing in this world that could have pleased me more."

On the day she was to be married two weeks later, Lorna received a frantic letter from Aunt Julia in London, demanding an explanation of what had happened to her family.

"She'd die if she knew I was with child," Lorna whispered to her father as they sat together on the settee in the parlor, finishing their third cups of tea.

Richard turned from the window, fidgeting nervously with his pocketwatch. "If the carriage doesn't get here soon, you'll be delivering that child before he's legitimized." He shook his head as Arthur and Lorna began laughing at him. "Scandalous," he said, hiding a smile. "Shocking. My poor wife must never learn any of this or she'll be on the next steamer out—speaking of which, I shall miss *my* ship if the carriage is much later."

"We'll miss you, Richard," Arthur said unconvincingly. "No one to keep us in line, so to speak."

"My heart's not strong enough to handle the pair of you," Richard said. "The mere prospect of even another month on this island gives me the shivers."

The private Roman Catholic ceremony in the istana chapel was simple and intensely personal, performed by the elderly priest Charles had retained. Ross could not believe it even as he repeated his vows—that this free-spirited beauty who had blown into his life, chasing away with her entrance all the clouds of his past, actually belonged to him. It was a fact he had not yet had time to savor, to let penetrate into the depths of his being. And now there would be a child . . .

A crowd of native well-wishers awaited them outside the chapel, and the river was strewn, the trees adorned, with masses of orchids, lilies, jasmine, hibiscus, and kambodja blossoms. A public reception was to be held in the istana courtyard, and suddenly, encountering the throngs of exuberant citizens, Ross was concerned about the strenuous evening he and Lorna would have to face.

"Are you sure you want to go through with this?" he asked her as she knelt to receive a bouquet of miniature orchids from two young girls.

"I would not miss it for anything," she said, burying her face in the exquisitely scented flowers. "And Jason said I'm in perfect health."

Ross nodded, his hand resting protectively on her shoulder. His heart was full. For once, there was not a cloud in the sky. And as he glanced back at the small chapel behind them, he felt an uplifting of his spirit, a quiet but powerful realization that though he, in the course of his life, had lost faith in God, God had clearly never stopped watching over him.

Epilogue

The old myths did not die easily on the island. The old legends, the false beliefs, did not fade away even with the advent of the school that Lorna had urged Ross to support during the first five months of their married life together.

She paused halfway to the wooded hillside shrine, her hand pressed to the ache in her lower back. Despite the efforts she had begun making to eradicate superstition among the people, the islanders still worshiped their animistic deities and expected her to make the traditional pilgrimage to one of Penala's many shrines in this, her sixth month of pregnancy. Fortunately, it was an easy climb, not a fraction as strenuous as the ascent to the isolated Temple of Two Hundred Steps that she'd made months ago.

She actually enjoyed the unhurried hike, and her mind felt deliciously clear. The child growing inside her thrived on the fresh island air and physical activity, not to mention the love of its two prospective, doting parents.

She waved down at the thicket of trees below her. Ross was there somewhere. He couldn't bear to let her out of his sight these days, and she and Amayli were constantly having to give him a detailed accounting of Lorna's proposed activities for his approval.

Lorna was happier than she had ever dreamed possible. The love between her and Ross seemed to deepen with each passing day. Their mutual commitment to their unborn child and to the island added an unexpected dimension to their relationship that could only strengthen with time. He was not only her lover, but also her mentor, her confidant.

The White Tiger had never been found, although its disappearance had stirred the hopes of a spate of treasure hunters all the way from Australia to Ireland. Lorna had to laugh when she learned that Captain Stokker was offering his maritime services and battered sloop for an exorbitant fee to scour the coastal waters for the statue.

She and Jason Parker had tried, unsuccessfully, to locate her, but Lorna hadn't given up hope of finding her. At this stage in her pregnancy, she desperately craved another woman who was practiced in motherhood to discuss with her the various aches and anxieties she was experiencing.

The well-worn footpath ended abruptly. The priest in the bamboo temple bowed deeply as she approached, and he sprinkled her path with dried petals and holy water. She was the Ranee, and inside her womb she carried the heir to the Raj. She had brought the island good fortune.

She ensconced herself carefully in the god seat, feeling deliciously irreverent as she kicked off her sandals and sat back to marvel over the sudden bout of gymnastics of her unborn child. In her hand she held the complete and revised manuscript of her father's book, *The Eden Flower*, which he had finished only last night.

She read until she reached the last page, the sun lowered in the sky, and her husband, frantic with concern over her prolonged absence, arrived to escort her back to the island.

"You aren't supposed to be here, Ross. It's not permitted unless you're making a petition."

He helped her up, grinning as she placed his hand upon her stomach and the baby gave a strong kick. "I suppose it's impossible to hope you'd stay home and knit booties like a normal expectant mother?"

"Booties in this climate? Is that what you expect of

me?'' She leaned back against his arm and stared up at the crimson sky, her own face aglow with happiness. Below them the night-blooming flowers were just beginning to unfurl and drench the air with their fragrance.

Ross took a deep breath and stood with his arms locked securely beneath her belly. ''All I expect of you—all I want—is that you love and never leave me.''

She turned to glance up at him, her eyes gazing into his. ''I have loved you from the day I met you. Surely you must know that will never change.''

A sudden breeze ruffled his hair, wafting to the shrine the hint of a dry monsoon. ''I know that without you and the child we've created my life would be incomplete, no matter how many personal successes I achieved.''

She shook her head to stem the tears of happiness that threatened to fall. ''We'll have to hurry if we hope to beat the wind down the river.''

''Give me your hand going down the hill. You've finished reading your father's book?''

''Yes. Just now. I recognized us in it.''

''And?'' He gazed down into her serene face, aching to defy the priest watching them by taking her into his arms and kissing her with all the passion she unfailingly aroused in him.

She took his hand and smiled, lacing their fingers together. ''It has a happy ending, Ross. That's all I'm going to tell you.''